Maurice

THE WHITE WITCH

Francis felt a chill of that loneliness which he had just told Jenny need not be too bad. The war. He had once more forgotten the damnable war. The portrait finished, he must pack up and go. A cloud came over the sun and everything except Jenny withdrew to a great distance from him. When Jenny too had gone he would possess nothing but his memory of her, and his memory of the weary man sitting at the great desk, and smiling as he turned to give the seal to his son. They became one in his thought; all he had.

The sun came out and he got up laughing, mocking at himself, once more in possession of his great possessions. A little girl of eight years old, a small child; what a fool he was! Yet as they strolled together back to the house he said, "Don't forget me, Jenny."

"I never forget anybody," said Jenny.

Also by the same author, and available in Coronet Books:

The Child from the Sea
A City of Bells
The Bird in the Tree
Green Dolphin Country
The Herb of Grace
The Heart of the Family
Gentian Hill
The Dean's Watch

The White Witch

Elizabeth Goudge

CORONET BOOKS
Hodder Paperbacks Ltd., London

First published by Hodder and Stoughton Ltd 1958
Coronet edition 1964
Second impression 1967
Third impression 1968
Fourth impression 1969
Fifth impression 1974

Printed and bound in Great Britain for
Coronet Books,
Hodder Paperbacks Ltd,
St. Paul's House Warwick Lane,
London, EC4P 4AH
by Hazell Watson & Viney Ltd,
Aylesbury, Bucks

ISBN 0 340 02410 0

For
JESSIE MONROE

AUTHOR'S NOTE

It has been said that every book has many authors, and this is especially true when a story has a historical setting. The history books play a large part in its making. I would also like to acknowledge my debt of gratitude to Charles Leland's *Gypsies*, which provided me with several gypsy legends, and to Charles Williams's novel *The Greater Trumps*, without which I should not have known of the existence of the gypsy tarot cards. And I would like to apologise for the many mistakes I must have unwittingly made, for only the story-teller who is also a competent historian can give a story of this sort to the reader without a quaking of the knees. One conjecture of mine I know may be incorrect. I have made Oliver Cromwell capture the Royal Standard at Edgehill. It is not known who captured it, though it is a historical fact that Captain John Smith rescued it again.

I am grateful to the translator and publishers for permission to quote from *Visions from Piers Plowman*, a new rendering of Langland's original, translated by Nevill Coghill and published by Phoenix House.

SONG

And can the physician make sick men well?
And can the magician a fortune divine?
Without lily, germander, and sops-in-wine?

With sweet-briar
And bon-fire
And strawberry wire
And columbine.

Within and out, in and out, round as a ball
With hither and thither, as straight as a line,
With lily, germander, and sops-in-wine,

With sweet-briar
And bon-fire
And strawberry wire
And columbine.

When Saturn did live, then lived no poor,
The King and the beggar with roots did dine,
With lily, germander, and sops-in-wine,

With sweet-briar
And bon-fire
And strawberry wire
And columbine.

Robin Goodfellow; his pranks and merry jests. 1628.

CONTENTS

PART ONE

PART TWO

PART THREE

PART ONE

CHAPTER I

THE CHILDREN AND THE PAINTER

Two children stood gazing at the world over their garden gate. They were just tall enough to rest their chins on top of it, but Jenny, being half a head shorter than Will, had to stand on tiptoe. Behind them the small manor-house where they lived, built of ship's timbers and warm red brick, glowed in the September sunshine, and the garden was on fire with autumn damask roses and marigolds. They could hear the bees humming over the clove gilliflowers under the parlour window, and the soft whirr of their mother's spinning-wheel; for Margaret, their mother, sat just inside the open window with Maria the dog asleep in a pool of sunshine at her feet. Her children were aware of her gentle eyes upon them, and her anxious love. And Will resented it. Jenny, incapable of resentment, nevertheless thought it a pity that love must be anxious, for anxiety was such an imprisoning thing.

It was many days now since she and Will had been allowed outside the garden gate by themselves; and their father had told them that this war was being fought for the liberties of the people. Will kicked the gate, not caring that he stubbed his toe, and Jenny said, "Hush, Will!" for she knew that the angry sound of his shoe against the wood had hurt their mother. The whirr of the spinning-wheel had checked for a moment and she heard Margaret catch her breath. The width of the grass plot, with the medlar tree in the middle of it, was between them, but she did hear the small sound, just as she had heard Will sobbing on the day when he had gone bird's-nesting alone and had fallen out of a tree and hurt himself. She had this gift of hearing, not with the ears of her body, but hearing, and between Margaret, herself and Will the bond was closer even than is usual between a mother and her twin children who have never left her even for a night. Jenny knew that her mother loved Will more than she loved herself, but this she thought right and natural, for Will was the son and heir.

There was really no reason why the children should be shut in the garden, but Margaret was always at the mercy of Biddy's tales. Biddy, their cook, was a very virtuous old woman, but like so many good women she was ogre-minded. She was seventy and had been good for so long that she suffered now from a natural ennui. Ogre-collecting relieved the ennui and also gave her considerable power over her mistress and the children, who shivered in delicious terror whenever Biddy came home from market with a fresh crop of stories. She was a marvellous raconteur and though her descriptions of local hangings and witch hunts were nowadays at second hand, for she did not at seventy get about quite as much as she had done, they remained those of an eye-witness.

But just lately the supply of murderers, thieves and witches in the neighbourhood had been running a little short, and Biddy regarded the war as a godsend. Not only was it a nice change, with the perpetual comings and goings of the Squire and his friends, and the militia drilling on the common and five dead in the first week while they were trying to get their eye trained on the target, but it had provided her with a whole new crop of ogres of a most distinguished type, a pleasing change from the gypsies and tinkers of pre-war days. The Bloody Tyrant and Rupert the Robber were familiar figures now to the children and their mother. Their ghastly appearance was known to them in intimate detail, even down to the twitch in the Robber's left eyelid and the Bloody Tyrant's wet red lips. They knew their habits too, from the boiling down of disobedient little children into soup to the disembowelling of captured prisoners. . . . And they might be here at any moment now, for the war was three weeks old. . . . Margaret and the children took pinches of salt with Biddy's tales, as they had always done, but Margaret found that in time of war salt has a habit of losing its savour.

And so she had confined her children to the garden, though no danger threatened them except from their own militia; and the militia had shelved the war for the moment to carry the harvest. In the country at large little was happening as yet apart from local skirmishes, and in the Chiltern country nothing at all, for here the division was not so much between Royalists and Parliament men as between Parliament men and those whose politics consisted of a passionate desire to be let alone to live their lives in peace. Margaret wished with all her heart and soul that her husband belonged to this latter party. But Robert Haslewood rode with John Hampden, and Margaret's heart was laid open to Biddy's tales.

The children gazed at the common beyond the garden gate. The peachy smell of gorse came to them. A lark was singing in the cloudless sky, and the heat-mist was blue over the beech-wood that filled the valley to the left. In the hot stillness they could hear the jays calling in the wood, and the drumming of a yaffingale. One might see him if one was there, and the squirrels too.

Will lifted his chin from the top of the gate and pushed it forward in a truculent manner. "Tomorrow," he said, "I shall go into the wood."

"Mother won't let you go," said Jenny.

"Tomorrow Mother has no more authority over me," said Will. "Tomorrow I shall be breeched and next week I shall go to school."

He looked down with loathing and scorn at the childish coat he wore, skirted like a woman's. His breeching had been postponed far too long because through the months of preparation for war his father had been so anxiously occupied, and away from home so much, that even the breeching of a son and heir had hardly seemed important. But tomorrow Robert Haslewood was coming home, bringing with him a sword from London. And tomorrow the tailor would bring Will's doublet and breeches, made to measure on the large side. And the barber would come too, to cut off his curls, and healths would be drunk all round and Will would be a man.

Behind them in the house they heard the opening of the parlour door and the soft voice of little Bess, the still-room maid, saying, "Madam, Madam, the rose jelly is coming to the boil!" The whirr of the spinning-wheel ceased and Margaret rose hurriedly, for Bess was not yet competent with the jellies and preserves. They heard the rustle of her dress and the crackle of Bess's starched apron, and Jenny could hear the gentle lovable clicking sound of Maria's nails on the polished floor as she padded after her mistress. There was a soft flurry of exit and the closing of the parlour door. The children looked at each other. Their mother's eyes were no longer upon them and her anxiety was now centred on the rose jelly.

A sense of release came to them, and a deep welling up of life.

Holding on to the gate, Will suddenly pulled up his knees and shot out his behind, delighting in the rending sound that announced the bursting of gathers. Returning his feet to the ground again he wiped his dirty, earthy fingers all over the fair curls that would be cropped tomorrow, finishing them off on the white collar round his neck. Then he spat at a passing bumble bee and missed it by only an inch. Tomorrow he would be a man and would not miss.

"I shall have a sword tomorrow," he told Jenny. "And I shall go into the wood now."

"You said you were going tomorrow," said Jenny.

"I shall go now," said Will.

He glanced over his shoulder, but the windows were blank. He unlatched the gate and slipped through.

"Me too," pleaded Jenny. "It won't hurt Mother, for she won't know. We'll be back before the jelly's done. Me too, Will."

"You're only a girl," he retorted. "*You'll* never be breeched."

Nothing stings so sharply as the truth. From the hampering abundance of petticoat round Jenny's thin legs there was no release to be looked for in this world, and judging by the pictures of angels in the family bible, not in the next either. A lump came in Jenny's throat, but she did not argue with her brother, for Margaret had taught her by example that in humility and gentleness lie a woman's best hope of frustrating the selfish stubbornness of men. She turned away from the gate and walked slowly towards the house. Her gait cried aloud to Will that soon she would have lost her playmate and would be alone. The pain that was already in her heart stirred sharply in his.

"Come on then," he said roughly. "Better come with me than go snivelling indoors to Mother."

Jenny never snivelled, but again she did not argue. She slipped quickly through the gate and shut it softly. They ran along the rough road that crossed the common until it dipped down into the wood, then left it and ran in among the great beeches where no one could see them. Then they walked slowly, swishing delightedly through the dead beech leaves and savouring the great moment. Will took his sister's hand now, with that air of protectiveness that was always his when he needed the comfort of her stouter heart. It was always eerie in the wood; and nowadays one could fancy Biddy's ogres lurking behind the trees.

Will at eight years old was a plump little boy, stocky and strong, dirty and dishevelled of wicked intent but not responsible for the gaps in his teeth and the number of freckles across the bridge of his nose. Jenny had shed her first teeth very tidily at an early age and her new ones were all in place, pearly and well-spaced. She was an orderly child. The white apron she wore over her long full-skirted blue dress was spotless, and so was her white cap. Her hornbook hung demurely from her waist. She was smaller than her brother and not at all like him, for her thin face was pale and her hair dark, cut in a fringe across her forehead, fell in soft ringlets on her shoulders. She had about her a delicate air of remoteness, like a shy bird that has touched down for a moment only in a strange land, but it was misleading. She was not as delicate as she looked and morally she was fast growing into one of those competent women who are in control of their circumstances. She held Will's hand firmly and soon it ceased to tremble in hers.

When he no longer felt afraid, Jenny's delight in the wood took hold of him. Her moods frequently took hold of him, for they were still very much one child. Reaching for air and light, the beech trees had grown very tall. One's eyes travelled up and up the immense height of the silver trunks, past the various platforms of green leaves to where the blue of the upper air showed through them. The final platforms were so high that the blue of the blue-green pattern seemed no further away in space than the green; but one tree had decided to be content with a lowly position, had grown only a short height on a slender silver stem and then spread out her arms and wings like a dancing fairy. Below on the floor of the wood the colours showed jewel-bright above the warm russet of the beech leaves. The cushions of moss about the roots of the trees were emerald and there were clumps of small bright purple toadstools, and others rose-coloured on top and quilted white satin underneath. The children stood still, watching. In the bole of another tree a round hole had been nibbled larger by small teeth to make the entrance to a squirrel's nest and was smoothly polished by the rub of fur. They saw a couple of squirrels and the yaffingale.

As they listened the muted autumn music of a deep wood, hidden within its distances, seemed to flow out to them like water from a hidden spring; the rustlings and stirrings of small creatures, the wind that was in the upper air only and stirred merely the highest patterns of the leaves, the conversational flutings of the birds, the strange sigh that breathed now and then through the wood, as though it grieved for the passing of summer. All the sounds came together and grieved them also, but quietly, for summer comes again.

"It makes my ears feel clean," said Jenny, and Will nodded. His own ears had the same rinsed feeling, but he was inarticulate and would not have been able to find the words to say what he felt. But he had imagination and suddenly it leaped into life. If words to describe what he saw or felt did not come as easily to him as they did to Jenny, his sense of drama could always take hold of a scene or situation and dispose it imaginatively about himself. This he could do with a great sense of his own kingliness at the centre of his world. With an airy leap, surprising in one so sturdy, he landed under the dancing beech tree and held out his arms beneath hers, laughter sparkling all over his freckled face. Then he girdled the trunk three times at breakneck speed, calling out to Jenny, "Who am I, Jenny? Who am I?"

She had no doubt as to who he was, for Cousin Froniga had just been reading them *A Midsummer Night's Dream.*

" 'Sweet Puck' !" she cried. " 'Are not you he?' "

"Come on!" he called to her, leaping off down the slope of the wood.

> "Over Hill, over dale,
> Through bush, through brier,
> Over park, over pale. . . ."

His voice died away and Jenny gathered up her skirts and ran after him, her hornbook swinging madly and her cap on the back of her head. The beech leaves crunched gloriously under their feet and the jays began calling again in the depth of the wood. They were coming to the bottom of the slope, and through the thinning trees they could see the fields of standing corn and the pastures where the sheep were feeding, the long azure distance to the east, and to the west the tall hill blazing with gorse and crowned with thickets of hawthorn that were already glowing crimson against the blue of the sky. They ran faster and faster, Jenny overtaking Will, and because they had not been in the wood for so long they forgot about the treacherous dip in the ground, like a deep ditch, that hid itself beneath the drifted beech leaves. Jenny fell first, catching her foot in her troublesome petticoats and pitching headlong. Will, running so fast he could not stop, tripped in some brambles and went head over heels after her, yelling with dismay. There was an answering shout from somewhere above them in the wood and both, as they fell, were aware of the man leaping down upon them, the terrible man dressed in black velvet, with pearl earrings and dreadful gleaming eyes and cruel red lips. They saw the forked black beard and the tongue moistening the lips as he sprang. He was just as Biddy had described him. Half dead with terror, upside down among the beech leaves, they shut their eyes and waited for death, for it was the Bloody Tyrant.

"You're not hurt, are you?" enquired a voice. "You fell soft."

Jenny felt herself picked up, carried to the further side of the ditch and set gently down. The owner of the voice returned to the bottom of the ditch and disinterred Will. "Come on, son," he said. "And stop yelling. The little girl never uttered a sound."

Will too was lifted up and set beside Jenny. Shivering with terror they stood there while hands felt them. "No harm done," said the voice. "What's the matter with you?"

Will, though he had stopped yelling, kept his eyes screwed tightly shut, so as not to see the knife, but Jenny opened hers so as to see it, for it was always her way to look hard at what frightened her. There was no knife. She looked up into the face of a smiling, grey-eyed young man with close-cropped hair. He had no earrings in the large ears that stuck out in such a reassuring manner at the side of his head, and he was not dressed in black velvet, but in grey home-spun wool, with a plain white square linen collar such as her father wore. She smiled. Her relief reached to Will and he unscrewed his eyes. His face was not white, but scarlet and burning, and there were tears on his cheeks. He looked at the man, and then, dreadfully ashamed, he hung his head and tried to rub the tears away on his sleeve. But the more he rubbed the more they seemed to come, until at last he was sobbing uncontrollably.

"Will's not breeched yet," said Jenny quickly.

"There's no shame in tears when a man's not breeched," said the stranger. "But what frightened you? The fall, or me pounding along so noisily to pick you up? I'm always a clumsy fool."

"Both," said Jenny. "Will and I thought you were the Bloody Tyrant."

She looked up and saw that he had stopped smiling. He looked both angry and sad. "So you thought I was an ogre?" he said. "It's amazing what feats of transmogrification imagination can perform."

Jenny did not know what he was talking about, but she did think it very odd that she should have seen that dreadful man in black just as clearly as she was now seeing this kindly one in grey.

"Imagination," he went on, "is the greatest power on earth for good or ill. Now then, son, try to imagine you were breeched yesterday."

"I'm being breeched tomorrow!" gasped Will, and hid his shame in the crook of his elbow.

"Tomorrow?" ejaculated the stranger. "Then I've had a lucky escape! If today was tomorrow you'd have drawn your sword and run me through!"

This remark conjured up such a pleasing picture that Will looked up, smiled a little and accepted from the stranger the offer of a severely folded clean linen handkerchief.

"You're painting a picture!" ejaculated Jenny.

"Come and see," said the man, and led the way to where he had been sitting on a fallen tree-trunk at the edge of the wood. A canvas on an improvised easel stood in front of the tree-trunk and was splashed with colour. The children stood and looked at it and the man stood and looked at the children, his merry smile back again about the corners of his mouth and in his eyes. The little boy was merely gaping with astonishment as he stared for what was obviously the first time at a landscape painting, but the little girl was neither gaping nor staring, she was looking, and what she felt shone in her face in a way that touched the man's heart with nostalgic sadness.

Through her eyes he saw his picture, and the world too. He had painted the scene with the whole of his considerable skill and deep delight in the beauty of earth, and it was a good picture of the English countryside in early autumn, but seen now through her eyes the green of that sunlit field had an eternal freshness and the sky, depth beyond depth of blue, was one that would never be clouded. The boy who had become himself had once been as happy as this child in the unconscious conviction that he and his immortal world would never know parting or change. What was art but an attempt to recover that faith? It was a sort of denial of the fact that one's eyes and the loveliness they looked upon would soon be lost in the same darkness.

He stopped looking at his picture and looked at Jenny. He wished he could paint her. She'd probably be dead of the small-pox a year from now and no record left of those bee-brown eyes, a warm brown banded with gold. Bee-brown pleased him, for a bee is one of the symbols of courage, he remembered. Women used to embroider a bee on the scarves they gave their knights. She had not cried, like the unbreeched boy, but now that the shock was over he was coming back to normal more quickly than she was. Though she had forgotten her fright in the joy of the picture, her body had not forgotten it. The colour had not come back to her thin sweet lips and there were dark smudges under her eyes. He did not suppose she ever had roses in her cheeks, but she did not need them with that smooth skin the colour of pale honey. Her face was too broad across the cheek-bones and too thin beneath them, but for all that it was the loveliest child's face he had ever seen, even lovelier than the face of the other little girl whom he had painted. . . . He loved these serious little girls.

"You haven't put the sheep in," she said.

"They kept moving, and I'm not clever enough to paint people's portraits unless they stand still."

"Do you paint people's portraits?"

"Yes. I'm a journeyman portrait painter. I travel all over the country, just like the tinkers do, only instead of mending pots and pans I paint portraits."

"Oh!" said Jenny, and her face was transfigured as a brilliant idea came to her. "Would you paint Will after his breeching? Would you paint him in his breeches and sword?"

"If I did, would your mother give me a silver piece for it?" he asked.

"Mother would give all she's got for a picture of Will," said Jenny with conviction. "And I think Father would give a silver piece."

Will smiled benignly. His distress was now a thing of the

past and he was sitting cross-legged on the ground, his red cheeks pleasantly dimpled as he gazed with rapt eyes at the landscape. But he was not seeing the landscape. He was seeing himself tomorrow in his breeches and sword. The painter glanced at him, well aware of what he was seeing. A typical male of the baser sort, none too brave, complacent, happy in the knowledge that his excellent opinion of himself was shared by the females of his family, yet withal a nice though somewhat toothless small boy who might yet make a man if sufficiently maltreated at school. His cheeks had soft down upon them, like ripe peaches, and his eyes were a bright speedwell blue. In order to paint the girl he'd be willing to paint the boy too if he kept his mouth shut. They were utterly unlike, but they seemed much the same age.

"Are you twins?" he asked.

"Yes," said Jenny.

"Then I won't paint one without the other. Two silver pieces for the two of you."

"That would be wasting Father's money," said Jenny with strong commonsense. "I'm not pretty, Biddy says, and I'll never be breeched."

"Both or neither," said the painter obstinately.

Jenny knew how to deal with obstinate men. Her father was always very fond of his own way, and so was Will. "We'll see in the morning," she said gently. "Will is to be breeched at nine o'clock and afterwards we're going to open a bottle of Cousin Froniga's metheglyn to drink his health. If you come at half-past nine, after the metheglyn, Father is more likely to do what Mother wants than if you came before."

"It will have to be a punctual half-past nine," said the painter, "for otherwise there won't be any metheglyn left for me. Where do you live?"

Will looked up with wide-eyed surprise, for he thought everyone knew where he lived. "At the manor," he said with hauteur. "My father is Squire Haslewood. My father is coming back from the war just for my breeching."

"It is as yet a leisurely war," said the painter.

Jenny looked quickly up at him, for the laughter had gone again both from his voice and his face. He had been putting some finishing touches to his painting while he talked to them, but now he had stuck his paint-brush behind his ear, his hands hung idle between his knees and he was frowning down at them. Jenny had the sudden tight feeling in the throat that was hers when her father was trying to make up his mind whether it was his duty to give Will a thrashing, or whether it wasn't. Then the painter came to a decision.

"I'll come," he said. "Hadn't you two better go home now?"

"Yes," said Jenny. "Mother will be anxious if she misses us."

She curtseyed to him carefully, holding out her skirts as she had been taught, her grave face absorbed in her task. He slipped his hand into an inner pocket of his doublet, took something out and handed it to her with a bow. "Take great care of it," he said.

"It's an elf-bolt!" ejaculated Will.

Jenny looked at the little flint arrow-head lying in her palm. She had always longed for an elf-bolt. How many hundred years ago had a fairy loosed this from his bow? Elf-bolts were the most precious of precious things. She looked up at the painter with eyes like stars.

"I found it when I was a boy," he said, smiling at her.

"I'll take great care of it," she said. "Thank you, sir."

"Goodbye, sir," said Will. He too had been well trained and he had a pretty bow. He was not aggrieved that only Jenny had an elf-bolt, though his mouth drooped at the corners. The painter could find nothing in his pockets suitable for Will except a little seal made from a bit of polished red stone. He hesitated, loath to part with the trifle, then gave it to Will. Though commonplace, he was a nice little boy, and the curve of a child's mouth is prettier up than down. The wide half-moon of Will's mouth turned a somersault and his dimples showed again.

"It was given to me by a very brave man," said the painter, "and it will belong to a brave man again once you're breeched."

Will went scarlet, but as he pocketed his treasure he said to himself that he'd keep it always in the pocket of his breeches and then he'd always be courageous; for the crest upon it was a little lion.

The children went away and the painter sat listening with his eyes shut until the chiming of their voices had become an indistinguishable part of the music of the wood. The drawing of the one music into the other had been beautiful, as lovely as the fading of prismatic colours into the light, or of the morning star into the blue of day. It is when loveliness withdraws itself that one's heart goes after it. "Peace," he thought. "Gone away like those children through the wood—so easily—do we call ourselves sane men?"

He opened his eyes and saw the picture he had been painting and found it so crude that it set his teeth on edge. The red of the hawthorn berries looked like dried blood and the high white clouds like puffs of cannon-smoke. He dropped it face downwards on the beech leaves, put his brushes and paints away in the saddle-bag in which he kept them, kicked to pieces the easel he had made out of bits of dead wood and thrusting his hands deep into his pockets sat looking out broodingly upon the sunlit scene that he had painted. It did not allow him to brood long. A man can read the darkness of his own thoughts into a representation of nature, but not into nature herself, for she will not be so soiled. Ten minutes later she had had her way with him and he sat so bemused by her beauty that he had forgotten the reason for his coming to this place.

A thrush was singing near him, and nearer still, which was strange for the shy thrush, repeating his stave of song not twice but over and over. Just as the music of the children's voices had withdrawn itself into the music of the wood almost imperceptibly, so this song was detaching itself from it, coming to him as solacement for the loneliness that the other had left. In his bemused mind they seemed connected. The children's voices and the bird's song. The bird's song and the children's voices. He roused himself and turned his head, hoping to see the creamy speckled breast, the brown silk feathers and the bright benign eyes of the courteous thrush, and saw instead a tall gypsy standing under the trees, a little turned from him, and whistling to a thrush within the wood with so perfect a reproduction of the bird's own note that the bird was answering him. The painter listened a moment to the melody and counterpoint, delighting in it, and then, for he had been told to wait here for a gypsy, he added a whistle of his own, the robin's. He was not a musician and his whistle was only a parody of the real thing. The gypsy, not deceived, turned towards him with a shy half-smile. "For how long has he been there, aware of me?" wondered the painter. "And I never heard him come. But one never does hear them. They're soft-footed as the rabbits." Aloud he said, "The high hills are a refuge for the wild goats."

And the gypsy replied in a slow deep voice, in perfect English, "And so are the stony rocks for the conies." Then he held out his hand and the painter took a packet from the inner pocket of his coat and gave it to him. The gypsy bowed and would have gone away at once, but the painter stopped him. "In a few days' time I think I may have more information to send," he said. "Could you meet me here at sunset in four days' time?"

"*Rai*, it is your part to command me," said the gypsy respectfully, and then, a little unwillingly, for a passer-by in the field could have seen them together in the shadows of the wood, he obeyed the other man's gesture and sat down beside him on the tree-trunk. The painter had no misgivings, for he had not yet learned the single-mindedness of the fighting man; an arresting scene or face or figure could still make him forget that he was one.

He had forgotten it again now, captured as he was by the beauty of all three. The brilliant day was spread like a banner behind the remembered face of the fairy child and this figure of legend dressed in the colours of winter woods and calling him *Rai*. He thought that the child and the man, with their air of remoteness, were both of the type who would prefer their background to be a hiding-place rather than a foil, but they had such quality that the brilliance of the day was less arresting than they were. *Rai!* The title of respect touched him, accustomed to respect though he was. His cheerful and slightly arrogant self-confidence did not leave him, for it was an integral part of him, but measured against the gypsy's grave humility it seemed to come as far short of it as did his own stockiness beside the height of the other. He was instantly attracted to the man. He was like a fir tree, lean and tall, his brown weather-beaten skin the colour of the trunk, his patched worn clothes faded from their original black to the deep green of the needles. Like the fir tree he looked tough and strong and ageless, yet because it was impossible to think of him as young he was probably old. His hair and beard were grey and the lines on his face were deep. And some time or other, for some offence against the law (though it was hard to think of him in connection with offences), his ears had been cropped. He looked a part of the tree-trunk he sat on, of the wood behind him and the fields he looked upon, more so than any gypsy the painter had ever seen. He was the perfect gypsy. Possibly that was because he was not a gypsy. The painter thought to himself that just as a great sinner called of God is more likely to become a great saint than the average respectable man, because of the fierce love and courage needed to carry him through his purging, so a man who chooses an alien people to be his people must undergo so radical a change that he becomes more like the ideal of the breed than they are themselves. "And why do I know he's not a gypsy?" wondered the painter. "Not his grey eyes, for not all of them are black-eyes. The genuineness of his humility, I think. However humble he may choose to appear, the real gypsy has in his heart of hearts nothing but contempt for the gorgio. This man has never felt contempt even for a worm under a stone. Say something, you fool. Make him look at you."

"It's a grand day," he said.

The gypsy turned and smiled at him. He had a charming smile, but it seemed something exterior to himself, like sunshine flickering over rock, and it did not touch his eyes. He had the slightly dazed look of a man who had suffered much. "And a grand countryside," he said. "You are a painter, *Rai*?"

"How do you know that?"

"Your hands."

The painter looked at his hands and laughed, for they had paint on them. He was a messy worker. "You're observant," he said.

"I am accustomed to look at a man's hands to tell his trade," said the gypsy. "But I did not need the paint on your hands to tell me yours. It is the shape of them, the broad palms, the short strong fingers. That is the artist's hand, not, as men think, the thin long hand." He spread out his own, which were like the hands in an El Greco painting, but stained and crooked with much labour. "And I am a tinker—Bartholoways the Tinker."

"To me, John Loggin," said the painter with a smile. "You have another name among your own people, I know. A gorgio must never hear a Romany's real name."

"To know a man's true name is to have power over him," said the gypsy. "Such power can be abused. Therefore the Romanitshel only tells his true name to those whom he can entirely trust." He looked again at the painter, and this time the air of remoteness seemed to fall from him a little, and his smile touched his eyes, as though it came this time from within. "My name is Yoben."

The painter bowed. It was as though a king had presented him with a fabulous jewel. "Mine is Francis Leyland."

"It is safe with me," said Yoben. "But I doubt if it is safe to sit here talking for so long in broad daylight on the edge of the wood. I mean safe for the work we have in hand. Our personal safety is of no account."

Francis smiled. Yoben might have passed beyond the point when a man cares whether he lives or dies, but he had not. Life was good to him. He answered softly, "I had forgotten the damn war."

"It will not allow you to forget it for long," said Yoben grimly. "On Thursday, *Rai*, after sunset, and further within the wood. You see that tree there, where a squirrel has built his nest? I will be there after dark." He got up, smiled at Francis and moved away among the trees. The rustling of the beech leaves as he disappeared into the wood was so faint that it might have been a bird or small beast vanishing there. A bird, Francis decided, for he heard the thrush's song again. He sat listening until the last note had been drawn back again into the music of the wood. Then he got up, picked the offending picture from the beech leaves, slung his saddle-bag over his shoulder and tramped down into the grassy hollow, and up the far fields towards the common above. The village possessed two commons, one presided over by the manor and the other by the inn where he had left his pony and his second saddle-bag. He walked along whistling, delighting in air and light, and yet beneath his happiness was a vague feeling of uneasiness. He had undertaken the work he was doing light-heartedly, counting the cost in terms of danger but not in anything else. . . . It was awkward to have lost his heart to a little girl whose father was his political enemy.

CHAPTER II

YOBEN AND MADONA

I

Yoben, his share of the day's labour finished, sat a little apart from the rest on a tree-stump, his short clay pipe in his mouth, his patched cloak pulled round his shoulders against the evening chill. He was often apart. He had been accepted by the dark-skinned, black-eyed, fierce Herons, but not absorbed. He had come from the north ten years ago, travelling with old Righteous Lee, the Tinker. Righteous had stolen a pony on a dark night and when they were caught with it Yoben had taken the blame, for the old man had a great fear of choking his life out on the gallows. Yet Yoben had not swung for it. Something about him at the trial, something arresting in the quality of his patience, had disposed the judge and jury to leniency and instead of hanging he had had his ears cropped and twelve months in jail. When he came out again Righteous was dead, but his sister, old Madona Lee, who had married Piramus Heron as a slip of a girl and was still alive at seventy despite his beatings, had been at the prison gate to meet Yoben. She had taken his hand in hers and kissed it, and then taking the diklo from her own head had tied it over his to hide the mutilation of his ears, and thereafter the Herons accepted him as one of themselves.

Though always a little apart from themselves. They did not know where he had come from before he joined Piramus, and he never told them. And they did not know where he went when he left them for perhaps weeks at a time. If they had to move to a fresh camping place while he was away they laid the patrines for him—those secret little signposts of crossed sticks and bent flower-stalks that any Romany could follow for miles over the hills—but they never asked him questions. They respected his reticence and admired his skill and generosity. He was a fine worker in metal, for old Righteous had taught him his own trade well. He could earn good money and never spent it on himself. He had the gift of tongues. In the Romany tongue, or the tinker's Shelta, or the gorgio's own language, he could be equally persuasive, and sometimes when he sat alone with his book on his knees he could be heard muttering in a fourth and unknown tongue. That the black book was full of spells the Herons did not doubt, but they did not fear them, for if Yoben was a Chovihan, he was a white wizard. The heart of a man who is ready to give his life for his friend is never black.

The hour was good and Yoben's brown taut face relaxed in pleasure as he watched the scene. Only he felt the autumn chill that had come after the heat of the day, the rest went barefoot in the cool grass. They had come to this camping place only a few hours ago, travelling up to the high country of the Chiltern heathlands from the valley below. It was familiar to them, and the children's voices were high and excited as they played about the hollow tree and the dew-pond that they loved, picked harebells and wild thyme. This was one of the few parts of the country where this particular gypsy tribe could live openly, without fear of persecution. There was gypsy blood in the Squire's family, and though he was ashamed of it, he protected them. Looking down upon them from the rising ground above, Yoben thought their tents, pitched only an hour ago, looked as though they had always been there. Accustomed to inhabit not a house but a scene, the gypsies had the gift of making themselves an integral part of that scene, as house-dwellers become a part of a room they are fond of. The rounded tents, with the coarse brown blankets pinned over the bent hazel rods with the long thorns of the wild sloe, looked like large mushrooms on the grass, and the old thorn trees, crab apples and bramble thickets that sheltered them seemed growing there for the purpose. The gypsy pack-ponies were by the dew-pond, cropping the grass. Eastward, beyond the camp, another meadow sloped gently to Flowercote Wood. Behind the wood a mass of apricot-tinted clouds was piled against the deep blue of the sky. There had been a thunder shower, and the hint of a rainbow lingered still over the wood.

The fire had been lit and the flames flowered in the blue smoke. About it the gypsies moved in the old once-gaudy clothes that had faded now to the soft earth colours that were all about them : deep crimson of the berries on the old thorn trees, dark brown and faded blue and purple. Of them all, only Alamina Heron, Madona's grand-daughter, struck a bright note of colour with the strings of coral beads she wore and her bright green skirt. She was singing as she hung the black pot on its hook over the fire, her swarthy face golden in the light of the flames. She had a voice like a blackbird's, full and lovely, but to Yoben's sensitive ear of a too insistent sweetness. . . . Had she and the blackbirds in the copse been silent he could have heard the lark that was above him in the sky. . . . Then he reproached himself, and shut his eyes that he might hear her better. Her soaring voice, against the murmur of the men's talk and the laughter of the children, was as beautiful as herself. Later, when he had left them and gone away through the twilight to Froniga, he would hear the lark.

He opened his eyes and saw Madona sitting beside the fire. Her voluminous old brown cloak was round her and under it nestled Alamina's three children like small birds beneath sheltering wings. With that picture in his memory he got up suddenly and went away. Of them all only Madona truly loved him with that quiet unalterable love with which he loved her. He walked slowly up through the green field dwelling upon that picture of Madona, worshipfully intent upon it even though he was going to Froniga. Though the two women whom he loved were not on speaking terms they seemed always together in his mind. He carried one to the other, as he was now carrying the picture of Madona to Froniga's cottage, and would presently carry memories of Froniga to Madona at the fireside.

He walked up through the meadow, facing west towards the afterglow, moving slowly and listening to the lark. As he walked, the green grass that grew near the dew-pond and in the hollow gave way to rough tussocks of tawny stuff matted here and there with the springiness of heather. When he reached the crown of the land he paused and looked about him. The country now seemed almost flat, for one hardly noticed the folds and hollows with their copses and bramble thickets, and the great cool sky arched over the upland plain with a majesty that imposed its own stillness.

The dark branches of orchard trees were etched against the west and pinpricks of light showed among them, for the village for which he was bound was here an oasis in the plain. To the left the tower of the church rose above the massed darkness of the churchyard yews, to the right an old rutted lane was deeply sunk between its hedges of sloe and hawthorn. It led across the heath down to the great river in the valley, the Thames with its silver loops lying among yellow irises and sedges, and no man knew how old it was. The whole of this land had a feeling of antiquity. Yoben had plied his trade in many shires, and had travelled roads that had not been new when the Legions tramped along them, but in no other stretch of country had he such a sense of the past. He was at a loss to account for it; unless it could be that the immensity of sky, the wide landscape and the great winds that could at times roar over the heath, destroyed the sense of cosiness which in the dales of a hilly country can shut out the thought of past and future.

The nearest cottage was Froniga's, for she lived at the edge of the village looking out over the wide plain as a cottage at land's end looks out over the sea. Her front door opened into the strip of flower-garden which separated her cottage from the heath upon the east and the lane upon the north, but to the south there was a herb garden and small orchard, and he made his way towards the gap in the bramble hedge and the stile that gave access to the orchard. Only Froniga's better-dressed callers entered her cottage by way of the lane and the front door. Vagabonds like himself came in through the gap in the hedge.

Though he was on fire now with his eagerness, he nevertheless paused at the stile, a dark shadow under the darker shadow of the huge old elder tree that grew there, and dread took hold of him, for there was no light in Froniga's cottage. It was some while since he had visited her, and in his wandering life he could get no news of her. She was fearless and wilful and she lived alone. He was always anxious for her. . . . He must find out.

He climbed over the stile and made his way among the old orchard trees. Above his head he could see the glimmer of apples, some of them small and jewel-bright, others large circles of dim gold among their withering leaves. The trees had been so twisted by winter storms that they lay this way and that, and one lay along the ground, but still it bore apples of a moony green. Growing over it was a bush of autumn musk rose, glimmering with ivory flowers. It was wet from the rain, and a gust of scent came to him as he brushed against it. There were beehives under the trees, and in the rough orchard grass he trod upon fragrant growing things, bruising them. Froniga was a noted gardener and herbalist, skilled in all healing arts, with fingers that were not only green but enchanted, and her small domain always seemed to him almost intolerably prolific.

He was, he supposed, a little jealous of her passionate love of plants. He came out from the shadows of the orchard into the herb garden, and the pungent scents of wet lavender and rosemary, germander and mint geranium. But the rectangular beds were all in good order, he noted with relief, and on the rim of the well sat a large white cat. But cats are heartless creatures and the placidity of Pen was no indication of her mistress's state. Over the cottage roof a star shone in the sky, and the tall old plum tree stood as always like a sentinel beside the southern gable. He came to the kitchen window and looked in. The fire was burning on the hearth and the stone flags of the floor were scrubbed and clean. There was a pot of basil on the window-sill and Froniga's spinning-wheel was in its usual place by the east window. No harm had come to her. She was merely out. His step was light with relief as he went round to the back door, lifted the latch and walked in. He doubted if even a civil war would ever teach Froniga to lock her door.

Two worn stone steps led down into the kitchen, lit by the flames of the fire. The little room had something of a festive air, for a kettle hung over the fire, the hearth was swept and a pile of apple logs was set ready beside it, with the settle at right-angles to it. The table was laid with home-made bread, butter, cheese and apples in pewter dishes. Rushlight candles were set ready for lighting and beside them in a pot was a bunch of harebells. Drawn to the table were two high-backed chairs of polished walnut. It was a comfortable room, for Froniga was not a poor woman, as poverty was counted in the year of grace 1642. Whom was she expecting? It could not be himself, for he had given her no warning of his coming. He stood for a moment in uncertainty, his head bent that he might not knock against the bunches of herbs that hung from the ceiling. Should he go? He did his best not to be seen in her company, for he was a Romany tinker and she, though she would passionately deny it, was a Rawni. He was very careful of the reputation with which she herself delighted to play battledore and shuttlecock. He had half turned to go away again when he heard her step on the flagged path outside the door.

"*O boro Duvel atch' pa leste!*" she said.

Bowing to her, he returned the ancient Romany greeting. "The great Lord be on you!"

She dropped her cloak on the floor and came into his arms with the simplicity of a child. She could be a woman of wiles when she wished to be, she could queen it with any woman in England and be snow or fire as the occasion demanded, but with Yoben she was always without guile. He had an honesty and humility that seemed to free some spring of freshness in herself, and an undemandingness to which she would gladly have given all that she proudly withheld from the greed of other men. Ten years ago, when she had first known him, it had puzzled her that he would not take it. "I am a man to whom the love of woman is forbidden," he had said to her then, and she had answered, her eyes full of pity for the torment that she felt in him, "There are more ways than one of fulfilling love, and the hardest way can be the best."

He did not ask her what it was, and she did not ask him why it was that way that they must take. They each had in their natures, as the fruit of adversity, a deep unhurried calm. Time was a flower that unfolded very slowly and kept its best secrets till the end.

"All is well with you, Froniga?" he asked anxiously.

"I never ailed in my life," she said.

"The days are anxious," he answered.

She laughed and leaned away from him. "Most of my days have been anxious, but I've always been the equal of my days."

The last daylight and the firelight together illumined her face, and looking at her he thought it was the strongest face he had ever seen in a woman, almost too strong for beauty and yet beautiful. She had never told him her age, but he judged her to be now about forty, for she had not been young when he had known her first ten years ago. She had a square brown face with high cheek-bones and determined chin. Her mouth was wide, with the lips set firmly. It was a gypsy face, but in her long-tailed dark eyes she showed her mixture of race, for they were not the changeful glittering black gypsy eyes, but soft and steady. Yet they had the strange penetrative quality of gypsy eyes, and her smile when with those she trusted had the joyous Romany frankness; for with her too guile was the result of oppression and not native to her character. She was tall and upright and carried herself superbly, if arrogantly. Her hands were not gypsy hands. Van Dyck would have delighted to paint them. She had always liked to dress plainly, but had loved bright colours, and he was surprised to see that she had now adopted the Puritan style of dressing, with her shining black hair hidden under a linen cap, plain white collar and cuffs on her grey gown, and a large white apron. He smiled, for that was typical of her. She never sat on the fence. Yet she cared little for politics and was not religious in the accepted sense, and he wondered what had induced her to hide her hair and exchange her green gown for a grey one.

"So you are a Parliament woman," he said.

"My cousin Robert Haslewood rides with John Hampden," she replied.

So that was it. Her relations with her father's family at the manor were nearly as full of sparks and prickles as her dealings with her mother's family down by the camp-fire, but she was fanatically loyal. Her loyalty to both strains in her blood, and her refusal to break with either, were responsible for the isolation in which she lived; they and the power that was in her, for people felt awe of her power.

"And you?" she asked challengingly.

"I have no politics," he said briefly. "You expect company?"

"Yes," she said. "You."

"But you did not know of my coming."

"However far away you are I always know when you turn towards me. If it is only your thoughts that turn, my thoughts too have only the one haven, but if it is your body also, with the distance between us lessening with every passing minute, then my heart grows lighter with every step you take. On the morning of the day that you will come there is no heaviness left in me."

In this sort of knowledge she was entirely Romany. Though the love between them was equal, he had no knowledge of it when in absence her thoughts turned his way. He felt himself a clod beside her, yet he delighted in being her foil; as the earth might delight in the contrast between itself and the green fern rooted in its homeliness. "I miss your green gown," he said.

She pushed him gently from her. "I have supper to get. In the room above you will find all you need put ready. Here is hot water for you."

She poured water from the kettle into a pewter jug and carrying it he unlatched a cupboard-like door and climbed up the steep dark stairs that led to the room above. It was not Froniga's room, which led out of it, but was used by her as a storeroom. A few early apples lay in rows on the floor and bunches of winter cherry and honesty, that Froniga called herb of the moon, hung from nails in the rafters. The silver and orange gleamed in the light of the rising moon, seen through the window, and moonlight washed the floor. Yoben caught his breath. After a parting, well-known rooms and familiar places take on such fresh beauty that one might be looking at them for the first time. A small truckle-bed stood under one of the dormer windows, for Froniga often had sick children under her care, and on it lay a finely-laundered white shirt. On a table beside it stood a basin and ewer, soap and a towel, two silver-backed brushes, a candle in a pewter candlestick and a tinder box. On the wall above hung a small steel mirror.

He lit the candle and made a fastidious toilet. In his roving life he could keep clean after a fashion, for he was healthy enough to enjoy bathing in running streams, but a tinker's trade is not of the cleanest and Madona was too old and Alamina too lazy to enjoy the washing of shirts. Froniga knew what a luxury her father's shirts and brushes were to him. The towel he used smelt of the woodruff that she kept among her linen and the soap of the oil of roses used in its making. The water was rain-water, soft as silk, the fine linen of the shirt almost as soft as the water to his chafed skin. He lingered over his toilet, to give Froniga time for her preparations. All that she did was done to perfection, but though she was competent she was not quick and hated to be hurried. When he went downstairs again lighted candles stood on the kitchen table and she was ladling broth out of the pot that hung on a hook over the fire, with her big white apron tied over a green gown.

"Now that's better," he said with satisfaction. "I do not know you in the sober dove-colours."

"You prefer me in parrot-colour?" she asked, setting his bowl of broth before him. "Or in yaffingale scarlet? I have something in common with a yaffingale, I think, for I like to laugh, but though I have plenty of vanity I hope I am not as bad as the parrot, who must always be drawing attention to himself with his 'Pretty Poll'."

"Durer and Van Eyck would sometimes set a parrot in the corner of their pictures of the Blessed Virgin," said Yoben as she took her own bowl and sat down opposite to him. "In the Middle Ages the grass-green parrot was one of the symbols of the Queen of Heaven, who bestowed on man an endless spring. . . . But I'm telling you what you knew long ago?" he asked in sudden humble anxiety. He was so accustomed to conversation with Alamina's children that when he was with Froniga he would forget how great was her own store of information.

"No, I did not know that," she said. Then she looked up, her eyes dancing. "But I am now a Puritan, Yoben, and would scorn to wear green in honour of the lady upon whom you bestow such idolatrous titles."

Fierce anger flamed in his eyes. "If you must hide your hair under the hideous cap must you put your mind in bondage also?" he asked. "When I came here last you were a woman of tolerance."

She looked at him in surprise, for she had never known him lose either his courtesy or his temper. She could lose her temper, but he, she had always thought, was the most patient man on earth. And now he was really angry, with that hurt anger which a man feels when a blow had been struck at his deepest beliefs. Yet even as she looked at him with astonishment the angry light went from his eyes and they were gentle as ever. "Forgive me, Froniga," he said.

She smiled, lifted his hands to her head with the gesture of a queen about to remove her crown and took off her cap. Her hair had only been loosely rolled up inside it and fell on her shoulders, black and shining. He had not seen her with her hair loose before and he gazed at her with a boy's shy awe. Aware of her beauty, she lifted her hair about her like a cloak. It was unusual hair, straight but curling at the ends. Something like panic took hold of him, and he got up quickly and pulled the curtains across the windows.

"Yoben," she said, "I do not care if the whole world sees us here together."

"It was not that," he said. "War makes men and women fanatical and your appearance just now would commend itself to no Puritan."

But it was not entirely that either. Straight hair curling at the tips and long-tailed eyes were the recognised marks of a witch, and he had seen many a witch-hunt in his time. "Never let your hair down again," he said curtly. "It's not safe."

She looked at him keenly and turned the talk to trivial things until she had him laughing at her racily-told anecdotes and enjoying the good food. He did not despise gypsy fare. Snails are good to eat in winter, taken in a hard frost behind the stumps of trees, salted and made into broth, and hedgehog flesh is tender as chicken, but Froniga's broth of herbs and vegetables, her bread and cheese and syllabub, were fit for a king, and with the enjoyment of a boy and the elegance of a king he ate of them. As they talked she thought how strange, and how maddening it was that she should have loved this fastidious, knowledgeable, gentle and cultured man for ten years and still not have the slightest idea who he was, where he had come from or why he had chosen to turn himself into a gypsy tinker.

Their meal finished, she cleared the table and they sat together on the settle by the fire. Usually after a parting they had much to talk about, but tonight, though there was no less of love, there was a shadow of constraint, and she felt she could not bear it. She got up, took the harebells from the pot on the table and brought them to him. "Our Lady's Thimbles, that bloom in her honour," she said gently. "And they reproach me, Yoben. I spoke carelessly just now."

He took her hands, still holding the flowers, and kissed them, then put the harebells into the button hole of his old jerkin. The hurt was healed, but there was still a shadow.

"You have no love for Puritans?" she asked.

"I have no politics," he said again.

"But you have sympathies, and they are not with us."

"Need we speak of this?"

"Yes, we must, Yoben. Because of this war you think one way and I another, and I can't bear it."

He took her hands again. "You must, my dear. What else is there to do? Do you expect to convert me?"

"Leading your roving life, you do not understand what has been happening in the country," she said. "Do you think good men would fight their King unless they were forced to it? They have tried the other ways, and they were useless. Do you want to see England without her Parliament? Only Parliament can preserve the liberties of the people, but the King would rule alone, without Parliament."

"You speak by the book, Froniga," said Yoben. "You have been well taught."

She was suddenly angry. "Do you admire tyrants?" she asked. "And the King is pro-Papist. If he gets his way in England we shall have the fires of Smithfield again, and be at the mercy of Spain."

"The fine phrases roll out well," said Yoben drily. They were both silent, fighting their anger, but their hands still clung together. Yoben recovered first. "It has come upon us," he said.

"I know," she said impatiently. "Is it only today you realise we are at war?"

"I don't mean the war," he said. "I mean our time of judgement, yours and mine. These scourges that come upon us, wars and disasters of all sorts, they're the retribution that the sin of the world pulls down upon itself, and collectively we're all guilty, though individually we may be innocent. Men choose one side or the other, making the best choice that they can with the knowledge that they have. Yet they know little, and the turns and twists of war are incalculable. They may fight for a righteous cause and yet at the end of it all have become as evil as their enemies, or they may in error espouse an evil cause and in defence of it grow better men than they were before. And so the one war becomes each man's private war, fought out within his own nature. In the last resort that's what matters to him, Froniga. In the testing of the times did he win or lose his soul? That's his judgement."

His voice trailed away into a silence heavy with dread and sorrow. Froniga drew her hands gently from his and sat looking into the fire. Why must he treat her in this way? Why, year after year, must he withhold his confidence from her? How can one soul help another's darkness with only conjecture for a candle? In the depth of her love for him there was an anger that had nothing to do with the war. He had refused her all the satisfactions of love. He was neither husband, lover nor intimate friend. He was simply a man arriving from nowhere as the fancy took him to talk about green parrots, and then vanishing into nowhere again, and that was supposed to satisfy her. She did not know which type of man was the most selfish, the sensual man who used a woman until she was broken, or the intellectual who demanded her sympathy yet defrauded her of her rights until she withered like a plant denied the sun and rain. Her anger died and she was suddenly ashamed. Both were weak men, yet both were men in need, and that was the plight of every human being born into this world. There was no remedy except mutually to accept the one and give to the other. And if this was a time of judgement, it was no time for sitting in judgement upon the failings of another, and that one the dearest to one's heart upon the earth. She must do the best that she could with her small candle of conjecture.

"One life knows many judgements," she said. "They are like the chapters in a book. What if every chapter but the last is one of defeat? The last can redeem it all. And God knows the heart that in its weakness longs for Him. Patient still, He adds another chapter, and then another, and then in the hour of victory closes the book."

He smiled, and she knew with gladness that she had taken the right path with her candle. "You always know where the salve is needed," he said. "If we could all see the hidden wounds of others as clearly as you do, 'Love your enemies' would not be so hard a command to keep."

She gave a sudden cry. "Don't speak of enemies, Yoben!"

"You've only just realised it?" he asked.

"Yes," she said. "And now it's your turn to comfort me."

"There's comfort," he said. "It's this. If the large conflict divides us, the smaller one unites us, and it is the smaller one that is the greatest in God's sight."

He got up to go. He had stayed only a short while, but the usual light-hearted hour that they spent together by the fire was not possible tonight. He took her in his arms and they clung together. He whispered something about another meeting and then withdrew himself and went away. She did not go with him through the garden, as was her custom, but stayed where she was, listening to his footfall on the flagged path by the well. He might come again tomorrow, or the day after, but things would not again be as they had been. So this was civil war. She had not known it was so bitter.

2

Yoben walked back over the field towards the distant glow of the camp-fire. The dew had fallen and silvered the grass almost as brightly as starlight washed the sky. The planets blazed above him, and he stopped and looked up at them. The constancy of those great lights, sometimes veiled for a season and then disclosed again, lifted his mind from sadness and discouragement. Were night to be always lightless, life itself would be that much darker. He could remember nights in prison made endurable by the stars seen through the small barred window, and other times when moonlight in a room where he lay sleepless had seemed to lift him on a tide of peace. His was a mind that had always needed symbols. Cut off from the sacraments of religion, he had clung to those of nature. In the stillness he could hear an owl hooting and the distant bark of a dog, but no other sound. In a world so still it was hard to believe in the reality of war.

When he reached the camp only Madona was still sitting by the fire. The three loves of her life were now her great-grand-children, Yoben and warmth. When she was not caring for the children she would sometimes nod by the fire all day, but at night she would become wakeful and alert and her mind would wander back over the long ways of the past, her own and that of her people, and in the light of her memory events that had once been bitter were so no longer. Yoben loved to sit by the fire with her at night and share the richness of the purged and sweetened past.

"Life is good by the fire, Yoben," she said, as he sat down beside her. "It's good to have fire when the days draw in." She picked up a handful of fir-cones and threw them on the embers, and in the light of the flames he could see the opening of her tent just beside them and within it the three children, Dinki, Meriful and Cinderella, lying asleep under her brown cloak. Waking or sleeping they seemed always under that cloak; except when they were away in the woods and fields, when the old woman would sit disconsolate, the folds of the cloak drooping from her shoulders like broken wings. Without Madona the children would have been comfortless indeed, for their mother Alamina took her duties to her offspring as lightly as she had come by them.

Yoben took off his own cloak and put it round Madona's shoulders, for she had nothing to keep her warm but the tattered remnants of an old red shawl, and at their backs the night was growing chill. She raised her arm, with that protective gesture he knew so well, and lifted the cloak about his shoulders also. It had been made for him in the days when his body had been more adequately covered with flesh than it was now, and with Madona a wraith there was room for both. She laughed happily and pointed to the glowing fir-cones. "Fire flowers," she said. "Nothing more fair to see." He smiled, watching them a moment where they lay in their glowing nest, each bract delicately outlined in golden fire. About them licked small tongues of flame, blue and crocus-coloured. No, there was nothing more fair to see, unless it was the night sky above them; or Madona's face in the glow of the flames.

Madona Heron was eighty years old and had a face of transmuted tragedy. Ten years ago it had expressed only the nobility of selfless endurance, but now it expressed also peace and delight. For nearly a lifetime she had endured without complaint every sort of ill-treatment from her husband Piramus, a man of violent temper and cunning cruelty, she had borne many children and mourned the deaths of most of them, she had put up with cold and exhaustion, near-starvation, persecution, in a perpetual cycle, and taken it all as merely her lot. And now her long patience had brought her at last to the point where the sense of personal struggle ceases for a soul and she is passive and at rest in other keeping than her own. Madona lived now as though lifted above life. Piramus no longer ill-treated her because he got no kick out of it; she was detached as a cloud in the sky. As she never considered herself at all, she was unaware of what had happened to her; she only knew that life was good. Yet she did not, like so many old people, cling to life, because she clung to nothing. Yoben, understanding where she stood, rejoiced in her joy. It was so seldom that a soul lived long enough in this world to attain such heights in a body that allowed her to enjoy her peace. For, say what men would who had never so suffered, detachment from severe physical pain was impossible unless the body died under the torture. It was when the iron touched your own flesh—your flesh—he wrenched his mind back to Madona. She had never ailed more than a little. Her black eyes were still clear and bright, and though she was frail as a brown autumn leaf she held herself upright and still moved with ease. Her face was very thin and the fine bones showed clearly through the wrinkled skin, the firelight glinting on the outlines of the high cheek-bones, aquiline nose and square chin and showing pits of shadow about the sunken eyes and in the hollowed cheeks. Froniga might one day look like Madona if she lived as long and selflessly. In the silence that had fallen between them he remembered Froniga coming in warm and glowing in her white cap and grey gown, and then Froniga in the green dress with her black hair tumbling on her shoulders.

"Is it well with my sister's child?" asked Madona.

"It is well," said Yoben, and then added for the hundredth time, "but it would be better if you and she could be known to each other."

To this Madona replied for the hundredth time, gently and inexorably. "Her mother married a gorgio. Her mother broke the Romany law and thereafter dared to wear a green gown. No Romany who breaks the law must ever again wear a green gown."

"It is not justice to punish Froniga for her mother's fault," pleaded Yoben yet again.

"Let her redeem her mother's fault by leaving the house-dwellers and becoming a true Romanitshel and I will take her to my heart," said Madona.

"But the house-dwellers are also her people, her father's people," said Yoben.

But Madona had the gypsy's fine disdain for everyone not connected with the Romany world. "I spit upon her father's people," she said serenely.

Yoben, as before, gave it up. Madona was the greatest woman he had ever known, or ever would know, but in matters of religion she was a fanatic, and the Romany law was her religion.

"It is a fair moon," he said, changing the subject to one very near her heart. "And the stars like glow-worms up there."

Madona turned her face up to the sky and the diklo fell back from her straggling white hair. Her lips parted and the outlines of her face softened as she smiled. She adored the moon. She gloried in all the works of God, but in making the moon she thought He had surpassed Himself. One of the things she enjoyed about Yoben was that he listened when she talked of the moon. The other men did not. To them it was no more than a useful light to go poaching by. Only Yoben agreed with her that moonrise was a lovelier thing even than dayspring, and that it was natural that the old should wish to live long enough to see just once more that silver light pouring from the sky.

"Nearing the full," said Madona, "and the weather set fair. Night after night now she'll show us the dearie things of earth, the fields fashioned of light and the trees from darkness; we'll not lose them."

"Tell me about her," said Yoben. "Tell me as you tell the children."

"You've heard me telling the children as many times as there are stars in the sky," said Madona.

"Once more," pleaded Yoben, knowing how she loved to follow the gypsy rôle of story-telling, and flung some more cones on the fire, so that the flames leaped up again. Madona replaced her diklo and spread her hands to the blaze. They were so thin that the light seemed to shine through them.

"The Sun was lonely," she began in her deep husky voice, half-intoning the words. "The great are always alone, poor souls, sad and alone in greatness, and who more lonely than the Sun? Only the Sun, driving his chariot through the fields of heaven. So many thousands living in his light, but only the one Sun. In his loneliness he thought he would take him a wife, and for nine long years he drove his nine great horses through heaven and around the world, but neither in the fields of the one nor the other, neither among the stars nor the flowers, did he see a maiden as lovely as his sister Helen with the silver hair. The more he looked at her the more he loved her, for indeed the Lord God never made a creature fairer than she. But when he asked her to marry him she said, 'Sun, my brother, your purity lights the world. If we commit this sin there will be darkness upon the face of the earth.' And she turned her face from his mid-day splendour and withdrew herself.

"So the Sun drove up and up the steep of heaven until he came to the throne of the Lord God (sanctified in heaven and upon the earth), and there he bowed himself and poured out the gold flood of his supplication, begging that he might have his sister Helen to be his wife. And the Lord God took him by the hand and led him into hell, and the Sun covered his bright face with his hands and could not look upon the desolation of that place. And then the Lord God took him into Paradise, and he stretched out his arms, and his heart was near breaking for the beauty and the peace. And then the Lord God led him back into the fields of the sky and they stood there together and the Lord God said, 'Choose'. And the Sun looked up and saw Helen afar off, and he said, 'Hell'.

"But the Lord God (sanctified in heaven and upon the earth) was not minded that the fair world He had lifted out of darkness into light should be plunged again into the bitter cold by the sin of a man and a woman, and stretching His hand across Heaven, He took Helen and flung her into the sea, and she became a silver fish, beautiful and delicate, sickle-shaped, swimming this way and that and giving light to the monsters of the deep. Then the Sun rose and blazed across heaven, descending pale with grief towards the west, where, plunging into the sea, he went to look for his beloved among the monsters of the deep. Then the Lord God (sanctified in heaven and upon the earth) took Helen in His hand and tossed her into the sky again, and she hung there, delicate and pale, a sickle curve of trembling light. The Lord God spoke, and the earth shook, and the mountains bowed their heads, and the stars hid their faces. 'Golden Sun and silver Moon, for eternity you must follow each other with your eyes through space without meeting in the fields of heaven. Then will your purity endure for ever, lighting the world. But you will wander for ever. There will be no respite for you, Sun and Moon.' "

Madona had been a harpist and singer in her youth, and her music still lived in her plaintive story-telling. Yoben sat silently when she had finished, thinking of these people whom he had adopted as his own, and of this story of theirs. How old was it? Some seven hundred years ago, it was thought, the Romany people had travelled from North-West India, bringing that story with them. They had journeyed through Persia, Armenia and Greece, gathering words from the languages of those countries into their own beautiful language, one of the eight Indian languages of the Aryan stock. They had spread themselves through all the countries of Europe, and in every country, it seemed, they had a different story to tell of where they had come from and how they had got there. Madona knew many of these legends and had told them to Yoben and the children, but they had all grown from the sun and moon story, they were all variations of the theme of penitent pilgrims destined to wander because they had sinned. "We expiate our sin," they had said to the Emperor Sigismund, and to the Pope too when they had journeyed into Italy. "Wandering, we expiate our sin." It was in the hope that in sharing their wandering he might expiate his own that Yoben had joined them. He had been a young man then and now he was old, and the end was not yet. His heart would have failed him had he known it would be so long.

Eleven tolled from the church tower among the trees. "Will you not sleep, Madona?" he asked.

"Here by the fire," she said.

He replenished the fire, fetched from her tent an armful of the dried river mint and hay that was her bedding and helped her to lie down upon it, covered with his cloak. She often had a fancy for sleeping in the open. Her body had been so toughened by endurance that cold dews and night airs caused her no discomfort, and out in the open she could see the moon.

Yoben stepped over the sleeping children in the tent and sat down beside them. He was not yet ready for sleep. He sat and watched them with mingled love and exasperation where they lay cuddled upon the heap of bedstraw, thyme and sweet wood-sorrel that Madona herself had picked and dried to make their bed; for it was upon bedstraw, thyme and woodruff that the Holy Babe had lain in the manger and Madona hoped (unavailingly) that upon such bedding holy dreams might visit them for their edification. But Dinki, Meriful and Cinderella were impervious to edification.

Dinki and Meriful were five and seven years old and Cinderella was four. They were nut-brown, and the two younger ones were plump as young partridges. The firelight flickered over their sleeping faces, touching the rounded curves of their dusky cheeks with colour and glinting in the shadows of their hair. By day their hair was seen to be as full of dust and foreign bodies as a last-year's bird's nest, and of much the same consistency, but by night the tousled soft dark rings had a mysterious beauty. Awake they looked the imps of mischief that they were, but asleep, with their sparkling black eyes closed and the long curling lashes lying on their cheeks in their own deep shadow, their faces had an angelic pathos. Cinderella had her thumb in her mouth. Her hand looked like a fat little pin-cushion of acorn-coloured satin, with five dimples in the fatness where the knuckles were. Dinki had pillowed a flushed apple cheek on a palm so dirty that it looked black. Meriful had thrust a slim brown foot from beneath the cloak. It was clean, for he had been paddling in the dew-pond, and was entwined with spray of Convolvulus. He only of the children was slim and delicately made, and already tall for his age. Asleep, his aquiline face looked proud as that of a young Pharaoh, yet gentle and pathetic too. Awake, he was the worst of the three. Yoben sighed and drew a fold of the cloak over the beautiful foot that he had last encountered as it kicked him in the shins. The bruises were still painful. Parental chastisement was needed, but the fatherhood of the children being uncertain, it had been allowed to lapse. Yoben was the only person, apart from Madona, who regarded Meriful, Dinki and Cinderella as being of any importance, and Madona was too old now to be much of a disciplinarian. She got most of the love and Yoben most of the kicks. But he was not unloved. Stirring in his sleep, Meriful flung out a hand that lighted on Yoben's. It stayed there, clenched firmly upon his thumb.

With his free hand Yoben took a shabby book from his pocket and held it so that the light of the moon and the fire fell upon the worn yellow pages. Yet he scarcely needed the light, for he had said the words day by day for such an eternity of time that he could have said them in his sleep. As he prayed he was aware of the eternal ascension of earth's praise, the adoration not of men only but of all created things. One was even more aware of it in silence and stillness than when the birds were singing and the trees bowing to the wind. He lost himself in it and the children came with him; he drew them with him in their sleep, Meriful holding to his hand.

"Laudate pueri Dominum: laudati nomen Domini," he murmured. "Praise the Lord, ye children : praise ye the name of the Lord."

"Sit nomen Domini benedictum: ex hoc nunc, et usque in saeculum.

"A solis ortu usque ad occasum: laudabile nomen Domini."

When midnight struck from the church tower he put the book away, gently disengaged his hand from Meriful's and lay down beside him. But though the flow of praise still held him, giving him peace, he could not sleep. Beyond the peace his anxiety for Froniga waited, and the times were evil.

3

Deeply anxious for him, she could not sleep either. She got up from her green-curtained bed and, wrapped in her cloak, leaned at the open window of her room, and almost instantly she was happier. The vast dome of the sky, arched from horizon to horizon over the heathland, would have been terrifying but for the moonlight that rained down with such gentleness upon the flatness of the crouching earth. The beauty that emerged from the flatness, her plum tree set with stars, the shapes of distant woods, the tower of the church rising from the churchyard yews and the faint glow of flame from the camp-fire down in the dingle, seemed to Froniga to have been drawn upwards by the moonlight as flowers are by the sun. But sunlight can tarnish, while this beneficence gave to all it shone upon a quality of unchangeableness. The plum tree in bright sunshine was of the earth, but in this moonlight its ebony and silver had an immortal look, as though it were not a tree but a spirit. Froniga had been told that to the blind moonlight has sound, and shutting her eyes for a moment she wondered what that sound could be. Music, brought down from the stars? A chime of far-away voices, like friends greeting each other in another world? Or a murmuring of reassurance, like the wind before the dawn? Something like that, some visitation of eternity giving a meaning to the flux of things.

Her eyes still closed she became aware of distant sound stealing into the silence, a rhythmic muffled beat, heard and then not heard, that might have been the rolling of a drum. Only the sound had an eerie quality that did not seem earthly. She listened intently and found herself listening only to the silence. "A running that could not be seen of skipping beasts." Then it came again, very faintly, and this time it might have been summer rain visiting the leaves, then more strongly, and the light rain had become a storm that was still on the far side of the heath. And then it was the skipping beasts again, running, coming nearer. She opened her eyes and her heart missed a beat with terror, for it was the unicorn galloping across the heath, his tossed mane silver in the moonlight, his silver hoofs scarcely touching the milky whiteness of the field. With white neck arched he wheeled round almost beneath her window, with two other dark shapes galloping after him. One gave a shrill neigh that was like a trumpet call and then all three pounded away again into the distance. She laughed, for they were gypsy pack-ponies, one white pony and two black ones, who by day were bony unkempt creatures hardly worth the stealing. But by moonlight, as horses do, they came into their own and showed themselves as creatures more akin to it than men are, mystical beasts before whom a man by night can feel afraid.

Froniga stood where she was until she could hear them no longer, and wondered if it was Yoben now who was listening to the sound of the skipping beasts. She went back to her bed and lay down, seeing nothing now from her high window but a cluster of stars. In the stillness she was aware of the ascension of earth's praise. She was not a woman who prayed very often, but she prayed now, not in her own words but in words to whose beauty the repetition of the ages had given an almost starry lustre.

"Praise the Lord, ye children: praise ye the name of the Lord.

"Blessed be the name of the Lord: from henceforth, now, and for ever.

"From the rising of the sun unto the going down of the same: the name of the Lord is worthy of praise."

She spoke the words aloud, again and again, and soon she was asleep.

CHAPTER III

MARGARET

Margaret Haslewood was dressed before seven o'clock the next morning, seated in front of her mirror and coiling her corn-coloured hair into a knot at the back of her head. Her hair was her great beauty and it was with a sense of exasperation that she hid it beneath her big white linen cap. She had looked pretty in the old days when she had dressed her hair in ringlets about her face and worn be-ribboned gowns and rustling stiff silk petticoats that had helped to support her always tottering self-confidence. She was a slight, pale woman, past her first youth, and the plain gowns that Robert her husband insisted upon now he was a Puritan made her look like one of her own servants. She found it difficult to order them about nowadays and she was blighted by her cap. Her cousin-in-law, Froniga Haslewood (she disliked using the gypsy form of Veronica, but Froniga insisted on it), was more than past her first youth but was not in the least blighted by her cap, and wore her grey gown with such an air that she would have cowed any number of servants; only, as is the way of things in this contrary world, she had none to cow. "There's one thing," thought Margaret, "if the clothes don't suit me as well as they do Froniga the—the—rest of it—suits me much better. Froniga to call herself a Puritan! There was a man at her house last night, Biddy says. She brings shame upon us all and upon the Cause for which we fight."

Margaret had only the vaguest idea what that was, for she had not much head for politics. She doubted if her husband had either, and he had taken no interest in them until that day when he had heard that the King had imprisoned John Hampden. Charles's extravagance had involved him in such financial straits that he had imposed a forced loan upon his subjects. It was illegal and John Hampden would not pay it. Robert had exploded into rage, not so much because of the unconstitutional behaviour of the King as because he had dared to lay a finger on John Hampden, who had been Robert's hero since they had been at the Grammar School at Thame together and Hampden, the senior boy in the school, had shown kindness to the terrified new boy. Robert's parents had not known that the boys must provide their own candles at school, and that first cold winter morning, when the bell rang for work at six o'clock, he had had no light to con his Latin by. He had wept, seven years old and parted from his mother for the first time, and John Hampden had comforted him and shared his own candle with him. It was an action typical of him. Robert was a hero-worshipper and from then onwards he had been Hampden's man.

Through the years of his boyhood and young manhood he had worshipped from a distance, for the wealthy Buckinghamshire landowner, with a descent nobler than that of the King himself, was far removed from the humble country squire, but he had estates in Oxfordshire and after his release from prison Robert saw him sometimes and came more and more under his influence. Hampden's beliefs became his beliefs, and his beliefs Margaret's, so far as she could make head or tail of them. The trouble between the King and a large section of his people, she understood, was both political and religious. Politically Hampden and John Pym and the men who stood with them maintained that the King had no right to execute policies which ran counter to the advice of Parliament, or to dissolve Parliament as and when he wished. Religiously, the Calvinist doctrine of the equality of all men before God, held by the Puritans, could not be reconciled with Charles's belief in special divinity resident in the person of the King. The choice, Robert would tell Margaret, was thus inescapable, for it was between justice and injustice, tyranny and liberty.

Margaret tried hard to feel that it was inescapable, and to feel the same enthusiastic dedication to a cause that he felt, and that had made a new man of him; a finer man, she knew, but sterner and more removed from her, not the close companion that he had been in the early days of their marriage. And he was away from home so often that much responsibility devolved upon her now, and she disliked responsibility. Sometimes she felt that she hated all the great men, Pym and Hampden and the rest of them equally with the King's men. Their anger, righteous or otherwise, flaming out in stirring speeches, had upset the whole country, and they had no thought for the repercussions in the lives of quiet people like herself. Dimly she wrestled sometimes with the problem of these repercussions. That the courage of John Hampden should have spoilt her happiness seemed altogether a bad thing, yet could evil come out of such good? Was it perhaps good that she should be lonely and overburdened? Perhaps the responsibility for repercussions did not belong so much to those who caused them as to those who received them? A speech made in Parliament could, like a stone dropped in water, cause a ripple like a wave in the life of an obscure woman the speaker had never heard of, but she supposed it was she to choose whether the wave should lift or drown her.

She got up from her mirror and fastened her big bunch of keys to her waistband. The sunlight gleamed upon them and her heart lifted a little, for it was a fine morning, the day of her little boy's breeching, and Robert was coming home. She would forget the war and try to imagine that this day was one of those that she and Robert had enjoyed when there had been no separation between them; or one of those they would enjoy together in the future when they had come together again. For perhaps if she could breast this wave she might grow into a new woman who would fit the new man as well as she had once fitted the old one.

The sunlight shone on the carved four-poster, the press, the dressing-chest and stools that had come down from father to son with the house itself. The bed-curtains had been a wedding gift from Froniga. On pale green linen, woven by herself, she had embroidered gilliflowers, paggles and roses. They were hangings fit for a queen's bed, but Margaret found it difficult to rejoice in them as she should. Biddy, who had lived for most of her life in this house and been cook to Robert's mother, had told her that when they were young Robert had wanted to marry his cousin Froniga. It had been in poor taste, Margaret thought, for Froniga to embroider hangings for a bed in which she might, if she had chosen, have spent her own wedding night and borne her own children. Margaret had embroidered the bedspread herself, but she was not such an exquisite needlewoman as Froniga and the linen was puckered in places.

She opened the door into the further room where the children slept, went in and softly drew back the bed-curtains. They were still asleep in a four-poster almost as large as hers, the dog Maria tucked in between them. There was room for a couple more children in the big bed and it was a shame to Margaret that her physical frailty should have produced only two. For years Froniga had dosed her with tansy, for the herbalist Nicolas

Culpeper (in whom Froniga had great faith) had said, "Let those women that desire children love this herb; it is their best companion, their husbands excepted." But it had been no use. After Jenny and Will there had been no more children, and Maria was a poor substitute.

She was also, today, something of a problem, for she was an aged King Charles spaniel, acquired as a puppy in the days when Robert was taking a less unfavourable view of the royal family than he did now, and she had been named after Queen Henrietta Maria. No man likes to be reminded of opinions that are no longer his, and upon his last homecoming Robert (who did not like dogs in any case) had said sternly to Margaret, "Get rid of that old bitch." But Margaret, disobeying him for the only time in her married life, had not done so because the children loved Maria. The worried frown that lived now permanently on Margaret's forehead deepened. . . . Maria must be kept out of the way. . . . Standing beside the bed she looked at her children, especially at her adored little son, lying on his back in a lordly attitude, outflung arms claiming much more than his half of the bed, his cheeks poppy-red, the curls that must be cut off today, a little damp upon his forehead, his breath coming sweetly and evenly between his parted lips. Jenny lay slim and straight upon her side, one hand under her cheeks, her face pale, her dark hair tucked neatly away under a frilled nightcap. Asleep, she looked much older than she was, not the least like either of her parents, but with some faint unidentifiable resemblance to Froniga. Margaret could not love her quite as she loved Will, who had her corn-coloured hair and blue eyes and his father's stocky figure and was altogether an enchanting mixture of the Haslewoods and her own family, the Coplands of Birch Hall. You could, so to speak, take Will to pieces and know exactly where each bit came from, and when he was put together again he was a knowable, lovable, perfectly ordinary small boy. But Jenny, apart from that vague likeness to Froniga, bore no likeness to any Haslewoods or Coplands that anyone remembered. She had reached very far back into time for her brown eyes and hair, that disconcerting air of remoteness, and the brains that Margaret was afraid she was going to develop very shortly. No Haslewood or Copland within living memory had been troubled with more brains than are necessary for the conduct of life in a gentlemanly or lady-like manner, and Margaret thought it was best that intellect should stop just there. An excess of it led to eccentricities and abnormalities, even if they were those of genius, and Margaret did not think such things should be encouraged. Jenny was lovable, and Margaret loved her dearly, but she was neither knowable nor ordinary.

"I wish I could kiss them awake, like I used to when they were babies," thought Margaret yearningly. "They would wake up and find themselves in my arms, and then they would burrow in as though they wanted us to be one person again. Life was warm and cosy in those days. The whole of our life seemed like a nest."

She straightened her shoulders and compressed the tenderness out of her lips. She must no longer pamper her young. Will was to be breeched today and Jenny was to don her first pair of adult corsets. She must remember what her husband said, that the children had in front of them a life of hard endeavour in the service of God and must be trained accordingly. . . . Whom the Lord loveth He chasteneth, but she hated to think of Jenny in corsets. . . . Spare the rod and spoil the child, and the rod was not spared at school. . . . With all the appropriate texts stabbing her heart she pulled back the bedclothes and said severely, "Children, get up at once. Jenny—Will—Maria—at once."

All three woke. Will opened his eyes, gazed belligerently at his mother, then rolled over on to his front and buried his scarlet face in the pillow, pulling up his knees and uprearing his buttocks in the manner of an affronted caterpillar. Jenny sat up and smiled sweetly but vaguely. Maria crawled after the warmth that had been so ruthlessly withdrawn from her, crept under the bedclothes at the bottom of the bed and remained hidden. She was devoted to the children, but now that this new Puritanical discipline had descended upon the house she knew when to dissociate herself from them.

"Children!" ejaculated Margaret.

Jenny instantly slipped out of bed and stood shivering in her night-shift, for the morning was chilly. Her mother noticed with a pang that she still had the mobile and expressive toes that very small children have. They curled upwards distastefully from the bare floor. But only with her toes did Jenny express unconscious rebellion. Without being told she went to the corner of the room, poured cold water out of the ewer into the basin, slipped off her night-shift and began to wash herself.

She was a biddable child, but her mother always had the slightly uncomfortable feeling that she was biddable because she chose to be. Should she choose one day not to be, Margaret did not at all know what would happen.

"Will!" said Margaret sharply.

The arched protuberance rose a little higher. Margaret summoned all her resolution and smacked it hard, but instead of sinking, the arch rose higher still. Surely, thought Margaret in despair, he was not going to force her to punish him on his breeching day.

"Will!" she said. "It's your breeching day!"

The arch sank slowly and with one long roll, like that of a porpoise, Will revolved over the side of the bed, came right way up on the floor, grabbed a towel, draped it over his shoulder, advanced his right foot slightly and placed his left hand on his hip. "Who am I?" he asked.

"Will!" said his mother sharply. There were times when thinking who he was all day was almost too much for her. "I've no time for nonsense. Get washed and dressed. If you don't hurry Mr. Lovejoy will be here with your clothes before you're ready."

"I might dress, but I won't wash," said Will. "Men don't wash. Who am I?"

"Do as I tell you at once, Will," Margaret was trembling and there were tears in her eyes. The church clock struck seven and there were only two hours of his childhood left to her. She had hoped that after breakfast he might have sat on her lap for the last time and been the loving little boy that he could be at times. But now they seemed heading for disaster.

Jenny, who had been combing her hair, ran round the room and plunged her comb savagely beneath his left armpit. " 'Speak, hands, for me!' " she hissed.

" '*Et tu, Brute!*' " sighed Will, and sank to the floor, where he lay with one arm doubled under him and his eyes staring horribly.

" 'Liberty! Freedom! Tyranny is dead!' " cried Jenny. " 'Rise hence, proclaim, cry it about the streets.' " And she returned placidly to her toilet.

Margaret left the room. She had to go because her tears were spilling over and her children must not see her weakness. Also she was furious with Froniga, whose habit of having the children to her cottage and reading Shakespeare to them, to rest their mother, was not resting her. The children were over-stimulated. And she did not want them to read Shakespeare, who had been dead for nearly thirty years and was now out of fashion. And what Froniga really wanted to do, she was sure, was not to rest her but to take her children away from her; because they were Robert's children and Froniga wished now that she had married him.

Struggling to control herself, she went slowly down the oak staircase, that was the glory of the house. The carved terminal post was crowned with the unicorn's head that was the family crest, and the balustrade was arcaded. The stone-flagged hall below was patterned with light, for the doors of parlour and dining-parlour were open and the sunshine streamed in through their windows. Good smells rose up to meet Margaret : bread baking in the kitchen, where Biddy could be heard singing among her pots and pans, furniture polish, the scent of the gilliflowers in the garden, and keener and more fragrant even than these, the scent of herbs. Margaret wiped her eyes and saw Froniga standing in the hall with a basket on her arm. For a moment such an early arrival on the part of Froniga seemed the last straw and then, suddenly, she was glad. Froniga was so capable. She took the last few stairs almost at a run and found herself, surprisingly, in Froniga's arms.

"What is it, my dear?" Froniga asked gently. She thought Margaret a poor fool and did not suffer her very gladly, but she was fond of her. Beneath the jealousy of the one woman and the impatience of the other there was an affection stronger than either of them realised.

"It's Will," sobbed Margaret.

"Who is he?" asked Froniga.

"Julius Caesar," said Margaret. "I can't think why I'm crying. But Jenny pretended to stab him and he pretended to die. I hate this war and I hate Shakespeare. He says men don't wash—I mean Will does."

"Leave Will to me," said Froniga. "Look, I've brought you a basket of strewing herbs."

"Thank you," said Margaret, struggling for cordiality. Strewing herbs had gone out of fashion, and she seldom used them, but Robert was fond of them, and she had forgotten that he was. Froniga had the irritating habit of knowing what she had forgotten and supplying it. But she managed to bend her head over the basket and sniff and make some appreciative murmuring.

In the basket were lavender, germander and pennyroyal, and sprigs of sea-green rosemary from the glorious bush that grew in Froniga's garden.

"It always seems so wrong to walk on rosemary," said Margaret.

"Not on great occasions," said Froniga. "Not when a little boy is to be breeched. You must have something to steady you, Margaret. Look, here's Biddy with tea for you. Biddy, keep the tea-leaves for me and I'll take them to one of my old dames."

Tea was a terrible price, and only the gentry could afford it. Both Margaret and Froniga saved their tea-leaves after they had been infused and gave them to their poor neighbours. Leaving the bustling Biddy to look after Margaret, Froniga slipped upstairs, for she had been aware as she talked of a small figure on the landing above. She loved Jenny only a little less than she loved Robert and Yoben.

"Cousin Froniga!" cried Jenny breathlessly, as she flew into her arms. "I can't get Will dressed. He keeps being one thing after the other. You'd think he'd like being himself on his breeching day, wouldn't you?"

"Those who dramatise themselves never like being themselves," explained Froniga.

She hugged Jenny and swept into the children's room. Will, attired in the minimum of undergarments, was standing on the bed brandishing his towel. "Praise be to God and little Laud to the devil!" he shouted. "Cousin Froniga, who am I?"

Froniga flushed angrily. The "mot" of the King's jester, that had cost him his place at court, had been bandied about with delight in Parliament country, but the imprisoned Archbishop had been born in Reading, not eight miles from them, and she believed in local loyalty. She lifted Will summarily from the bed. "Have you washed?' she asked curtly.

"No," said Will. "Men don't."

"There you are wrong," said Froniga, and hauled him to the basin of cold water. With his head pinioned under her arm she attended to his ablutions.

"I won't put those skirts on again," he said through the muffling towel.

"There you are once more wrong," said Froniga, and with deft movements she got both his arms into his long full-skirted coat, buttoned it up and reached for the hairbrush. Jenny watched in admiration, marvelling at her cousin's capabilities, determining to be like that when she grew up. And now Cousin Froniga had brushed Will's hair so that it was a mass of glinting curls all over his head. No one else could brush his hair like that. But it seemed a pity to be taking so much trouble when his curls were to be cut off in another two hours.

"If his curls are to be cropped they must be worth cropping," said Froniga, answering Jenny's unspoken thought, as she so often did. "Endings should have poignancy, a clear sharp cut between one fair thing and another, otherwise they are as dreary as the death of the wicked. . . . Children, listen!"

They ran to her at the open window. At first they could hear nothing, for they had not the keen hearing that Froniga had inherited from her gypsy mother, then faintly above the rustle of the wind they heard the sound of a horse's hoofs coming up the hidden hill to the left. "Father!" they cried, and flew helter-skelter from the room. Froniga smiled, thinking that the patter of an excited child's feet on the stairs is one of the gayest sounds in the world; not even the patter of summer rain on parched leaves, or the galloping of ponies in the moonlight, gave her quite such a feeling of expectancy. Of what? We live ever on the edge of expectancy, she thought, whether we know it or not; ever with our eyes on the line of light that shines through the crack of the door.

She set herself to the tidying of the room, for in the excitement of Robert's arrival the maids and Margaret would have plenty to do. Pulling off the bedclothes she found Maria, who instantly forestalled punishment by rolling on her back and gazing up with pleading eyes while tucking in her forepaws to expose an expanse of chest which she desired should be caressed. Froniga, stooping to rub the creamy-white chest, thought how intimately a beloved dog becomes an integral part of its home. Maria seemed always at the heart of Flowercote Manor. Wherever it was warm, in the children's bed, before the fire, curled round in patches of sun upon the floor, there was Maria, the complete sybarite, yet radiating warmth from her own enjoyment of it. Froniga lifted her from her comfortable nest and set her on the floor. Unresentful, she waddled towards the pool of sunlight by the window and lay down in the centre of it.

CHAPTER IV

FOR PARLIAMENT

Robert Haslewood was astonished at the beauty of the country through which he was riding. The beech-woods alternating with the park-like fields with their groups of tall silver birches and Spanish chestnuts, the patches of heath country and the sudden long views of far blue hills had been familiar to him from boyhood and yet it seemed to him that he had never really looked at them before. . . . He realised suddenly how much the last few years had changed him.

Until the death of his parents he had been an idolised only son and after that an adored husband. Life in his ancestral home had always been pleasant and his easy kindliness had won him the affection of his servants and tenants. His parents' death and his boyhood's passion for his cousin Froniga, five years older than himself, and her laughing rejection of it, had been his only sorrows. He had seen himself always through the eyes of his parents, his wife and his dependants, and moved through his comfortable days a paragon among men.

Then had come the first of two experiences that had shaken him so much that he had been bewildered by the shaking. They had seemed such small things to cause him such distress.

He had been in London during halcyon spring weather. Hampden had lately been on trial again for his refusal to pay the illegal ship-money tax, but this time the King had won his case by such a small majority that he had not been imprisoned. Robert had been in high good humour over this, and swollen with pride that he lived nowadays on terms of increasing familiarity with this great man, and on a warm sunny day had set out with pleasurable anticipation to watch John Lilburne whipped to the pillory.

Lilburne was a young Puritan who had been caught distributing the forbidden Calvinist literature, which Dutch shipmasters unloaded on lonely parts of the Essex coast. The Star Chamber had imposed a savage sentence and it was to be carried out today. Robert had been in the country when the earlier Puritan martyrs had suffered, Prynne, Burton and Bastwicke. It had been a great occasion. Rosemary and other sweet herbs had been strewn before their feet by the crowd and the excitement and edification had been intense, for the martyrs had preached eloquently from their pillories, and when their ears had been cropped the crowd had surged forward to soak their handkerchiefs in the martyrs' blood. Robert had been extremely sorry to have missed it, and was glad he could make good the omission now it was Lilburne's turn.

As a justice of the peace he had himself condemned men to the stocks, to be flogged or branded, even to be hanged, and that being his duty, and they felons, had thought no more about it. He had never personally supervised a flogging or hanging, but he had seen men in the stocks and the pillory often enough, had watched them with pleasure or ridden by laughing, and so he expected to feel no emotions now except the excitement of partisanship, of righteous indignation, of cheering crowds, and the pleasure (which he had never analysed) of watching another man's suffering out of the comfortable depths of his own security. And then, unexpectedly, something happened to him. His immunity failed him slightly; not a great deal, but enough to startle him as nothing in his life had startled him yet. To begin with, Lilburne turned out to be a young man, hardly more than a boy, and looked delicate and highly-strung, and from the Fleet to Westminster was a long way for a boy to be whipped. But he had courage and he managed it, though he arrived at the pillory exhausted and suffering, covered with mud and blood and not able to speak to the people just at once. He gasped out that he would do it later, but they put a stop to his gasps with a gag. But Robert, as he followed along with the crowd, did not manage it so well as Lilburne, for something about the boy, his eyes or his homely yeoman features, reminded him of Will, and so of himself, for Will was like him. This thing seemed to be happening to himself. Until now, miseries of all sorts were what happened to other people. If they bore their pain silently he thought no more about it. If fortitude failed them he felt a sense of personal outrage. But now it was as though this thing were fastening in his own flesh. When the boy was in the pillory he could not stand it. He was so sickened that he had to go away.

But he could not keep away, and later he went back. Lilburne was coming to the end of the allotted hours of his torture.

Because of his thirst and the heat of the day his lips were black and swollen. Some hostile elements in the crowd had pelted him with rotten eggs and filth. Flies crawled over his bruised face, feeding on the filth there, and his eyes were bloodshot. Robert met his eyes, and the pain went boring into his own head as though nails were being driven into his temples and into the back of his skull. He stood there till the end with the boy and watched when they took him away. Yet what kept Robert awake that night was not so much the remembrance of the boy's pain as of the time when he himself had ordered such punishments to be inflicted, had watched them with pleasure or ridden by laughing. What sort of creatures were men? What sort of a man was he?

After that he was swept up into the tragic march of great events. He was a member of the Short Parliament. He listened with his mind alight and his heart burning to the oratory of Pym and Hampden's reasoned arguments. He joined the march of the four thousand gentlemen of Buckingham along the frost-bound roads to London, carrying two petitions to the King, one "to declare their readiness to live and die with the Parliament and in the defence of the rights of the House of Commons", and the other a protest that "John Hampden, Knight of our shire, in whose loyalty we, his countrymen and neighbours, have ever had cause to confide", should have been accused of treason. He stood through that dreadful silence in St. Stephen's Chapel when King and Parliament stared at each other in hatred and hostility and the King turned on his heel and went out, never to return to his capital until he came back to die.

And then, in the early summer of this same year, when even those who had struggled hardest for peace had seen at last that war was inevitable, he had ridden with John Hampden to a meeting of the Parliament leaders at Broughton Castle.

"You're quite sure, Robert?" Hampden said. "You can still turn back. You are not yet committed to war."

But Robert, with a flash of insight, replied, "I am committed to commitment. A man must choose one side or the other."

Hampden said, "A great many respected and respectable men are sitting on the fence."

"Like the Church of Laodicea, neither hot nor cold," Robert replied. "I do not want to lose my soul."

Then he blushed hotly because though in the past he had

liked to talk about his possessions his soul had not until this moment figured in the list.

Hampden replied gravely, "No. In the last resort that is what matters to a man. You are committed then. *Vestigia nulla retrorsum.*"

It was his family motto. No way back. The words repeated themselves in Robert's mind, echoing to the beat of his horse's hoofs, as the sun sank behind the beech-woods and the windy twilight came down upon them. It was late evening when they came to Broughton in its green valley, but the full moon was rising among the scudding clouds and the fortress walls shone clear as in the day, mirrored among the water-lilies in the moat. The gateway had a warlike look, but within, the green lawns and the lovely Elizabethan house spoke only of peace. Hampden led the way beneath the great trees to the outside stone staircase that brought them to the hidden room on the roof that was the council chamber. It seemed to Robert a long climb, for his old peaceful life was gone now, fallen beneath him like a child's plaything. He would not have it again; and neither would England recover her peace in which his own had lain resting as though in the hollow of a steady hand.

But once inside the quiet room, with the door shut behind him, his mood changed. Most of the men in the room were insignificant country squires like himself, but there were a few others who were among the gre[illegible] their day, and when they bowed to him, making him one with themselves, awe and exultation took hold of him. He felt as a man might feel who goes on board a sea-going ship and as the vessel glides out from the harbour feels for the first time the lift of the sea beneath him. He was going somewhere, and it was not only the movement of history that he felt but the movement of his own soul that was a part of it.

He moved from John Hampden's side as the company gathered round the table and sat down among the unknown country gentlemen at its humble end. As they sat thus, the candles reflected in the table's dark polished surface and the wind sighing beyond the shuttered windows, he was more than ever reminded of a ship, with the captains of the fleet gathered together in the admiral's cabin.

Lord Saye and Sele, the owner of Broughton, sat in the place of honour at the head of the table, the light shining upon his inscrutable features. His enemies called him "Old Subtlety".

His suave and charming manners, his distinction and elegance, had their perfect foil in the men sitting one on each side of him. Upon his right sat the great John Pym, a large man with tousled curly hair and alert cunning eyes. His great intellect showed in his broad forehead and his resolution in his firm full mouth. Though he might be virtually king of England he dressed soberly, in respectable black with a plain linen collar. Upon his left sat a man whom Robert had seen before at Westminster, John Hampden's cousin, Oliver Cromwell, a colonel of militia and member for Cambridge. In appearance he was not attractive. He was tall and ungainly, untidy and none too clean in his person, his sallow face unhealthy and overweighted by a large red nose. Robert remembered hearing him speak in Parliament, but badly, for his voice was ugly and grating and he had no gift of oratory. Someone had said to John Hampden, "Mr. Hampden, who is that sloven?" And Hampden had replied with a flash of anger, "That sloven whom you see before you has no ornament in his speech; but that sloven, if we should ever come to a breach with the King (which God forbid!), will be the greatest man in England." Robert remembered that now, and when Colonel Cromwell rose to speak he watched him intently and it struck him that this was a man who knew his own mind, and that not with obstinacy but with judgement. His blue eyes were fearless and he looked like a man who had passed through fire, knew what he knew, and now within himself lived with assurance.

Robert's usually rather dull wits were immensely illumined that night, and John Hampden could have told him why. This latest welling up of men's love of righteousness, of their willingness to fight for it, was for most of them as yet untainted at the source and had its freshness. They had all of them, that night, according to their capacity, a touch of vision. They could still say, each man of himself, "He looked for a city which hath foundations, whose builder and maker is God." The vision would leave them, Hampden thought sadly, if they themselves by their own actions fouled the stream. And what men did not? That was their tragedy. Those were happy who did not live long enough to see what they loved fouled by what they were.

Robert saw the look of sadness on John Hampden's face and realised how hard it must have been for this man, unambitious and peace-loving, to turn himself into such a fighter as he had been through these past years. Wealthy, and happy in his life of country gentleman, in becoming a political leader he had had nothing to gain and everything to lose. Love of his country and of justice had compelled him to practise violence on himself. Robert realised as never before that his gentleness and charm were no indication of weakness of character. Cromwell's face looked stronger than Hampden's only because of its ugliness. Hampden's nose did not overweight his face because the strong cleft chin balanced it, but it was much the same nose. They both had fearless eyes, but Hampden's had deep pouches beneath them. He looked ill. He had never recovered, Robert knew, from his imprisonment, or from the death of his adored wife.

The meeting, the last of many at Broughton Castle, proceeded quietly. War was a certainty and it was now a question of getting hold of the militia and training them as a nucleus for the Parliamentarian army. As far as possible plans were made and means of communication agreed upon, and then the younger men went away into the night, leaving their elders to talk on into the small hours of the morning. Robert rode alone through the windy darkness. His mood of exultation held, so that he rode fast. Cottagers, hearing him go by, felt a vague stirring of uneasiness. The sound of a horse cantering in the night, heard through the rising wind, can arouse a sense of the numinous as surely as the first rumble of thunder before a storm. They did not at once go to sleep again. They lay listening to the wind, their minds turning this way and that, as they tried, in the way of men, to find some personal explanation of the impersonal sorrow that lay so heavily upon them.

Some weeks later Hampden raised the standard of Parliament on Chalgrove Field. From the villages and towns of Buckinghamshire and Oxfordshire men came flocking to his leadership. Country squires such as Robert came with their men behind them. Other groups were led by their clergy, Bible in hand. Many carried bill-hooks and cross-bows, weapons that had been stored in the churches, or had been family heirlooms, since the Wars of the Roses. Under the hot sun, surrounded by the cornfields, they pledged themselves to fight for the freedom of England, their cheers rolling to the ramparts of the beechwoods beyond the standing corn.

Through the weeks that followed Hampden struggled to discipline his Buckinghamshire country bumpkins, with whom Robert, though he belonged to Oxfordshire, had allied himself for love of Hampden, into an effective body of cavalry. He gave them his crest and motto for a standard, and uniforms of the green that had been worn by the medieval retainers of the Hampdens. Then with Lord Saye and Sele's Oxfordshire Bluecoats, the London Redcoats and the Warwickshire Purplecoats he marched north to the relief of Coventry, which was in the hands of the Royalists. They fought an engagement there, so small that it could not be called a battle, but it was the first blooding of the war. The King, after watching it, had ridden to Nottingham and raised the Royal Standard as a sign that now in bitter earnest the war had begun.

It was after this engagement that Robert suffered the second of his two disturbing experiences. He had taken no part in the fighting, for he had been left in charge in the rear. Finding his duty consisted of nothing more arduous than sitting on the baggage and watching them from afar he had been filled with a palpitating thankfulness that horrified him, when he remembered how he had yelled and cheered at Chalgrove. A few days later, coming out of the inn where he was lodging, he met the eyes of a well-dressed stranger going in. They confronted each other for a moment or two, each drawing back politely to let the other pass first, but the man's movements were merely mechanical and he was seeing not Robert but some vision within his own mind. Yet so fixedly did his eyes cling to Robert's that he seemed to be seeing his vision within them, and Robert was frozen in horror. This man's eyes, like Lilburne's, were bloodshot, but not with physical agony. His agony was of another sort. He was afraid. For most of his life Robert had subconsciously refused to consider fear; why should he when the things that were to be feared happened only to other people? But now he not only looked at fear, naked and appalling, but into it, deeper and deeper. The man moved and a moment or two later he found himself outside in the sunshine, walking fast down the street, but he was still looking into the man's eyes, and the eyes were still seeing within his that which the other feared. What was it? Sentence of death? Madness? The fearful mutilations of war? Whatever it was, it was within him that the other had seen it. Within him was death, and all that went with death. He carried within him, as a potential part of himself, all the disasters that happened to other people because there were no other people. There was no such thing as immunity. He knew now why he had always refused to consider fear, why he had lived his life on a plane apart, as though he were one of the immortal and indifferent gods. It was because he was himself afraid. He was guilty of what he most despised in other men, cowardice. He was a cowardly man. He was also, like all cowards, cruel; he rode past pillories laughing. Those with whom he spent his days esteemed him, he knew, for his kindliness. The indifferent gods could afford to be kindly. It cost them nothing and they were better served for it.

Sometimes his admiration for John Hampden would swing over into something almost like hatred, and he would wish that he had never gone to school without candles. The man had hooked him then and now he was dragging him in his wake through waters that were too deep for him. He wished he could speak of these troubling things to someone, but he was an inarticulate man and he was ashamed to try; for others had no doubt finished with these thoughts in adolescence and would laugh at him. He was as immature as one of his own children.

He was coming near home now and he began to think of them with a lifting of the heart. He loved them, he had always thought, only a little less than he loved Margaret. The three were his wife, son and daughter, loved in that order, and he had never questioned his affection for them any more than he had questioned the beauty of the country in which he had been born and brought up. They were his, and he had for them the right feelings because he was an estimable man. But this lifting of the heart was new to him, and surprised him. He was used to a sense of pleasurable anticipation in home-coming, but this was something more. It was, literally, a lifting, not into the indifference of the gods but into a new sort of vision, that was oddly opposed to his new vision of other people. Strangers seen in the streets seemed sometimes now not strangers at all, but intimately a part of himself, while he was looking forward to seeing his wife and children again not as part of himself, but as strangers whom he was eager to know. He supposed he had never known them because he had taken them for granted, just as he had taken for granted the country round his home and had not known it was so beautiful.

How deep the woods were, and how far and blue the distance. The trees were thinning and soon he would perhaps get his first glimpse of Froniga's cottage. Was it to be seen from the road? He had never noticed. Nor had he noticed how one rode into the sunshine and out of it again, just here where the trees were thinning. Sun and shade were dappled on the road, and there on the left, under the thorn hedge where the wood ended, was the patch of turf where the winter heliotrope grew. He had picked a bunch of it with Froniga on his tenth birthday. She had been fifteen then and a woman already. Though he had forgotten the heliotrope from that moment to this the smell of it seemed to drift across his face and he thought it would forever now remind him of Froniga. There was her cottage with its small steep thatched roof, upon which she grew patches of houseleek to protect her from lightning, and its two chimneys sticking up at each end like two ears, and the orchard trees beyond. No smoke came from the kitchen chimney. Was she at the manor? He recognised suddenly, soberly, how much he loved her. From her rejection his hurt pride had flung off to Margaret, been salved and comforted and achieved an apparent transference of love. But the achievements of pride are ephemeral. He loved Froniga.

Upon his right was a pond with a vivid carpet of green duckweed, and upon his left the village inn. Upon the bench outside the inn a man, a stranger, sat smoking a long clay pipe. Robert looked at him curiously, for in his own country he was accustomed to know every man he saw by sight. The stranger was just a stocky fair-haired fellow as he was himself. He wore rough country clothes and touched his forehead as a yokel might do, yet the half-smile on his face had the friendliness of equality. Robert smiled back and was surprised at himself, for he was not fond of strangers, especially not fond of them upon his native heath.

For this common, though common land and not his property, always felt to him like his own. In all beautiful countrysides there are focal points which are like the hub of a wheel. The place, out of past history or present beauty, exerts some magic. Men exiled from their country think of it when they think of home. The common by the inn was such a place. Robert rode slowly under the great linden trees near the inn, and past the hummock of ground where the stocks stood. Then he turned Diamond, his mare, off the stony road on to the springy turf of the common. The horse was tired, and so was he, yet a thrill went through them both, and before he could stop her the mare had broken into a canter. The cool morning air, crisp yet laced with sunshine, raced by them. Robert took off his hat and laughed as Will might have done. He was vaguely aware of streaming colour everywhere, purple and blue, red and gold, and before the end of the common was reached he quieted Diamond with hand and voice and gently reined her in. He wanted to see the colours drift to their appointed places.

The common, so crowded on fair days and Sundays, was deserted now except for the sheep cropping the turf. It was patched with heather, gorse, harebells and thyme, and down in the chalky hollows the traveller's-joy was silver among the crimson thorn trees. Upon every side the woods and hills rose and fell to the amazing blue of the distance. The woods were touched with colour here and there, faint amber and gold that from this distance seemed just a restlessness in the rounded masses of dull green, but near at hand the cherry trees on the common had a few leaves that were like vivid flames. The inn and the group of cottages that included Froniga's were half-hidden from him now by the linden trees, but there were a few others grouped round the common, thatched timber-framed cottages that seemed as much a part of it as the feeding sheep. Others bordered the lane that turned eastward towards the church.

Robert looked with affection at the old tower among the yews, and with annoyance at a plume of smoke rising from the dingle by Flowercote Wood. . . . The gypsies must be there once more. . . . They'd be poaching again and it was impossible for him, or his bailiff Tom Bellows in his absence, to condemn his own cousins to the stocks. They knew that. Only here did they dare to let their strange, persecuted underground existence come boldly to the surface. He swore softly, condemning to perdition his late uncle who had not even had the decency to move out of the neighbourhood when he had married Froniga's mother, Richenda Heron. He had taken a farm at the other side of Flowercote Wood and lived there disgracing his family and enjoying himself to the full until he had died of a surfeit of quodling tart and metheglyn at the age of forty. The headstrong beautiful Richenda had not survived him long, for she had been in nothing more headstrong than in her love for him, and Froniga at fifteen had gone to live at the manor to be turned into a lady.

This process she had endured with courage for ten years, until Robert fell in love with her. She alone had retained her serenity in the family disturbance which had followed. But she had been wilful. Flatly disobeying every command laid upon her, she had gone off to live her life as she wanted to live it; to be alone, and devote herself to the growing of herbs and the healing of the sick. At her age such behaviour disgraced her relatives and, like her father, she had not had sufficient tenderness for their sensibilities to move far; only to the cottage at the edge of the village, that looked out over the heathland like a cottage at the world's end looking out over the sea. Robert wheeled his horse round, trying to see it again, and he thought he could see a gable end between the branches of the orchard trees. He would go there tomorrow and sit with her in the small parlour fragrant with her herbs. Why not? She was his cousin. That he loved her was a mere commonplace. Many men had loved her and he imagined that she had treated them all as she had treated him, as small boys after the jam, to be spanked and set out of doors until they could learn to behave better.

He wheeled round again and rode down into the green valley that divided this common from the other smaller common by the manor. As the road rose once more he was in the beechwood where the children had found the painter. It wound steeply up the last bit of the way. How did it end? Robert wondered. Did the trees thin out gradually or did they form an arch at the top of the hill? It was ridiculous that he should not remember. He bent over to adjust a saddle-bag, then looked up to see an arch up above him filled with incredible blue. It seemed to be the end of the world. The wood ended suddenly, like a wall with an arch in it, and beyond that was blue. It dazzled him. He shut his eyes, and when he opened them again two little figures stood there in the archway, as though they welcomed him beyond the world.

He almost fell off his horse and strode a few steps forward, but though he tried to call to them he could not. He had been so pierced by the sight of his children that no words would come. Seeing them there was like seeing that tortured boy, or the man who was afraid; only this time he knew neither pain nor fear, but pure joy, and realised that in this world he might never be sufficiently flung out of himself to know it again. Within himself, he was too guilty now to know untarnished joy.

The children saw him and came speeding down to him out of the blue. He held out his arms and Jenny, who was quicker on her feet than Will, ran into them and he caught her up. Jenny, being a girl, had always been less important to him than Will, his son. She had seemed a pale little creature, all bunchy petticoats and shy brown eyes, but now, holding her, he forgot Will. Within the bunchy clothes her small body was compact and firm, and her pale cheek was warm against his. He kissed her and looked into her eyes and saw their shyness drowned in that brimming over of pure joy. But though he looked deep into her eyes he could not share it now, because he had returned to his habitual self-consciousness and joy was not their mutual possession, as fear had been his and the stranger's. But he could say, "*my* daughter", and in that way have his humble share in what she was. "My daughter," he said aloud, and though he spoke with a touch of boastfulness he was in fact experiencing his first spasm of true humility.

But Jenny was not self-conscious and prompted him to his duty with a gentle murmur. "There's Will," she said.

Robert set her down, keeping his left arm about her, and held out his right hand to his son. "How are you, Will?"

Will, poppy-cheeked and breathless from his run, bowed and said, "I'm well, sir. Are you well, sir? Have you my sword?"

"It's in my saddle-bag," said Robert, smiling.

"Could I have it now?" whispered Will.

"No," said Robert. "Not till you're breeched. But you can ride Diamond home if you like, with Jenny pillion behind you."

He lifted the children up to the saddle, and Diamond, who loved them well, turned her head and whinnied softly. She was chestnut, with a white star on her forehead, and like all horses she had a great gift for rising to the challenge of the moment. Though she was very tired she paced forward now with neck arched, as though there were bells on her harness and all of them were ringing. With Robert walking beside the children the four of them passed through the archway into the clear blue of the day and in front of them, beyond a bright patch of gorse, was the manor-house in its garden full of flowers.

CHAPTER V

THE BREECHING

I

The moment had arrived and the company were gathered in Margaret's bedchamber. Margaret stood with her husband by the window, her hand in his, pale but resolute not to weep, though she had a clean handkerchief handy. Froniga sat on Margaret's dressing-stool, her hands folded in her lap, the picture of serenity but with an unwonted tenderness about her lips. Jenny stood beside her, terribly constricted in the grown-up corsets she had just put on, and her new pink gown with the pointed bodice. Biddy, and the two young maids, Bess and Araminta, wore clean starched skirts and bodices, and clean mob caps and aprons, but Bess and Minta had already crumpled their aprons by wiping their eyes on them. Biddy, with her hands folded at her large waist and her usually merry old face puckered into a solemnity befitting the occasion, was dry-eyed. She had seen so many breechings. It seemed to her only yesterday that the boy's father had been sitting on that high stool, with the towel round his neck, only in his case Matthew Isard had been pomading his curls, not cutting them off. Old Matthew had scarcely altered a day since then. His withered-apple, toothless, smiling countenance was just the same, and so was the long apron with the deep pockets full of the tools of his trade that he wore over his mulberry-coloured jerkin. He, like Nathaniel Lovejoy the tailor, lived in Henley, four miles away, and barbered all the gentry, but not the lower classes, who were barbered at the local fairs or not at all.

Nathaniel Lovejoy had changed a little more since that earlier breeching, for he was an artist in his profession, and artistic sensibilities age a man. He was bald and his shoulders were bent. He wore spectacles on the end of his nose, for forty years of tailoring in his little ill-lit shop in Hart Street had strained his child-like pale blue eyes. He was a very good old man and he looked like a parson in his threadbare black clothes, with his thin delicate hands folded so peacefully before him. But there was nevertheless a look of pride about him, and his was the post of honour beside the big four-poster where his handiwork was laid out, the doublet and breeches that he had made to measure, and with them hose, buckled shoes and a little high-crowned hat.

The curls were all cut off and Bess, bursting into loud sobs, gathered them up and tied them in a silk handkerchief to be delivered to her mistress later. Will descended from his stool and held out his arms that he might be divested of his long skirted coat. Seated on the stool he had looked white and wan, and had kept his eyes shut, and now, with his arms stretched out, his face had an almost holy look. Margaret was sure he was sickening for something, and even Robert felt a twinge of anxiety. Froniga and Jenny knew that Samson asleep beneath the shears of Delilah had now become Isaac preparing for the sacrifice. The great moment had arrived, and Margaret, as was her right, stepped forward to assist Mr. Lovejoy. All the family gathered round. The babyish coat dropped to the ground for ever, as might the earthly garments of some saint bound for the bourne of heaven, and Will stood there in his little white shirt, so innocent and angelic of mien that even Froniga felt a prickling in her eyes. Mr. Lovejoy solemnly handed the doublet to Margaret, the hose to Froniga, the hat to Jenny, as being the more ladylike garments, while reserving to himself the honour of the breeches. Mr. Lovejoy had compromised well between Robert's politics and the happy nature of the occasion, for while the little suit was severely plain, with no lace upon it and no ribbons at the knee, it was yaffingale green, and the matching hat had in it a very small red feather.

"Now, my young master," said Mr. Lovejoy, and held out the breeches. Will stepped skilfully into them and Mr. Lovejoy whisked them into place with a practised hand. Then Margaret put on the doublet and Biddy fastened it, and Froniga knelt at Will's feet and put on the hose. The two young maids put on each of them a buckled shoe and Jenny handed him his hat. He was rosy and dimpling now, and enjoying himself immensely, and because it was suddenly such fun to be himself, he was, for once, himself. The women were all about him like honeybees, happy now and humming with laughter and talk. Only Robert stood aloof from the group, his hands behind his back, grave and unsmiling. Will looked up and over the bent heads of the silly chattering women, the eyes of father and son met and a secret smile came into the eyes of both. These women! Will pushed them from him, but gently, for he felt affectionate towards them, and Robert said, "Allow me, please," with a note of sternness, so that with the exception of Froniga they fell away like chivvied hens; and even Froniga moved backwards with something less than her usual stately dignity. Robert moved two steps forward and took from behind his back a sword-belt of green leather, and a little sword with a shining silver hilt. Will's blue eyes opened wide, as bright as stars, his cheeks crimsoned and his lips parted. He stood straight as a lance, feet together, his feathered hat in his right hand, his fair cropped head held well up, while his father adjusted the belt over the right shoulder and across the breast of the new doublet. Then, as his left hand closed over the hilt of the sword, he exhaled a little sigh and moved forward to stand beside his father, facing the huddle of women. As from a vast distance, across a chasm that could never again be crossed, he smiled at them with tolerant kindness. William Henry Haslewood was now a man.

With some ceremony, Will walking between his father and mother and Froniga and Jenny following, the company trooped down the great staircase. The unicorn upon the terminal post looked larger than usual, alive and interested. Jenny put up a hand to touch him as she went past, and the arched neck felt warm and smooth. Had she been able to stop a moment, she was sure she would have felt the muscles rippling under the skin.

Crossing the hall to the door of the dining-parlour Robert gave an exclamation of surprise and annoyance, for standing in front of the great stone fireplace were two men, one the stranger whom he had seen outside the inn and the other a sparrow-shaped, bright-eyed little old man in a black gown, with a red face and pointed white beard.

"Damnation!" muttered Robert to Margaret over Will's head. "Did you invite him?"

"No," she whispered. "Hush now, Robert."

Robert put a good face on it. Parson Hawthyn had been a part of his life for years. The old man had prayed beside his parents when they lay dying, had married him to Margaret and baptised his children, but his idiosyncrasies had always been something of an embarrassment to the formal Robert. And his latest quirk was now more than an embarrassment, it was an outrage. In Parliament country, in a village where the

Squire was doing his best to persuade able-bodied men to fight for Parliament, the Parson remained an obstinate Royalist. He was not aggressive—he was too humble a man for that—but when any parishioner asked for his opinion he gave it in no uncertain terms, apparently quite unaware that this was disloyalty to the Squire. And he was still appearing Sunday by Sunday to eat his dinner at the manor-house, as he had done for years past, as though the cleavage between himself and Robert were of no more importance than a disagreement upon the merits of ale and metheglyn. And here he was, unasked, at Will's breeching. The old man had no proper feeling, Robert decided angrily. No sense of loyalty, nor of manners. No delicacy of perception.

"It is my right," said the old man firmly. "I baptised the child."

His beautiful voice was clear and incisive, and immediately he spoke he became to the one to whom he spoke an authoritative and compelling power. Francis, who for the last ten minutes had been feeling like a needle hopelessly hooked by a magnet, stood unnoticed beside the hearth, his hands behind his back, congratulating himself upon detachment and smiling to see another man captured in his turn. Robert flushed like an embarrassed schoolboy, opened his mouth to protest and shut it again, his eyes held by the gay sparkle in the eyes of the other. It always struck him as slightly indecent that a man of seventy-five or so (no one knew how old Parson Hawthyn really was) should have such brightness in his eyes. If the old man had been feeling the sins and sorrows of the world as he should, decided Robert, his eyes would have grown dim long ago. His own eyes fell suddenly, for he had been seized by the ridiculous notion that Parson Hawthyn had looked right into his mind, and seen the boy in the pillory and the man who was afraid, and the two children standing at the door. He heard the old man speaking again, and his voice had undergone one of its sudden changes; it was low and almost caressingly gentle. "Sir, it is a pleasure to welcome you home. I know no greater pleasure." It changed again and had a suave courtesy like the sound of silk. "Madam, my felicitations upon this auspicious occasion." It deepened into authority. "Will, receive my blessing." Will bent his head and while the words of the benediction sounded musically in the room the stillness was so profound that Francis could have taken his oath that not a mouse stirred in the wainscot or a bee in the garden. Detached, a little beyond the orbit, his smile broadened to something like a grin. He had never seen such a consummate actor in all his life.

His grin faded. He was hooked again; drawn into the family circle by the old man's bewitching charm. He was being explained as a new friend, met at the gate, a journeyman painter. It was a long time since such a one had visited the village. Would not Madam Haslewood like portraits of the children? Then Will and Jenny greeted him with joy and in a few minutes not a man or woman in the room remembered that the country was at war.

2

"I have never tasted such metheglyn," said Francis to Froniga. "No, not even in my childhood, when all food and drink (always excepting gruel and parsnips) tasted divine. Did you make it?"

"Now why should you think I made it?" asked Froniga.

They were sitting together on the wide window-seat. Froniga had, in the kindness of her heart, thought to set the shabby young stranger at his ease but had found it was not necessary.

"Because you look like a woman of potency," said Francis. His eyes acknowledged her beauty with boldness, but when she looked at him with her strange moony dark glance the boldness fell away; but gracefully, respecting her wishes, and he did not drop his eyes or show embarrassment. He was, she perceived, perfectly at home where he found himself, and with an almost unrealised uneasiness she felt that he was more than at home, that in other circumstances it might have been he who would have been setting her at her ease, not she him.

"Do you use Queen Elizabeth's recipe, adding violets and gilliflowers to the honey and ale, the herbs and sweetbrier leaves? And do you tie a bag of cloves and mace to the tap-hole of every barrel?"

Froniga smiled. "I will not tell you what I do," she said. "My recipes are my secrets. But this I will tell you. The same garden nourishes the bees and the flowers they feed upon, and petals of those flowers go into any conserve or cordial that is made with their honey. That, I think, is important. Also the petals of the said flowers should be picked at the full of the moon."

He suspected that she was laughing at him, but he did not

mind. He saw that a bunch of violets was pinned into the bodice of her gown. "Those grew in your garden," he said. "Only a woman of magic could cajole them into blooming at this time of the year. They are just the colour of the shadows on your eyelids."

A sense of weariness came to Froniga. Here was another man. Would she never reach an age that would be a safe harbour from men? She had sailed into forty with high hopes, but it had made no difference. "Do you know much about unicorns?" she asked, for she had learned to change the subject immediately as soon as her eyes were mentioned.

Francis looked towards the beautiful carved stone over-mantel. Instead of the usual stylised interlacing bands, surrounding the family coat of arms, the carver had fashioned a wonderfully free and natural representation of leaves and branches, with small singing birds among them, and in the centre was a unicorn's head, looking as though it were appearing from among the branches of a wood. "Nothing except that there are none," he said. "But that's a very fine representation of a legendary beast."

"Jenny will tell you that our family unicorn is no legend," said Froniga. "And if you would like to see her face at its most charming when you paint her portrait, talk to her about him while you work."

"I will," said Francis. There had been no difficulty about a commission for both portraits. Robert, after the morning's vision of the two children at the door of Paradise, would not have separated them for the world. "May I look closer at that carving?"

They got up and moved towards the mantelpiece, revealing a patch of sun on the floor where Maria had been lying half-hidden by Froniga's skirts. She stretched herself the better to feel the warmth of the sun and Robert, moving backwards to make way for Froniga, stepped upon her tail. She sprang up with a yelp and snapped at him. She was not bad-tempered, but she was old, and she had always suspected that Robert did not like her. Now she knew it.

"That damn dog!" he ejaculated angrily. For the last ten minutes he had been in a bad mood, for apart from the normal reaction from the emotion of home-coming he was tired after his journey, so tired that the metheglyn, which usually cheered him up, had disagreed with him instead. It was annoying too that Parson Hawthyn and the painter had not followed the example of Matthew Isard and Nathaniel Lovejoy and taken themselves off once Will's health had been drunk. And another man fascinated by Froniga always hurt him intolerably. . . . As usual, he vented his annoyance on his wife. "Margaret! That wretched little bitch! I thought I had told you to get rid of her."

His spasm of irritation spent he would have recalled the words if he could. He was sorry. There was a sudden silence in the room. Every man and woman in it had remembered again what they had forgotten, that they were at war. Froniga spoke first, her voice as cold as the silence.

"Maria got rid of? Why?"

"You know perfectly well why," he muttered. He was feeling confused now and the room spun round him. Froniga's astonished eyes seemed to disappear and he found himself looking into a small furious face that for a moment he did not recognise. He also found himself being belaboured by a very hard pair of fists. They belonged to his gentle little daughter. For a moment he stood there, enduring her blows, seeing her agonised white face floating up at him as though on some dark wave, vaguely aware of Will, crimson-faced and terrified, clutching Maria to his chest.

He caught Jenny's fists and held them, though she fought to get them away. "Sweetheart, I didn't mean it," he said. "You can keep your dog. Put her down, Will. I didn't know you cared so much for the little beast. Sweetheart, be still." He had imposed stillness on Jenny, but she did not unclose her fists and they were cold in his grasp. She was no longer angry, but her eyes were full of fear. He drew her to the window-sill, sitting down with her on his knee. "Come, Will," he said, and Will, looking sullen, came reluctantly. A tactful hum of conversation had been set going in the room by Froniga and Parson Hawthyn, but he was not aware of it. He was aware of nothing but his children. He had come home to win and know his children, and Jenny in his arms in the beech-woods, and Will's eyes meeting his as he brought him the little sword, had seemed to augur so well. And now he had lost them. He kissed Jenny's cheek, but she did not return his kiss, and Will was still staring sullenly at the floor and pushing the strewing herbs about with the toe of his new shoe.

Robert put Jenny down and got up and went back to his guests, telling himself that next time he came home he would win them. Children, like small animals, soon forgave the blunderings of those who loved them. But he remained heavy-hearted. In efforts to know and love others we are betrayed by what we are, thought poor Robert, and what a man wants and what he is are parallel lines that never meet.

Francis turned to Margaret. "Madam, before I go may I show you a couple of portraits? I have them with me. I should like you to be sure that my style will please you."

Jenny and Will had gone out in the garden with Parson Hawthyn; Margaret, Froniga and Robert stood waiting together by the hearth while Francis went into the hall to fetch his canvases. The itinerant portrait painter was a familiar figure in the countryside, and though he was most often on a level with the puller of teeth and the journeyman tailor, he was occasionally some well-born seedy fellow who had fallen from grace. But this man was the reverse of seedy. Robert and Margaret were not, like Froniga, uneasy. Their simplicity took most things at their face value, and if this man had to be in and out of the house for the next few days they were thankful to find him so gentlemanly.

Francis came back with two small canvases under his arm and propped them up on the window-seat. One was a hastily executed portrait of old Sam Tidmarsh, the wheelwright and sexton, refreshing himself at the inn, with his mug of ale in one hand and his long pipe in the other. Sam Tidmarsh, with his grey beard jutting out in argument and his eyebrows shooting forward as though to join in, was obviously in a state of happy exhilaration. His nose and cheeks were rosy, his eyes cunning slits of blue between the half-closed lids. A twist of smoke rose from the bowl of the pipe and foam flecked the brim of the pewter mug, yet it needed only a half-glance at those eyes to know that he had paid for the filling of neither.

The other portrait was of a little girl of perhaps five years old, wearing a low-cut blue satin dress and with a small cap of seed pearls on her fair head. Her pale face had a look of remoteness, even as Jenny's had, but while Jenny's eyes and mouth held the promise both of anger and laughter should she be outraged or amused, this child's face was so grave and still that Froniga could not imagine any change in it except that of weeping. Nor could she imagine the face growing older, for it would not grow old.

"What a sweet little girl!" said Margaret.

"Very like our Jenny," said Robert.

"Heaven forbid!" whispered Froniga. "Who is she?" she asked the painter sharply and harshly.

Francis bowed to her, and smiled, and said, "You like my portraits?"

"Why do you ask?" said Froniga with a touch of anger. "You must know perfectly well that few men in England could so set out guile and mortality." And with the attention of the room focused upon her she left it as a queen might do, forgetting or disdaining to lift her skirts. They swept the fragrant herbs and she closed the door upon a gust of the scent that was so intimately a part of her.

Margaret flushed and Robert said, "My cousin is a law unto herself. The portraits are excellent. I don't, myself, see any signs of death in the face of Sam Tidmarsh."

Francis smiled and bent over Margaret's hand, made his arrangements for tomorrow, then bowed to Robert and followed Froniga out into the garden. But she was not there, and nor were the children and Parson Hawthyn. The garden was empty. He opened the gate and went out and saw the old parson walking along the road towards the village. He quickened his pace to catch up with him, for these flamboyant actors were always amusing. Yet as he came nearer he realised that there was nothing flamboyant about the old man's gait. He walked slowly, leaning on his stick, and his head was bent.

"Are we going the same way, sir?" asked Francis cheerfully from behind.

The old man turned and Francis, to his dismay, saw that tears were trickling down his red cheeks. The red was not that of health but of the mottling of hundreds of tiny veins, and the knuckles of the hand that held his stick were swollen with rheumatism. With his other hand he took out his handkerchief and with great simplicity wiped away his tears.

"I wept for the sorrow of it all," he said. Then he looked directly into the painter's eyes with sweetness and gaiety and Francis, after meeting his glance for a moment, looked away, for the old man's eyes seemed to penetrate to the back of his head.

"Yes, we're going the same way," said Parson Hawthyn. "For

you, young man, are coming back to my parsonage to smoke a pipe with me."

Francis fell into step beside him, cursing himself for a blind fool. The old man was no actor but one of those rare beings whose feelings gush out exuberantly from a truly benevolent heart. He had no need to act.

CHAPTER VI

THE BUTTERFLIES

I

It was Alamina's washing day, and from behind a blackberry bush her offspring watched anxiously. Alamina had no regular washing day, for she was a woman who disliked regularity, but when she did wash, which was seldom, she washed with a concentrated fury that embraced everything within sight, and she generally finished up with the children. But she was now only at the beginning of things. Several of the men had fetched water from the well at the inn for her in cooking-pots, and poured it into the huge tub. Alamina stood in the tub with cooking-pots and garments piled up on the grass beside her. She had kilted her skirt above her knees, and a brilliant orange diklo was tied over her beautiful untidy hair. Her coral beads swung as she moved, and when she bent over the tub the movement of the sunlit water sent waves of light rippling over her dusky sulky face. It gave a strange fitful lustre to her beauty. Alamina was always at her loveliest when she was in a temper and never more beautiful than on her washing day. She dragged the verminous garments into the water and trod them underfoot with savage triumph, her hands on her hips and her head flung back. Her full red lips were parted and soon, when the rhythm of the work took hold of her, she would begin to sing. That would be the children's moment to escape, if they could, for absorbed in song she would not be so likely to see them go. Escape was difficult on washing days because their usual harbours of refuge were denied them. Madona would not shelter them on washing day, and neither would Yoben. Total flight was their only hope, but it was not easy to achieve it, for Dinki and Cinderella were so fat, and Cinderella so young, that they could not run fast enough to escape pursuit, and though the slim Meriful was fleet as a hare he scorned to desert the other two. The three always held together like a trefoil clover leaf. In this one loyalty only could they be considered estimable children.

Alamina began to sing, a low angry mutter at first, scarcely a song at all, a sort of musical swearing. Then a few sharp trills found their way into the profanity, and then a few more, and then, like the sun bursting out from behind a cloud, came the full prima donna volume of her blackbird song. The children ducked and ran, but the sudden cessation of their mother's aria, and a piercing scream, told them how slender was their hope. Alamina had a terrible sixth sense that always knew when anything she wanted was eluding her, and it did not as a rule elude her for long. The children, sharp-eared as rabbits, could hear her light-footed swift pursuit after them like the wind in the trees. They could picture her too, the orange diklo fallen back from her streaming hair and her long brown legs carrying her forward at fearful speed. Yet they ran on, little Cinderella dragged forward through the air by a brother on each side. They had spunk and they always ran on, though the further they ran the worse was the beating when they were caught. Yet they ran on to the bitter end. That was their code.

Flowercote Wood was only a short distance away and they were in among the beech trees long before their mother caught up with them. They dived this way and that, trying to lead Alamina in the wrong direction, then lay down, then started up again. They were soon in a part of the wood that they did not know and there towering above them was a beech tree on top of a mossy bank. Its great roots sprawled down the bank, clutching at the earth below with splayed feet, and behind the roots and sheltering bracken there was a hollow place. They never needed to speak their thoughts to each other. Silently they squeezed in between the roots and clung together in the dark earthy space beyond. The tree was a hollow one and the earth had been tunnelled away behind the roots by a badger or fox. The hollow was warm and dry, with a floor of beechmast, and there were nuts that had fallen down from a squirrel's nest in the upper part of the tree. Meriful, Dinki and Cinderella felt entirely at home there, equally creatures of the woods, and if a passer-by had seen a glimmer of starry eyes behind the brake he would have thought them those of furry creatures.

They waited a long time and then crept out, hardly able to believe the wonder of the thing that had happened to them. They had outwitted Alamina. They were free in the world and could go where they liked.

"Which way?" Dinki asked Meriful, who with his hands in

his ragged pockets and his feet wide apart, was sniffing and listening. He always found his way as much by scent and hearing as he did by sight, and even more by his acquisitive instinct. If there was anything worthwhile to be had anywhere, Meriful could generally find his way to it. Cinderella was not interested in the way they were going because she had found a stick shaped like a baby, with two arms sticking out, and sitting among the beech leaves, her dirty blue frock trailing its rags round her, she was talking to it and stroking it. She had no toys. Romany children had never had them. Egyptian and Roman children had had their painted babies to rock in their arms and put to bed, but Cinderella had never had a doll. The boys had had their little pipes as soon as they were old enough to suck at them (though they only had the rare and precious tobacco in them when they could beg or steal a few shreds from Madona), but Cinderella had never had anything but feathers and nuts and bits of stick that she found in the wood. Most Romany children did not feel this loss, but in some vague way Cinderella did. She had a strong maternal instinct and was the only one of Madona's many descendants who was in the least like her.

"There's water near," said Meriful.

Dinki lifted his head and he too got the sound and scent of water. There were no streams in this high heath country and springs were rare, and he loved water, not dead and debased in a bucket to rob him of his comfortable dirt but living water that moved and sang. He whooped with delight and dragged Cinderella to her feet. She dropped her bit of stick, yelled and kicked his shins, but Meriful was already speeding ahead and gripping his sister by her fat wrist, Dinki hauled her in pursuit. She had no breath to roar, but the tears trickled down her bulging cheeks. . . . It was the nicest bit of stick she'd ever had.

Meriful, slim and long-legged, reached the spring long before the other two. When they caught up with him, breathless, and grubbier than ever from tumbling down and getting up again, he was sitting back on his heels, his thin hands laid one on each knee, gazing at it. The other two squatted down beside him and stillness and awe held all three. Cinderella still sobbed a little, but her tears had stopped.

The water bubbled up under a low stone-arched recess, built to protect it, and was beautiful and clear and cold. Above the arch the stone had been roughly carved, but was so worn by time and weather that it was difficult to see what the carving represented. The dome of the arch was moss-covered inside and ferns grew in the wet crevasses of the stones, and over it bent an elder tree weighted with bunches of black fruit. The children were quick to know that this was no ordinary spring. Not only was there the elder, that magic tree whose blood would run like that of a living woman should any mortal have the temerity to cut it, but the immense quiet of the place spoke of a presence here. No bird sang and no air stirred. The scent of the wet moss was drowsy and the soft bubble of the water was the only sound. But the children were not afraid, for under the protection of this presence they felt as safe as when they were clustered under Madona's cloak. They cupped their brown hands and drank some of the water, and Meriful held his hands in the spring because he had warts and he thought its magic might take them away. The warts were still there when he removed his hands but he told himself that he would try another day. One application might not be enough. Then they ate some of the elder-berries, and this they did not because they were hungry but because they thought the presence would like them to partake of the bounty of the place.

"What's that?" asked Dinki with his mouth full, looking up at the carving over the spring.

Meriful stood up and carefully traced the outline on the stone with his forefinger. "It might be a horse," he said. "Just the head."

Dinki also stood up and felt with his finger. "A little horse," he said. "A white one like our Baw."

Cinderella, still sobbing a little, picked some forget-me-nots to comfort herself for the loss of her stick and stuck them in her hair, which being so curly and matted always held anything thrust into it quite securely. Then she bent down and picked some of the pink-tipped daisies that grew beside the path. "Here's a path," she said.

"Look, there's a path!" exclaimed Dinki.

A well-trodden path led away from the well and disappeared from sight through a thicket of traveller's-joy. They looked at it with awe. They never trod paths, for paths led to houses, and they were frightened of houses. Only Meriful of the three of them had ever been close to a house and he only when he was a small child. He had been a peaky baby and of assistance to his mother when she carried him in Indian fashion in her shawl to beg from the gorgios. With the tears running out of her lovely eyes she had pointed to his rags and his thin legs, and his pitiful little face all blotched with weeping (for she had denied him his breakfast and given him a good spanking before they started out), and had always come away with the heel of the loaf and a silver piece. But Dinki and Cinderella had never been of any use to her for they had always been too fat.

"It leads to houses," said Meriful. "They come along this path from the houses to get water at the spring."

Cinderella dragged at his hand, pulling backwards, and then there rang out through the wood the sound of the church clock striking the hour. They had heard it before, of course, but distantly. This was close at hand. The notes of the bell seemed to fall through the leaves like stars, or like drops of water, cool and shining as the water of the spring. The children ran down the path but it was not the track through the wood that was drawing them but the living invisible link that united the well and the church. A gorgio's child might not have been aware of it but these children had an apprehension denied to children who live in houses. And they ran now without fear, even though they knew they were coming near houses, because the presence that had been at the well ran with them. The bare light feet of the three made scarcely any sound upon the path, and the feet of the fourth no sound at all.

The trees thinned out and in front of them was a stile and a low stone wall, and beyond the wall a sea of green grass and rounded green mounds, and grey stones that sloped this way and that like the toppling waves that Yoben had told them about, and beyond the grey-green sea were black trees and a huge grey mountain of stone. And now the children did feel fear, such fear that they stopped and clung to each other at the stile. For this must be a graveyard, that dreadful thing which Alamina had described to them but which they had never seen. Dead gorgios lay in those green mounds, and at midnight their skeletons came out and gibbered and danced on the graves. Their skeletons ran through the woods at night and fetched away naughty Romany children who would not obey their mothers, and crunched them up as easily as hazel nuts. That was what Alamina had said about graveyards, but Madona had said the dead are kind people and that if you make a hole in a grave with a stone and go there night after night soon you will hear them talking, and they will tell you where money is buried. Yoben, when asked, had said briefly that graveyards were gardens and women talked a lot of nonsense. So it was hard to know what to believe, and still clinging to each other the children crouched down and peeped through the stile.

Out there in the green sea the path branched into two, one leading to a cave in the stone mountain and the other leading out through a wooden gate to a group of thatched cottages. "Those are houses," whispered Meriful, "and that cave in the mountain leads into a church."

They looked at the path and the safety of it tingled in the soles of their feet. Upon the other side of the stile the air was very blue and there was laughter there. Suddenly feeling brave they got through the stile and ran through the green sea, and its terror curled away back from the path like the terror of the sea when the Israelites marched through it singing, and they came in safety to the cave in the rock.

Here they crouched down again, on the floor of the cave, for though they were no longer afraid their awe was great. "That's a door," whispered Meriful, for he had seen doors, though never a door as big as this one. It was not latched, and presently they crept forward and applied their eyes to the crack. Cortez, upon that peak in Darien, had felt no greater thrill. They leaned against the door and slowly it creaked open a few inches, and a few inches more. They stopped, all in delicious wonder and confusion, then leaned again, and laughed, and then they went through. Hand in hand they stood just within the door and gazed in amazement at this vast cavern in the mountain to which the small cave had admitted them.

It seemed to them so vast but it was in reality a small grey-arched Norman church, dim and cool and musty-smelling. The sun shone through the opaque green glass in the small windows as through water, and the green light lay gently on the worn flagstones, the old rood screen and oak benches. The church was full of shadows and hidden among them were old tombs and the escutcheons of dead knights. There was a stone pulpit and an altar with a silver cross upon it, for Parson Hawthyn was a Laudian and refused to take away the cross or any of the church ornaments, retaining the full ritual of the Church of England and wearing his surplice let Robert say what he would. The villagers did not mind what he did for he was beloved, and they were accustomed to his ways.

It was a long time before the children dared the shadows but presently, still feeling safety in the soles of their feet and aware of peace in the green light and laughter in the floating motes of golden dust, they essayed them. They found the lady first, lying on her tomb in her best gown with a ruff round her neck, her head on a cushion and her feet resting against a strange little horse with a thorn sticking out of his forehead. To begin with they thought the tomb was a rock and so they were not frightened. It was only when they stood on tiptoe and felt the strange shapes with their hands that they realised that a lady and a tiny horse had been turned into stone by some Chovihan. But still they were not frightened, for the magic felt good to them and they supposed the act to have been beneficent. They made their way from one wonder to the other, bobbing up and down among benches and tombs, flitting from the green sea light to the shadows again like bright butterflies in their gay rags. They lost all sense of time and they did not know that they were hungry.

It was Cinderella who all by herself discovered Madona. Parson Hawthyn had among other eccentricities a gift for carving wooden figures and making them gay with paint and gilding, and he had set a few here and there about the church. A couple of little cherubs sat upon a window-sill and looked down upon the font, and in various nooks and crannies perched birds: robins, chaffinches and kingfishers with hoods of blue. Cinderella did not see the cherubs, for she did not look so high, and the birds she took to be real birds, but what she did discover was Madona with a baby in her arms, almost hidden in a niche in the wall. She knew it was Madona, even though Madona's cloak was brown and this cloak was blue, because of the smile upon her face. Madona smiled just like that when some mother brought a new baby and laid it on her lap. And that was the way she smiled when Cinderella sat upon her knee. And that was the way Cinderella herself would smile if she could have that baby. She had wept for the loss of her bit of stick, but what was a bit of stick, even mossy and with two arms to it, to a baby like this, a real baby with a golden head and pink feet and a white diklo tied round its middle?

Scarcely breathing, her eyes like stars and her cheeks crimson, she stretched her hands up to the niche and touched the baby. She had meant only to touch but as soon as her fingers felt the wood she could feel the baby in her arms. She, who had never had a toy, knew suddenly, in a great gust of delight, the full passion of a little girl's love for a real doll. She must have it. Her fingers closed upon it. And then she felt an agony of apprehension. Was it fixed on to Madona's knees, or would it lift off? Madona's hands were curved beneath the baby, as though offering it to Cinderella, but, when it came to the point, would they let go? Cinderella gave a pull, but Madona's hands held tight, for though the two little figures were separate the paint had not been quite dry when Parson Hawthyn had laid the baby on his mother's lap. Cinderella began to sob with apprehension. Then she pulled again and Madona suddenly let go.

She ran to the lady's tomb and squatted down beside it to nurse her baby. He was about twelve inches long and the golden head fitted into the crook of her elbow as though it had always been there. She pulled up a fold of her ragged blue skirt and wrapped it round him as a cloak. She began to try and sing the song that Madona had sung to her when she was a baby, her tiny piping voice clear and true as a wren's. It was the lullaby that all gypsy mothers sang to their children, and they said it was the song Mary had sung to her Baby when they lived in Egypt. Meriful, hearing her singing, began to whistle the tune as he sat up above her astride the tomb, his orange tawny jerkin bright as a robin's breast in a green-gold finger of sun, whacking up the little horse and riding to the fair. Dinki was too busy to sing, for he was running up and down the pulpit steps, but the patter of his bare feet sounded like the song of rain on the leaves accompanying the whistling and piping of the robin and the wren. The music was so small that it made scarcely more sound than the unheard laughter that had come with the children out of the wood.

2

Parson Hawthyn's parsonage squatted comfortably among currant bushes, rose bushes and Michaelmas daisies. It was smaller than Froniga's cottage, but he lived alone and his kitchen and parlour, with one little room under the thatch above, were all he needed. Like most of the country clergy of his day he was very poor, but in his case his lot was mitigated by the fact that he had no family. Yet, for an educated man, such austerity was deplorable, thought Francis, as he looked about him in the parlour where they sat smoking their pipes together.

He himself was the heir to great possessions, and though he enjoyed escaping from them now and again, in escapades such as the present one, part of the pleasure of his escapades lay in the return to civilisation afterwards. Parson Hawthyn's mode of existence was not what he called civilisation. What would it be like to own only this one small shelter from the wind and rain, and fit it nearly as closely as a snail his shell? A tall man could not have stood upright in this low-ceiled room, and Parson Hawthyn had only to stretch out a hand as he sat on the settle and all his possessions were within his reach: his few books upon their low shelf, an empty tobacco jar beside them (Parson Hawthyn, refusing Francis's well-filled pouch, had scraped up its last shreds to fill their pipes), his inkpot and quill pen upon the table, his wood-carver's bench in the corner of the room. Doubtless he had a change of garments in the room above, and a few pots and pans in the kitchen, but there would hardly be room for more. His only luxuries seemed to be the books and tobacco (when he had any) and the rose bushes and Michaelmas daisies outside the open window. The casement with the small panes of greenish glass was set wide, so that they could see the butterflies hovering over the Michaelmas daisies and hear the humming of bees. There was no other sound, for even sound seemed at a minimum. Francis looked up and found the old man looking at him with a humble, almost apologetic look in his eyes.

"To you, who have only your pack on your back, I must seem to have much," he said sadly, for it seemed that his wealth grieved him. "I am often uneasy. Not only have I where to lay my head but I lay it on a pillow, and I possess blankets, and I have never known what it was to have my only meat the doing of the will of God. If you have that knowledge I envy you."

Francis swallowed some smoke the wrong way and coughed. "I have not that knowledge," he said. "Mere journeyman painter though I am, I have never been a poor man."

"Then you and I both have our full blessedness to come," said Parson Hawthyn cheerfully, and stretching out his hand he pulled a shabby old book from his shelf. He held it on his knees, stroking it gently, and Francis smiled, for their famous library was his and his father's most treasured possession. The old man opened the book and with an exclamation of distress smoothed the corner of a dog-eared page. Francis's smile broadened. Books were living things to those who truly loved them.

"Would it be blessed to be without books?" he asked.

"Ah, there you have me!" said Parson Hawthyn. "They are the best of the earthly meats. Yet it may be that if my head were not so full of other men's prayers I should come nearer my God in my own poor halting words; or, better still, my lack of them. Have you achieved silence in prayer, young man?"

Francis grinned. This was the most astounding old man. He kept no guard. At the manor an hour ago he had given himself with such entire wholeheartedness to the claims of the moment that Francis had thought him a first-rate actor, and now he was talking to a stranger picked up on the common as unreservedly as though he had known him all his life.

"We should pray for the poor," said Parson Hawthyn. "That is the first duty of a rich man; and I count you and myself among them if we have never wanted for a crust of bread or a book. If we do not pray for him, then when we give a coin to a poor man we shall do it with arrogance. Prayer, my dear sir, brings you to the feet of those for whom you pray. Have you read *Piers Plowman*?"

"No, sir," said Francis. A copy of Piers was probably among the books at home, but no one read William Langland these days.

"Out of fashion," sighed the old man, "like Shakespeare. But God will bring them again to our notice. Praise be to God that all that is of His inspiration is for ever safe in His keeping. William Langland was born in Oxfordshire, some say, at Shipton-under-Wychwood, though it was in the hills of Worcestershire that his vision came to him. Listen, now, to this prayer for poor men, and remember it when you lie warm in a dry bed with a nice bit of boiled bacon and a mug of ale snug in your belly."

He turned the pages of the book on his knee, yellow pages, speckled with rust like a thrush's breast, until he found what he wanted. When he began to read Francis thought that the hum of bees and the rustle of wind made the perfect background for the amazing beauty of his voice.

"Now, Lord, send them summer, some manner of joy,
Heaven after hence-going, that here have such default!
And have pity on the rich that relieve no prisoners

From the good things thou hast given, the ungrateful many;
But, God, in Thy goodness, give them grace to amend.
But poor people, Thy prisoners Lord, in the pit of mischief,
Comfort those creatures that suffer many cares,
Through dearth or drought, all their days here,
Woe in winter-time, for want of clothing,
And in summer-time seldom a full supper;
Comfort Thy care-stricken, Christ, in Thy Kingdom."

"That's good," said Francis. "I can remember the last line at any rate. If I don't pray much myself I do at least know I'd be a better man if I did.

Prayer . . . the soul's blood,
The land of spices; something understood."

"Who said that?" demanded the old man, pouncing on the words like a miser on gold.

"George Herbert," said Francis.

"Ah, I can't read the modern poets," said Parson Hawthyn wistfully. "The new books—they have been for years beyond my means. I have just the books my father left me."

Francis took a book out of his pocket and laid it on the table. "This is George Herbert's *The Temple*. It was given me to read on this journey by the father of a little girl I painted. It was his book. I'd like you to have it, and so would he."

The old man looked at the book as though it were a bag of gold. "I can't deprive you, sir," he whispered hoarsely.

"You're not depriving me," said Francis. "I've read it."

Parson Hawthyn blinked. Men who could so lightly part with their books were beyond his comprehension. "I thank you, sir, I thank you," he murmured, and placed George Herbert between Spenser and *Piers Plowman* on the shelf. "You give me great wealth for the gift of a book is the gift of a human soul. Men put their souls in their books. When one man gives another a book then three souls are bound together in that most happy thing, a trinity. What blessed thing is a gift! It was the old name for the Holy Spirit. The Gift. I have no way in which to reward you, sir, though you have my poor prayers, and I can show you my church. It is small, but the Normans built it, and many have prayed there through six centuries."

Francis was not interested in country churches but he was

interested in Parson Hawthyn, and they strolled out of doors into the sunshine of the little garden.

"Now here's more of my wealth," said the old man. "Butterflies on Michaelmas daisies. You know these daisies? Not all gardens have them, for it's not ten years yet since John Tredescant brought them into England from foreign parts. I know young John and he gave me a plant or two. They are new to you, I expect."

Francis smiled, remembering the banks of them in the royal gardens, and in his father's garden, and remembering too John Tredescant the elder, the king's gardener.

"They are beautiful," he said gently. "And so are the butterflies."

They were a wonderful sight, sunning their glowing wings on the mauve and purple and white of St. Michael's daisies; tortoiseshells and whites, peacocks and fritillaries and, loveliest of all, the painted ladies with their wings inlaid with the moon and stars. Francis searched his memory for the words he wanted, words that would once more bring that look of pouncing eagerness to the old man's face.

> "Of all the race of silver-wingèd Flies
> Which do possess the empire of the air,
> Betwixt the centred earth, and azure skies,"

he began, and stopped as Parson Hawthyn's round red face suddenly beamed at him like a lighted lamp. "But you know how it goes on, sir. Not at all complimentary to painters."

"Certainly not," said Parson Hawthyn delightedly. "No indeed.

> Painted with thousand colours, passing fair
> All Painters' skill. . . .
> Not half so many sundry colours are
> In Iris brave, nor heaven doth shine so bright,
> Distinguished with many a twinkling star.
> Nor Juno's bird in her eye-spotted train
> So many goodly colours doth contain.

No, sir, your painter's palette cannot produce such colours as these, such orange-tawnies and red-browns and azure-blue. And nor can my clumsy carver's tools make form so beautiful. But we'll learn sir, we'll learn. You see my autumn damask roses? They came from Mistress Froniga Haslewood. She grafted them for me from her own and her bees come here after them. There is not such another gardener as Mistress Froniga in the country."

They went through the churchyard gate and followed the narrow path that led among the graves. Just outside the porch Francis stopped and asked, "Who is that singing?"

They stood in the porch and listened. The piping was not bird music and yet seemed too thin and sweet for human voices. It was so unearthly that Parson Hawthyn could not speculate as to its origin but just stood listening, his face wrapt. Francis, his head still full of poetry, felt as though he had been caught away to Prospero's island. "Where should this music be? i' th' air or th' earth?" He tiptoed forward and looked through the crack of the door. The music instantly died away, but through the green gloom within there passed, like a ripple through water, a butterfly shimmer of colour. Then there was stillness. Nothing moved except motes of dust in a glancing sunbeam. Imagination, thought Francis. The metheglyn at the manor had been very potent, and poetry is heady stuff. He opened the door wide, and bowed, and Parson Hawthyn, still bemused, passed in.

But Francis must have been bemused too, for standing beside the old man in the empty church he mechanically took off his stiff Puritan hat, bowed to the altar and crossed himself. Parson Hawthyn suddenly ceased to be bemused and cocked a very penetrating dark eye at his companion, then as they moved about the church he thrust anxiety aside. The contradictions in this young man were disturbing but not his concern at the moment. His concern, now, was that he should spend a happy half-hour within the church. He showed him the bells, Marie, Gabriel, Douce and John, the cross, and the old painted panels set in the rood screen. They showed figures of the saints, for the church was dedicated to All Saints, but the colours were dim now, like the colour of the woods in winter. And then he showed him his own little carved figures, the birds and the cherubs and the Madonna in her niche; but these he showed with diffidence and some shame, aware how crudely he had painted them, and aware of laughter firmly battened down beneath the young man's compliments. He did not mind the laughter, but he did mind that his colours were so crude. When he thought of the butterflies he could have wept. "Patience," he said to himself, "for there is eternity. Shall we then dip our brushes in Iris, the rainbow?"

They were standing before the Madonna's niche and he was aware of an abrupt cessation of amusement.

"It's a poignant little figure," said Francis. "I've never before seen a Madonna with her arms laid empty in her lap like that. I see your meaning. Her glory was in giving."

Parson Hawthyn stared. Sure enough, the baby was gone from his mother's arms, that lay held out upon her lap and empty.

"No," he said, "that was not my meaning, though it is a good meaning. Someone has taken the baby. It does not matter. As you say, her glory was in giving."

They moved to the tomb of the lady and Francis asked, "Who is she?"

"An ancestress of the Haslewoods," said Parson Hawthyn, and added in a curiously triumphant tone, "She died young."

Francis was aware of delight. The lady had a small, child-like figure. There was a half-smile on her lips and she seemed to have closed her eyes not in death but in laughter, as children sometimes screw their eyes shut when joy is bubbling in them. Though it was fashioned out of stone the whole tomb had a golden look. Francis found himself smiling broadly. Delightful to die young and gay, as poppies do, dropping their petals on the grass as swiftly and happily as they opened them.

"She's enchanting," he said. "She and the unicorn."

He turned from the merry lady to look at the airy little creature who lay at her feet, at rest, but with neck arched and delicate horn pointed as though he might leap away at any moment. "Back to the wood," said Francis. "I liked him best, I think, in the Haslewoods' dining parlour, looking out through the branches. . . . Why . . . look here, sir! Look!"

Leaning over, with the interest of a fellow artist, to see how the genius of a sculptor had dealt with the unicorn's tail, he had caught sight of something behind the tomb, a brightness and a hint of colour. He beckoned to Parson Hawthyn and they both peered over the little lady's recumbent form and met the glance of six round dark eyes, bright with terror beneath matted shadows of night-black hair. The children had crouched down so low on the stone floor behind the tomb that they looked almost bodiless, three cherub heads that had fluttered down like butterflies behind the tomb. The smallest cherub was more easily seen than her brothers, for the blue garment she wore seemed to float her face upwards, as though on a wave of blue water, and there was a little bunch of forget-me-nots stuck in her hair. Her face was tear-stained and agonised with entreaty, her arms clutched across her breast as though hiding something.

"They've got the wooden baby!" laughed Francis.

Suddenly they were gone. The terror which had frozen them to the floor became active as soon as they heard the gorgio speak. They were out from behind the tomb and across the church and through the open door in a flash. For a moment the little figures stood out clear-cut against the dazzle of sun-shot blue that filled the dark arch of the door, and then the blue absorbed them and they were gone. The two men remained staring stupidly at the place where they had vanished. It looked now like the archway into another world, and they felt, old, soiled and shut out.

"I'm sorry," said Francis at last. "The young limbs! If I'd been a bit quicker I could have caught them and got your bambino back for you."

"No, no," said Parson Hawthyn gently. "You may be quick upon your feet, young man, but you'd never have caught a gypsy's child. They're fleet as hares. Let her keep her dolly. She'll cradle him well."

"That was stealing, you know," said Francis, amused.

"Not for them," said Parson Hawthyn. "The Romany people say that a gypsy boy was present at the Crucifixion and ran off with one of the nails before the soldiers could use it. The soldiers found another nail for their purpose, but God did not forget the kindly act, and allows the Romany people to steal from the gorgios when they wish, and does not account it sin. . . . So they say. . . . They are an adroit people."

They strolled out of the church and down to the gate. "You will have noon lunch with me?" asked the old man.

Francis made courteous excuses, for he had a shrewd idea that if he shared Parson Hawthyn's noon lunch there might be little left for Parson Hawthyn, and he had ordered a good meal for himself at the inn. The old man did not press him, remembering that the cheese was a little mouldy and the bread was stale. Increasingly, as he had talked to this plainly-dressed but exquisitely mannered and entirely poised young man, he had realised just how stale and mouldy the bread and cheese were.

At the parting of their ways he took Francis's hand and looked at him with smiling earnestness.

"'Manners makyth man,' sir," he quoted, "and being one of the fundamental things about us are more difficult to alter than the cut of our coat or our hair. For your own safety, sir, I would tell you that the more I have seen of you today the less have you reminded me of those mendicant daubers who paint portraits for a living."

Francis laughed. "It's for a wager," he confessed.

Parson Hawthyn's smile faded. "Do not forget, sir, that at the manor you were hospitably entertained."

Then he released the young man's hand, bowed and limped away towards his parsonage. His round, sparrow-like figure was a matter for mirth, but Francis did not laugh. The unease he had felt yesterday came again, deepening to a sense of fear; not physical fear, for he scarcely knew what that was, but the fear of destiny. In time of peace one worked it out quietly, aware that one's own character gave to it a measure of inevitability, yet aware too of a certain flexibility of choice. In war it might thunder down so suddenly that a man would have no time to choose what he would do.

CHAPTER VII

THE WHITE WITCH

I

Froniga, her basket on her arm, came out into the early morning sunlight and sat down on the edge of the well. She felt heavy and sad, for the perplexities that had kept her awake most of the night were still with her. There was Yoben. He had always said, he still said, that he had no politics, but politics had come between them. And Robert. Today he was taking Will to school at Thame and then rejoining his regiment. What would happen to him in this war? The strength of her love for Yoben had never diminished her love for Robert. In her youth she would have liked to marry him, but she had known her own strength and the harm it would have done to him. For she loved power and she had to rule. She would have ruled him and he would have been a child to the end of his days. And perhaps cruel to the end of his days. For the unkindness in him would have been strengthened by the shame of his subjection to her; he would have compensated himself by bullying those who were weaker than he was. She thought that he did not know about his cruelty, but she had known about it since his childhood, when she had found him cuffing his kitten after his father had thrashed him. She had not loved him any the less for it, knowing that all but the noblest of men and women are as cruel as they are self-centred. The cruelty of the weak may be more nauseating than that of the strong, because of its element of revenge, but the cruelty of the strong, who must fulfil their purpose no matter who or what obstructs it, can do more damage. It was that she was afraid of in herself, and because of it there was only one man of the many who had desired her whom she would have married, and that was Yoben, because she was aware of some dedication in him stronger than herself. She believed that was partly why she loved him. Her love for Robert she had never been able to explain to herself, for it had no passion in it, and Robert was not particularly attractive. It was perhaps the appeal of his ordinariness. He had never had the slightest understanding of her unordinary powers and with him she had found rest from them. What would this war do to his beloved ordinariness?

And she was anxious about Will, who would not find boarding-school a bed of roses, coddled and spoilt as he had been by his mother. And her darling Jenny. The parting from Will, the first parting of her life, was likely to tear her heart in two. Will's portrait had been finished yesterday and she hoped Margaret had had the intelligence to arrange for Jenny's to be started today, to distract her mind. She had carefully not suggested it, for resisting her suggestions was the only way in which poor Margaret ever showed any strength of purpose. Well, at least Margaret was not flighty, and would not start an affair with the journeyman painter. Now there was another perplexity. If that young man thought his stocky figure and blunt features made him look like a countryman he deceived himself. Had he never noticed how countrymen move? And did he suppose journeyman painters could paint as he did? If he supposed either of these things he was a fool, and fools are dangerous to those who harbour them.

There was a soft warm pressure against her leg and looking down she saw her white cat, to whom she had given the gypsy name of Pen, sister. She rubbed her gently behind her ears, and Pen jumped up and began to knead her lap with her paws, her whole body vibrating with joyous purring. Then with one quick trustful movement she coiled herself round into a snowy wreath upon her mistress's knees. She was not quite asleep, for there was a glint in her eye and she continued to hum. The doves who lived at the farm beyond the orchard were circling out from their cot, over the garden and back again, in a high silvery curve against the sky. The white gypsy pony whom she had mistaken for a unicorn was cropping the grass just on the other side of her garden hedge, and robins and chaffinches were hopping near her without fear. The creatures never feared her. One of her unordinary powers, and the only one that gave her nothing but joy, was her power over them. A wave of delight went through her and her worries were forgotten. Why worry? They didn't. Worry was sin, a part of man's rebellion against God and loss of trust in Him. They had not sinned. When they satisfied their appetites they were merely fulfilling the law of their being, not violating it. They did nothing to excess and knew no rottenness, and so they were wholesome, and she adored their wholesomeness. She could, she thought, live happily with Pen and the doves and the white pony until the end of her days, and miss none of her humankind but those very few to whom she had given the wholeness of her love.

Her eye fell on her basket and she remembered that she had come out to pick herbs and lettuce leaves and to look at her flowers, that she loved only a little less than birds and beasts, and much more than the majority of human beings. She made ointments and lotions and medicines for the sick, not so much because she loved the sick, though she did not lack compassion, as because she liked to see her herbs and flowers doing their work, loved to test and prove their potency. The dependence of men upon the creatures to whom they considered themselves superior filled her with delight. Animals, birds and flowers could live very satisfactorily without men, but men deprived of the creatures perished miserably.

She got up, and with Pen following her walked into her garden. It was a fragrant and musical place, humming with bees, with grass paths separating the cushions and knots and parterres of colour and scent. Froniga had more than a hundred herbs and knew all their names and just where to find them. She loved them all with passion, but best of all she loved her great rosemary bush, her lavender hedge and beds of mint geranium, that some call costmary and others Bible leaf, because a sprig set between the pages of one's Bible was sweet to smell in church, her germander and marjoram. Among her flowers were marigolds, paggles, daisies and gilliflowers. She had all the loveliest gilliflowers, sops-in-wine, Master Tuggie his rose, ruffling robin, queen's dainty and painted lady with her lovely white flowers stippled with cherry, and though it was not the season of their glory many of them were still in flower.

She walked slowly, intent as a mother in her nursery to see that no harm had come to her darlings, noting with fury where a slug had done damage, and with sorrow where a sparrow had forgotten himself. Pen was a garden-trained cat and never hurt a plant. Froniga gathered her herbs and lettuce leaves and then made some nosegays for Robert and Will to stick in their buttonholes, to refresh them upon their long hot ride to Thame. Robert's was very plain, just lavender, costmary and rosemary, small enough to carry in his pocket beneath his leather jerkin in time of battle. When she had made it, before she laid it in her basket she held it in her hands and murmured over it words of power that her mother had taught her. Will's nosegay was larger, and had a hen-and-chicken daisy in it, and a couple of paggles to bring him heart's ease in the first hours of homesickness. She said no words of power over it, only a little fairy blessing, for she had sat long last night with her Romany tarot cards spread out before her, and the shadows that had gathered behind Will's head had been only those of childhood's sorrows, that will pass, and behind them the sky had been blue. She could not have borne the darkness behind Robert's head had it not been for one rent in the clouds shaped like a doorway. For Yoben and for Jenny she had not dared to look into the future. She had thought she had the courage to face anything whatever for those she loved, as she did for herself, but she found she had been mistaken.

She stood and looked at her rosemary tree. It had grown here ever since she could remember and she suspected that it had been planted when the cottage was built, for of all the trees of divine power rosemary is the most potent in driving away evil, and few gardens were planted without it. Upon the journey to Egypt, Mary threw her blue cloak over a rosemary bush, turning the white flowers to the blue of her mantle, and when she returned to Nazareth she would spread her son's little garments to dry on a rosemary bush after she had washed them. Rosemary, dew of the sea, the freshest and sweetest-smelling plant in the world, is steeped in the mercy of Christ. Froniga's tree stood just under six feet high and had not grown at all since she had lived here, which proved that at her coming it had passed the age of thirty-three years, for rosemary never grows after the age when Christ died and never passes the height of Christ while He was a man on earth. Froniga planned to ask Parson Hawthyn to make a box out of the wood of her rosemary tree and to give it to Jenny when she grew up, for an old herbal of a hundred years ago had said plainly, "Make thee a box with rosemary and smell to it and it shall preserve thy youth." She greeted her tree and curtseyed to it. That it was a living personality she was convinced. Her religion was entirely individual, an astonishing mixture of Christianity, white witchcraft, Romany and fairy lore, and a quite sublime faith in her own powers. She was not given to self-analysis. If she had been she might have been shocked to find that she was more wedded to her spells than to prayer. White magic was more amenable than God. The good spirits would permit their power to be drawn with a human will, while God demanded of the human will that it be drawn into His. Froniga did know that much about God but had never set herself to consider her knowledge.

She passed on beyond her herb and nosegay garden to her rose garden, that in June was one of the loveliest in the neighbourhood. She grew her roses chiefly for medicinal purposes but for their beauty too; apothecary and rosa-mundi, velvet and village maid, damask roses for making melrosette, the musk rose for its scent that drifted on every breeze, maiden's blush and incarnation because she loved them. Of sweetbrier roses she grew a quantity, both for metheglyn and toilet waters. They hedged her whole domain as well as the herb garden and the cottage was named after them. She moved along the grass paths with reverence and awe. The rose was so immensely old. From the gardens of Damascus and Persia the garden rose had come to the walled castle gardens of England and to the poor plots of the peasants, and for how many centuries it had grown wild in the forests who could say? Its incense breathed from old legends and the dim ways of lost centuries were lit by its beauty. Cold never killed it, and storms did not tear it away from the stones where it clung. It mantled walls as though it loved them, and its flowers leaned in at cottage windows, with chin propped on the sill like a curious child.

Froniga left her rose garden and followed a daisy-edged grass path to the little front garden next to the lane, upon the east side of her cottage. Here there was a small grass plot, and a paved path leading from the gate to the front door, hidden deep within its honeysuckle porch. Flower-beds bordered the path and in them Froniga grew her primroses, jack-in-the-green, hose-in-hose and galligaskin, and the cowslips and wallflowers that she used in so many medicines and toilet waters. Violets grew under the cottage wall, but then violets grew everywhere in Froniga's garden. She could never have enough of them for conserves and jellies, and as an excellent medicine for hang-over. After a fair-day half the village came to Froniga for medicine for that purpose.

She knew Robert and Will were coming even before she heard the clop-clop of their horses' hoofs in the lane. She did not know, as she did with Yoben, when they turned homeward from a distance, but she knew when they turned the corner by the inn and rode down past the wheelwright's cottage to her own. She walked down to the gate in the sweetbrier hedge, unlatched it and went out to meet them.

Robert was riding Diamond, and Will was on his dapple-grey pony, who had been named by Froniga Pal, because he and Will were so devoted, as devoted as she and Pen. Jenny longed for a pony too but had not been given one because she was only a girl. Behind them at a respectful distance, Tom Fettipace, the groom and garden boy who was to bring Pal back from Thame tomorrow, ambled along on his chestnut pony Noah. When he saw Froniga he pulled his forelock and turned Noah aside to crop the grass by the side of the lane. Tom had great tact. Froniga noted his tact with approval and then looked at Will.

The tide of love can play queer tricks, for it never stays still, it is always coming in or going out, but it can come in so slowly that years pass before the one who loves realises that what was at first a thin bright line upon the skyline is now a brimming flood. Or it comes in suddenly like a tidal wave, and breaks in choking brightness over your head before you know where you are. Froniga had always had an affection for Will but now, from one moment to another, she loved him. He came riding down to her through the green tunnel of the lane, in and out of the dazzzle of the sunshine and the flickering of green leaves, and she did not even see his father. He was dressed not in the green festive suit but in breeches and doublet of severe grey. He was a sombre figure, for the bright little sword had been left at home and what was left of his hair was entirely hidden by his large black hat, an exact copy of his father's. The colour had gone from his poppy-cheeks, his usually sleepy eyes were wide open and unnaturally bright, and though he was smiling at her, he was keeping his dry lips tightly closed over the gaps in his teeth. He always rode well, but now his back was straight as a wand. His reins were skilfully held in one hand while he kept the other free to take off his hat to the lady. He came level with her, reined in Pal and removed his hat, and the sun shone upon the close-cropped corn-coloured hair. Froniga gripped her hands together that she might not touch his hair. Her arms ached with the longing to fling her arms around him and lift him off the pony, carry him indoors, hide him, not let him go to school, not let him be a man, anything to bring back the sleepy droop to those strained eyelids, and see the old gappy-toothed wet smile. She knew how it had been with him these last two days and nights. Since his breeching he had not slept with Jenny and Maria in the big bed, but by himself in a truckle-bed in his father's dressing-room. He, who had been accustomed to roar at pleasure, had not dared even sob in the night in case his father heard him. By day he had seen his mother weeping as she packed his saddle-bags and had realised at long last what it was that was going to happen to him; he was going away from the home he had never left, even for a night, into a far country. Jenny, drifting after him wherever he went like a shadow, he had scarcely spoken to at all, because he was now a man and she was only a little girl. His throat had ached because of the unnatural silence and every now and again his heart had pounded with sudden dread. But it was glorious to be a man and he would not have put the clock back for anything in the whole world, not even to sleep with Jenny and Maria again in the big bed. Suddenly Froniga realised that he would not, and she unclasped her hands and looked up at him and laughed. She had the most infectious laugh in the world and his tight lips had come open into the old smile. But it was nearly his undoing. His lips trembled. Quick as thought Froniga took a comfit from her large hanging pocket and popped it between them.

"I've a bag of them here for you," she whispered. "Look, I'll put them in your pocket. There's a marigold in them, darling boy—that's good for the spirits—and marjoram for your rumbling stomach, and here's a little nosegay with a blessing upon it to bring you joy; but don't let the other boys see it, dear heart. Keep it hid."

He crunched upon the comfit, finding it indeed most comforting to the spirits, and then whispered, "I've another thing."

"Show it to me," she whispered back.

He took the little seal out of his pocket. "The painting man gave it to me," he said. "It's a seal. It has a lion on it."

With great kindness he held it out so that she might hold it. She took it, closed her hand upon it, and for a moment almost lost consciousness of the place where she was. She saw a splendid room with a painted ceiling and gilded furniture. Outside the window were great lime trees. She saw the weary man writing at a desk. At his knee stood a small, sturdy little boy. He took something off his desk and gave it to the child, and the tenderness of the smile that flashed across his face enchanted her. At the same time the familiar warning flashed through her mind. "Quick, quick, give it back or you're undone."

She gave it back and said, "Take great care of it, Will. Such gifts are precious."

"Nothing for me, Froniga?" asked Robert.

He had dismounted, with amusement in his eyes. The immense value which she set upon gifts and tokens of all sorts always amused her family, and she was accustomed to their laughter and was in her turn amused by their amusement. How little did they know! If they could for one moment close the eyes of their bodies and see with their other eyes, what then? They would see their thoughts alive, passing out from them to stifle or refresh the multitude of human spirits about them, spirits of those whom the world calls living and of those whom the world calls dead, some of them delicate and young and harmed so easily. And the others, the spirits of beasts and birds, of flowers and trees and houses, and the sprites both good and bad. And the great ones, those who had chosen God and endured the proving. And those who could not be named for terror because they also had chosen what they loved. If they could see their memories, not what they thought them, a mere drift of smoke from a snuffed candle, but the reflection in the glass of the spirit of something alive for ever. And the life of the so-called inanimate things, even a little red seal, able to absorb something of the life of an eternal moment and transmit its power. Gifts and tokens were not little things. But for nearly all of them their other eyes opened only in sleep, and in waking they forgot what they had seen. And those who could see in their waking moments knew, if love of power had not destroyed their sense of danger, that they must look only so far and no further. Awareness of much was permitted them, but of experience only a very little. Froniga still knew where she must stop.

"A nosegay, of course," she said. "Do I ever let anyone I love go from me without a nosegay?"

She brought it to him and put it in his buttonhole, and suddenly with a stifled cry he flung his arms round her. It was his custom to kiss her at greeting and parting, but always with cousinly correctness. Not like this. He had not kissed her this way since their youth, and she felt the fire in his body as hot as it had ever been. She was as sensitive as she was strong, and though her spirit rose quietly to the mastery it did so with anguish. The unassuaged passion hurt her and her pity flowed. She returned the kiss but her lips remained cool under his and her hands on his shoulders held and steadied him. Her great soft eyes, when he looked in them, did not mirror his own. He felt, as she had willed that he should, that he had not called her from the depths of herself.

Crimson with shame, Robert flung away from her and turned to his horse. She ran into the cottage to fetch the stirrup-cup of home-brewed cowslip wine. When she came back he was mounted and in command of himself, and looking the typical Puritan of years to come, his face white and grim below his black hat, his figure stiff and angular in the hard plain clothes. Will, beside him, was trying to look exactly the same. She realised with a sinking of the heart that this new seeking after righteousness had a harshness about it that was as alien to her own spirit as it was to that of England. It was coming up like an east-wind blight that drained the colour from the world and silenced the bird song. . . . She had a sudden longing for her old green gown.

Her men-folk tasted the stirrup-cup and handed it back to her with polite but distant smiles. Already they had receded a long way from her. Then they moved off and trotted up the lane, Tom Fettipace wheeling in behind them. The greenness came down like a curtain. For a little while she heard the rhythmic beat of the horses' feet, and then that too was lost in the voices of the birds and the sound of the wind in the trees. The childhood of Will Haslewood and the youth of his father were immortal for ever, but they had become now what men call memories.

2

Froniga wasted no time in mourning for them, for she took an austere view of time. It was of course an illusion, but the wrong use of an illusion can be very serious. An illusion exists to be converted into something useful, and the minutes and hours of her morning had to be converted into medicines and lotions for the sick.

Bending her head, for she was too tall for her own low

doorway, she passed into the dimness of the honeysuckle porch and down the two worn stone steps into what she called her parlour, though it would have been more accurate to call it her dispensary. There was no apothecary nearer than Henley, and he had his hands full with all the ailments of that busy little town. The ailments of the village were attended to by Froniga and Margaret, though very few trusted Margaret. There was also Mother Skipton, but people only went to her under cover of the dark. If an illness baffled these three women the patient either went to Dr. Appleby at Henley or died. Frequently both.

The parlour, like the kitchen, had a stone-flagged floor and whitewashed walls, and from the low beams that crossed the ceiling hung bunches of herbs. A log fire burned here too, for Froniga infused her herbs over its heat, and her patients liked to sit on the bench before it while they told her how poorly they felt. There was an oak table where she sat to do her work, and two presses where she kept all her medicines and lotions, ointments, comfits and preserves. In a carved oak chest she kept her green gown and her precious herbals, chief among them John Parkinson's *Paradisi in Sole Paradisus terrestris* and *Theatrum botanicum*. She regretted that he should have dedicated these two glorious books to King Charles and Queen Henrietta Maria. But she continued to use them, for a fellow herbalist is never an enemy.

Froniga had studied all the known doctrines of healing, her favourite being the doctrine of signatures. She felt it was only commonsense to believe that God had written upon every tree and plant a sign by which man would know the ailment it would cure. Hawthorn bore thorns, for instance, so that he should know that distilled water of hawthorn flowers drew both thorns and blisters from the skin. The purple stains upon iris petals showed them to be a proper cure for bruises, and the spotted cowslip was the obvious cure for spotty complaints. There was, of course, a difficulty here, for the hawthorn is not the only tree to bear thorns, and the colour of the bruise is found in other flowers beside the iris, and which of them was it the intention of the Almighty that one should use? Trial and error frequently settled this point, and if in doubt Froniga turned to the stars for help. The young Puritan herbalist Nicolas Culpeper (he who advocated tansy for childbearing) had worked out in very accurate detail the exact relation, in his opinion, between the stars and the herbs, and between the planets and the parts of the body which they governed. He had written it all down for her when she had visited his medicinal herb-garden at Spitalfields. The position of the stars at the time the patient was taken ill could determine both what was the matter with him and what treatment should be given to him. But it was a complicated doctrine, and though Froniga was a clever woman she found it difficult.

The doctrine of the five humours she left to the medical profession, for she did not approve of the extensive blood lettings needed to let out an over-dose of this humour or that, and the new theory of the circulation of the blood discovered by a Dr. Harvey, who had been a physician to Lord Bacon, she thought utter nonsense. Many people agreed with her, and since he had published his book on the subject, Dr. Harvey had been pronounced crackbrained and his practice had fallen off considerably.

There remained Froniga's own precious and peculiar knowledge, written down in no book. Her mother had taught it to her father, and her father had taught it to her. He had not used it, having no wish for such power, but only through him had her mother been able to hand on her knowledge to her daughter, for the spells of a white witch or wizard must be handed on from man to woman and woman to man, or they lose their potency.

She hung a pot upon the hook above the fire and put into it the herbs she had picked in the garden. Equal parts of samile, milfoil and bugle, in white wine, was an unequalled remedy for the treatment of wounds, of which she had had several lately, from local skirmishes and accidents of the militia, and would have many more as this wicked war went on. As one of her herbals expressed it, this was a remedy that "healeth all round most perfectly, bugle openeth the wound, milfoil cleanses the wound, samile healeth it". Leaving the herbs to simmer she took the lettuce leaves from the basket and turned to her table, where last night she had left ready her pestle and mortar and a dish full of snail shells. She made an excellent soporific of pounded lettuce leaves, which was both for internal and external application. The soles of the feet have great affinity with the head, proved by the fact that wet feet produce a running cold, and she always insisted that her soporific should be rubbed on the soles of the feet as well as drunk. Snail shells pounded fine were excellent for rupture, and there would be many ruptures in this war, while anxiety and wounds caused much sleeplessness. To her basic remedies she would add when the time came those herbs which the planets told her were particularly potent at the moment when the illness or the wound was suffered. And always over each medicine she would murmur her beneficent spells.

As she pounded lettuce leaves she was thinking of a case which was causing her particular anxiety. Little Joe Diggar was having convulsive fits and they were not yielding to treatment. She had suffered much with him lately. It was part of her healing art to feel in her own body something of the pain of those she was treating, and so she knew he was no better. She had tried every remedy she knew of except one. The prescription for this one began, "Take the skull of a man or woman, wash it clean and dry it in the oven after the bread is drawn." She shrank from it, but if relief did not come quickly the child would die. She supposed duty compelled her to try this last remedy. It was in one of her herbals and was, she knew, considered efficacious, nor had she heard that any spiritual harm came to the patient after the remedy had been applied. Nevertheless she did not like having dealings with death when she was trying to preserve life. The snail shells were different, for she used only the shells which the blackbirds had emptied for her. She never herself destroyed a snail. And she felt a further reluctance. Skulls did not lie about in the hedgerows and she knew of only two places where she could procure one. She must either go and dig one up from the churchyard or she must apply to Mother Skipton, who doubtless always had them by her, as she used them in her various arts and most likely helped herself from the nearest gibbet as occasion required. The former course held no terrors for Froniga, but she did not want to disturb the peaceful dead in the churchyard. It seemed a desecration, even though the life of a child was at stake. But some poor creature who had died on the gibbet had been already much disturbed and a little more or less was not likely to distract his spirit overmuch. Moreover he had not been buried in consecrated ground. But still she could not make up her mind. When she was practising her healing art she was always very aware of the good spirits, and there was one, truly beneficent and always merry, whom she felt to be very much with her when she cared for the children of this place. As she pounded she asked this spirit to vouchsafe to her some sign as to what she must do.

She was draining off the lettuce juice from her mortar when she became aware of a slight darkening of the light. She looked up and her heart gave a bound of delight. The creature standing in the doorway might have been Oberon. The light was behind him and at first sight she saw only the outline of the small figure, with wisps of flimsy garments floating about shapely limbs, garments that might have been made of spiders' webs. The little head was held proudly. A transparent silvery crown was on the dusky hair and it seemed that huge earrings hung from fawn's ears. Then she saw more clearly, and the spiders' webs were orange-tawny rags, the earrings were bunches of elder-berries and a silvery crown of traveller's-joy was twined round the head of her cousin Meriful Heron. She had seen him often, but he had never come to her house before and she held out her hand with a cry of welcome.

"What is it, dearie little son?" she asked in the Romany tongue. "What can I do for you? Come here, little *tschavo*, little son."

He came to her cautiously, stepping on tiptoe, his eyes enormous with astonishment at the strangeness of her room. She marvelled at the beautiful contours and dusky shadows of his face. He laid his hands palm upwards on her lap. "*Rawni*, I have warts," he announced proudly.

"They are fine warts," she said admiringly.

"I wish them gone," he said in a kingly manner. "Twice have I dipped them in the spring of the little horse, but they are still with me."

She realised, humbly, that she had been mistaken in the source of his pride. She had thought him proud of his warts, but his pride was in himself. It was doubtless he who had crowned himself with the exquisite silver crown.

"I can cure your warts," she said, and rising she took from a pewter pot on the mantel a piece of lard with the skin on it. With this she rubbed his warts, then, taking a hammer and nail from a box on the table, she bade him follow her. They went out of the door and round to the south window of the cottage, where, murmuring a fairy spell, she nailed the lard upon the wooden frame of the window. "In a few days' time this lard will have disappeared, Meriful," she said. "The sun will have melted it and the birds taken it away. As the lard disappears, so will your warts disappear. Do you understand?"

He nodded gravely. He understood perfectly. He took the

bunch of elder-berries off his right ear and gave it to her as a token of gratitude. "The magic is good," he said, "and that which you purpose in your heart is good, *Rawni. O boro Duvel atch' pa leste.*" And suddenly he had vanished. He went so silently she did not even hear the creak of the garden gate. She looked at the bunch of elder-berries, even bigger than those that grew on her own tree. He had plucked them from the tree that grew over the spring in Flowercote Wood. Traveller's-joy grew there too, cobwebbing the bushes round about as though it were the spray of a fountain. Holding the berries in her hands she was aware of the bubbling spring, the cool fresh scent of the place and the clarity of the laughter. You could not speak of the sound of laughter when you heard nothing, but the laughter that lived there always seemed to have the same cleansing power that the water possessed. She believed that the beneficent spirit had answered her through the child. "That which you purpose in your heart is good, *Rawni.*" She would go to Mother Skipton. But she would not go under cover of the dark as the villagers did, for she would not put herself under the domination of the dark. She would go in the daylight, and if she was seen, what of it? The only eyes to which a sensible woman should pay the slightest attention are those that see the heart.

CHAPTER VIII

THE UNICORN

If Will's childhood had passed into memory on the day he rode to Thame, so had Jenny's. The day of her father's and Will's departure had not been unbearable because she had been busy with her mother. If Margaret felt sorry for herself about one thing, then she felt sorry for herself about all the things, and the parting from Robert and Will had made her so acutely aware of her weak heart and delicate digestion, the tiresomeness of the young maids and Biddy's rudeness, and the jelly that had not come out right, that she had ended up on the sofa in tears, and Jenny had had to read to her and wind her wool, and run her errands, and the time had passed as quickly as it always did. But at night, when she climbed into the big bed with Maria and there was no Will, she became, as never before, aware of time. She must lie in this bed in the dark for nine hours without Will, and then she must get up and dress and go through the hours of the day—and there were fifteen hours in her day—without Will. And she must live for weeks and months without Will; and when he came home he would be different and he might not want her any more. And then she would have to live the rest of her life without him.

The bed seemed enormous. Maria was beside her, but Maria was asleep and dreaming of rabbits and not able to share the misery through which Jenny was passing. No one could share it. The bed bigger and the room beyond the bed got bigger too, bigger and darker, a cavern of loneliness, and out of it there led that passage of the endless hours. Though she was lying in the bed she could see herself walking down that passage, on and on for ever, and always alone. Time was loneliness. She had not known before that people lived alone, or that they lived for such a long time.

And then she was no longer watching herself going along the dark passage, but was actually there, plodding on and on in the cold emptiness, trying to get to the end of time because when time ended loneliness would end too. At the end of time there was a door, and on the other side of the door was Will, not a strange Will who had come back from school, but the Will who had come with her from her mother's womb and had been the other half of herself. She must get to the end of time. But a cold wind was blowing against her, and though she fought and struggled she could not prevail against it, and suddenly her feet went from under her and she fell headlong, screaming as she fell.

She sat up in the big bed, shivering and drenched with sweat. The church clock was striking twelve and she had heard nine strike and ten, but not eleven, and so though she had thought she was too tired to sleep she must have dozed a little. Had she been screaming in a nightmare or had her mother called her? Mother! She had forgotten her mother. She was suddenly as hot with shame as before she had been cold with misery. Mother too was alone in her big bed. She ran across her room and opened the communicating door softly. She would curl up in her mother's arms, as she had done sometimes when she was smaller, before her mother had begun to be so strict with her, and then neither of them would be lonely.

She crept across the room to Margaret's bed, longing for the warmth and comfort of it, a host of loving words crowding up behind her eager parted lips, and drew back the bed-curtains gently. The window curtains were not drawn and through them the moonlight shone upon Margaret's face. She had cried herself to sleep and was now as deeply and happily asleep as a child. She looked a child, with her fair hair escaped from her nightcap and her wet lashes lying on flushed cheeks. Jenny stood looking at her with a strange adult tenderness in her dark eyes. She touched her mother's hair gently but she did not attempt to waken her. She realised that the days when she had curled up in her mother's arms were over, like the days when Will had been a part of her. It was she now who would take care of her mother. They would love each other always but they would live alone. She crept back to her own bed again and gathered Maria into her arms, and realised for the first time the extraordinary truth: a dog in its utter ignorance of the mind and soul can seem nearer to one than a human being who knows a little of both and knows it wrong.

The morning came and she remembered that she must have her portrait painted. It was her turn now. Margaret was in bed with a headache, but Biddy dressed her in her new corsets and her new pink gown with a bunch of flowers pinned to the bodice, and brushed her hair and polished it with a silk handkerchief so that it shone like glass. Jenny was not looking her best as she came out of her room to go downstairs, for her dark eyes had a lost bewildered look and there were shadows under them. Her lips, usually parted in readiness for the fun that was just round the corner, or to tell about the fun that was just over, were set together in a thin line. She went slowly down the stairs, holding up her skirts, and Maria came after her. The house was filled with sun and the warmth brought out the smell of the old ship's timbers of which it was so largely built. It was a good fragrant smell, the smell of home. On some of the old beams fragments of carving still showed, and others had boltholes in them. The old warn treads of the staircase, leading her gently down step by step, the smell of the warm timbers and the sound of Maria coming flipperty flop behind her brought her some comfort. She was sick at heart with loneliness, but Maria was there, and she was on the verge of knowing what good company the spirit of a house can be.

She walked into the dining-parlour, where the man whom she knew as Mr. John Loggin was setting out his paints. Leaning against the wall was the unframed portrait of Will. He was sitting proudly, his head up and his hand on the hilt of his sword. His eyes looked straight into Jenny's, but his serious mouth did not smile. A wave of misery broke over her. It would have been a relief to cry, but she could not. Instead she bent her head and made a stiff wobbly curtsey to Mr. John Loggin. Her curtsey was as changed as her face. There was no grace in either and dismay fell upon Francis, for this stiff lifeless doll was not the child whom he wanted to paint.

He lifted her out of her curtsey, carried her to the window-seat and sat down with her on his knee, keeping his hands about her waist. "What's this?" he asked, feeling the whalebone under her gown. "What's all this scaffolding?"

"My new corsets," said Jenny with a touch of weary pride. "I had them on the day Will was breeched, didn't you notice?"

"No, I didn't. You hadn't a face to match them then. I won't paint you in corsets. Take them off."

"Then my gown won't stay right," objected Jenny.

"I'm not here to paint your gown," said Francis shortly. "Nor to paint that face you're wearing. I'm here to paint Jenny. If the face and the gown belong to the corsets, then for the dear love of God take them off and I'll paint my Jenny in her shift."

This was a new Mr. Loggin, imperious, and accustomed to be obeyed, but Jenny was not afraid of him. He was on the verge of laughter and the arm he had put round her held her with a gentle strength that was new to her. The look in his eyes was new to her too, because until now she had had no need of compassion.

"I'll go upstairs and put on my old gown," she said patiently.

"Be quick, sweetheart," he said, and kissed the top of her head so lightly that he was sure she did not feel it. She nodded and slid down off his knee, but she had felt the kiss and that also was new and strange. Will had gone riding to a new country, but her new country was coming to her.

When she came back again, wearing the blue gown she had worn in the woods, she looked more like herself. There was more light in her eyes, and when she saw that the picture of Will had now disappeared her lips parted with relief.

Francis posed her on a high chair, Maria at her feet, and set to work, deeply thankful that Margaret was the type of fool who took to her bed with a headache when her menfolk left her for war or school. Her mournful face when he had been trying to paint Will had nearly driven him distracted and caused him to paint what he considered a shockingly bad likeness. He had flattered Will. The ordinariness of the urchin was his chief charm, but he had missed it and given the boy the poise of a king's son. That had pleased the parents, of course, especially Robert Haslewood, who had been subtly flattered by it. "They say Will's like me," he had remarked several times over, and several times over Francis had assured him that Will was the image of his father. Robert had smoked his pipe on the window-seat through most of the sittings, relaxed, self-satisfied, and most extraordinarily expansive. He was not usually much of a talker, but Francis, when he wanted to be, was the master of every social art. He could extract information with so much charm that his victim was unaware that he had been asked a single question. And so it had been in one way a successful portrait, and for its success, as well as for its lack of veracity, he hated it.

But now, with Jenny, he had nothing to think of but Jenny. Once or twice Biddy put her head round the door, but he took no notice, and seeing that all was well with them she went away again. The room was warm and quiet, and as he worked he told Jenny one of the stories by Charles Perrault, who was charming all Europe now with his fairy tales. He told her of Puss in Boots, of whom she had not heard before, and she smiled and a little colour came into her cheeks. But she happened not to be very fond of cats and Puss did not quite restore her to the Jenny of the woods. Then he remembered Froniga's advice.

"Of course cats cannot compare with unicorns," he said. "Have you ever seen one, Jenny?"

"Not yet," said Jenny. "They're shy, you know."

"So I've heard," said Francis.

"But my great-grandfather saw one," said Jenny. "You see, he belonged to my great-grandfather."

"Now, how did he come by a unicorn?" asked Francis.

"My great-grandfather Walter Haslewood was a merchant adventurer," said Jenny. "And when he was a young man he built himself a ship and he called her the *Unicorn*. He had a unicorn for a figure-head and he painted it white with blue eyes and a scarlet tip to its horn, like a real unicorn's. He said a ship was better than a wife because it didn't talk. He sailed in it for years and years. He sailed to the West Indies in it and he fought the Spaniards in it. He sailed to El Dorado in it and he loved it more than all the world. How can you paint me while I'm talking?"

"Because I'm not like your great-grandfather. I like a talking woman and I paint best what I like best. Go on."

She was the Jenny of the woods again, and without knowing it he had set her in sunshine against the carved overmantel, where the unicorn looked out through the shadowed leaves, a child glowingly alive against the mystery of her dreams. She was entirely unself-conscious, thinking not of herself but of the story she was telling him. The flowers that had been a tight little posy in the other gown were now released and free and she was holding them in her hands on her lap. Her hair was ruffled and the old faded blue gown a little tumbled, as though she had just come from the woods. If he could only paint what he saw it would doubtless annoy her parents, who would have liked a well-dressed tidy child, making a pair with the correct stiff little boy in the other portrait, but it would be the first portrait to give entire satisfaction to himself.

"What happened to the ship?" he asked.

"She got old," said Jenny, "and she'd been hurt fighting the Spaniards, so she wasn't seaworthy any more, and my great-grandfather was in a fine taking, because he could not live without his unicorn. Then he thought what to do. He brought her up the Thames to that place just below Henley where the old ships are broken up, and he made them take her to pieces very carefully, and then he loaded the pieces on wagons and brought them out here and used them to build this house. And so he still had the unicorn. He put the figure-head on the stairs. I'll show it to you. The paint's worn off it now and it's a bit battered but you can see it's a unicorn."

"Did he bring back gold from El Dorado?" asked Francis.

"He brought it back from somewhere,"said Jenny. "He made the house very beautiful with it. They say in the village that there are bars of gold hidden in the house now, but we can't find them. Biddy and Will and I have looked everywhere, but we think bad fairies must have taken them."

"Just as well," said Francis. "Gold is always a source of trouble. What did your great-grandfather do after he was settled in the house? Marry a dumb wife?"

"That's just what he did do," said Jenny, delighted with his perspicacity. "No one would marry her because she was dumb, but my great-grandfather liked her being dumb because he said a talking wife would be the death of him. She was called Anne and she was pretty, and little of stature and very merry. She was sixteen when my great-grandfather married her and when she was eighteen she died, but before she died she had two little boys, twins, one was my grandfather and the other was Cousin Froniga's father."

"And so your great-grandfather did not see a real unicorn but only his ship?"

"Oh no, he saw a real one too," said Jenny. "The day before my great-grandmother died he saw it in Flowercote Wood, white and shining under an elder tree, but when he came to the elder tree it had gone and in its place there was a spring of water. He built an arch over the spring and carved it with a unicorn's head. The spring never runs dry and the village people get their water there."

"And he buried his little dumb wife in the church," said Francis.

"Yes," said Jenny. "And he had a carving of her put on top

of her tomb, with the unicorn lying at her feet. And then he married another wife."

"Dumb?"

"No, he couldn't find another dumb one. She was the talking sort, but she brought up the little boys very nicely."

"And what did your great-grandfather do?"

"Died."

"And where's he buried?"

"Beside the dumb wife under the paving-stones."

"And where's the talking wife buried?"

"Out in the churchyard, and all the Haslewoods who came after her are buried there too."

"And has your cousin Froniga ever seen the unicorn?" asked Francis.

"I asked her once," said Jenny. "And she laughed and she would not say."

"It's the usual type of family legend," thought Francis. "Before a death the creature is seen. Yet probably all the old seaman saw was sunlight or moonlight glinting on a gypsy's pony." But he was grateful to the unicorn for having transformed Jenny. She was sitting still now, smiling to herself as she thought about it, and he painted quickly and steadily, absorbed in the child and her beauty. He had forgotten himself and presently he had forgotten Jenny. He and she had ceased to exist as separate entities. They had become merged together in something else, the creative act that was the expression of his love for this child.

He was aware of a sense of weariness, of shadow and disintegration. The one thing was once more becoming three things: himself, the picture and Jenny. The patch of sunlight in which he had set her had moved and she seemed lost in the shadows of the wood behind her. She sat courageously holding the pose, but her lips were white.

He flung down his paint-brush, cursing himself for a fool. He picked her up, carried her across the room, lifted her and Maria after her over the low sill of the wide window and set them down right in the middle of the clove gilliflowers. "Stay there till I come back," he commanded. Then he strode out of the parlour and across the hall and flung open the kitchen door.

"Biddy, a cup of milk and some honey cakes for your little mistress. Cold pasty and some ale for me." He spoke pleasantly, for in an age when great men were accustomed to treat their servants as dirt beneath their feet, courtesy to inferiors was one of his eccentricities, but he spoke as a man speaks who is not accustomed to speak twice.

"Hoity-toity," said Biddy, and withdrawing her floury hands from the dough that she was kneading she placed them on her hips.

Francis's jaw dropped for a moment in sheer astonishment, then his mouth set like a trap. The quality of his silence was something Biddy had not met before; her eyes met his for a moment and she hastened to do his bidding.

"Put them on a tray and I'll take them myself," said Francis curtly, and with his hands in his pockets he surveyed the kitchen with an artist's appreciation. He liked the rosy glow of firelight reflected in the gleaming pots and pans, the deep shadows and the rich autumnal colour of golden pumpkins, red apples and pots of jelly that glowed like ruby wine. The Dutch painters were right, kitchens were beautiful things. He must paint a kitchen. Until now he had been chiefly a portrait painter, but he had painted a few classical pictures slightly less vulgar than the goddesses that Rubens had set sprawling all over the ceiling of the King's banqueting hall, and perhaps a shade more intelligent than the allegorical masques that they were perpetually performing at court, but, he thought now in all humility, he must learn to paint the reality of simple things as Rembrandt did. There was just one thing to be said for Protestantism; in banishing the madonnas and the classical allegories from so much of European art it had opened the door to the forgotten beauty of the windmills and the cattle in the fields, ships, copper pots, baskets of red apples, and a woman's shapely hands kneading the dough.

He was aware of the scrutiny of three pairs of eyes fixed upon him in an unblinking stare. They were those of the two little maids and the kitchen cat. He was unembarrassed, for to him these personalities were merely pleasant notes of colour, rose and lavender skirts, tortoise-shell fur and silver whiskers. He took the tray from Biddy, waited for the door to be opened for him and passed gracefully away, his head in the air, planning the picture that should make him as famous as Rembrandt. Biddy fell upon the little maids and soundly berated them. She also slapped the kitchen cat. Having thus re-established her authority she continued once more to knead her dough.

Jenny had picked herself up out of the clove gilliflowers, for she did not want to hurt them, and with Maria was sitting on the grass waiting for Francis and watching a host of small white butterflies hovering over the lavender.

"Lonely, Jenny?" he asked.

"No," said Jenny. "There were the butterflies. Shall we go in the arbour?"

She led the way along a grass path between clumps of Solomon's seal and dame's violet to where cool vine leaves hung over an arbour of trellis-work. There was a wooden seat inside and a small table, where Francis put the tray.

"Honey cakes!" ejaculated Jenny. "I'm not allowed them except on Sunday."

"You're allowed them now," said Francis firmly. "And so is Maria."

Jenny took one and munched delightedly, sharing it with Maria, her legs swinging as she sat on the high seat, and Francis champed happily on the cold pasty. He had sat in many arbours with many pretty women, always entirely at his ease, always master of the situation, and with the woman, figuratively speaking, at his feet, but never with such content as with this small woman, who was by no means at his feet and never would be. He found that he wanted to talk to her. He seldom talked to women, not even to the beautiful but boring woman to whom he was betrothed. He kissed them and joked with them, but did not exert himself further. But Jenny and her cousin Froniga were as much unlike the women he knew as Rubens's banqueting hall was unlike the kitchen he had just seen.

"You did not speak the truth about the butterflies," he said to Jenny. "They did not stop you feeling lonely without Will."

Jenny munched more slowly, considering this. "I forgot about Will while I watched them," she said.

"Beautiful things can do more than help you to forget," said Francis. "Animals, trees, flowers, if you respond to them, look at them in a certain sort of way, forgetting yourself and loving the thing you look at as though it was the only thing alive in the world, something else comes alive, something between you and it, making you and it one with itself, not three any more but one. I don't know what it is, except that to me it's the most important thing there is. Once you've found it you don't feel so lonely."

"Maria seemed important this morning," said Jenny. "More important than usual, and so did the house."

"They are important," said Francis. "But not so important as this living thing, this companion that comes when you respond."

"Were you lonely when you were a boy?" asked Jenny.

"Yes. I had no mother and no brothers or sisters. Then I began to look at things and sometimes to paint them, and then this companion came."

"Does he always come when you paint?"

"As soon as I forget myself."

"Did he come this morning?"

"Yes."

"First there were three of us and then there was one of us."

"Yes," said Francis, and wondered how much she had understood of what he did not understand himself. He noticed that she had called the third one he.

"Have you finished my portrait?" asked Jenny.

"Not quite," said Francis. "But I'll finish it tomorrow."

"Mother will be well tomorrow," said Jenny. "She'd better come and watch. It will stop her thinking about the war."

She spoke with maternal tenderness, for since last night her attitude to Margaret had undergone a revolutionary change. Anyone who spoke a sharp word to Margaret now in Jenny's presence would do so at their peril, and if she thought it good that Margaret should be with them tomorrow, with them Margaret would be. Francis felt a chill of that loneliness which he had just told Jenny need not be too bad. The war. He had once more forgotten the damnable war. The portrait finished, he must pack up and go. A cloud came over the sun and everything except Jenny withdrew to a great distance from him. When Jenny too had gone he would possess nothing but his memory of her, and his memory of the weary man sitting at the great desk, and smiling as he turned to give the seal to his son. They became one in his thought; all he had.

The sun came out and he got up laughing, mocking at himself, once more in possession of his great possessions. A little girl of eight years old, a small child; what a fool he was! Yet as they strolled together back to the house he said, "Don't forget me, Jenny."

"I never forget anybody," said Jenny.

CHAPTER IX

THE BLACK WITCH

That afternoon Froniga packed her basket full of little gifts, both for her cousins the Herons and for Mother Skipton. She put in it a packet of borage and hyssop to make a medicinal tea of which her aunt Madona was very fond; for though Madona would never see her she would occasionally accept a gift, and sometimes send one in exchange, just to show Froniga that if she would repent of her wickedness in wearing a green gown and return to her mother's people, she should be forgiven. There was also a pot of ointment made from hog's grease and broom flowers for Piramus's gout, and again for Madona a bottle of aqua-aurea made from her own lilies-of-the-valley, for heart weakness and headache. For the gypsy girls she had made nosegays of thyme, mint and lavender to bring them sweethearts. Madona's nosegay was of rosemary and costmary; rosemary, strong and holy to ward off evil, and costmary because it grew in ancient Egypt, and by way of Egypt, Madona believed, her people had come from India. Then she had apples and comfits for the children, and for Mother Skipton melrosette made from her own roses, the tea-leaves Biddy had given her and some little cakes of her own baking. Upon the top of the basket she had lain vine leaves from the vine that grew on the cottage wall.

Then she set out. It was a grey, still day with a cool tang in the air, a day such as she loved. The swallows were gathering to go away to the moon. A row of them was sitting on her own roof-tree and she looked up at them and wished them godspeed. Modern scientific knowledge had not penetrated as far as the village, and Froniga still believed they went to the moon, and loved to think of them there, nesting in its dim green valleys, singing by its still waters a song they did not sing on earth. In winter it was a joy to look up at the moon and think of the flight of the swallows as a Jacob's-ladder between one world and another. As she walked down Pack and Prime lane the scent of the flowers in her garden drifted after her and was lost only gradually in the fresh earthy smell of the lane and the scent of coming rain. Between gaps in the hedges, where the holly trees were twined with traveller's-joy, she could see the serene pale gold of the shorn harvest-fields lying like water between one wood and another. A lark sang out of sight in the grey sky, a yellow-hammer chattered of his bread and cheese at the top of a tall holly, and on all sides were the soft murmurings and rustlings that with the scents and the cool air of the grey days spread a net of magic for the unwary, so that they forget why they came and where they go and are likely to drift like thistle-down where the unseen tides of joy choose to take them.

"Not yet," said Froniga, and turned her attention to the ruts in the lane. The increase of wheeled traffic was not good for the roads and lanes of England and she regretted it. People were growing too soft now, riding in coaches instead of braving the weather on horseback as their fathers and mothers had done before them. She remembered her mother on horseback, lissom and light, and she was sad because Madona would not see her and of all her mother's people only the children loved her.

She came to a wide gap in the hedge and went through it into the field, and there below her in the hollow was the encampment. Her heart ached as she stood looking down on the round tents, the grey smoke of the camp-fire weaving lazily among the trees, the moving figures, and heard the strange lilt of their voices, the twang of a harp, a snatch of song and the laughter of their children. In dreams she saw those colours, those faded crimsons, greens and blues, and heard the songs they sang and crept nearer and nearer to their fire. In her youth there had been nights when she had almost run off to them, so wild had been her longing for the stars over her head at night by the fire. But love had withheld her, love of the house roof and the earth of the garden, that love of home and work that came from the other strain in her blood, but it did not prevent the aching of her heart, and also the feeling of shame. They were a persecuted people down there, safe only in this countryside where Robert protected them. They knew hunger, fear and danger as she would never know them, and she was one of those who have a hidden contempt for ease and safety.

Behind a blackberry bush near her she saw a shimmer of blue, and heard a tiny musical sound that was like no bird she knew. Her feet soundless on the grass, she went forward and looked round the bush. Her cousin Cinderella was sitting cross-legged on the ground, singing to the doll she was rocking in her arms. Her song was muted and almost wordless, but Froniga recognised it as something she had known when she lay in her own mother's arm. Cinderella was amazingly dirty, but the rose of her cheeks was visible through the dirt, and her parted lips stained with blackberries reminded Froniga of the fallen damask rose-petals that lay on the grass in her garden. She was looking down at her doll, rocking it with ineffable love, entirely absorbed in this new joyous passion of maternity. Froniga was neither surprised nor shocked to see that the doll was the bambino from the church; she knew the nefarious habits of her relations and she was not enough of a church woman to have a sense of sacrilege. Indeed she thought the bambino most suitably placed where he was. It had always hurt her that Cinderella had no toys.

"Cinderella," she whispered softly.

Cinderella looked up and a slow smile spread from her sloe-black eyes to her lips, and from thence to her dimpled cheeks and then all over her body. Her very toes curled with her smile and she hugged the bambino more closely to her. Her cheek resting on his head she whispered, *"Rawni!"* and her maternal love seemed to flow over Froniga too. Then her eyes went to the basket. Froniga sat down on the grass beside her and waited with a beating heart for the miracle to happen.

Sometimes at home, looking out from a window of her cottage, she would see a flock of little birds fly out of a bush, as though they were leaves blown by a sudden gale, and drift down upon the thistle seeds lying in the grass in the field. They had been invisible in the bush, and upon the grass they were almost invisible too, until they all flew up again and returned to their bush. In some such magical way, when Froniga came, the gypsy children were suddenly all around her, as though the wind had blown them. She would hear their voices calling like birds in a wood, and see the tall grasses bend and a shimmer of colour along the hedge. Then she would hold out her arms and presently the littlest one would be on her lap, and her arms would encircle two more, and the rest would be strewn over the grass about her, their bright eyes fixed on her face and their fingers pointing to the basket. Then she would open the basket and give them the apples and comfits she had brought them, and they would crowd round her munching, and chattering softly in their own language, just as the birds did, and her heart would be so shaken by maternal passion that if she could she would have fled with them all back to the cottage and hidden them there, behind the ramparts of the sweetbrier hedges. They would have been with her for ever and there would have been no waking from the dream.

Would she dream today? Would she once more be the mother of many children? With Cinderella nestled against her she shut her eyes and heard the high calling of the birds in the wood. She half-opened her eyes and saw the shimmer of colour and the popping up and down of elves in the grass. She held out her arms and opened her eyes wide, and there they were again. The littlest was in her lap, its thumb in its mouth, its bright beady eyes peering up at her through a thatch of matted hair, and the rest had pressed in as near as they could get. "*Rawni! Rawni!*" they cried. "Open that basket quick!"

She opened her basket and gave them apples, heart-shaped comfits of sugar and rose-water, candied rose-petals and violets and red candied cherries. They opened their mouths like young birds and she rejoiced in them as she fed them. Will and Jenny did not rouse in her quite this delicious joy. Though no child was intimately known to her, and all of them together not as dearly loved as Jenny's little finger, yet they made a mother of her, as Jenny and Will could not do. There was about them, somehow, an immortal quality that matched her own immortal longings. In the presence of these children she believed that somehow, somewhere, she would yet be a mother.

"*Rawni*, has the piece of fat nearly melted? For see, my warts have nearly gone!"

She inspected Meriful's hands and found them nearly, but not quite, wartless. "Another day of sunshine and they will be gone," she said with decision, and popped a cherry into Dinki's mouth. He was pressing against her knee, and with him was a very small boy called Goliath, brother to Acorn who was sitting in her lap. She asked their names of one and another just to hear the music of them; Swallow and Shani, Everilda, Leondra and Stari. They were all very grubby, but living their out-of-door life in the sweet-smelling summer they smelled only of summer; of hay and clover, wood-smoke and the straw of their beds. Then another smell came to her, the smell of unclean old age, and she knew her dream had ended. She kissed Cinderella, lifted Acorn from her lap, and rose slowly to her feet, bending her head to shake out the folds of her skirt. When she lifted her head the children were gone and confronting her was her uncle by marriage, Piramus Heron, with a few paces behind him Alamina, three or four young gypsy girls and Logan, Piramus's nephew, a heavy black-browed bully of a man whom she disliked intensely. Down by the camp she could see other figures, wary but expectant.

She met her uncle's hostile eyes and held them with hers, half smiling at him. Although she judged him to be almost entirely evil, she had a lurking admiration for him. He was old, his black beard streaked with grey and his powerful head a little sunk between his broad shoulders, yet he held himself upright and his dark cavernous eyes had a fierce light in them. He had a heavy cruel jaw under his beard but he had laughed in his day, if only devilishly, and the laughter lines were scored as deeply on his face as those of age. He wore his filthy clothes with a rakish air, gripped his cudgel-headed stick as though he meant to use it and carried with him an atmosphere of undinted pride that called to the very same thing in Froniga. She gave him a greeting and curtsied to him, but without taking her eyes from his, acknowledge his right to her curtsey but refusing his domination. She could see the anger in his eyes and knew how he longed to assert his patriarchal right to wring her neck; with exhilaration she knew herself only just strong enough to prevent his doing it. She took the pot of ointment from her basket and gave it to him. He took it with a growl of thanks and for a moment something else gleamed in his eyes, a recognition of their mutual power and a gleam of respect, Then he turned away and went off down the slope of the field, and immediately Alamina and the girls drew nearer, eager as the children, but without the children's simplicity in greed. Froniga disliked the contrast between the soft silk of their wheedling voices and the acquisitive sparkle of their black eyes more than she had disliked her uncle's anger; though less for its hypocrisy than for the fact that by it she was outlawed. Their guile, kept for the gorgio only, was as much a barrier between her and the camp-fire down below as the circle of their bodies. Sometimes she wondered what would happen if she broke through the two barriers and ran down there and found Madona.

She gave them comfits and nosegays and sent dutiful messages to Madona, and as she walked slowly away from them she thought sadly that she could feel their strange hatred like a knife between her shoulder-blades. She went through the gap in the hedge and walked on down Pack and Prime lane towards Mother Skipton's cottage. She walked quickly and did not look back until the lane turned left, when she stopped a moment to get a glimpse of her cottage. In this flat countryside it was often possible to see it from a distance, and there is a thrill in being abroad in the world and seeing a loved home far off waiting for you. She could see the house-leek growing on the thatch and the chimneys like the two cocked ears of a rabbit, and she saw Logan loitering along in the lane behind her. She turned quickly and walked on.

Though Froniga and Mother Skipton had lived for many years with only a couple of miles between them they had never met each other. One walked abroad by day and the other by night, so that they had never met even by chance. The villagers seldom mentioned Mother Skipton in Froniga's presence, so that she did not even know what she looked like. This complete separation between them was natural, for they were like the reverse sides of a coin, divided by their very closeness to each other. It was, she thought, a horrible closeness, just that hair's breadth of difference between them of a woman who has gone too far and a woman who still knows where to stop. As she walked a great distaste and reluctance grew upon her. It seemed to be pressing her back, asking her questions. Once she had stepped over the dividing line between white and black would she be able to get back? Was she strong as she thought she was? Had she misunderstood the message that Meriful had brought her? Was it possible that deep within her she had buried an almost unacknowledged curiosity to explore the darkness of the other, and might that have prompted her to misunderstand? "But there's the child," she answered. "Whatever the danger to myself, I must go on for the sake of the child. If I can hold my own against the evil of Piramus Heron, I can confront anything." She lifted her head arrogantly and went on.

The lane turned and twisted, and beyond a field full of thistles she could see a sombre wood. At the edge of the wood was a cottage with sloping walls and rotting thatch. Its one chimney leaned at a crazy angle and the dormer window of the little room in the roof seemed on the point of falling out. As she walked across the field she could see a garden choked with weeds and could picture the woman who lived in such disorder, the usual miserable old black witch, dirty, mumbling and toothless, with perhaps a beard on her chin and a mangy black cat at her heels. Reluctance returned to her, and then was lost in curiosity, for she had reached the broken gate into the small garden. What herbs did Mother Skipton grow?

She lifted the latch and went in and walked slowly up the narrow path, lifting her skirts to avoid the slime of many slugs. There were plenty of plants and herbs growing among the dank weeds that choked the beds, but, as she had expected, there were no yellow flowers, for black witches dislike the colour of sunshine, and there was no rosemary, lavender or mint geranium, and no rue. But the occult things were there in plenty, henbane and hemlock, mandrake and nightshade, fox-gloves and wolf's-bane. Just brushing by them she felt a heavy drowsiness upon her, and nearly stepped upon a large toad who lay on the path beside the well. The stones of the well were wet and slimy, and such an unhealthy smell came from it that as she passed she took out the little posy of rosemary that she always carried within the bodice of her gown and inhaled the clean strong scent. Immediately her drowsiness left her and she came alert and watchful to Mother Skipton's door.

It surprised her, for it was painted green and the doorstep had been scrubbed. On one side of the door hung a bird cage with an insulting and raucous jackdaw inside, and on the other side there grew a root of that rare mysterious new plant, the love apple, that would in later years change its name to tomato, its fruit already flushing scarlet. Froniga gazed at it with admiration but with awe, for it was said to be a most potent plant, possessed of strong tonic qualities, a relative of the mandrake. It was not certainly known whether its power was for good or evil and so she had not yet dared to plant it in her garden. Still looking at the love apple, she lifted her hand to knock at the door, but before she could do so it was quietly opened.

"Good afternoon, Mistress Haslewood," said Mother Skipton pleasantly. "Won't you come in?"

Although restored by the rosemary, Froniga was on the verge of being taken aback, and did not immediately answer. Across the scrubbed doorstep the two women looked at each other.

Mother Skipton was neither old, toothless nor unclean. She was of medium height, thin and angular, with a yellowish skin stretched rather tightly over the fine bones of her face. Her straight hair was coiled neatly within a linen cap, and though her brown homespun gown was patched and worn it was clean and tidy. Froniga had steeled herself to confront evil, as she did with Piramus, yet she felt in this woman only a vast weariness. Nevertheless her face was not entirely pleasant. Though Mother Skipton was smiling her strained colourless lips were mirthless and between them the white teeth showed unpleasantly pointed. The almond-shaped long-tailed eyes, just the same shape as Froniga's only not quite so large, compelled one to look into them deeper and deeper, yet they seemed dark pits of nothingness. Froniga felt that she was being sucked down into their nothingness and it took all her willpower to look away. She must say something.

"You recognise me," she said, "but we have never met."

"When evening comes you do not always draw your curtains," said Mother Skipton. Her voice was light and dry, and reminded Froniga of the rustling of parched leaves that are dying for lack of rain. A faint suggestion of something a little like panic quivered down her nerves, and she turned to the love apples.

"They are beautiful to look at," she said.

"And most refreshing to the taste," said Mother Skipton, and picked one and handed it to her.

Froniga knew it was a test of her courage. Would she eat the fruit of her enemy? She ate it, finding the love apple cool and invigorating. She thought it more like a pomegranate than an apple, and the plant itself had a pungent smell not unlike the scent of geranium. She thought it not evil though most potent. "What colour are the flowers?" she asked.

"Yellow," said Mother Skipton shortly. "Small and undistinguished. I dislike the flowers. Will you come in?"

She stepped back from the door and Froniga followed her into the dark little room. The floor was of trodden earth and the smoke from the meagre fire could scarcely find its way up the crooked chimney. It seemed that Mother Skipton slept as well as lived in this room, for there was a cupboard bed in the wall. The place had the dank sour smell of poverty, and as Froniga sat on the black cracked settle beside her hostess, she realised how much her successful leechcraft must have injured this woman, who had been making her potions before she herself had set up in business. Yet she was not conscious of hatred, only again of the great weariness. Mother Skipton probably lacked the strength to hate, even as she lacked the strength to weed her garden. Yet there was nothing reassuring in her weariness. She was like a spent snake. What she gasped for was not compassion but the power to hate again.

"What do you want of me?" she asked.

"Your help," said Froniga.

"That's a strange request for a rich woman to make of a poor one," said Mother Skipton.

Froniga had never considered herself rich, quite the contrary, but looking round the bare little room she recognised the truth of the accusation, for accusation it always is to those who believe they have a soul to lose. With another tremor of nerves Froniga realised that of the two of them, Mother Skipton was in some ways nearer blessedness. "Have you not noticed," she said, "that the appeal for help is made far more from the rich to the poor than from the poor to the rich? The well-to-do are often singularly lacking in practical efficiency."

"Certainly without serving men or maids most of them would die," agreed Mother Skipton. "But not you, I think."

"No, I can cook and clean and shoe a horse with anyone," agreed Froniga, "but I cannot cure a little boy of convulsions, and I have tried every remedy I know except one."

"You need a skull?" asked Mother Skipton, and rising from the settle she moved to a cupboard in the wall beside the fireplace.

"If you have one to spare," said Froniga, and took her purse from her pocket.

"I have several," said Mother Skipton, "and I do not wish to be paid for the one I will give you. We are two sisters in the study of the occult arts and one does not take payment from one's sister."

She spoke with an icy pride which Froniga understood and respected, even though the word sister stuck in her own proud gorge. She stood up, slipped the purse back in her pocket, and said, "Thank you."

Mother Skipton unlocked the cupboard with a key that hung at her waist, and opened the door. It was a deep cupboard, and though it was hard to see in the dim light, Froniga thought she saw a root of the terrible mandrake looking like the corpse of a dead baby, some small wax images and many strangely shaped phials. Such a sickly stench came from the cupboard that Froniga for a moment swayed where she stood, then the cupboard door was quickly shut again and Mother Skipton stood before her holding a skull in her hands, no gallows skull but that of a child of six years old.

"To cure a child of convulsions the skull of another child is more efficacious than that of an adult," said Mother Skipton.

Froniga took the little skull into her hands and knew even as she took it that it was to happen again; twice in one week. For a moment she fought against it, but she could never stop it. It came rarely, but she could never prevent it except by putting away from her the thing that she held, and this thing seemed to be holding her. She saw the churchyard at night, lit by a full moon, and a woman's figure bending over the newly made grave. She looked a frail woman, but some demoniacal energy seemed to enable her to shovel away the earth and break open the lid of the coffin. Through the voiceless screaming in her mind Froniga became aware of a piece of common knowledge that had long ago been assimilated by that same mind. At the Witches' Sabbatical they are anointed with an ointment made from the juice of smallage, wolf's-bane and cinquefoil, the meal of wheat and that fat of children dug out of their graves. It was Hecate's prescription. . . . Let go, or you are undone. . . . But she could not let go for the thing held her as though her fingers were a part of it. . . . I can't let go. . . . The scene changed and she saw a dark wood lit by a flickering fire. How tall and gaunt she was, that woman who stood by the fire, her face veiled, and to her they were coming up the aisles of the wood. They were laughing, but there was no more joy in their laughter than there was in Mother Skipton's smile. It sounded like cracking ice. And she was laughing too, with burnt eyes and parched throat, as she ran with them up the aisles of the wood, and in her laughter also there was no mirth. There seemed a pressure of ice about her heart and she had the sensation of loss and helpless misery. She was familiar with it, as are most men and women at certain times of their life, but never like this, never before without hope . . . Let go. . . . But she could not let go. She stood by the fire and she faced the woman with the veiled face. All about her was the sour smell of dirty clothes and sweaty hair. The hopeless laughter rose higher but she could scarcely hear it now because of the screaming in her head. The restless bodies pressed upon her but she was not conscious of them, she was conscious only of the veiled face. For the veil was slipping. . . . If you look upon that face you are lost. Call upon God. . . . I have not done so in the days of my security, and why should I insult Him by doing so in my danger? I will let go in my own strength or not at all. . . . But I can't . . . I know now what it is to have gone too far. And the veil is slipping from that awful face. I am undone by my pride, I am undone. And the veil is slipping. . . . Shut your eyes. . . . But she could not shut her eyes. The burning balls were standing out of her head so that the lids could not cover them. . . . Jenny. Yoben. Parson Hawthyn. . . . The thought of them came to her like a fresh breeze. The skull slipped from her hands and fell with a crash to the ground.

She was once more standing in the dark and dreary room looking into the emptiness of the other woman's eyes, and again came that feeling of being sucked down. This woman was stronger than she was. She was stronger than Piramus Heron. Her emptiness was far more evil than his cruelty and anger. Compared with her he was no more than a naughty child. Terror, the first real terror she had ever known, took hold of Froniga. The sweat was trickling down her back and her knees were shaking. And her body had escaped her control. She could neither bring her eyelids down over her aching eyes, so that she might no longer stare into the eyes of this other woman, nor force her legs to carry her from the room. They were drawing nearer and nearer to each other, the small distance that divided the two sides of the coin was disappearing and they were becoming one. Froniga put out a hand blindly, to ward off the contact, and then found that the hand had been taken. Mother Skipton had mistaken her gesture and was holding her hand. Without any effort of her will she was able to look at last away from Mother Skipton's eyes, and look down. Resisting a panic-striken urge to pull her hand away, she looked steadily at their clasped hands. Sisters. Mother Skipton was holding to her now in a way to which she was accustomed. Sick people often held her hand like this, holding to her strength in their abysmal weakness. Suddenly she forgot everything about Mother Skipton except that, like all the half-starved, she was very anaemic. She looked round and saw her basket standing on the floor beside her.

"I've brought a few things for you," she said, and letting go of Mother Skipton's hand she picked up the basket and put it on the battered old table, wondering how best she could avoid hurting the other's pride that was so like her own. "I've time and strength to make these things," she said, as she set the little cakes upon a platter of vine leaves. "They are dependent each upon the other, time and strength. When you've no strength you've no time. When you are weak it takes so long even to light the kitchen fire."

"It can take hours," said Mother Skipton slowly.

"Take a spoonful of melrosette night and morning," said Froniga firmly, placing the golden pot beside the cakes. "Red rose leaves boiled in purified honey. Roses are for comfort and honey for cleansing, and both together for strength. And here are tea-leaves. They have been used only once and there is still much virtue in them."

"I've never tasted real tea," said Mother Skipton.

"You know how to infuse it?"

"Yes. I know."

"I'll fill your kettle for you before I go," said Froniga gently. "Do you draw your water from the well?"

"Yes."

"But it's unclean. There is a sweet fresh spring in Flowercote Wood."

"I cannot walk so far," said Mother Skipton. "And I prefer my own water."

The momentary acquiescence of her physical weakness had gone out of her and she was no longer to be dominated. Froniga went into the garden and let down the bucket and drew up some water from the well. Then she filled Mother Skipton's kettle and coaxed her sulky fire into a semblance of life. There seemed no more she could do. Just outside the door she paused, looking back. The light of the beautiful luminous grey day, flowing in past her, lit up the cakes lying on their platter of vine leaves, green leaves edged with crimson, and the golden pot of melrosette. They seemed to gather all the light to themselves, so that it was hard to see the still figure standing in the shadows beyond them. The skull still lay on the floor and neither woman spoke of it, for it seemed a symbol of the failure of both to achieve any dominance over the other. Froniga turned away silently and picked her way down the overgrown garden path. She went through the gate and latched it behind her.

CHAPTER X

PARSON HAWTHYN

I

"My soul is escaped even as a bird out of the snare of the fowler; the snare is broken and I am delivered." Once out of sight of the cottage she picked up her skirts and ran up the lane the parting of the ways, and then along the path through the fields that led to Flowercote Wood. She did not stop running until the trees of that happy place had closed in safety around her. Then she sat down upon a fallen tree-trunk and began to laugh and cry together. She laughed because she, Froniga Haslewood, had run away for the first time in her life. She cried for her sister. And she laughed and cried together from sheer relief. "The snare is broken and I am delivered."

"But not by my own strength," she acknowledged, "for she was stronger than I. And not by the grace of God, for I did not call upon Him." Then by whom? By remembrance of the three clearest spirits whom she knew, Jenny, Yoben and Parson Hawthyn. And what is a clear spirit but a channel of the grace of God? She sat still digesting this fact, and there began to come to her a first dim realisation of God's humility. Rejected by the proud in His own right by what humble means He chose to succour them; through the spirit of a child, a poor gypsy or an old man, by a song perhaps, or even it might be by the fall of a leaf or the scent of a flower. For His infinite and humble patience nothing was too small to advance His purpose of salvation, and eternity was not too long for its accomplishment.

Froniga got up and put the thought of humility firmly from her; it had in any case done no more than touch her in passing, and by the time she had told herself she had no time to waste she had forgotten how potent a touch can be. She walked on through the wood, thinking of young Joe. She was going to cure him, of course. She never—practically never—failed in any purpose to which she had set her hand. She had been mistaken in the means, that was all. "The magic is good. That which you purpose in your heart is good, *Rawni*." She had mistaken the guidance of the good spirit. It was the magic of the elder tree by the well that was good, and the good purpose of her heart was the healing of the child. A potion made from those elder-berries, infused in the water from the well, was all that was needed for Joe. She would go to the well at once.

As she went on through the wood she had a growing sense of brightness. Darkness had seemed about her as she ran through the fields, but here under the trees the silver light seemed to gather and sparkle. All things were brilliant in its clarity: the moss and the jewel-like toadstools, the flowers that grew along the edge of the wood and the bumblebee banded with gold who bumped against her shoulder. Yet the grey day remained the same, shadowed and cool with its promise of rain, and she knew that her sense of growing light was something that another would not have shared with her. She believed herself passing from the influence of one spirit to that of another, and the other was somewhere ahead of her, laughing among the trees. She could not hear the laughter any more than she could see the tides of joy to which she had now abandoned herself, letting them carry her where they would, but the sparkle of the light seemed the perfect expression of them both.

She took no path through the wood, for she was being carried. She found herself on the edge of the wood, where she picked some tall spires of candlewick glowing with light, the mauve stamens of the yellow flowers each tipped with coral, excellent for chest ailments, but when she had finished delighting in them she was deep in the heart of the wood, gazing entranced at a branch of honeysuckle that carried the marvel of scarlet berries and creamy flowers both growing on the same twig. Then she was somewhere else and was soon quite lost, and she heard the birds chuckling, but here in this wood the tides of joy had a focus and she was not surprised when she found herself at the spring.

She sat by it for a while, soaking herself in the quiet of the place. The tides of joy were here a still pool and the unheard laughter was a star in the midst of it. The sparkle that had been in the wood was here a little dimmed, as though it had fallen as dew. There was no sound except the bubble of water. Even the chuckling birds were now silent.

As the children had done, Froniga cupped her hands and drank some of the water of the spring, and reaching up she picked a cluster of elder-berries and ate them, gratefully acknowledging the hospitality of the spirit of the place, and then she filled her basket for the child. "And now I have nothing in which to carry the water," she thought. But this did not disturb her, for she had only to sit and wait and one of the village women would come along to fill her pitchers at the spring, and lend her one of them. Even those who had wells in their gardens never failed to come to the spring several times a week, for they would not dream of mixing their dough with any water but this. There was no bread anywhere so light and crisp as the village bread.

She sat and waited and saw that up above the trees the grey sky had a tinge of gold. The church clock struck the hour of vespers and soon after she heard the uncertain feet of someone old coming down the path. In a moment or two she looked up into the rosy face of Parson Hawthyn. He wore his cassock, hitched up out of the way. In one hand he carried an earthen pitcher and in the other a leather bottle.

"I came here to get water for a potion and I have nothing to carry it in," she said. "May I borrow your bottle?"

"Allow me to fill it for you, Mistress Froniga," he said courteously, and bent over the spring. He had known her for years and called her by her Christian name, yet she did not know if he liked her. She suspected that he disapproved of her. As a rule she was indifferent to the opinions of others, but today, after what he had so lately done for her, she felt less indifferent than usual. She got up, and when he had filled the bottle and the pitcher it was his turn to stand and look up into her face, so short was he. He turned his head sideways in a sparrow-like manner and said gravely, "You have been much in my thoughts today."

"Why was that?" she asked.

"I do not know," he said. "You, I expect, do know. Your knowledge is great."

"And such as you do not approve," she said, to test him.

"Froniga, disapproval is one of those things which I've thrown overboard. One does, you know, lighten the ship in old age. My dear, I shall carry this bottle of water home for you."

"Then let me lighten the ship by carrying the pitcher," said Froniga. "We will go back by way of the parsonage and leave it there."

He accepted gratefully, for he suffered from shortness of breath and carrying water did not agree with him. The false pride that will not be helped was another thing he had shed with old age. They walked slowly along the path together and Froniga said, "But there must be many things of which as a parson you should disapprove. Sin, for instance."

"I don't disapprove of my sin," he said. "I detest it. Disapproval is far too emasculate an emotion with which to confront sin."

"Witchcraft, then," said Froniga.

"That's sin," said Parson Hawthyn uncompromisingly.

"White witchcraft?" asked Froniga.

"Froniga, I lack knowledge of the art, and I speak under correction, but I should say—when practised by a silly woman, rubbish, when practised by a wise one, dangerous unless she possesses the virtue of humility in marked degree."

"In that case she might not be able to instil faith and confidence in the sick," said Froniga shortly.

"I have always felt that that might be her difficulty," said Parson Hawthyn, and looked up at her with such merriment at having scored a point that she laughed and changed the subject.

"This path is no place for argument," she said. "I am always happy on this path. Are you?"

"I am happy anywhere," said the old man simply.

"You were not happy at Will's breeching," Froniga chided him.

"The sun is still there, Froniga, even if clouds drift over it. Once you have experienced the reality of sunshine you may weep, but you will never feel ice about your heart again."

Ice about your heart, squeezing it, squeezing love out. The long arctic night without sunshine, so that you must light a bonfire in the dark wood. The crackle of the flames had been like the crackle of breaking ice. The sweat started out on her forehead and she found that they had passed out of the happy wood into the churchyard and that she was looking at the very spot where she had seen the frail figure stooping over the grave.

"Was a child ever buried there?" she asked. "Look, there, under that crab-apple tree."

"Yes. Ten years ago," said Parson Hawthyn.

"And was the grave violated?"

"I feared so."

"You made no enquiries?"

"The soul of the child was safe and enquiries would have distressed the parents. If it was that poor woman, I prayed for her. You have been to see her today? There now, my dear, be careful of the water. Let me carry it while you open the gate."

She opened the churchyard gate and shut it, and then stood waiting for him while he carried the pitcher to the parsonage. She rubbed her hot cheeks ruefully, for she had betrayed herself in spilling the water. When he came back he smiled to see her rosy face. "My dear," he said, "your transparency delights my old heart. You are not, yet, thank God, a subtle woman."

He limped along beside her talking of the blackberries at the bottom of his garden, for he was not an inquisitive man. His one leading question had been asked with a purpose. The misery of Mother Skipton was one of the clouds. If Froniga visited and pitied her he might know one day where to look for an ally. It was Froniga herself who brought the conversation back to its starting point.

"What do you believe, sir, about black witchcraft?"

"I hold the accepted view," he said gravely. "I believe that evil spirits who have left this world, but desire to continue their evil practices within it, take possession of men and women who are willing to yield themselves for that purpose."

"It is also believed by many that only by burning the body of the black witch or warlock can you destroy the evil, and therefore the burning is justified. Do you believe that too?"

"Certainly not," said Parson Hawthyn. "Burning was never the Gospel method for the casting out of devils."

"But is burning so much worse than beheading or hanging?" asked Froniga. "Surely you don't disapprove of those?"

"My dear, I have already told you that I disapprove of nothing. I loathe, detest, hate and abominate the block, the gibbet, the rack, the pillory and the faggots with equal passion," said the old man vehemently. "Not only are they devilishly cruel but they are not even commonsense. They do not lessen the evil in the world, they increase it, by making those who handle these cruelties as wicked as those who suffer them. No, I'm wrong, more wicked, for there is always some expiation made in the endurance of suffering and none at all in the infliction of it."

Froniga was startled into complete silence. Never before had she heard such extraordinary statements. They had left the village and were taking the short cut through the fields to her cottage, walking more and more slowly as they became more argumentative. Looking at him she saw that Parson Hawthyn's usually gentle face had become stony with rage. Even his voice had become hard and rasping. She wondered how he proposed that law and order should be maintained in the land without those props of society that he had mentioned.

"I grant you we must have prisons," he growled. "Humanely administered. Even then I tremble for the souls of the gaolers. We are all of us so near the beast. Look at yourself, a lovely and cultured lady, yet able to sleep at night, calm as a white unicorn, with a loaded gibbet not four miles from you. Look at myself, walking with the same lovely lady and behaving like a mangy old bear with a sore head."

He looked himself again. His growling turned to chuckling and she laughed too, but she was not quite mollified, for she had always congratulated herself upon being an unusually humane woman.

"We all of us need to be toppled off the throne of self, my dear," he said. "Perched up there the tears of others are never upon our own cheek."

The anger went out of them both and they walked silently through the grey-gold twilight. The trees round Froniga's cottage had taken purple veils to themselves and from out of the shadows came the white form of Pen to welcome her mistress. The birds had gone to sleep and the only winged creatures stirring were the moths, furry brown, or white with the greenish tinge of lilies upon their whiteness, or the faint gold of corn. The first drops of the rain fell as gently as the touch of their wings.

"May I know for whom you will mix the potion?" asked Parson Hawthyn diffidently. "I would not intrude upon your secrets, Froniga, but I would be glad to add my poor prayers to yours."

"It is for Joe Diggar's convulsions," said Froniga, and the truth compelled her to add a little tartly, "The words I say over my potions are not what you would call prayers."

"Are they not?" said the old man. "Whatever you say, you offer it, do you not, together with yourself and your labour, for the well-being of the child?"

"Yes. I do that," said Froniga.

"I'll do the same tonight, in the church. You can think of me there, and I will think of you. Now don't laugh and say there is no labour attached to my part of the bargain. The labour of keeping my body out of my bed, after nine of the clock, is greater at my age than you would believe at yours. But remember, Froniga, the well-being of the child may not necessarily include prolongation of his earthly life. *Dominus vobiscum*, my daughter."

He bent to stroke Pen, handed her the leather bottle and was gone, limping away through the shadows. Preceded by Pen, with plumed tail raised, Froniga walked slowly through her orchard and garden and let herself into her cottage with a sigh of relief, sniffing its homely scent of herbs and wood-smoke, apples, and the ship's timbers that had been built into its walls. She did not know, as they knew at the manor, what ship had built her home, but she had her ideas about it. Not a sea-going galleon like the *Unicorn*, but a small stout rivercraft that had plied up and down the Thames from the Port of London with treasure from the East—tea, cinnamon, pepper, cloves and green ginger—until it was tired out with all its labours and was glad to be becalmed upon the flat heathland, under the great skies. When her room was warm, as now, she could fancy she smelt the cinnamon and ginger, and they gave a sharp, racy tang to the cool scents of the English herbs that hung from the beams. It seemed a long time since she had been in her room and she had such a sense of port after storm that she locked her door to increase her feeling of safety. She made up her fire and lit her candles, and then, suddenly aware of how the warm light would be shining out into the twilight, she drew her curtains.

She put the elder-berries to simmer in the spring-water over the fire, ate her supper and washed up the dishes. Then she strained the liquid from the berries and bottled it in a clear crystal bottle, murmuring her spells as she did so, reaching out to the good spirits, and especially to that one good spirit, whose power was hers as she murmured to them. They liked to do good on earth, but they could not, she believed, without the loan of her spirit and her body. What danger could there be for her? She thought of Parson Hawthyn with a spirit of irritation that passed quickly into a sense of vivid companionship. Her own work done she sat down, shut her eyes and tried to see him where he was in the church. Where did he kneel? At the altar? By the tomb of her little grandmother? Our Lady's niche? But she could see nothing, only darkness, and she abandoned the attempt. Darkness, she imagined, was what he would prefer her to see, and as she let it possess her she found surprising strength in it. There was darkness and darkness, one of life and one of death, and this of life was good.

Presently she got up and tidied the hearth for the night, and quite unconsciously she reverted to the good old custom in which she had been brought up, but had abandoned as her self-confidence increased, and made the sign of the cross in the ashes. It was now impossible for the cottage to catch on fire. Then she laid the branch of a broom tree with which she swept her floors across the threshold of her back door, to ward off the evil eye. Evil was already warded from the front door by the clump of Christmas roses planted there for that purpose. They had grown beside the stable door at Bethlehem. A child, a little girl, who had gone with the shepherds into the stable, had cried because she had nothing to give the Baby; not even flowers, for it was winter. But Gabriel had led her out and touched the cold snow beside the door, and out of it had grown a clump of snow-white Christmas roses.

Froniga went upstairs to bed. Nothing on earth could harm her now, for the protection was threefold. Her head on her herb pillow, she slept soundly.

2

In the church Parson Hawthyn sat up stiffly and rubbed his rheumatic knees. He felt cold and stiff and his hour of prayer had brought him no personal satisfaction, plagued as he had been with indigestion, wandering thoughts, a depressing sense of personal failure and the growing conviction that Joe would die. The apparent failure of prayer never disturbed him, convinced as he was both of its hidden worth and of the adorable perfection of the will of God, but he was distressed because Froniga would be distressed. Slipping once more to his painful knees he tried to pray for her too, and for the child's parents, and this time, as he struggled to compose his thoughts, they ceased to wander, were gently taken hold of and spun together, as it seemed, into one thread that tautened and drew out into a spinning line of wonder. He crawled up it as a spider might do, taking those for whom he prayed with him, though aware that in his case the line was not of his own spinning, up and up while the wonder deepened into joy and the joy into worship. He hung for what seemed a timeless moment upon the point of worship and then the thread snapped, and he fell, so heavy was the weight of his sin.

He hoisted himself back upon the bench again and thanked God for the mercy that had been vouchsafed to him. He had not been kneeling in any of the places where Froniga had tried to picture him, but in the dusty corner where the sexton kept his branch of broom. He always said his private prayers here, for he felt that the spiders and the mice who shared his affection for this particular corner were more suitable companions for his unworthiness than Our Lady of Heaven, or even that happy little creature Anne Haslewood. As for mounting up the steps to the altar, he seldom dared do that unless robed in the vestments of a priest. These gave him both anonymity and confidence. Wearing them he was no longer that despicable sinner John Hawthyn, but the priest of this parish, one with all the priests of this parish both past and to come, robed in the mediatorial office of Christ Himself, so lost in it and dignified by it that his individual frailties ceased to exist. But in private prayer these both frightened and humbled him, and he felt more at home among the mice.

He listened companionably to their rustlings and squeakings, removed a spider from his neck with affectionate gentleness and watched with pleasure the flight of a white moth across the dusk. To another the church would have seemed dark, but to him it seemed almost luminous, so deeply did he love its darkness that, like the habitual barrenness of his prayer, seemed not a wall but a curtain. In his self-confident days he had tried sometimes to part the curtain, but not now. His belief in what was behind, that made him able to describe himself in all sincerity as a happy man, nourished itself upon the fact of the curtain. If it were ever to be drawn aside it would be from the other side, not this, and it would be no more his hand that drew it than it had been his hand that spun his thoughts together into that line of light.

He got up and made his way through the shadows to the door and opened it. The white moth came with him and fluttered out through the porch into the grey curtain of the rain. With his old cloak about him he stumbled through the churchyard to his cottage. It felt cold and damp in his little living-room. The fire had gone out and a draught came down the chimney. The door did not fit well and there was a pool of rain on the floor. For a moment he was visited by a sense of depression because autumn was here and winter not far behind and it might be a very long time before he felt really warm again. Then he thrust the thought aside with shame. He had a bed to sleep in, even if he was not always very warm in it, and many poor wretches had not even that.

> Now Lord, send them summer, some manner of joy,
> Heaven after hence-going, that here have such default!
> And have pity on the rich—

Suddenly he remembered how rich he now was. Upstairs he had a tinder-box, a candle and a new book. Entirely forgetting his need of pity, entirely forgetting the poor, he dropped his wet cloak on the floor and clambered up the crazy little staircase to his attic bedroom with the greed of a miser scurrying to his gold. He lit the candle, undressed quickly and slipped into his poor bed with its hard straw mattress and worn patched blankets that had lost their warmth. Eagerly he pulled the book from under his pillow. He looked first at the fly-leaf, where there was a puzzling inscription. In a beautiful spidery handwriting was written, Charles R., and under it the initials F. L. The explanation that occurred to him was so fantastic that he did not accept it, yet so precious to him that he did not entirely thrust it away. He turned to his place in the book. He was reading only one poem an evening, lest he should finish the book too soon. True, he would be able to read it over and over again until he knew it by heart, for the book was his own, but for him there was never anything quite to equal the first reading of a poem that set free the imprisoned music in his own mind. For Parson Hawthyn was more poet than scholar. He read less for information than for the relief of his own inarticulateness. The chimes were there but he needed another to set them ringing for him. And this man, being a priest also, knew his innermost thoughts.

Aaron

> Holiness on the head,
> Light and perfections on the breast,
> Harmonious bells below, raising the dead
> To lead them unto life and rest.
> Thus are true Aarons dressed.

Profaneness in my head,
Defects and darkness in my breast,
A noise of passions ringing me for dead
Unto a place where is no rest.
Poor priest thus am I dressed.

Only another head
I have, another heart and breast,
Another music, making live not dead,
Without Whom I could have no rest:
In Him I am well dressed.

Christ is my only head,
My alone only heart and breast,
My only music, striking me ev'n dead;
That to the old man I may rest,
And be in Him new dressed.

So holy in my head,
Perfect and light in my dear breast,
My doctrine tuned by Christ, (Who is not dead,
But lives in me while I do rest)
Come people; Aaron's dressed.

He put the book under his pillow and blew out the light. He was too tired and chilly to sleep, but that was of no consequence, so happy was he. There were only two more days to wait and then he would once more mount the steps of the altar in Aaron's robes.

CHAPTER XI

TOOTHACHE

"Jenny."

She was employing the last few minutes before bed-time in picking a bunch of wild flowers for her mother. They grew here in a patch of grass in the front garden, near the hedge, where their seeds had blown through from the common and rooted with that sturdy determination which plants show when the initiative has been with themselves. She was sitting on the grass and binding them together with a bit of blue ribbon when she heard her name spoken on the other side of the hedge. Parting the branches she made a window in them and looked through. Francis was on his knees on the other side of the hedge. She smiled, for she was not surprised. Her portrait was finished and she and her mother had said a polite farewell to Mr. Loggin, who was now leaving the neighbourhood. He had bowed and kissed their hands in a formal manner, but somehow she had not felt that was her last sight of him. It had not seemed a suitable farewell. This one was much better, looking through this leafy window into the illimitable golden world where Mr. Loggin belonged, from the quiet green bower where she belonged. He was not looking himself. One cheek was larger than the other.

"Have you toothache?" she asked.

"Yes, little witch, I have."

"Cousin Froniga will take it away."

"Jenny, can you read?" he asked abruptly.

"I can read a little," she said.

"What do you read?"

"We've got a book," she said with pride.

"Foxe's *Book of Martyrs*?"

"Yes."

Francis groaned. "Nothing else?"

"The Bible. And Cousin Froniga has the plays of Mr. William Shakespeare, and Sir Walter Raleigh's *History of the World*. She reads them to me, and I like them better than the *Martyrs*."

"So I should hope. Jenny, I am going to send you a book of fairy stories. There will be one in it, an old Saxon story, called *Beauty and the Beast*. When you read that one you are to remember me."

"But I won't forget you," said Jenny. "I don't forget people. I told you so."

He did not doubt that, but one day they might execrate him to her, and she had been brought up on the devilish Foxe. "You'll like the beast," he said. "He wasn't as bad as he seemed. Goodbye, Jenny."

"Goodbye," said Jenny.

She smiled at him through the leafy window, but without sorrow. He did not belong to her safe green world, he belonged outside it, and in her fledgling state she loved only those who belonged. But she was aware of bounty in him. He was to give her a book, and still smiling at him she tried to remember what else he had given her. An elf-bolt. And in the garden, on the day he had painted her, he had talked to her as no one else had ever talked to her, not even Cousin Froniga; as though she were a grown-up woman. Her eyes both widened and darkened and her smile faded, as though she looked from her window not at him but at the years that had yet to come. It was he who pulled the green branches across and got up. . . . It was too early yet, and he was to blame that he had forced that look of maturity upon her face.

He walked quickly, for he was anxious to be gone. He had nothing to do now but collect his pony from the inn and ride to Henley. In that Parliament stronghold he might collect a little information to offset his failure at the village. He was useless as a spy, and Suckling had been quite right when he had betted him a small fortune that he would be. Well, Suckling needed the gold and he'd pay it over gladly as the price of withholding the knowledge he had gleaned from the innocent Robert. If Yoben had gone that night to the edge of the wood he had had a fruitless vigil, for at the last moment Francis had decided not to join him there.

His tooth was throbbing again. Damn the thing! Great though his possessions were they did not include good teeth. In that respect many a rogue and vagabond was better off than he. Curse the thing! Could Froniga Haslewood really cure toothache? There was no harm in asking, and anyway she was a pretty woman and he would like to say goodbye to her.

He had already packed his saddle-bags and it took him only a few minutes to harness his pony and say goodbye to them at the inn. Then he led his pony down the lane to Froniga's cottage and fastened the bridle to the gatepost. He stood under the honeysuckle porch and knocked gently and she opened her door almost at once. She wore a green gown and had discarded her cap. Her shining dark hair was coiled at the back of her head, her eyes were bright and ardent and there was colour in her cheeks. She held her head in a challenging way and her smile was a little mocking. Her beauty and dignity, together with the shock of this transformation of a Puritan woman into something distinctly other, was enough to knock a man down, but except for the sudden leap of light into his eyes, and a smile as mocking as her own, the experienced Francis gave no sign of shock. He bowed to her, said, "Mistress Haslewood, I crave your assistance," and pointed dramatically to his bulging cheek. But she had seen it before he spoke, and in a moment her glowing ardent glance had become the coolly appraising one of the professional woman. "A compress of toothwort," she said instantly. "I have been expecting this. My jaw has been aching all afternoon. Come through into the kitchen."

Francis went down the two steps into the parlour, and followed her through into the kitchen. Here the candles were already lit and smelling deliciously of the rosemary that had been used in their making to disguise the smell of the tallow. The table was laid for supper, and from the pot hanging over the fire there came a most savoury smell of stew. Standing by the fire was Yoben. The severity of a first shock can make the succeeding one seem as nothing, and Francis smiled at Yoben as though the meeting had been only what he was expecting. His smile was not returned. Yoben bowed, but stiffly, and without kindliness that Francis remembered. He felt most deeply for Yoben in his predicament and admired the dignity with which he sustained it. To his mind there was only one thing more maddening than to have such a situation interrupted by another man, and that was to have it interrupted by another woman. . . . Or there might be a third thing, and that was to be in love with a woman like Froniga, who could forget all caution and consideration for her lover just because she had caught sight of a swollen cheek. . . . These professional women were the very devil.

"Sit here by the light," she commanded. "Open your mouth."

Francis did as he was told, casting a comical look of apology at Yoben over her shoulder as she bent to look at him. The other man's face softened a little, and when Froniga commanded him to take the stew off and put the kettle on he did so with resignation. "It should be drawn, but not with that abscess," said Froniga. "I will take away the swelling and the pain and then in a day or two you should seek the aid of a surgeon. I picked the last of the toothwort in the garden this morning. It is fortunate that I have not yet used it, for I have many sufferers from this complaint. There, Yoben, hanging from that hook."

Francis was not a student of wild flowers and he looked curiously at the fading bunch she took in her hands. Upon each strong stem tooth-shaped flowers of a yellowish white grew one above the other to the summit. He touched one, then pulled it, and it came out with no difficulty, like the loose milk-teeth he had once removed with no trouble whatever. He groaned softly, for his present molars were of a different character.

"When you go to the surgeon it will come out as easily as that," said Froniga, putting the flowers in a basin and pouring hot water upon them. "The virtue of the herb will loosen the roots as well as driving away the pain. Under what planet were you born?"

"I have no idea," said Francis. "I am no astronomer."

"You must at least know the date of your birth," she said with a touch of impatience.

"January the twelfth."

"Capricorn," said Froniga. "I thought so, for you are not handsome." She was merely murmuring to herself as a doctor might do who notes that the pulse is rapid, and she looked a little hurt when both men laughed. Then she became absorbed in adding a few sprigs of some other herb to the concoction in the basin. The second herb was something to do with Capricorn, Francis supposed.

"I will tell you a little more about those born in the winter solstice," said Yoben to Francis. "They have fine libraries. They can make good painters or musicians, though they are perhaps more critical than creative. They are thoughtful under their cheerful manner. They fear poverty. They never meddle with the affairs of others and they are loyal friends."

The two men looked at each other and Francis said, "That is a perfect description of myself—especially the last sentence."

"You wrong me if you think I invented it," said Yoben. "Mistress Haslewood will bear me out that I did not."

"No," said Froniga. "Open your mouth, please."

Francis opened it, and quick as lightning she clapped one toothwort poultice inside his mouth and one outside, and then before he had time to yell with the pain she had caused him she bandaged a strip of woollen material tightly round his jaws and clamped them shut. As she did so she murmured some sort of incantation in a strange language. His skin crawled. Was he about to be turned into a toad? She could be a ruthless woman, he perceived. He looked at her, sparks in his eyes, and was met with answering sparks. Then she turned her back on him and busied herself with preparations for supper. Yoben resumed the clay pipe he had laid aside and left Francis alone to recover himself.

He recovered quickly. The pain ebbed steadily until it was merely a dull ache, and then no ache at all. A sleepy sense of well-being grew in him, a drugged contentment. He drifted out of it into a new sort of awareness, not of himself but of the other two. The awareness was vivid, and had a quality of vision about it. Yoben had begun to talk gently to Froniga, his eyes following her as she put apples on the table, honey and bread and a bottle of wine. She did not look at him, yet Francis was almost painfully aware of her absorption in Yoben than he was of his in her. He was aware of their love with a sense of shame, not so much because he had interrupted what he guessed was their goodbye feast, as because he knew that he himself was incapable of such love; incapable of it even for Jenny if he should meet her again when she had become a woman. Both of them belonged to that rare order of beings who can truly love, perhaps only a few, and never easily, but those few with a painful depth, cutting channels that would never be silted up and never erased. They were not critics to hold others at arm's length, not artists to make use of them or egoists to exploit them, they were seers to see the eternity of the human spirit and to recognise those whom to love and be loved by was a part of the eternity of each.

Froniga came to him, took off the bandage and removed the poultices. He moved back into himself and felt he had been away for hours.

"Toothache gone?" she asked.

"Gone," he replied.

"Then we'll have supper."

"You and Yoben," he said, "but not myself. It's getting dark and I'd like to reach Henley tonight. My pony is tethered to your gate."

"Leave him there till you've eaten," said Froniga.

"And then spend the night with me," said Yoben. "Have you ever slept in a Romany tent? You'd enjoy it this weather. Continue your journey in the morning. It would be better so."

Francis knew, meeting his eyes, that for some reason or other it would be. He realised too that they wanted him to eat with them and that he was hungry. For the last two days toothache had put him off his food. Froniga ladled the stew into their bowls and he picked up the horn spoon she gave him and fell upon it.

"Chicken?" he asked a little later, though uncertainly. The delicious meat was more tender than chicken. It tasted like a mixture of pheasant and sucking pig, and the herbs that Froniga had cooked with it were perfectly blended.

"Hedgehog," said Froniga, smiling. "I am half a gypsy and Yoben brings me a hedgehog sometimes. I have a weakness for it. He prepared it for me."

"And how do you prepare a hedgehog?" asked Francis. "Pluck it?"

Yoben laughed. "That would be a painful business. When you find your hedgehog, rolled up in a ball, rub his back with a stick until he opens out, then hit him hard on the head and he is dead, poor fellow. Then coat him with clay and bake him in your fire. After a while take him out, tap the clay ball and prickles and skin come away with the clay. What Froniga does with him then is her own secret." He lifted his glass. "There is an old Romany blessing. 'The Lord love you, and may you always have a big hedgehog in your mouth.' "

"I return the blessing and drink to you both," said Francis. "But the hedgehog I wish for you is a symbolic one—the gold at the foot of the rainbow—whatever blessing you each want most in life." He looked at them as he drank to them. Yoben was smiling with tolerant amusement, as though in dealing with toasts and good wishes they played with a boxful of children's toys, but Froniga, he saw, took such things seriously, and her eyes were troubled.

She was indeed troubled just now. The blessing she had always wanted was to be herself a blessing, but Joe Diggar had died. It was true he had died peacefully, with no distress, and looking as though the eyes of his soul had opened on a merry land, but still, he had died, and she was disturbed by her own failure to heal him. Was her power to bless leaving her? Parson Hawthyn, when she had sympathised with the failure of his vigil in the church, had replied tartly, "Failure? How can I fail when I am nothing? There is but one power that is our own, Froniga, the power to offer the emptiness that we are, and we make idols of ourselves if we think we are the only instruments of salvation ready to God's hand."

In her heart, though not to him, she had acknowledged her pride. She did truly seek the welfare of those she loved and served, but she wanted it as a tangible thing, visible gold placed in the crock by herself.

"If I ever paint you, Mistress Froniga," said Francis gaily, "I shall put in the corner, where Dürer sometimes put a parrot when he painted the Virgin, a crock of gold."

"You had better put my pot of basil," said Froniga with a touch of bitterness. "It is the symbol of poverty, and I need poverty. No, not as you need it, who were born under Capricorn and cling to your material possessions, but as those do who were born under the Archer and have powers within themselves that are beyond the ordinary. Our love of riches is a more subtle one than yours, our pride more dangerous."

Yoben watched them with tenderness from a far place. He imagined that he had long ago lost everything, including his self-respect. . . . The fact that he clung to the love between himself and Froniga with every tentacle of his being was a matter that he had somehow overlooked. . . . He wondered what these two would think of him if they knew his story, but it was typical of him that his question caused him no distress beyond a humble sadness, for having been able to accept the fact of himself, he was able to accept with equal humility any judgement that might be passed upon him. Froniga's, he knew, would not be harsh and would not shake her love for him, and it would have been an ease to him to have it, but an ease that he would purchase with too much pain for her.

"Come back when the war is over and paint Froniga," he said. "Paint her as El Greco would have done, painting the bones of her beauty and the texture of her mind in colours that are not of this world. You like El Greco?"

"I do not," said Francis. "And I will insult no beautiful

woman by painting her as though only her bones and her intelligence interested me. Nor will I paint her as though she sat in the shadow of death. In the light of immortality too, I grant you that, but her immortal soul is not what chiefly interests me when I am confronted with a beautiful woman."

"Nor does it interest Rubens," said Yoben with humour.

"Rubens?" ejaculated Francis with contempt. "I did not say that a painter should deny a poor woman her soul."

"What should he do then?"

"Be a realist like Rembrandt. He paints what he sees with such loving clear accuracy that the beauty that is not seen shines through it."

"He was not painting in the days when I knew Europe," said Yoben, "and neither was Velasquez, but I have heard men talk of him. They say he paints the dignity and chivalry I used to know in Spain. And who is this Anthony Van Dyck men speak of?"

"A Dutchman, a follower of Rubens, but he does not deny the soul. You seem to talk much with the gorgio, Yoben."

Yoben smiled serenely. "Yes," he said. "And you, Mr. Loggin, have studied masters of whom the generality of journeyman painters are for the most part ignorant."

Froniga had been listening with amusement, but now her face changed, became alert. "Listen," she said.

They listened, hearing a sound familiar now in the countryside, men marching and the sound of their singing. It was a gay song, the "March along, march along," of the Royalists. The singing and the sound of tramping feet in the twilight that was drawing on to dark had a strange beauty. It held them for a moment entranced, until they realised it was coming up Pack and Prime lane. "Your pony!" said Froniga to Francis. "Bring him into the garden. Never mind my flowers. Take him down into the orchard. Yoben, stay here."

Both men obeyed her. It was light enough for Francis to lead his gentle old pony along paths rather than flower-beds as he took him down into the orchard. He hooked his reins over a branch and sat down on the fallen apple tree. The tramping men came past the cottage and he heard them laughing and joking between their bursts of song. He realised that they were just a party of young men out on a spree, searching for a drink and without warlike intentions. They must have come from one of the Royalist houses of the neighbourhood, from Wallingford

Castle or Greenlands. He saw a glow of light among the trees as the inn door was flung open. No harm would come. Squire Haslewood was not at home and the old landlord, Sam Tidmarsh's brother, would not care whether he served friend or foe provided they paid good money.

Francis forgot them and abandoned himself to the joy of the moment, forgetting past or future, for like all artists he could do that if the moment had sufficient beauty. As the darkness deepened he could see the stars through the branches of the apple tree above his head. Near him was the waterfall of the musk roses. Froniga's kitchen window, across which she had drawn her red curtains, glowed deeply, and the whole beauty of the night seemed fitting itself as a frame about her cottage. That was as it should be, he thought, for it sheltered the farewells of a rare pair of lovers. Yet he did not feel lonely or shut out, for the rosy glow in the window seemed shining upon him out of his own future.

CHAPTER XII

FOR THE KING

A shadow moved and Yoben was beside him. "Come now, my friend," he said, and laid his hand on the pony's bridle. They went quietly through the garden and out into the lane, walked down it for a while and went through a gap in the hedge into the fields. Owls called about them and the air was cool and sweet. They walked in silence until Yoben said, "I waited for you the other night."

"You knew why I did not come," Francis stated rather than asked.

"You had broken your enemy's bread and tasted his salt."

"Yes."

"There is no room for squeamishness in war," said Yoben harshly. "We must win this struggle. If we are defeated England is lost, not only to the King but to God."

Francis stifled a feeling of dismay, for this was a new Yoben. He felt rather than saw the hardening of his face and the fierce light in his eyes. He had hoped that all the religious fanatics were on the other side, for extremists set his teeth on edge. Well, one's friends could not be cut to one's private and personal pattern and a bottle of sloe gin was worth three of blackberry cordial any day.

"Don't you know that the odds are against us?" Yoben went on. "Parliament holds London. Their potential both in money and men is greater than ours. Unless each man fights this war with all he has and is, denying himself even the right to his private chivalry, we shall lose it."

"We shall win it."

"What with?"

"Private chivalry. This so-called Puritan army is a rabble. There are many gentlemen and fine soldiers among them, I grant you, but not enough to leaven the dough. And who are the King's men?"

Francis paused, and bit off the arrogant words, but the silence in their place was almost red-hot with a pride so fierce that it was a match for Yoben's fanaticism, and immediately dissolved it. The kindly man whom Francis had known until now slipped over the fanatic like a scabbard over a sword and he said courteously, "Men like yourself, the sons of noblemen, courtiers and poets, and the Catholic gentry who for years have been the flower of the King's army and have been tempered by martyrdom." A warm note came into his voice. "I grant you it is a fair chivalry, and its gallantry will warm our hearts, but its numbers are too few to allow themselves the luxury of individuality. The spies, even the amateurs, must bring back some information or, I say again, we shall not win this war." His tone again changed quickly. "Do you know the King is on the march?"

"No!" said Francis. "I imagined him still at Nottingham."

His mind went quickly back to that stormy day in August when the King's standard had been hoisted at Nottingham. While his little army cheered him, Charles had stood beneath the standard with the face of a man stricken with mortal disease. That he should march so soon was the last thing Francis had expected.

"That young genius Prince Rupert has prevailed," said Yoben. "A quick smashing blow at once, before Parliament can fully gather their forces, is the best chance."

"I must get to the army," said Francis impatiently. "Where is it?"

"I have my sources of information," said Yoben with a smile, "But a Romany tinker cannot know everything. I only know the King is marching west—possibly on Derby. If you were Rupert, what would you do?"

Francis, remembering the pitifully small company of men who had gathered about the standard at Nottingham, replied tersely, "Find some means of increasing the size of the army."

"I'd do the same," said Yoben. "I'd march through the country with all the verve and dash I could encompass, gathering in the loyal gentry as I went. I'd get Derby. I'd get Chester. If you have Chester you command the northern approaches to Wales. I'd recruit all the Welshmen I could; they've no staying power, but if you're out for a sudden smashing victory they're your men. From the borders of Wales I'd turn south-east towards Birmingham, and for my battleground I'd choose the Midlands."

"Why?" asked Francis.

"It's open country, suitable for Rupert's shock tactics. A

quick victory, Oxford and Reading in our hands, and the way would lie open down the Thames valley to London. That would be my plan."

"Taking my chance that it's also Rupert's I'll ride north-west," said Francis. "Can I get a good horse in Henley? Why did you prevent me going there tonight?"

"Not only for the pleasure of your company when I go there myself early tomorrow morning," said Yoben, "but because Henley is in confusion tonight; troopers from Greenland House gave it a taste of street fighting. Those men at the inn are a few of them. They'd marched up Pack and Prime lane from Henley. By tomorrow Henley will be itself again and you'll be able to take your pick of good horses at the Bell Inn. The landlord is a Royalist."

They had been standing still under the stars, absorbed in their talk. Now they were silent, looking down at the Romany tents and the glow of the camp-fire below them, and Francis, with his capacity for living in the moment, was instantly absorbed by the thought of the night's adventure. "Will they accept me or knife me?" he asked with interest.

"With me, you'll be accepted without question," said Yoben. "I did them a favour, once, and so now I and my friends are sacrosanct for ever. That's a Romany characteristic."

"And yet you affect to despise chivalry," said Francis lightly.

"I did not say that," said Yoben soberly. "God forbid that I should despise any fair thing, but we cannot fight wars with roses in our hands."

The faint twang of a harp greeted them as they came down the slope, and Alamina's voice singing. The gypsies had finished their evening meal and men and women together were sitting about their camp-fire. They looked at Francis as he and Yoben joined them but neither singer nor harpist checked their music and the rest moved only to make room for the newcomers. Francis sat down beside Yoben, his mind flaming with excitement as he looked round the circle of firelit, savage, tragic, exquisite or dreadful faces floating against darkness above a mist of colour and smoke; flame-colour and the greens and blues and crimsons of their lovely rags; smoke of their windy fire and short clay pipes. How could he stamp this scene on his memory so that he should never forget it, burn it in so that he should see it as he saw it now when he should get his paints again? He couldn't. That was the painter's tragedy. Such wild and living scenes were more easily captured in music than in paint, for music moved like wind and water, but paint imposed its own stillness upon memory. The eyes of these people had a terrible sparkling brilliance, and their dark faces, smooth as acorns or wrinkled like the bark of trees, had a shimmering vitality that was like light on water. The harp-music thrummed eerily, and when the woman's wild beautiful voice sank from recitation to refrain they all joined in softly, rocking themselves as they sang. Then suddenly excitement seized them, and they swayed with strong rhythmic movements, their singing swelling like the rising wind in the trees. Then the song ended, their bright eyes turned upon Francis in eager curiosity, and in the silence Yoben introduced him to them, with sonorous words and expansive gestures which seemed to satisfy them, for they smiled at him and gave him the post of honour next to a vast and wicked old man, with fire lurking still in his sunken eyes and sardonic humour in the gouged-out furrows of his face. He lit Francis's pipe from his own, deigned to accept a gift of gorgio tobacco from the stranger, and signed imperiously to the harpist to play again.

As Francis began to recover from the tremendous impact that the scene had made upon him, individual faces caught his attention. The old white-haired harpist was blind, he thought, for his eyes had no light and his dark hawk-like face had the rapt and fierce attentiveness of a man whom nothing can distract from his inward vision. But the eyes of the singer went boldly from face to face, glorious sparkling pagan eyes. He thought she was one of the most beautiful women he had ever seen, her body soft and graceful and so young that it did not offend with its voluptuousness. Her smooth dark skin had a tinge of colour on the prominent cheek-bones and her full lips were red as rose berries. The masses of dark hair that shadowed her forehead gave mystery to her face. She had the same strong square face that Froniga had, but it was without the fine drawn look of race and character that distinguished Froniga's. It would thicken and coarsen with the years. Having met them once, he did not again want to meet her eyes, and he looked instead at the strong pillar of her throat, the gold and rose of the fire reflected in the smooth skin. Her beauty troubled him profoundly, gave him a vague feeling of treason, even though he was more repulsed than attracted by her, but he had to return to it again and again. When he looked away from her, studying other faces, he felt the pull and knew she had willed it. He was not delivered from her spell until Yoben touched him, laying his hand on his arm and keeping it there, as though compelling his attention, though he did not speak.

Francis had known there was an old hooded crone sitting upon the other side of Yoben, but the smoke of her pipe and Yoben's had drifted between them and he had not seen her clearly. Now, leaning a little forward, he saw that with her cloak fallen back from her white hair she was looking at him with a grave and sweet attention, tinged with astonishment, that reminded him of Jenny. He forgot Alamina, for what he was looking at was a beauty from beyond the world, shining through a flesh so disregarded that it had become scarcely more palpable than a fine glass full of light. He felt the familiar thrill of joy, the most intimate and searching that he knew. Here again was the cup held out. He never drank from the cup, or even wanted to, knowing that in this world he could not. Sometimes a star shaped it, or a phrase of music, but this was the first time that a human being had shaped the cup. Something had happened to this old woman which made her more powerful than any star. So rare was her quality that one could not disbelieve what she held. She smiled at him, and he answered her smile, not returning it but answering it, for their brief interchange was a conversation. She said, "You are a gorgio, and a most surprising creature, but because you are his friend I hold you in my heart." And he replied, "It is so with me that what he loves I must love too." At that she smiled again and lifted her cloak slightly, as though it were wings, and he saw two small creatures nestling against her, one on each side, fast asleep, circular as winter robins. Then he saw a third child, more delicately made, sitting between the old woman and Yoben, a boy beautiful as a young thrush, whose sleepy head lay against Yoben's shoulder. He too seemed included in the gesture of the lifting wings that sank down now as though failing and drooping, and there were fear and entreaty in the old woman's eyes. He leaned forward and looked into them, and pledged himself.

He settled back into his place and did not again look at Madona. What she had asked of him, what he had promised, he had no idea. He put the strange little interlude from him and became absorbed once again in the faces round the fire and the new song Alamina was singing. He imagined it was a love-song this time, low and soft and lilting.

An hour later, when the gypsies had gone to their beds and the fire had died down to a deep coral glow, he left the tent he was to share with Yoben and went to see that all was well with his pony. He found him well cared for, caressed his rough head and walked on a little further down the slope of the field, enjoying the coolness of the night and the brilliance of the stars. He stood for a while in stillness and peace, listening to the owls and the rustle of the wind in the trees. He had a sense of unreality. The whole of this strange night seemed like a dream. Then he turned to go back. Something moved, some shadow slipping from the deeper shadow of the hawthorn tree upon his right, some shape of beauty as lovely as the stars and the night. She came into his arms without his having realised that he had opened them to her and for a moment or two she was part of the dream. Then the darkness seemed to blaze and crackle into fire as the woman's body burned and glowed in his arms that had become hoops of steel about her. He kissed her mouth and her eyes and the glorious column of her throat over which he had watched the firelight ripple. Watching her from the other side of the camp-fire he had felt repulsed, but now they had met in the fire and it had welded them together.

Out of the midst of it, as his arms lifted her, she laughed suddenly, a low laugh of triumph with a note of cunning in it. Looking down into her face, that was laughing up at him, he saw her eyes sparkling like black diamonds, with no humanity in them. What was he doing with this creature in his arms? She was half siren and half animal, neither evil nor good, elemental and utterly alien to him. With an exclamation of disgust he flung her away from him and saw the triumph in her eyes turn to hatred. She stumbled and fell to the ground. He turned and left her there.

He walked away and the quiet of the night flowed over him again, but he could not feel it. He could feel nothing but her hatred. Furious that it should affect him so, he plunged his balled fists angrily down into his pockets and found them empty. He had had a few loose coins in one of them and with amazing skill she had picked his pockets while she was in his arms. His disgust turned to amusement, and the ugliness of the little incident sloughed off him as he laughed. By the time he reached Yoben's tent he had almost forgotten it.

Yoben had spread their beds of dried bracken, river mint and wild thyme and almost at once Francis lay down and pulled the blanket over him while Yoben, wrapped in his cloak, sat at the opening of the tent smoking his pipe. Francis could see his fine profile outlined against the glow of the dying fire outside, and presently he asked, "Who is that old crone who sat beside you, with the children under her cloak?"

"Madona Heron. Her sister was Froniga Haslewood's mother."

"What is it about her that sets her at once so far, and yet brings her so near?"

Yoben was silent a moment and then said, "I can only explain Madona by saying that there must have been in her all her life, whether she knew it or not, that complete willingness which is the soul of courage, as it is the soul of prayer. And so she is very near perfection. She is so far because that is so rare, so near because perfection has finished with the sin of separateness."

"She can foresee the future?" asked Francis.

"I believe so," said Yoben. "She is doubly foreseeing, I suspect, for being both a Romany and a saint. But she makes no parade of it."

"No," said Francis, remembering with what simplicity she had extracted his promise from him. He was silent again, and then he asked, "What were the songs that siren sang to us tonight?"

"She sang first one of the legends of her people. There are many, but nearly all have the central idea of a people condemned to wander the face of the earth in expiation of their sin. She told how the gypsies were among the first people God made, and how Cain married a gypsy. The years passed and they became a great people with a great king, named Caspar, who with two other kings followed a star to Bethlehem and found Christ. When Caspar came home again he converted his people to the Christian faith and they remained devout Christians until the Saracens attacked them in Egypt, when they surrendered to their enemies and denied Christ. Now they must travel for ever in penance for their sin, but they are so hardy that when all other people of the world are worn out they will still be travelling round with tents and wagons. Then she sang a love-story. A gypsy girl loved a gorgio, who was imprisoned by his King. When she heard of it she went to the King and begged that he might be set free. She was an expert needle-woman and could make a beautiful cloak in one day. The King said he would set her lover free if she could make him seven cloaks in seven days. She made six but fell asleep for weariness while she was making the seventh, and the King would not free her lover. She died of grief and was changed into a spider, and to this day she spreads out her threads when the sun shines, and the dewdrops on them are the tears she has wept for her lover. The story is a beautiful one, but has nothing to do with Alamina. Except as a dramatic performance she would weep for no man's death, and she never forgives."

"I will remember your warning," said Francis drowsily, and settled himself in his sweet-smelling bed. He was nearly asleep when he opened his eyes again and saw Yoben still sitting by the opening of the tent. He was no longer smoking, but holding a small black book in his hands. The stars and the dying fire gave little light and he must have known by heart the words he was mumbling so softly that Francis could catch only a few of them. His face was so absorbed that to watch it seemed an intrusion and Francis turned over upon his other side. He thought he knew now why he had been so instantly attracted to Yoben. They worshipped God after the same manner.

2

Francis woke before dawn and looking through the holes that the field-mice had nibbled in the tent just by his head saw the morning star blazing in a clear sky. Ten minutes later he heard the first sounds of life, a dog barking and the cries of children, and then with the first faint light the whole camp exploded into activity like a hive of angry bees. He and Yoben made their toilet quickly; it consisted of straightening the clothes in which they had slept.

"I have only one thing against this countryside,"said Yoben, "there is so little water. You never see a stream and we are always dirtier here than anywhere else. The tribe will be leaving this camp today. Will you help me take down the tent?"

They went out into the crystal world, cold and still, and found a brightly coloured maelstrom of activity at the centre of the crystal. The fire had been brought to life again by the women and a black pot hung over the flames. Tents were being taken down, rolled up and stowed in tilt-carts and wagons, pots and pans and bedding going in after them. They ate, dipping hunks of coarse bread in the stew, and then the fire was stamped out and the stewpot put away in the beautiful painted wagon that belonged to Piramus and Madona Heron as the elders of the tribe. The ponies were caught and harnessed, the old and infirm and the small children were piled into the carts on top of the household gear, a gypsy boy went to the bridle of each pony and the cavalcade surged into movement up the green slope of the field, making for the wide gap in the hedge that led into Pack and Prime lane.

There was something thrilling and dramatic about the exodus, and Francis could have cheered as he stood watching with Yoben. Each cart and wagon, loaded to capacity, the pony straining gallantly between the shafts and the gypsy boy egging it on with cries and cracks of his whip, took the green slope like a ship in full sail, rocking from side to side, gay and reckless. Each lurched through the gap in the hedge dangerously but triumphantly and turned skilfully into the lane. There was little laughter of song, for the gypsies travelled for the most part silently, bearing themselves with immense pride and dignity, but the jingling of the harness, the creaking of the carts and the rhythmic cracking of the whips made music. They were bound for the leafy valleys below Nettlebed, where Yoben would join them in a few days' time, after he had mended a few pots and pans down Henley way. They would travel there before the gorgios were out of doors, passing through wild Highmoor, where lived the fierce Celts who fought with everyone, and with the gypsies worse than all, before the sun was fully up. In the deep valleys they would hide themselves, doing what trade they could in the villages round about with fortune-telling, the mending of pots and pans, the selling of love-potions and the meat skewers and pegs they made from close-grained elder-wood, and when things got too hot for them they would come back again to Robert's green fields, where they were always protected. It added to the drama of the occasion that they went to danger. Before the cavalcade returned again some of the men, caught thieving, might have swung for it, and others been clapped in the stocks or deported. Each man as he rocked up the hill and out into the lane knew that it depended on his own quick wits whether he came back again, and laughed at the knowledge, and women knew that they might come back weeping, and held their heads all the more arrogantly now. They were a proud people, who had been persecuted for centuries, and they knew how to breast the wave.

Last of all came Piramus and Madona, a handsome boy leading Baw the white pony that Froniga in the moonlight had mistaken for a unicorn. They came more slowly, as befitted their dignity. The rising sun glinted upon the red and blue paint of their wagon and upon the scarlet scarf knotted round Piramus's throat. He looked magnificent in a tattered black velvet doublet that he had stolen from a gorgio he had knifed in the back, and his fierce dark face had in the morning light a look of nobility, so proud and hawk-like was it. He held the reins in his left hand, while his right hand rested regally upon the knife in his belt. He was a consummate actor. Looking neither to the right not to the left, he passed by, and Yoben and Francis might not have existed, for all the notice he took of them. But Madona bent forward and smiled at them, her old face soft and tender. She sat as though enthroned, Cinderella on her lap, Dinki leaning against her knee and Meriful wedged in next to Piramus, but there was nothing self-conscious in her queenliness. It was her own as the scent of a flower is its own, and she knew nothing about it. When she had gone the world seemed to the two men suddenly rather cold. Then they too, Francis leading his pony, went up the green slope and through the gap in the hedge, turning to the right towards Henley.

They walked at first in silence. Yoben was thinking how the jingling cavalcade was awakening Froniga. It was passing her cottage, and in her small room with the high dormer window she was lying and listening to her kinsfolk passing by. Only a few feet separated her and Madona. He held them together in his thoughts, as always, praying that one day they might have a deeper unity. Francis was thinking of Yoben. How in the world had this cultured Catholic gentleman come to be a Romany tinker? He supposed he would never know. Yoben was one of the most trusted of the Royal agents, and good spies have a great capacity for keeping their own counsel.

"Won't you load your gear on my pony?" asked Francis, for Yoben was walking along like Atlas, his shoulder bowed beneath his tinker's equipment.

But Yoben, smiling, shook his head. "They're a part of my body," he said, "and I carry them as a snail his shell."

They were passing a tumbledown cottage in a dark garden, and Yoben crossed himself.

"A witch?" asked Francis, a gleam of amusement in his eyes.

"Yes. Did you not feel the evil?"

"I ate too large a breakfast. A man full of rabbit stew feels no influences, good or bad. You ate nothing."

"It is Sunday," said Yoben briefly.

"I had forgotten," said Francis. "I am not as devout as I should be. I am not, as I think you are, fighting this war for religious reasons."

"There is no valid reason for fighting this war except the religious reason," said Yoben curtly. "What does it matter whether King or Parliament is supreme? Change from one supremacy to the other and you merely exchange one tyranny for another. Basically this war is part of the great European struggle; is Europe to be Catholic or Calvinist? In such a struggle the duty of all Catholics is clear."

"Like so many of us, you over-estimate the Catholic sympathies of the King," said Francis. "He protects us for the Queen's sake, but he himself will never be a Catholic, and if he wins this war England will be no nearer to the true faith than she is now."

"And how near will she be if the Puritans win the war?" asked Yoben bitterly. "The Church of England, the Church of such men as the King and Archbishop Laud, is not hopelessly far from the true faith, but the so-called religion of those appalling Puritans is little better than devil-worship. And the King is pro-Spanish. A man must take his stand upon one side or the other, and there is no doubt upon which side he stands."

"His Majesty is marvellously accomplished at keeping a foot in both camps," said Francis gently. "Indeed there are times when his friends think with despair that he has as many feet as a centipede. Yoben, do not think that I am casting any slur upon the King's integrity. I am not. In the last resort he would die for the essentials of his faith. But he believes in diplomacy, and diplomats are always—if I may coin a word—centipedal. And I would not describe all Puritans as heathens. Through all the self-righteousness which you rightly describe as devil-worship, the vulgarity, the ranting, the fanaticism and the blood and thunder, there runs a stream of sheer goodness."

Yoben's anger fell from him and his face wore again its habitual look of gentle melancholy. His mind had gone back to a conversation he had had with Froniga. "You are right," he said. "As a man is, so is his cause, a mixture of good and bad. There is seldom a clear-cut line, so that a man can say, upon this side is the evil and upon that the good. We long for such a division, but it is not often given to us. If it were it would make our task too easy."

"Our task?" asked Francis.

"Our task of perpetual choice by which we win or lose our souls." His voice broke off like a snapped thread. They walked on and Francis could think of nothing to say. It was Yoben who broke the silence, asking courteously, "If you do not fight this war for the religious reason, then for what reason do you fight it?"

"I've not come within ten miles of a fight yet," said Francis, laughing. "But if I ever have the luck to find myself in a charge of Rupert's, it will be because loyalty to the Crown is in the family tradition and we are a family who do not break with tradition. But I have a further reason. When as a very young man I first went to Court, the King was not yet thirty. He showed me great kindness and I loved him. I love him still. He never loses men's love, though he does at times break their hearts. I was a romantic youngster. The whole Court was romantic. We were sodden with it. The masques and the dancing, the music and the verse-making, the whole flowery Arcadia, flowed round us and built up the walls of the ivory tower in which the King loved and dreamed his dreams. He shared them with me. The whole of England was to be an Arcadia, a united people enjoying the blessings of peace and prosperity (who would appear crowned with flowers in our masques) under his absolute authority, worshipping God as King and Archbishop bade them, as united in religious as in secular obedience. His people were, to the King, a sacred trust from God, and his people were to look upon him as God's own representative, ruling them by divine right. It was all a delightful rose-coloured short cut to Utopia, and when we looked out of the windows of the ivory tower the rose-colour lay like pretty clouds over all the darkness of the land. What went on under it we had no idea. We have now. Human nature is intractable stuff, hard jagged stuff, the sort of stuff that dreams are wrecked on. Yet still for me, as, I believe, for the King, there is the dream. The perfect England. It is a lovely land.

It is better to die for a broken dream than for no dream at all."

The lovely land, thought Yoben, and the fair city. His own passionate dedication to the ideal of a united Christendom purged of heresy, the Holy Catholic Church untorn by dissension, was the same dream. "He looked for a city." But it lay beyond the confines of this world.

"Look below you," he said quietly.

Francis had not been watching the way they were going, and the vision of the city took him by surprise. They stood on the slope of a wooded hill, and at their feet was Henley. Above them the sky was bright blue, but below river-mist still hung over the little town, not hiding it, but softening with its silver gauze the outlines of roofs and chimneys and the soaring church tower. Through the silver gleamed the red of the tiled roofs, the blue plumes of smoke from newly-lit fires, the glint of latticed windows facing the sun. Beyond the little town woods rose again to the skyline, so that it seemed to lie protected in a green cup. Francis knew many of these country towns of England, though not this one, and loved all that he knew. Italian towns clung courageously to the summits of steep hills, and many French towns studded the plains like jewels in a green shield, but most English towns found comfortable hollowed places, with water handy, and curled themselves round in them like cats, and like cats dreamed there in the sun. He knew just what he would find below him : old wide streets meandering gently as streams down to the river, bow-fronted shop windows, a couple of inns with painted signs and galleried yards, a few fine gentlemen's houses facing the streets, with behind them hidden walled gardens of ancient beauty. There would be taverns too, and poor wattle-and-daub cottages jostling each other on each side of narrow dirty cobbled lanes, but they hid themselves behind the seemly parts of the town like children behind their mother's skirts. If there was no cathedral in this town, that great church down there was as fine as a cathedral, and over the river there would be a grand old bridge. There would be a wharf too, where barges from London set down their sea-coal, that had come to London by ship from Newcastle, and others that took on cargoes of sheep's wool and the woven cloth that was made in nearly every cottage of the Chilterns. Below them the church clock sounded the hour, and then a trumpet sounded. It seemed a signal for the crowing of cocks and the barking of dogs, and the dissolving of the mist into thin air. The town took on firmer and clearer outline, and they went on down the hill.

"In a minute of two I shall leave you," said Yoben. "Ask your way to the Bell Inn."

"I'll see you again?" asked Francis.

"Can you doubt that?" replied Yoben. "Even at our first meeting were you not aware of permanency? Goodbye."

He turned up a narrow lane to his left and vanished almost as suddenly as he had vanished into the wood. Francis listened a moment, almost expecting to hear the blackbird's song, but he heard instead the church bells ringing. Leading his pony, he walked on down to the main street, where in the cool fresh sparkle of the morning everything was just as he had expected it to be—only, if anything, more delightful. The bow-windowed shops were shuttered, as it was Sunday, but front doors had been set open, and through some of them he caught a glimpse or two of those hidden gardens, and could smell breakfasts cooking. He paused before a little old shop wedged like a crooked dwarf between two top-heavy timber-framed houses, that looked like spindly giants about to fall forward on their faces, and read over its window the legend, "Nathaniel Lovejoy. Tailor." A little bespectacled old man, with bald head and bent shoulders, as gnome-like as his shop, was sweeping his doorstep with a branch of broom. His face seemed vaguely familiar, but Francis could not remember where he had seen him.

"What is the name of this street, sir?" he asked courteously.

"Hart Street, sir."

"Could you direct me to the Bell Inn?"

The old man looked at the soberly dressed young Puritan and a gleam of recognition came into his eyes. "Better not go to the Bell, sir," he said. "There are King's men there." His voice sank to a rapid undertone. "They came from Greenlands, sir. They'd heard there were arms hidden here, in the tavern by the river. There must be a spy about, sir, or how did they know? For it was true, sir. We'd collected arms from all the churches and manors round about. They took the lot. Our Henley men weren't behindhand, they set about them, but we'd not the weapons, you see, sir, not like they had. There were men killed, sir, in this very street, and several wounded. I never thought to see such a thing in Hart Street, I never did. There was blood all over my doorstep, sir, there was indeed. But I washed it off, and you can't see it now. They were searching houses till late last evening, looking for arms. What'll they do today?"

Francis smiled reassuringly into the old man's troubled eyes. "March away, now that they've got what they wanted. Where is the Bell Inn, so that I can avoid it?"

"It's up Bell Street, sir, that turn to the right. You'll excuse me, sir; my porridge is on the boil."

He knocked his branch of broom against the doorpost and went in and shut the door. Francis retraced his steps, turned to the right and led his pony over the cobbles of Bell Street, where the pigeons were strutting in and out of sun and shade and the tall half-timbered houses reached up to the sky, cutting patterns in the blue with their chimneys and gables. The church bells had fallen silent and there was no sound but the whirring of the pigeon's wings as they rose about him in a silvery cloud. He walked on up the street and under the archway of the inn into the cobbled yard.

He found a small company of Royalist Troopers there, singing and whistling, polishing their arms and grooming their horses, getting ready for the road again. He strolled into the midst of them with his pony, his high hat upon the back of his head, a disarming grin on his face, and slapped the nearest of them heartily upon the back. As he had expected, this was one of the lighter moments of war, and he met with no worse than shrill whistles and catcalls, some good-natured cuffing and the instant removal of his hat from his head. He saw it spinning into the midden with no regrets, for it had been damned uncomfortable. All the same, it was an illuminating experience, for a man who had seldom been treated with anything but the most obsequious deference, to hear the uninhibited comments upon a homely face and figure which for lesser men are a commonplace, and he'd had enough of it by the time an erect soldierly figure appeared in the inn doorway and a voice bawled at him, "You there, you rascal, what's your business?"

"Captain John Smith, sir," he shouted back in delight. "In the King's name!"

Captain John Smith was well known to him, one of those Catholic officers of whom he and Yoben had been speaking, men of good birth who were professional soldiers because other professions were closed to Catholics, but who had to keep their religion secret lest the men under their command lynch them, as many of their number had been murdered for their faith, but who continued in unshaken loyalty to the King and were the best officers he had.

"Come inside, fellow," he said curtly, and turned on his heel.

In the inn parlour, where the royal arms and monogram were carved over the fireplace in commemoration of the King's visit to Henley ten years ago, Captain Smith sat down before a table and motioned to the shabby Puritan to stand before him. "What's your business?" he rapped out.

"John," said Francis, "I want a wash, a suit of decent clothes, and a good fast horse to get to the King. Can you oblige me?"

Captain Smith stared hard at the face of the man before him, his jaw dropped and then he laughed. "How was I to know you, my Lord, in such a guise?"

"I had a bet with Suckling that I could turn myself into a first-class spy," said Francis. "I've lost. I was a fool—fiddling while Rome burns. John, do you know the King has left Nottingham?"

"Yes, my Lord. I was riding with this troop to join the King when a spy we have in these parts brought news of the weapons hidden in the tavern, and we stopped to teach Henley a lesson. You'll ride with us?"

"At once?"

"In a couple of hours. The men need a meal and I have to arrange for the accommodation of some wounded. And also—" He paused and looked at Francis. "Did you know, my Lord, that whenever possible Mass is said in the crypt of the inn? There are Catholics in the neighbourhood, and they come here secretly. There is a hidden entrance to the inn from a back street. The landlord is a Catholic. It is not always possible to get hold of a priest, especially now, but today we are lucky. In half an hour. Will you come, my Lord?" He smiled. "The landlord will fit you out with garments less unsuitable than those you are wearing."

"I've just time to wash and change," said Francis soberly.

Twenty minutes later he was kneeling in the crypt of the inn, sunk, it seemed to him, in the depth of the earth. The Bell was very old, and the crypt was supported on columns and vaulted like a church. It smelt dank and musty, and was only fitfully lit by the candles on the altar and a couple of sconces fixed to two pillars. The altar was a table of dark oak, spread with a fine linen cloth, and behind it on a wall hung a crucifix. Dim figures whom he could hardly see were kneeling near him and he could hear the slow footfall of others coming cautiously down the winding dark stairs. It seemed impossible that up above him there was still the bright sunlight, the cheerful little town and the troopers in the cobbled yard. Even the war seemed remote. He felt as far removed from it all as though he were in one of Saint Martin's caves at Marmontiers, or in the catacombs of Imperial Rome, or further back still, in the cave at Bethlehem. Awe fell upon him. He did not hear Mass often, and when he did it was in the garish brilliance of the Queen's Chapel at Whitehall, as one of a perfumed silken crowd who whispered to each other, swayed and rustled and were seldom still. Here the stillness was profound. It weighed upon his eyelids and he closed them. "Out of the deep have I called unto Thee, O Lord." The deep of the caves of the earth, the deep of pain and grief, of battle and sudden death. When one had never learned to pray, and suddenly longed to do so, what a comfort were the prayers of other men. "If Thou, Lord, wilt be extreme to mark what is done amiss, O Lord, who may abide it? . . . with the Lord there is mercy." A man came and knelt beside him and without looking he knew it was John Smith. For a few moments there were no more footsteps on the stairs, and then slow footsteps that seemed to come from far off, from beyond time, like footsteps from another world, and the closing of the door. He felt rather than heard the priest moving between the kneeling figures towards the altar, felt it as a sense of expectation and of blessedness. The stillness deepened and seemed to glow, and then a voice that he knew began to intone the introit of the Mass.

Francis found that he was not surprised, and when he looked up and saw Yoben's tall figure at the altar it was with a sense of comfort and homeliness. John Smith's shoulder touched his for a moment and his sense of surety was increased. From the ends of the earth they were coming to this hiding-place in the deep, from the past and the future. Death could not touch the safety of this place or break the bond between them. They were a vast multitude, yet the deep from which men call to God could hold them all, and the deep was home. Within it they were knit together into one body.

It was over, and they were filing out as quietly and silently as they had come. Yoben stood by the door, the light from one of the sconces falling on his face, and Francis was startled to see it ravaged, as though the hour of peace and blessedness he had given to others had been an hour of torment for himself. As Francis passed him their eyes met, and Yoben's seemed full of shame and entreaty. Francis wondered if this was the first time for many years that Yoben had said Mass, and if he had only done so today because another man had failed. He seemed to be asking for pardon and understanding. Francis could only guess at his thoughts, smile at him and pass on in pity and wonder.

Half an hour later the King's horsemen clattered out of the inn yard, along Bell Street and out into Hart Street. The church bells were ringing again and churchgoers stopped to look at them with awe as they trotted by, for they were a goodly sight. The two men who rode at the head of the troop had plumed hats upon their heads, with bright scarves crossing their chests, and rode well upon fine horses. The shining dignified troop jingled down the broad, winding street and under the tall tower of St. Mary's Church, the bells ringing out over their heads. The two officers lifted their hats in honour of the Virgin as they passed beneath the tower, and again in honour of her mother as they trotted over the beautiful old bridge and passed the chapel of Saint Anne that was built upon it. The Thames stretched wide and lovely upon each side of them. Francis turned to John Smith and smiled as they rode through the water-meadows towards the beech-woods, the little town left behind them, for a sober excitement drummed in his blood. Soon the sound of the bells was also left behind and they seemed to have the fresh green world entirely to themselves. They trotted on, a beautiful, orderly cavalcade riding to join the King.

PART TWO

CHAPTER I

PRELUDE TO BATTLE

I

It was Saturday the twenty-second of October and the King's army was marching towards London, about fourteen thousand of them, ill-equipped but enthusiastic. So far they had done well. In a brilliant march, screened by Rupert's cavalry, they had come by way of Derby and Stafford to Shrewsbury, then up to Chester, then back to Shrewsbury again, gathering in the local gentry as they went, and hordes of little dark Welshmen armed with knives and clubs. From Shrewsbury they had marched through Bridgnorth to Kenilworth, and now with the Avon behind them they were marching towards Edgecott. Somewhere, they knew, the enemy was on the move, trying to bar the way to London, knowing as well as they did that if they could reach London and capture it, now at once before Parliament could gather further strength, they would have won the war. Apart from a brilliant little cavalry engagement of Rupert's they had seen no fighting yet, but they knew it was coming. Rupert, scouting on ahead with the cavalry, was jubilant. He had got the armies where he had wanted them, in the open country of the Midlands. Victory now, and the way to London lay open.

To the west the afternoon sun lay level across the glorious plain of Warwick, ahead the hills rose against the sky, splashed with the crimson and gold of autumn. The weather was set fair, but the wind blew keenly from the north and the King drew his cloak more closely about him. He was sad and preoccupied, though he spoke occasionally to his two excited young sons, Prince Charles and Prince James, or to Sir Edmund Verney, his standard-bearer, or to one or another of the splendidly dressed young men who rode with him. They were a gay crowd, hard put to it to keep their horses to the slow pace of the infantry and the gun-teams, and Francis, Lord Leyland was harder put to it than anyone. He wished he were on ahead with Rupert. It was an honour to be a member of the King's bodyguard, but so far a tame one. He was riding now beside the King. "Sir, when the fun starts, may I join Rupert?" he asked.

Charles eyed him coldly. "If it's fighting you want you've merely to remain at your post. Do you imagine that I propose to put myself in a place of safety when my army is engaged?"

So glacial was his tone that Francis murmured an apology, drew back a little and rode on in silence, though he had an overwhelming desire to shout and sing. He had known he was a man born fearless but he had not known he would so delight in war; or at least, he corrected himself, in the exciting preliminaries. How he would feel when the fighting started he had yet to discover. But he realised how the gaiety of the young men about him must fret the King. For him this was no adventure but a tearing apart of his personality, a sort of death. His idea of kingship was a mystical one; he was himself his people; and now his people, his being, were divided and at war. Francis remembered with what desperation he had worked for peace. "Our very soul is full of anguish," he had written to Parliament, "until we may find some remedy to prevent the miseries which are ready to overwhelm this whole nation by a civil war." But when men are fanatically wedded to opposing ideals there is no remedy, thought Francis, except to fight it out.

He looked at the King. His tiny indomitable figure was upright and alert upon the magnificent black horse. The King rode well. In his youth it had been thought that a boy so ill and weak would never be able to sit a horse, but in that as in other things his courage had been the conqueror of his body. No man in his kingdom now was a finer horseman than the King. Like his bodyguard, he was splendidly dressed, with just that added shine and sparkle that seemed to make him the central point of the blue and red and gold of the autumn day. Beneath his crimson cloak the silver cuirass gleamed in the sunshine, and his sword and spurs and the harness of his horse were twinkling points of light. The crimson and white feathers in his hat lifted in the wind and there were pearls in his ears. But his face was white and still, with sharpened contours. He was at all times a rather humourless man, but today his heavy-lidded eyes and pursed mouth looked as though laughter would not visit them again.

Like shadow running over a sunny landscape a misery that

was not like his own began to eat up Francis's excitement. He had a sense of fear, as though at the approach of something beyond endurance, and then a feeling of hopelessness. One did this thing and not the other, made a mistake in a moment of weakness, and the choice of the moment became a long, relentless and bitter road. Nothing was so relentless as consequences. If one could bear them alone until the end it would not be so bad, but no one was ever alone for weal or woe, least of all a king. No choice that a king could make could ruin himself alone. Ruin. Was that what the King was thinking of as he rode? Francis was ashamed of his own eagerness of a few moments ago. A man should not rush too eagerly upon danger, for it was none too easy to keep one's footing in it.

He rode on chastened, aware now of the cold wind and the fatigue. And then at a turn of the road lightness of heart returned, for they had ridden into the middle of a pack of hounds out at exercise. There was barking and yelping, the laughter of the cavaliers as they quieted their restive horses, and the profane shouting of a large red-faced country gentleman standing at the top of a bank.

"Who is he?" asked the King sternly.

The red-faced gentleman was struck silent in mid-oath. He looked at the little man on the black horse, so extraordinarily small in comparison with the immensity of his dignity, so deeply sad in his brilliant setting. He dragged his hat from his head and turned to Francis, who had dismounted and was standing beside him.

"Squire Shuckburgh," he whispered hoarsely.

"Present Mr. Shuckburgh to me," said the King. "Sir, how can you find it in your heart to amuse yourself so merrily while your sovereign rides to fight for his crown?"

"Dawgs, sir, is dawgs," said Squire Shuckburgh, standing hat in hand at his King's bridle. "They must have their exercise though the kingdom be split in two."

"For whom do you fight?" asked Charles. "For your King or for the rebels?"

"For neither, sir," said Squire Shuckburgh. "I'm a peaceable man."

"Will you not fight for your King?" asked Charles.

Mr. Shuckburgh raised his troubled eyes and looked at the man above him. Charles was smiling. His dark eyes had come alive in his face and the charm that had won so many to love him took Mr. Shuckburgh captive. "I will, sir," he said. "Give me leave to take these dawgs home and I'll be back, with what men I can muster. Where shall I find you, sir?"

"I lie tonight at the home of Mr. Toby Chauncey at Edgecott," said the King. "Join me there in the morning."

Mr. Shuckburgh bowed and drew back and the cavalcade rode on. No one had any doubts as to the loyalty of Mr. Shuckburgh. In these matters the King had a sure instinct. The sun went down and the north wind was edged with sharper cold. In the deepening shadows they came to the manor-house of Edgecott, grey and remote under the great elms, but glowing with firelight and candlelight. Within, with the doors shut and the curtains drawn against the wind, with food and warmth and welcome, the spirits of the young men soared again and the older men thought of the morrow with resolution. Mr. Shuckburgh had seemed a happy omen.

Francis lay that night in the King's room, wrapped in his cloak, on a pallet bed stretched across the doorway, while the King, who had removed only his armour, lay sleepless in the great curtained bed. On a table beside him lay, as always, his two watches and his silver bell. His wax lamp burned in a basin at the foot of his bed. Francis knew he was sleepless because of the quality of the silence in which he lay, not like that of either sleep or death, with neither rest nor forgetfulness in it. Francis could not sleep either, strung up as he was by the tenseness of the King's silence. Against it he heard the noises of the night, the moan of the north wind, the scurrying of mice in the wainscot, the creaking as the timbers of the old house stretched and settled themselves again after the coming and going of many men, the occasional movements of the sentry outside the door and the friendly murmur of the wood fire on the hearth. Somewhere outside in the night were fourteen thousand men, sleeping in out-houses and barns, cottages and stables, on the leeward side of ricks, around bivouac fires lit in sheltered places and in deep ditches covered with the autumn leaves. The sentries were alert, guarding the guns, and somewhere Rupert and his scouts were on the watch. And somewhere too another army was encamped under the stars, some of them sleeping, some of them waiting sleepless, as he and the King were waiting, for what the morning would bring.

There was a clock somewhere below in the great house and he counted the hours. Midnight. Now it was Sunday morning.

One o'clock. Two o'clock. Soon after that came the first eerie cock-crow of the false dawn, and then the sound of a cantering horse. Francis heard a movement and saw that the King had left his bed. "Light the candles," he said.

"Sir, it may be nothing. Do not disturb yourself yet."

"Do as I say."

Francis lit the candles on the sconces round the wall, threw fresh logs on the fire and stirred it to a blaze. The King put a comb through his long hair, settled the jewels in his ears and glanced at himself in the polished steel mirror, but he had lain so still that his clothes were not disordered. Then he sat in a high-backed chair, elegant and cool, his hands on the chair arms, his eyes studying the point of one shoe, only the slight twitching of a muscle in one cheek showing that this moment was different from any other. No one ever saw the King anything but calm and controlled.

The horse came nearer, and the beat of his hoofs, now loud and clear, now muffled by the sound of the wind, seemed to merge all at once into the sound of feet running upstairs and the challenge of the sentry outside the door. "Let him come in," called the King.

It was Mr. Toby Chauncey himself, fully dressed as were most men in the house that night, with dispatches from Rupert. The King read them. "I will hold a council of war here in this room at once," he said to Mr. Chauncey. In a few moments his commanders were with him. Francis, standing behind the King's chair, listened with one half of his mind to what the King was saying, while the other half was absorbed in the beauty of the scene; the candlelight and firelight gleaming on the grave bearded faces, the rich crimson of the brocade bed-curtains and the bright hilts of the swords.

"The enemy are at Kineton, seven miles away," said the King. "We are thus between the enemy's field army and London. My nephew does not counsel a march on London with the enemy at our heels. He thinks we should give battle now and wishes me to march as quickly as possible to his support at Edgehill. The enemy will then be below us in the plain. What is your opinion, gentlemen?"

They were of Rupert's opinion, and after only a short discussion left the King to get a little rest before the morning broke. He wrote a letter to Rupert and then lay down again. The thought of the coming battle seemed to have brought him comfort. "Francis," he said, "If I can win an overwhelming victory it will end it. If God will grant me victory today, my people will be spared the misery of a long war. I have a righteous cause and a just God in Whom I put my trust." And then he slept, and did not wake until Francis drew back the curtains and let in the first light of the dawn.

2

While the King slept, Robert, with a couple of his men behind him, was riding through the narrow lanes carrying dispatches from Colonel Hampden to Lord Essex, Parliamentary commander-in-chief at Kineton. Colonel Hampden and his Greencoats, with the baggage-train, had been delayed by various mishaps. They were making what haste they could, but he wanted Lord Essex to know that they were a day's march behind the main army. Robert rode fast through the winding lanes, his way lit by a fitful moon. The cold north wind stung his nose and ears and probed with icy fingers even through the thick cloak he wore. He rode virtually alone through a country where at any turn of the road he might encounter the enemy's scouts and get a bullet in his chest. He thought that open battle might be better than this; you could at least see what came at you.

But the hours passed and no harm befell him. Just at dawn he found himself at the edge of a little wood, uncertain of the way. He and his men dismounted, for the lane they had followed had petered out into a rough track through the wood and now it ended in a stubble-field. Except for an occasional sigh in the trees everything was still, grey and cold, the flat fields rolling away shrouded in mist, until they lost themselves in the shadow of the great hill that reared its long crest against the sky as if it were a vast tidal wave. For a moment Robert almost cringed, feeling that it might indeed come roaring down upon him. He was exhausted and his mind was playing strange tricks. "Can this be Edgehill?" he asked one of his men. He had heard strange tales of Edgehill. Once, men said, the land had ended at that vast cliff and the plain where he stood had been under the sea. Where the stubble-fields now stretched sea monsters had had their lairs and fish had woven in and out of the stems of oozy woods, and high above them little sea-horses had drifted through the blue water like flocks of small birds in the upper air. Looking at that terrible cliff, or wave, he could almost feel that the old days were back again.

"That's Edgehill, sir," said the man.

"Then we are not far from Kineton?" asked Robert.

"No, sir, but we've took the wrong turn. Kineton must be a mile or two behind us."

But they did not immediately turn back. They could not take their eyes from the great hill. Behind the crest of the cliff the sky was lightening. Up on the hilltop the north wind had carried away the mist and the skyline gradually became clear and black against burnished silver. Then it seemed to toss and waver as though black spray lifted against the silver. One man gave an exclamation and Robert stared amazed. "Sea-horses," he thought stupidly. Little sea-horses turned dusky by the night's enchantment had taken shape along the skyline and drifted there like blown spume before the wind. "Enemy scouts," said the man who had exclaimed.

Though it was not likely they could be seen in the misty valley, they drew back into the shadows of the wood. Without doubt it was the enemy. As the light strengthened they could see the plumed hats and the gleam of armour. They could see also the curved necks of the horses and their flying tails as they cantered along the crest of the hill, more and more of them, a whole company of horsemen, an unearthly frieze of dark beauty against the now brilliant sky.

"Not scouts, sir," said the other man excitedly. "Cavalry. Rupert's." He growled in his throat. "Trust Prince Robber to pick that hilltop before my Lord of Essex has had time to take his nightcap off."

"Hold your tongue," said Robert sharply. The dilatoriness of Essex, who hampered his own personal movements by carrying his coffin and winding-sheet wherever he went and those of his army by a too-careful taking thought for all eventualities, was well known to his men, but not to be commented upon by the rank and file. "Kineton as fast as we can." Then he wheeled his horse round and rode quickly back into the wood, his men behind him. Once beyond the wood and back on the right road they flogged their tired horses to a canter. If the army was still asleep it must be wakened quickly.

It was full daylight when they galloped into Kineton and found the little village the centre of a vast military camp. Trumpets were sounding, camp-fires were alight, horses were being fed and watered and breakfasts were being cooked, but all in a leisurely manner vastly removed from that frieze of black horses along the edge of the hill. Robert reined in his tired horse, jumped from it and accosted the cavalry officer strolling towards him.

"Sir, I must speak with my Lord of Essex at once."

"Dispatches from Colonel Hampden?" asked the officer, eyeing Robert's green coat.

"Yes, sir, but more than that. The enemy cavalry are taking up their position on Edgehill."

The officer began to run, Robert after him. They ran down the village street to a house where a sentry stood on guard before a door. The officer spoke to him and they were admitted. They went down the passage within and another sentry admitted them to a low panelled room where the commander-in-chief sat with his chief officers. The room seemed to spin round Robert as he stood before the Earl, handed him Colonel Hampden's dispatches and told him his news. He was so tired that he stumbled over the words. Then a hand gripped his arm, the fingers biting into his flesh like steel, and a harsh voice began to rap out questions. Out of the sea of faces one came close to him, peering into his own, the strong ugly face of Oliver Cromwell, the great beak of a nose red with anger, the keen eyes snapping. Abruptly he let go of Robert's arm and turned to the courteous elderly gentleman behind the table. "My Lord, we must act at once. Drive the cavalry off the crest before the main army joins them."

"The main army are probably there already," said the Earl suavely. "Let us do nothing hastily, Colonel Cromwell. If we must accept battle let it be on no disadvantage of ground. We will hold a council of war at once. Captain Haslewood, send one of your men back to Colonel Hampden, bidding him make all possible speed."

"I'll go myself, my Lord," said Robert. A wild hope was in him. If he rode back to Hampden he might miss the battle.

"No!" said Cromwell, before the Earl could speak. "We need every good officer we can lay our hands on. The army is an untrained rabble." His voice rose to an almost hysterical trumpet note. "This battle has come too soon, but the God of Hosts will not desert His people."

"Captain Haslewood, you will despatch one of your men to Colonel Hampden as I bade you," said the Earl; "take a little rest yourself and then give us the benefit of your services. Colonel Cromwell, the enemy are as inexperienced as we are. I pray God we may have a great victory. Decisive victory now would end the war and prevent incalculable suffering."

Upon the sadness of his tone Robert and his companion closed the door behind them. Probably they were saying the same thing in the enemy camp, Robert thought wearily.

"My lodging is next door," said the officer, hustling Robert down the passage. "I'll get you food and leave you to rest while I get my men together. Then I'll fetch you, for I'll be glad of your help with my troop. As Colonel Cromwell said, we're an untrained rabble. How we'll stand up against Rupert's cavalry God only knows." But he spoke quickly and cheerfully, his face flushed and his eyes sparkling. The expectation that was in Robert a paralysing coldness creeping through his body seemed in this man to be a dancing fire. "Why?" thought Robert. "Why am I not as other men in this matter of war?"

A little later, having done his best to swallow some cold meat, bread and ale, he was lying on a hard straw mattress in the garret of a small cottage. He had taken off his boots and his cuirass and covered himself with his cloak, but sleep was out of the question. He lay staring up at the rotting thatch above him. Why had his first fight to come upon him like this? If he could have faced it with his wits about him, and his body in good shape, he might have had a chance of acquitting himself well. What chance had he now, aching, sleepless and weary? What damnable luck! Could he get out of it? No! *Vestigia nulla retrorsum.* He had committed himself. If cowards could find no joy in battle they could at least cling to commitment and drag themselves, like a man on a ladder, from one hand-hold to another of the things that honour compelled them to do. He thought of his children, standing in the blue door at the top of the hill, and then for no apparent reason he thought suddenly of the young man who had painted that excellent likeness of his son. He had seldom been so attracted to anyone as he had been to that young man. Well, he was out of it, jogging along some country lane on his pony, his saddle-bag full of canvases, brushes and paints, or else sitting on a fence admiring the landscape and smoking his pipe. He could have sat on a fence too, John Hampden had given him the chance. He could have been at home in his garden, tidying up the autumn flower-borders. Did he want it? No. All about him now was an increasing roar of sound, horses cantering up the village street, men marching and singing and trumpets sounding. The flimsy cottage where he lay shook as the gun-teams went by. The web of sound gathered about him and took him prisoner. He felt that same sensation of being lifted and carried forward that he had felt in the council room at Broughton. It was the movement not only of history but of his own life. In a moment he was on his feet and buckling on his armour. His throat was dry and his fingers fumbled at the buckles, but he had not now the slightest desire to be left behind. When his friend came bounding up the rickety stairs to fetch him he was ready, his orange scarf, badge of a Parliament man, crossing his breast above the bright cuirass, his pistol in his holster and his sword at his side. Every trace of weariness had left him.

CHAPTER II

EDGEHILL

I

By the middle of the morning the whole Royalist army was in position on the crest of the hill, the infantry in the centre and the cavalry on either wing. The King's tent was pitched in the centre and he stood before it, with the two young Princes and his bodyguard around him, watching the enemy marching into position on the plain below. He wore silver armour with a black velvet surcoat and the Collar of the George hung round his neck. Over his head the wind lifted the rich folds of the Royal Standard. Beside it was his standard-bearer, Sir Edmund Verney, his face sombre and still. He was a Puritan, but he loved Charles. He had lately written to his friend Edmund Hyde: "My conscience is only concerned in honour and gratitude to follow my master. I have eaten his bread, and served him nigh thirty years, and will not do so base a thing as forsake him; and choose rather to lose my life (which I am sure I shall do) to preserve and defend those things which are against my conscience to maintain and defend." The King looked calm and almost cheerful and there was not one of the men about him who did not believe that in a few hours' time they would have won this fight. As far as they could tell, the two armies were numerically much the same, but they had superior cavalry. And the enemy, when they attacked, would have to advance uphill. And above all they had Rupert.

" 'Tis a fair view," murmured the King.

It was one of the grandest in England. The day was still grey and cheerless, but it was now clear of mist and from where they stood they could see right across to the Welsh hills. To the right was Tysoe church among the trees and to the left the Vale of the Red Horse, with the figure of the horse cut in the cliff above. Knowing the strength of their cavalry, that horse seemed to many of them a good omen. Down below was a chequer-board of meadows and shorn harvest-fields, with the road winding through them towards the roofs and church tower of Kineton, and marching up this road, and deploying to either side of it, were the enemy. In the clear air they could see the regimental banners and the glint of light on the helmets and cuirasses of the pikemen. Francis imagined he could make out the huge weapons of the musketeers and the heavy bandoliers across their chests, but this imagination was unusually vivid this morning. The grey uniformity that Cromwell was later to insist upon had not yet submerged the army, regiments were still distinguished by their colours, and everywhere was the bright gleam of the Essex orange scarves. The army might have been an autumn wood upon the march. The wind brought with it the rumbling of the gun-teams and the sound of cheering. An hour passed like a few minutes and the army was in position, well out of range of the King's guns. Then came stillness and silence, and creeping eerily into it the sound of the church bells of Tysoe and Kineton ringing their people to prayer. Then they too were silent and the only movement to be seen down below was that of the Puritan preachers going up and down the ranks to pray with their men. Francis had forgotten it was Sunday. He crossed himself and then put his hand within his surcoat. Hanging round his neck on a chain was a little relic which his father had given him. He fingered it, murmuring an Ave. For a brief moment he thought of Jenny, and saw her face smiling at him through the hedge when he said goodbye. Then he remembered her father, his enemy. Was he down there? Was one of those orange scarves bound over Robert's beating heart, as his own blue scarf was crossed over his that pounded with excitement? When the blue scarves met the orange it would be as though the sky fell over the autumn woods.

The King had called a council of war and was going into his tent, followed by his two sons, his commander-in-chief, old Lord Forth, Sir Jacob Astley, commander of the infantry, Lord Lindsey and the others. Rupert, his white poodle Boy at his heels, chose to saunter last into the tent, arrogant and splendid, his great height dwarfing the men about him. He turned his head as he went in and Francis saw his face, thoughtful and austere with straight nose and thrusting lower lip. Rupert was a thruster. It was his good looks alone that made him a romantic figure, for there was nothing romantic about his temperament. He was a professional soldier concentrated upon work only. In his leisurely stride there was concealed impatience, for these old men, Forth and Astley and Lindsey, drove him mad, and so had his uncle just lately, with his perpetual bargaining for peace. But he was only twenty-three and when his eyes met those of Francis a grin spread over his face. Not much longer now; he would see to it that caution did not get the better of these old fogies. The tent-flap dropped behind him and the young men about Francis broke into eager talk.

It was easy to see what was happening. The cautious Essex was not going to advance uphill. There would be no battle to-day unless they abandoned their splendid position and went down into the plain to meet him. "We cannot march away from the rebels," said the excited young men about the King's Standard. "We must go down."

The King was soon back. "I shall give them battle," he said.

In a short time the whole army was moving, with all possible speed, for if Essex were to attack while they were struggling down the hill it would go ill with them. Charles and his commanders had put their trust in Essex's well-known hatred for sudden offensives, but even so they spent a terrible hour hauling their guns down the hill with the infantry scrambling where they could and the cavalry making their way down the steep rutted road. But Essex made no move, and by early afternoon the whole of the King's army was marching to battle stations.

"O Lord," cried old Sir Jacob Astley aloud as his men gathered behind him, "Thou knowest how busy I must be this day. If I forget Thee do not Thou forget me. March on, boys!"

When the men were drawn up in position the King rode from regiment to regiment, and the cheering roared down the lines. The cavalry, commanded by Rupert on the right wing and Lord Wilmot on the left, fretted and chafed, their harness jingling and rattling as the horses neighed and tossed their heads. Then came a maddening delay, the King's commanders insisting that he take up a place of safety on the slope of the hill, behind the army and not in the midst of it. He resisted, then gave in. Cursing under their breath, his young bodyguard had to turn and ride back with him. "O God," groaned Francis, "I'd give my immortal soul to be with Rupert." He was almost weeping as he wheeled round again and looked out over the two armies below. It was a spectacle of great beauty. A faint gleam of sun lit rank upon rank of shining armour, tossing plumes and restless horses, blue scarves and orange scarves, shining forests of tall pikes and huge muskets, and guns crouching like beasts low to the earth, their gunners beside them with flares in their hands. The blood in his veins seemed to have turned to fire, and the body of his horse too seemed a body of impatient fire between his knees. It was three o'clock in the afternoon, and the guns roared out. When they were silent the trumpets sounded and Rupert's cavalry wheeled in to the charge.

Francis could have kept his station if they had not yelled as they rode, and if his own horse had not neighed and reared up madly. He could not hold it in, or he did not try to; he could not remember afterwards what happened between the moment when the trumpet sounded and the moment when he found himself galloping and yelling with Rupert's men. Those few minutes had seemed to fall right out of time. But that charge was something he never forgot; not even the horror of what came afterwards ever dimmed its brilliance in his memory. It seemed to him then, and ever afterwards, to be one of the most exciting things that ever happened to him. His spirit seemed to whirl out wings and flash to the very height of being. He wouldn't have cared if he had plunged from that height into the heart of darkness. He was utterly reckless. The speed, the pounding hoofs of the horses, the wind rushing by his ears, the unity that there was between his own body and that of his horse, the hot blood of the one seeming to rush into the veins of the other, was a oneness of intoxication. Bent low in his saddle he yelled with the rest, aware of the pale gold of the stubble-fields beneath them, of the silver and blue racing over it like the tide over the sand. But there was a cliff rising up before them, the bodies of men and horses, orange scarves crossing silver armour. "Have at them! King Charles! King Charles!" yelled Rupert. They dashed on without slackening speed and crashed into the living barrier. There was a brief bedlam of clashing arms and screaming horses, a swaying backwards and forwards of blue and orange, and the charge went on. It had scarcely checked at all. Riding as madly as their pursuers, the Parliament cavalry fled across the field towards Kineton. They were brave men, but a charge like this was something new in the history of war. Never before had men and horses been wielded by a genius of a commander into such an appalling battering-ram. And a strange and fearful thing had happened. Just as the yelling cavaliers came charging down upon them, a troop of their own horse suddenly left them, discharging their pistols on the ground, and wheeled round to join the enemy. They were a troop raised by Sir Faithful Fortescue to fight for the King in Ireland, and then conscripted to fight against him. But Sir Faithful had bided his time and led his men back again to their true allegiance.

For Francis there had been no check at all, for he and the men about him had seemed to cleave through the barrier like a scythe through grass. And then it seemed to him that he was alone, pursuing one man alone across the plain. He could see the poor wretch bent low over his horse's neck, riding for his life, see the torn end of his orange scarf streaming out behind him. But there was no pity in Francis, only a savage and cruel exultation. He was gaining on his enemy. In another minute he'd be slashing at him, he'd have him down. He pounded on and was almost on top of him, his sword-arm raised, when the man looked round, his exhausted face grey with terror, blood trickling from a cut on his forehead and dripping off his chin, his mouth open and his eyes staring. Yet even in his distress Francis recognised Robert Haslewood; it was scarcely recognition, it was more like a flash of intuition, of warning. He swerved aside, yet even so they jostled each other, their eyes meeting in mutual hatred. Francis galloped on, aware of a feeling of sickness. He did not know where he was going. He only knew he had left the other behind and could not stop his horse.

He became aware again that he and the other were not alone in this plain, that there were galloping horses all about him and that the charge had become a rout. He heard Rupert's voice shouting angrily, "Stop! Get back, you fools, get back!" He saw the tall figure of the Prince on his huge black horse, his face congested with anger as he tried to get his men back to the battle behind them. To unleash such a charge was one thing, to stop it was another. Francis was one of the very few who understood that victory was in danger of turning into disaster. He managed to get control of his horse, wheeled round, and rode with Rupert back into the fearful fight behind them.

2

From his post of observation on the hilltop, the young Princes and his bodyguard beside him, the King watched the battle open according to the accepted pattern, which had altered little in centuries of warfare. The artillery duel, which with so few cannon as he and the enemy possessed could do little damage, was a modern accretion and nothing more than the overture. The next step was the advance of the infantry, to become locked in a clinch with the enemy infantry, and the simultaneous charge of the cavalry upon the flanks. The cavalry were all-important. Their aim was to drive the enemy cavalry off the field, wheel round and attack the enemy infantry in the rear. If they could do this the battle was as good as won. So important was the cavalry charge that a large reserve of cavalry was kept in hand, to charge a second time if the first failed.

"Three o'clock," thought the King. "Only two hours of daylight. If it is to be done it must be done quickly."

The trumpets sounded and the battle began. The roar of the guns was followed by the rattle of musket-fire, then a pause as the musketeers drew back behind the pikemen to reload, then musket-fire again and the rolling forward of both masses of infantry. Meanwhile the cavalry under Rupert and Lord Wilmot had charged. Rupert had transformed the cavalry charge. He had trained his men to ride home at the gallop without halting to fire their pistols, which was the usual practice. They themselves, not their firearms, were to be the weapons. The King watched Rupert's men ride off with a sense of trust in Rupert, but he looked towards the left with more anxiety, for Lord Wilmot was an undependable young man. His men charged magnificently, but the King noted that they had ridden at the easiest target, a detached troop of enemy horse, not at the main body, as they had been told to do. Then the King was aware of a further failure of discipline. The cavalry reserve commanded by Sir John Byron, a man as wild and hot-headed as Lord Wilmot, and many of his young bodyguard, following Francis's bad example, were galloping off without permission. Nevertheless as he looked down over the field the battle seemed going well, for the Parliament cavalry were streaming away towards Kineton, hunted by Rupert and Wilmot on either side, and the infantry, his standard in their midst, were pressing the enemy steadily back. It was going well. It was going magnificently well.

Then, looking to that dangerous left, he saw a large troop of enemy horse on the move. They were the men whom Wilmot should have attacked and had not, and the reserve who, unlike his own men, had obeyed orders. They wheeled round and charged the flank and rear of his infantry. And his own cavalry were lost to him. They were no more than blown autumn leaves far away on the plain. Suddenly a fearful change came over the whole battle. The Royalist infantry gave way against the unexpected cavalry charge, and the Parliament infantry attacked afresh, confident now of victory. The King saw his standard swaying above the fight, and wondered how it fared with Edmund Verney fighting down there for love of him. Then the standard fell.

No man in the King's domains had a higher courage than his own. In a short while he was where his standard had been. The silk had been torn away and captured by the enemy, but the staff lay on the trampled earth, still held in the severed hand of Sir Edmund Verney. All about the King was a fearful scene of carnage, for his raw untrained troops, facing their first battle, had taken terrible punishment. Lord Lindsey had been mortally wounded and his son captured, but Lord Forth and Sir Jacob Astley survived, and two regiments, the Prince of Wales's and the Duke of York's, who had not taken the first shock, came in from the right and fought mightily about the King. The two young Princes, left behind on the hillside with Boy the poodle, watched their own regiments defend their father with bursting pride, and watched once more the turning of the tide, not quickly this time, but slowly and inevitably. For Essex had used his last reserves. The tremendous resurgence of courage and resolution that had flared about the cool and gallant figure of the King was something he had no more strength to combat, and the Royalist cavalry whom Rupert had been able to lead back from the charge were fighting with all the more fury because they were so few and so late. The Parliament troops drew back over the mounds of the dead. They had had enough.

"One more charge," cried Rupert, riding with Falkland backwards and forwards across the field, trying to gather together the scattered cavalry. "One more charge. Have at them once more and we win the day."

But not even Rupert, not even the King, could rouse their men to fight any longer. Darkness was coming upon them. There was confusion everywhere. Officers had lost their men, and men could not find their officers. The horses that still lived were foundered. They had time now to see the dead, and the badly wounded who had not yet been able to die. Even the intransigent Lord Wilmot could do no more. "My Lord," he said to Falkland, "we've got the day. Let us live to enjoy the fruits of it."

But they had not got the day, nor the fruits of peace that Charles had so desperately hoped for. The two amateur armies had fought a fine battle for their first, but neither side had won it, and the fruits of it could be nothing but continued fighting. Under cover of the darkness the two armies drew back to their original positions, the Parliament men to Kineton and the King's men once more to the crest of the great hill.

3

"Which seems like home to us now," murmured Francis. He was one of the favoured few who sat with the King, Rupert, Boy and the young Princes about the camp-fire on the heights. All round them the dark moonless night was studded with these fires, but no singing came from them and only occasionally the low growl of voices. The men were too exhausted to sing. They wanted only to eat and rest. The horses too were still and motionless. Here and there they could be seen against the glow of fire, their weary heads hanging. The King and those with him were glad of the warmth of the flames, for the north wind was blowing keenly and it was freezing. "Thank heaven for the cold," said Rupert. "It will save many a poor fellow down there from gangrene."

It was the first remark he had made for a long time, for he was eating his heart out with frustration and furious anger with Wilmot, who had not backed him up when he had tried to rouse the men to charge again. Victory had been within their grasp then and they had flung it away. What could a man do with these amateur soldiers who stopped fighting because they were tired? Did they think war was a game of golf? And those cavalry of his, he thought he'd trained them better than that. He'd dinned it into them often enough that to drive the enemy horse off the field was not an end in itself; the double back and the attack on the enemy's flank were what they were there for. But they'd gone on galloping hell for leather over the plain as though they had meant to gallop over the edge of the world. Partly inability to stop and partly loot, he supposed. Plenty of loot at Kineton. When would he learn that loot is as much a part of any soldier's bloodstream, be he amateur or professional, as are courage and loyalty? And they could not try again next day, for Colonel Hampden had arrived at Kineton with two fresh regiments. They had no fresh regiments, they had thrown in all they had. Nothing to do now but lick their wounds quickly and march on London while Essex was slowly licking his.

Francis looked down into the great pool of darkness below. Small glow-worm lights were moving there, where men were giving what help they could to the wounded. The pall of darkness studded with those twinkling lights would have been beautiful had one been able to forget the agony it covered. All joy in battle had long ago fallen from him. He was unhurt, and he he had acquitted himself well, but he was more wretched than he had ever been. He had seen many cruel things in his life. He had seen Strafford lose his head and Father Ward pay the penalty of his courage at Tyburn, but in the fight that was just over he had seen more fearful sights than these. Yet what was haunting him most was the mutual hatred with which he and Robert Haslewood had looked at each other when he spared his life. There was reason for Robert's hatred; under cover of apparent friendship he had entered the man's house as a spy. His own momentary hatred had been, he supposed, for the detestable reason that men do often hate those whom they have injured because they make them feel despicable.

"Have they found Verney's body yet?" asked the King.

"No, sir," said Rupert.

The King roused himself and began talking cheerfully of incidents in the battle that were good to think of now. The courage of young Charles and James and the imperturbable way in which Boy had guarded them. Old Astley's prayer. The knighting upon the field of battle of Mr. Shuckburgh, who had duly turned up with his men and fought with savage enjoyment. And last of all there was the fact of his own preservation, when he had stood where his standard had been and not one of the musket-balls that whistled round him had touched him. This, he thought, was an omen that God was on his side. His exquisite charm played over them and he had them happy before he went to rest in his tent. Francis, when he lay down wrapped in his cloak beside the fire, was able to forget Robert and fall asleep.

CHAPTER III

THE ROYAL STANDARD

I

In the upper room of a Kineton farm-house Colonel Hampden sat working at a rough table, papers strewn before him. He and his Greencoats, though they had made all haste with the baggage-train, had arrived too late for the battle, but not too late to defend the field base of Kineton from the attack by the Royalist cavalry who had not turned back with Rupert. He had driven them off and they had not had their loot. Now his men, exhausted with the long march, were sleeping, and he himself free to forgo sleep and grapple with business. He was not by temperament a fighting man, in spite of his great courage, but he could handle all questions of finance and organisation with wisdom and clearsightedness. He was not a man of divided loyalties like Essex, he was convinced of the righteousness of his cause and had already suffered much for it, nor was he cold and impersonal like Pym; he loved men and was loved by them. And he was no fanatic. A devout but tolerant Puritan, he was not attracted by the harsh creed of the Independents that appealed so strongly to his cousin Oliver Cromwell. The name that he had already earned for himself, the Patriot, described him well. He had no axe to grind. He loved England. His integrity and idealism shed a light upon his cause which was a beacon to many.

Another half-hour of concentration and his mind was suddenly weary. He put his papers together, laid down his pen and went to the window. The house was at the end of the village and looked out over the plain below Edgehill. In the windy darkness he could see the lights glimmering over the battlefield, and far off the glow of the King's camp-fires. Sadness fell upon him. That great battle and no decision. What would be the end of it all? Would he live to see it and would he want to see it if he did live? He shivered in the cold air from the ill-fitting window and drawing back into the room became conscious of the sounds of the night: the whine of the wind round the house, the beat of the sentry's feet below the window, the heavy breathing of exhausted men asleep in the hayloft which opened out of his room. Now and then there was a stifled groan. Only a small proportion of the badly wounded had as yet been brought in, and they were at the further end of the village, but a few of the men sleeping in the house, his own Greencoats, had slight wounds. Who was that man groaning? He opened the communicating door and went in, carrying his candle, shading its light with his hand. The loft was full of men lying where they had dropped in exhaustion. The loft was bitterly cold, but the atmosphere was foul and stuffy, catching Hampden by the throat. The groans had stopped when he entered, but he soon found one man who was not sleeping. He was lying on his back in the hay staring up at a hole in the roof. In spite of the blood-stained bandage round his head Hampden recognised him at once and remorse stabbed him. He had sent Robert Haslewood on ahead with dispatches and then in all the turmoil of subsequent events had neglected to find out what had happened to him.

"Robert, you fool!" he exclaimed, for the instinctive reaction of even his great mind was immediately to put the blame on another. "What are you doing in this foul den? Why didn't you call out to me? What a fool you are, Robert. You're not badly hurt, are you?"

"No," said Robert dully. "Only a scalp wound."

"Then get up, man, and come to my room next door."

He helped Robert to his feet, took him to his room and made him lie down on his bed, covering him with his cloak. He took wine and bread from a tray that had been brought for himself and made him eat and drink a little. "What happened, Robert?" he asked gently. But Robert, though he did as he was told with the docility of a child, would not or could not answer. Hampden let him alone, hoping he would sleep, and went back to his work.

He was immersed in it again when he heard the challenge of the sentry below his window, and then someone leaping up the steep stairs. The door was flung violently open and a tall cloaked figure entered. Something hurtled through the air and fell upon Hampden's table on top of his papers: a bundle of rich silk, torn, bloodstained and dirty. He looked up from it to see his cousin Noll Cromwell towering above him, his fists resting on the table, his eyes glaring down into his. He was immensely relieved, for he had not been able to find out how Noll had fared in the battle. He was even relieved to find him in the grip of one of the blind furies that did at times take hold of him, for only an uninjured man could have been possessed of such rage an energy.

"Sit down, Noll," he said, though knowing his cousin incapable at present of such a course. He lifted a fold of the silk and his candle gleamed on the golden lions of England. He dropped it again and said with awe, "The Royal Standard. I did not know we had it."

Colonel Cromwell's powerful face was congested with anger and the intensity of his feeling, his big ugly nose blotched with purple, his eyes bloodshot. "The standard is all we have got," he said thickly. "We've not got victory. I tell you, John, we could have had it three times over. If that fool Essex had attacked Rupert's cavalry on the heights, before the main army joined them. If he had attacked them when they were struggling down the hill to the plain. If our cavalry could have held against Rupert's cavalry." He paused, breathing hard, and his fist came down upon the table. "The cavalry, John. There's the crux. You, Essex, Pym, you command this army, I command a mere troop of your horse, but take it not ill what I say, without cavalry to match Rupert's you will not win this war. We can copy his tactics, give him a taste of his own medicine, use men and horses like a battering-ram as he did today, only if we have men of a like temper with his. And what are our troops? Old decayed serving-men, tapsters and such kind of fellows. Do you think the spirit of such base and mean fellows will ever be able to encounter gentlemen that have honour and courage? You must gét men of a like spirit, of a spirit that is likely to go as far as gentlemen will, or else you will be beaten still."

Hampden said, "You could forge cavalry of such spirit, Noll."

"I could forge an army of such a spirit," said Colonel Cromwell.

The rage had spent itself, but he still stood towering over Hampden. He moved and the candlelight sent his tall shadow leaping up over the ceiling. Hampden was oppressed by the great shadow, the brooding presence.

"Sit down, Noll," he said again, impatiently.

This time Cromwell obeyed him, but Hampden was in no better case, for now it was his cousin's eyes that tormented him, intolerably blue and deeply penetrating. They seemed to transfix him, as though he were an owl nailed up on a barn door, even though he realised that they were not even seeing him.

"Men who would obey me like my own sword in my hand," said Cromwell. "My colonels would be butchers' sons and my sergeants men from the plough. The rank and file could be the scum of the earth for all I'd care, but I'd forge such a spirit in 'em that for fighting power they'd be the equal of any gentlemen upon the face of the earth." His face hardened. "These young men, these sons of the noble houses, they're few. Those born valorous are always few. They go first and fall quickly. You're left with the rank and file who learn their valour under the cat and gallows threat. But they're tough. They last and they breed. Discipline 'em, teach 'em to make a conscience of what they do, and you'd have an army that would win the war."

Both men were silent. Hampden was realising afresh what he had always known : that Noll Cromwell, hitherto so clumsy, so unhappy, so unsuccessful in much that he had attempted, was one of those men whom war reveals as of greater stature that they or anyone else had dreamed of. Cromwell was silent because he was suddenly dog tired. Hampden had forgotten and Cromwell had never noticed the man lying on the bed. They were both startled when Robert's almost spectral figure appeared beside them. His eyes had the glitter of fever and his limbs were shaking so much that he had to prop himself on the table with both hands.

"It would take more than the cat and the threat of the gallows to make a valorous man out of me," he said to Cromwell. "You saw me. You know." He spoke tauntingly, his voice rising hysterically, and raising his fist he shook it in Cromwell's face.

"He's delirious," said Hampden.

Cromwell got up, seized Robert's wrist and held it, looking at him steadily. A smile of extraordinary sweetness flashed across his face. He could show at times the cruelty of a bigot, he could impose his will on others at whatever cost of suffering, but his complex nature was not without a noble pity and understanding of men.

"I saw you," he said, "and I tell you that even out of *you* I can make a man of iron." He dropped Robert's wrist and pointed to the mound of torn silk lying on the table. "I must deliver that rubbish to my Lord of Essex. You can bring it to me in the morning. Now go and lie down. Good night, John." He stalked from the room, and the spurs that he still wore clattered on the stairs as he ran down them.

Robert went back to the bed and lay down. When ten minutes later Hampden went to look at him he was deeply asleep. Hampden smiled. Noll had given his orders to Robert as though he were his to command. Well, let him command Robert if it was for the man's good. The thought came to him, "he must increase and I must decrease", and he accepted it without bitterness.

There was no room on the narrow bed for himself as well as Robert. He fetched some straw from the loft next door, spread it on the floor and lay down upon it. He was abominably cold and also extremely hungry, but Robert had had the last of the bread and wine. He remembered with a quirk of humour that he was a millionaire. Certainly war was no respecter of persons. How was the King faring up on the windy height? Suddenly he remembered the Royal Standard. He pulled it from the table, spread its heavy silken folds over him and went to sleep.

2

Colonel Cromwell, unlike his cousin, had the ability to command comfort. He had slept well upon a mattress of goose-feathers and was now finishing a breakfast of bread, eggs and ale in the pleasant parlour of a petrified old lady whose house he had commandeered the night before. After a few hours' sleep he had risen before dawn and had prayed for an hour. The Lord had granted him much consolation and the knowledge that he was a chosen instrument for the Lord's work. What if this first battle had been indecisive? There would be other battles. The army was the Lord's, doing the work of the Lord, and the Lord would not desert His people. Nor, he was convinced, would the Lord delay much longer in removing the Earl of Essex from the command of His army. The conviction had come to him while he prayed that the elimination of Essex was only a matter of time, and the thought had brought great peace to his soul. His servant came in and told him that an officer of Colonel Hampden's wished to see him. "Bring him in," said Cromwell.

A moment later Robert stood before him, the Royal Standard rolled up inder his arm. "Put it here," said Cromwell, clearing a place on the table. "And sit down."

Robert did as he was told, but Cromwell made no attempt to look at the standard again. He and his men had captured it yesterday and he had thought John might like to see it before he delivered it to Essex, but it meant nothing to him. It was Robert who, last night, had meant something to him. Robert had seemed a symbol of all the terrified undisciplined fellows who must be given strength and valour if they were to be of the slightest use to the Lord. He had felt that he had to get his hands on him. "I know your face," he said. "Apart from yesterday, have I seen you before?"

"At a meeting at Broughton, sir," said Robert.

"I remember you now," said Cromwell. "I remember that I marked you particularly. There was that in your face which made me aware that upon that occasion you felt much zeal for the cause."

Robert's blanched face went scarlet, but he said steadily, "And I feel it still, sir."

A change had come over him since last night. He had managed to get hold of a clean bandage and had spruced up his uniform. He was ashamed, weak and wretched, but he was doing the best that he could, holding himself well and keeping his hands steady, and his eyes clung to Cromwell's like those of a dog to his master's. Cromwell's firm grip last night, his kindness and certainty, had in some way integrated him. In the midst of his weakness he felt the beginning of a new strength, not the inspiration that Hampden's integrity had given him, and would give him again, but a sort of stubbornness. He might be a fool and a coward, fool enough to take a spy into his house and give him military information, craven enough to set the men he led an example of flight in battle, but even weak fools can manage to hold on if strength is given to them, and the man in front of him had given him strength. If he could be always with him, he would not fail again.

"I wish I could serve in your troop, sir," he said hungrily.

"Certainly not," said Cromwell curtly. "You will remain where the Lord has placed you and serve Him in His strength."

Suddenly his blue eyes kindled. He put his arms on the table and leaned forward. Within him he felt that deep glow and tremor, that movement of the spirit, that since those days of dereliction, of repentance and new birth that now lay two years behind him in his life, was more and more transforming him from the clumsy ineffective man he had been to the inspired leader that he would be. Unconscious of himself, with persuasive and winning charm, he spoke to Robert of the strength of the Lord, of zeal for the Lord and abandonment to His service. Within a mere twenty minutes he had transformed a weak and malleable young man into a disciple almost as fanatical for the cause as he was himself.

3

Out in the street again, blinking stupidly in the sunshine that had banished yesterday's grey clouds, Robert found himself accosted by a tall young officer, rosy-cheeked, cheerful and smiling. The sun gleamed warmly on the orange Essex scarf that he wore prominently across his breast.

"I am from my Lord of Essex," he said courteously. "He has heard that the King's standard was captured in yesterday's battle. He wishes me to enquire which of his officers has it in his keeping and to bring it to him. Can you help me, sir?"

"Colonel Cromwell is about to take the Standard to my Lord of Essex," said Robert bemusedly, but pleased to be so much in the counsels of the great.

"Then if you will direct me to Colonel Cromwell I can save him the trouble," said the officer.

"He lodges in that house with geraniums in the window," said Robert. "And you will find him within."

The officer bowed, smiled at Robert with heart-warming friendliness, and walked to the house with the geraniums. He found the door ajar, went in, and knocked at the door of the little parlour. On being bidden to enter he did so, and saluted the large ugly man behind the table with as much respect as though he were the commander-in-chief himself.

"Colonel Cromwell, I come from my Lord of Essex. He sends you his felicitations upon the gallant part you played in yesterday's battle. He understands that the Royal Standard is in your keeping. It could be in no more trustworthy hands than yours, but it would give him much pleasure if it could be delivered to him. I was commanded to ask for it in his name. You will forgive me, sir, if I intrude upon you."

Cromwell had scarcely as yet returned to earth, and to that acuteness of mind that was his when earthbound. He did not know the officer by sight, but the young men about the commander-in-chief were not yet personally known to him. He was touched by the young man's deference. He also suffered from a twinge of conscience. Essex should have had the captured standard in his hands before this. He handed the standard to the officer with an apology to the Earl. The young man bowed and withdrew. Out in the village street again he found it a scene of confusion. The amateur army had not had time to sort itself out yet after its first battle. The wounded were still being brought in from the battlefield, men and horses were jammed together in the narrow way, some going in one direction and some in another. The young man with a bundle under his arm and an orange scarf across his chest was scarcely noticed as he threaded his way through the crowd. He came to the end of the village and found his horse where he had left it, tethered to an apple tree at the back of an orchard. Making a wide circuit to avoid the battlefield, he cantered fast through miry lanes to Edgehill. By noon that day Captain John Smith had delivered the Royal standard into the hands of the King.

CHAPTER IV

POSTMAN'S HORN

I

Two months had gone by since the battle of Edgehill, and on a cold December morning Parson Hawthyn had just finished setting his house to rights. He had made his bed, washed the pewter plate and leather mug that had held the crust of bread and the draught of ale he had had for his breakfast, swept the floor and dusted his books. Leaning his branch of broom against the wall he looked out at the day. It was a morning of mist and hoar-frost. Every twig and blade of grass had clothed itself in white samite, every spider's web was a delicate filigree of spun glass. The shining mist was thin, soon it would have slipped down from the sky to lie like lamb's wool on the distant woods; against it the sun hung like a pale gold shield on a silver curtain. It was an exquisite morning, but cold, and having thanked God for the beauty, Parson Hawthyn wondered if it was his duty for the children's sake to light a little fire. He was the village schoolmaster, as well as the parson, and every morning for an hour or so his room was crammed so tightly with small children that on all but the coldest mornings the proximity of their bodies gave them all the warmth they needed. But today it was indeed very cold. Parson Hawthyn's rheumatic joints were painful and his fingers numb. If a fire was necessary for the children's sake he would himself be very grateful for it. With the fair next week it would be a pity if any of them caught cold. They looked forward to the Christmas fair on the common from one year to another. He went out to his kitchen and brought in an armful of apple logs that Froniga had given him, and a basketful of fir-cones and dried moss, and knelt painfully down before the hearth.

He had just got the fire burning merrily when the garden gate creaked and the first of the children arrived. They gave shrill cries of delight when they saw it and held out their small podgy chilblained hands to the warmth, chirping like sparrows.

More and more children came stumping in, pummelling and shoving their way to the hearth until the space before the fire was one mass of solid child, so integrated and so excited that Parson Hawthyn feared he would never get it separated again into its component parts. He regretted his action. The coming fair was excitement enough without his having added to it a sweet-smelling, brightly coloured fire of cones and apple-wood.

"Children, fetch your benches from the kitchen," he said loudly above the hubbub, but no one took any notice. They were all little children. The bigger boys, if their parents were at all well-to-do, tramped the four miles to the Grammar School at Henley, in winter leaving their homes long before daylight and munching their breakfasts of bread and cheese as they went, and the sons of poor men started early to work on the land and herd the sheep. The bigger girls helped their mothers at home, spinning and carding wool, weaving and knitting stockings. Oxfordshire wool and cloth were famous not only in England but also on the Continent.

So it was well to get the little children out from under foot to the village school, whether they learned anything or not. They learned a good deal from Parson Hawthyn, in spite of the fact that in his old age he had lost the trick of discipline. He found it increasingly difficult to make himself heard, and his rare applications of a ruler to a pink palm did little to increase the pinkness. Applications of the flat of his hand to the sterns of little boys was equally ineffective as a punishment, for his rheumatic knees could not bear up beneath their wriggling weight and at the crucial moment their sterns would disappear from sight and he would look helplessly down at them giggling on the floor. But the children loved him and for love of him they would try to learn their letters and the Lord's Prayer from their horn books, and before they left school the more intelligent were able to repeat their catechism and grace before meat and to learn a few psalms and hymns and proverbs by heart. And they would listen to him spellbound while he read to them. When he read aloud from the Bible or from Spenser's *Faerie Queene* he had no difficulty in making himself heard. Even when they did not understand a word the magic of his voice held them still.

"Now, my dears; now, my dears," he said, trying to raise his voice above the hubbub. "Come now. If you will be good children and fetch the benches and con your lessons well you shall roast some chestnuts at the fire before you go."

This was a treat reserved for the days before Christmas. With fresh cries of delight they retreated from the fire. The little boys ran to fetch the benches and the little girls began to remove their hoods and cloaks and to shake out their bunchy skirts. Parson Hawthyn loved to watch them emerging from their wrappings and to see them in their sober little homespun skirts and bodices of grey or blue or brown. These were separate garments, for only gentlewomen might wear gowns all of one piece. Some of the skirts were patched and darned and the aprons they wore over them were none too clean, but the children were most of them healthy and rosy, for unless the harvest failed they did not go hungry. Their fathers might pasture their hogs upon the beechmast in the woods and gather firewood there, and all had their strip in the common field where they could sow barley and oats, peas and beans. Robert was a good squire, and in bad times Parson Hawthyn would starve himself rather than let a parishioner go hungry.

The boys came back with the little benches, made by Parson Hawthyn himself, and they were placed two for the boys on one side and two for the girls on the other. The children were packed upon them as tight as sardines and school began with the handing round of horn books and the recitation of the Lord's Prayer. Everybody knew that and the noise was very great. Catechism was almost as noisy, for though not all could answer the questions, those who could not were able to produce swishing noise by swinging their own legs, and squeaking noises by pinching their neighbours' legs. Then came more recitation. It was proverb day and proverbs were short and easy. "So much is mine as I possess and give, or lose, for God's sake," they piped shrilly. "He that can quietly endure overcometh. . . . All fear is bondage." Beyond the window the mist was thinning and some timid sunbeams slanted into the room and touched the children's heads. Carroty heads, gold, chestnut and nut-brown heads shone and gleamed; one seemed a smooth cap of silver gilt and another was aureoled with flame.

And then through the children's piping came threading the sound of a horn. At first it was so faint and far away that it seemed unearthly, like a fairy huntsman in the woods. At first only Parson Hawthyn heard it, and a thrill went through him, so lovely was the music, so fitting as an accompaniment to the children's voices and the shining day. Then the children heard the horn too. One by one their voices fell silent, though their mouths remained wide open with astonishment. Then their eyes sparkled and their cheeks grew pink with excitement. It was the post!

Tobias Shakerley, the postman, came so seldom that he was a figure of wonder and awe. Choosing a fine morning for delivery, he would come cantering up out of the valley from Henley, upon his piebald pony, clad in yellow and green like an elfin rider, with his mails upon his back and his horn slung over his shoulder. If he had a letter for any farm or manor he would wind his horn as he approached and everyone would drop whatever they were doing and run, for there might be a letter from that seafaring husband not heard of for two years, from a lover at the war or a young son at school. The letters, written so seldom and costing so much to send, would be long and detailed, for it would be some while before the writer could afford to send another. They would be read and re-read, carried about in the bodices of women's gowns, laid away in drawers upon sprigs of lavender, and then, when years had passed and there were enough of them, sewn into patchwork quilts or tied up in bundles with ribbon and laid away in secret recesses of escritoires. But they were never destroyed. They were more precious than gold and the man who brought them was a messenger from heaven.

"He'll have gone to the manor with a letter from Master Will," said Patsy Shandy excitedly.

"Noa!" said her brother scornfully. "Master Will he'll be back home for Christmas. He'd not waste good siller on a letter and him soon back home."

There was a burst of excited voices, then a period of intense listening as the children tried to make out the direction from which the horn was sounding now, then more thrilled conjecture. "He'll be at Farmer Rennie's to say his daughter's wed." . . . "Noa, he's at the manor. It'll be from Squire." . . . "But Squire's home." . . . "Noa! Squire ain't been home since Edgehill fight. That'll be from the Earl of Essex to say Squire's dead." Parson Hawthyn was as excited as any, but now he intervened. "My dears, my dears. It is nothing to do with us who has a letter and who has not. Let us see now if we can remember the twenty-third psalm. Patsy, let's see if you can say the first verse. Patsy, my dear!"

"The Lord is my shepherd," shrilled Patsy, then her voice rose almost to a scream, "Sir, sir, postman be coming here!"

"No, no, my dear," said Parson Hawthyn. "No one ever writes me a letter."

But now all the children were yelling together, and through their yells came the sound of a horse cantering and the shrill winding of the horn. Then with a flash of yellow and green Tobias Shakerley drew rein at the gate. In a moment all the children had surged out of the cottage, some through the window and some through the door, and were surrounding Tobias with wild excited cries. "Who be for? Parson? Who from? Where from? Lemme see it! Lemme hold it! Be Betsy Rennie wed? Be Squire dead? Be the war over? Lemme see! Who be for? Be there a seal on it? Lemme see seal! Lemme see!"

Parson Hawthyn reached over the children's heads and took the large square packet from Tobias Shakerley. It was tied with ribbon and heavily sealed. "Who be from, sir?" cried the children. Parson Hawthyn shook his head, for he did not know the writing.

"The seal might tell ee, sir," said Tobias helpfully. It was not his custom to ride on until he had found out all he could about the letters he had delivered.

Parson Hawthyn looked at the seal and saw the unicorn upon it. The Haslewood crest. He handed up a coin to Tobias, put the letter within the breast of his cassock and led the way back to the schoolroom. "Who be from, sir?" chorused the children. "Who be from?"

"I do not know," said Parson Hawthyn. "And I do not mean to read my letter until school is over. The twenty-third psalm, children, please. Beginning with Patsy, you will repeat a verse each. Now, Patsy, back to the first verse."

But school was disorganised by the excitement of the letter. The children could not remember the psalm, and when he tried to prompt them Parson Hawthyn could not remember it either, although he knew it so well he should have been able to repeat it in his sleep. The letter was like a leaden weight against his heart. It could not be from Will, for he would be home in a few days. Robert's handwriting he did not know, but why should Robert write to him? He feared that Robert was dead and that someone else, using his seal, had written the bad tidings to him that he might break them to Margaret. He knew there were bad tidings in the letter. He and the children abandoned the twenty-third psalm and tried the one hundred and twenty-first, but they fared no better. In the end there was nothing for it but to send the children home early. They were reluctant to go, without knowing what was in the letter and who it was from, but after he had divided the chestnuts amongst them to be roasted at home, and given them an apple each from the basketful Froniga had brought him for his own consumption, they were mollified and ran off munching and chattering, to pursue the sound of Tobias's horn all round the parish.

2

Parson Hawthyn drew up his chair to the fire and threw a few more fir-cones upon it, for he felt very cold. Then he took out his letter, broke the seal and drew out the many pages, written in a crabbed and rather childish hand, the fist of a man who does not write letters very often. He looked at the signature. Robert Haslewood. He broke out in a perspiration of relief, immediately as hot as before he had been cold. Robert was alive. He thanked God for it. But why should Robert be writing to him, and at such length? He felt uneasy and turned back again to the beginning of the letter. It was written from London and began,

"Reverend Sir, as I fear it may not be possible for me to return to the manor for Christmas I write you this letter in order to send you my greetings, wishing you joy and all the compliments of the season. Also, knowing how kind a concern you have for the welfare of the family, I think you may like to know how it has fared with me up to the present."

Parson Hawthyn paused to breathe a sigh of relief. His uneasiness had been unreasonable. This was a letter of friendship to rejoice his heart. He and Robert might not see eye to eye in these days, but Robert knew his old friend loved him. Parson Hawthyn spread the pages on his knees and prepared to go on reading in a calmer spirit.

"You will have heard, sir, how after Edgehill fight both armies were too crippled to continue further hostilities; how the King's army fell back upon Oxford and ours upon Warwick and Coventry. Of that painful matter, the fall of Reading to Prince Rupert, I will not speak. The devil is in that young man, but the Lord will be revenged in due course. The power of the Lord will overthrow him, and his enemies will eat him up. Indeed the power of the Lord has already aided His people. I refer to the failure of the King's march upon London. Competent authorities are of the opinion that had the King not delayed so long at Oxford, had he marched sooner, things might have gone ill with us. But the Lord permitted some hesitation to fall upon his spirit. He dallied, prating of peace, and meanwhile our glorious army marched again, blocking the approach to London, and the defences of the city were by the power of the Lord greatly increased. When the King reached Fulham Green our army, increased in numbers by the addition of the London trained bands, confronted him. His own men were footsore, and others of our men were coming up behind him. Nevertheless the enemy unlimbered their guns and we thought a battle was imminent. Then the King perceived the hopelessness of his position. He withdrew his army and marched back to Oxford, where as you doubtless know he has gone into winter quarters like a fox into its lair. It is expected, the weather being inclement, that there will be little fighting now until the spring."

Parson Hawthyn thanked God for that but he sighed, for this letter appeared to be less about Robert's welfare than that of the army for whose comfort he held no brief. He returned to the letter.

"And now truth compels me to go back a little way and tell you of an evil mischance that befell us in the midst of victory. Two of our glorious regiments, the London Redcoats and Colonel Hampden's Greencoats, myself with them, were guarding the crossing of the river Brent at Brentford. One morning early, in thick fog, Prince Rupert's cavalry attacked us. I may say without conceit that having rallied from the shock we made a magnificent fight of it, and should have made short work of that young man had not a regiment of Welshmen come to his assistance. The Welsh, when the blood is hot within them, are of the devil entirely and we suffered a grievous defeat, and I a wound in the shoulder, not serious, but painful enough to make me keep my lodging for the present. These setbacks, never permanent with the Lord's people, are sent us as a trial of our faith. Surmounting them we are the mightier for our fall, for the Lord of Hosts is with us and the God of Jacob is our refuge. And now, sir, I come to that portion of my letter which is the purpose of it. It will, I fear, give you pain, but I write it at the dictates of my conscience, putting pen to paper to make my wishes known."

Parson Hawthyn's sight was never very strong and he found now that he could no longer see. And he was cold again. When men spoke of following the dictates of their conscience he always turned cold; in his experience it so often meant that his conscience would presently start dictating differently. He waited, praying for strength, found that he could see again and read on.

"I must tell you, sir, that God has had much mercy upon me, granting me a great enlightenment of the spirit. After Edgehill fight I was in much despondency, but He led me to strength and comfort. He led me to a man as great as any I have known, to a Joshua among the Lord's people, to Colonel Oliver Cromwell, of whom if you have heard any evil you will know it is a lie put about by the devil himself. Through him I was led to the Lord's chosen, to that sect called the Independents, to whom alone the Lord has revealed His will in these troublous times, who are a chosen instrument unto Him for the delivery of this unhappy country from an evil and popish tyranny. Sir, I have found strength and peace and a courage not my own. Sir (I say it with all humility, for the glory is the Lord's), I stood my ground at Brentford. I owe to the Lord much service and this I would perform. Zeal for the Lord consumes me. I would have the Lord's house, where you serve and where I worship, a place purged of idolatry. I command you in the name of the Lord that the painted panels in the screen, and those heathen images which you have set about the church for its defilement, be removed and burned. And I command you, once more, as I have commanded you before, that the Lord's table be placed where it should be, in the centre of the church, and that the cross upon it be removed and taken to the manor. The matter of the melting down of it for a purpose pleasing in the eyes of the Lord I will attend to when I come. I forbid you to use the Book of Common Prayer. It is the devil's book. Henceforth you will not patter and mutter like the priests of the great whore but pray as the spirit moves you, and preach the word of God and minister to the people in a plain black gown. Sir, I remain your faithful friend and servant, Robert Haslewood."

Parson Hawthyn sat for a few moments gazing at the dying fire. Then he pulled himself to his feet, gathered his old cloak about him, and with the letter crumpled up in one fist went out into the sunshine, which he did not see, and crossed the churchyard to the church. In his accustomed spidery corner he fell to his knees and prayed that he might be able to pray. His prayer was not, he thought, answered. Nothing was given to him but desolation. He sat back on the bench behind him, the crumpled letter upon his knees. He looked at it stupidly for a while and then thoughts began to form slowly in his mind. That Robert had suffered a conversion, that he had in truth had an enlightenment of the spirit, he did not doubt. The letter was sincere. He believed that Robert had indeed found the strength that God alone can give, and that he gave thanks. He was no bigot. He believed that truth is a great globe and that men see only that part of it upon which for them the light shines. He believed that through any creed held in sincerity the finger of God can reach and touch a man. He believed that if men struggled to find the light, they would reach the light, not only in spite of but through their mistakes and limitations. But there was one way in which they would not find it, and that was by turning back on the path upon which for them the light shone and taking another man's path for the sake of expediency or peace. He recalled the words of Sir Thomas More. "I never intend (God being my good lord) to pin my soul at another man's back, not even the best man that I know." That to him was the sin against the Holy Spirit. That was loss of integrity, the way down into darkness, and he was not going to take it.

He raised his head and looked about him. The slanting sunbeams touched the small carved figures that he had made. In themselves they were of no importance. The birds and the angels he had made only to teach the children to praise God for creation, to teach them the care that the angels had for them. Our Lady in her niche and the saints in the screen were only painted wood. Even the cross upon the altar, the symbol of man's redemption, was a symbol and no more. Were the altar taken from the window of the morning and placed in the centre of the church he would still stand there as Aaron. If his surplice was taken from him he could still say, "Come people; Aaron's dressed," for he was a priest whatever he wore. If he used other words than those of the Book of Common Prayer he would still be praying. It was not that. It was that the ritual of the Church of England was her ritual. To forsake it was to forsake her, and the Church of England was for him the path upon which the light shone.

He got up and with a heart full of dread, and at the same time full of peace, went out into the churchyard. Standing in the lane outside his cottage he realised again that it was a beautiful day. The sun was free of the mist now, and the melting hoar-frost had strung every twig with orbs of light. Looking out over the fields he saw something moving in the distance against the softness of the winter trees. He could just make out the bent necks of the horses pulling the chariots and the tiny distinct figures of the charioteers, bright notes of colour in the blue and misty landscape. Not chariots, but wagons. It was the gypsies arriving for the Christmas fair on the common. He sighed, for he did not like the fairs. They were exciting, they could even be beautiful, but they always led to trouble.

3

When the sun set that evening the gypsies were once more at home, settled as comfortably into the hollow by Flowercote Wood as though they had never gone away. It was a clear frosty evening and their fire crackled and burned merrily, orange and gold against the dim blue of the twilight. The women sang at their work and the children laughed about the fire. Madona sat holding her thin hands to the blaze and called, "Alamina." Her granddaughter was, she knew, in the tent behind her, but there was no answer to her call. She repeated it sternly. "Alamina. I call."

Her power was still great, and Alamina came reluctantly and stood beside her. She was dressed, Madona noted, in her best. She wore her coral necklace and her green skirt and her bodice was laced with blue ribbon. She was combing her hair, a thing she did only upon the rarest occasions. The frost had got into it and it clung crackling to her comb. Sparks came from it and there were sparks in her eyes.

"*Tshai*, oh my lovely daughter, where are you going?" Madona asked sternly.

"Oh my *pûri-dai*, oh my lovely grandmother, that is nothing to you," said Alamina cheekily.

She laughed, her white teeth flashing, and the strands of her dark hair seemed to stand out all round her head like spitting snakes as she combed. Madona wondered, not for the first time, how she had come to be the mother of the mother of this creature of lightning and storm.

"You are not yet of the devil, daughter," she said, "but you are not good, and that which you purpose in your heart is not good. Feel after no evil things, my daughter, go to no evil places, for the fingers of the *beng* creep this way and that, thin and searching, and not easily to be torn away once they have fastened on you."

She looked up earnestly at Alamina, but Alamina had disappeared.

She was already running over the field, her flying feet leaving light prints in the frosted grass. In the west the sky was smoky orange. It was growing cold, yet she needed no shawl, for she was on fire and sparkling with the sweetness of the revenge to which she ran. Nevertheless, when a little later she walked up Mother Skipton's path she felt a slight shiver of apprehension, for the lights had gone now from the west and it seemed very dark in the little garden. When the jackdaw, hanging in its cage outside the door, squawked loudly, she jumped. She knocked at the door and called softly, *"Tshovihawni! Tshovihawni!"*

Mother Skipton opened at once, for she had learned never to keep anyone waiting lest being afraid they changed their minds and went away. "Have no fear, pretty child," she said gently. "Come in and tell your trouble. There are few troubles I cannot help. You are in love?"

Alamina stepped in and she shut the door, then held the candle up to look at her visitor. When she saw her the expression of her face changed, for this bold beautiful gypsy was not the lovesick village girl she had expected to see. She let the motherly gentleness slip from her face as though it were a veil. Eye to eye they looked at each other, taking the measure of each other. Alamina was no longer apprehensive, for this dry brittle woman was so frail she could have taken her in her hands and broken her. Mother Skipton realised that this was a tough customer and she must bargain first. "Show me the colour of your money," she said, and when Alamina laid a silver piece on the table she went on, "That is not enough, for you want nothing so easy as a love philtre. You want to work your vengeance on a man. Is that not so? Two silver pieces."

Alamina laid down the second coin, but her upper lip lifted a little over her teeth and Mother Skipton realised that not by hook or by crook would she get three. She swept the two into her pocket, unlocked the cupboard beside the hearth and took from it a lump of yellow wax. Kneeling before the hearth she held it over the smoky fire in an iron pan until it was soft and malleable. Then she took it in her hands and said to Alamina, "Sit here beside me on the settle." Alamina did so and they sat knee to knees, the dark, empty, almost blind-looking eyes of the woman meeting and holding the sparkling bright eyes of the girl. "Tell me what he did to you, why you hate him and what he looks like. You need tell me only briefly, for looking in your eyes I shall know much that you do not tell me."

While Alamina told her story the other woman's fingers moved over the wax, kneading and moulding, but her eyes never left Alamina's. In the depth of their emptiness something seemed to come into being, some dark intelligence that was without light but was intensely alive. It seemed reaching out to Alamina, searching into her mind and groping there, so that her mind went blank. She choked over a word, gasped and was silent. Then terror gripped her, drenching her body with sweat. She longed to take her eyes from the other eyes, cease to acknowledge the dominance of the evil there, to scream and run away; and she could have done so, for her will was strong, but she fought the longing down. If she escaped, she would not have her revenge. She reached out for it and her fingers met other fingers, thin and cold. Yet Mother Skipton was still holding and moulding the wax. The moment when she could have escaped passed. The fear left her and she began speaking again, though her voice trembled and her words did not come easily.

"That is enough," said Mother Skipton presently. "You have done your part well. You can lean back now and watch me."

Alamina leaned back, immensely tired but immensely pleased with herself. She watched Mother Skipton at work and presently she laughed maliciously, for the little figure was unmistakable, stocky and strong, yet somehow with an air of arrogant grace. "*Tshovihawni*, you are clever," she said.

"It is not I," said Mother Skipton briefly.

She worked on in silence for a few moments, then laid the

image in Alamina's lap and took a thorny branch from a pot beside the hearth. "It is finished," she said, "and here are the thorns. You can stick them in yourself, knowing that each thorn pierces his flesh, his mind, his heart. Put them where you will."

"He will have much misfortune?" asked Alamina eagerly, as she jabbed in the long cruel thorns of the wild sloe.

"He will have misfortunes small and large, the small ones vexing and laughable in their frustration, and men hate to be so frustrated. There will be two great griefs, sharp as those two great thorns you are pushing in the heart, now at this moment, and it is you who will bring about the second one, you yourself. There's joy for you, *Tshai*!"

"And after that?"

"After that, long darkness."

"Death?" asked Alamina eagerly.

"Why should you wish him to die? Death ends misfortune."

"That is what the old say," retorted Alamina. "For the young, life is sweet. I wish him to die."

"I do not know what the darkness holds," said Mother Skipton with a touch of weary impatience. "Give me the image that I may put it in my cupboard."

"I will keep it myself," said Alamina, and her hands closed upon it.

"That you cannot do. If those who came to me took away the images I should be betrayed."

"If it were to be stolen from your cupboard by another, and destroyed, then the darkness might not end in death."

"It will not be taken from my cupboard by another," said Mother Skipton sharply. "Give me the image at once, and go. I have finished with you."

Her will compelled Alamina. She relinquished the image, watched the witch lock it in the cupboard, and went away into the night.

CHAPTER V

THE FAIR

The fair was held two days later, on St. Thomas's Day. It was one of two fairs held yearly on the common, the other being on Midsummer Day under the patronage of St. John the Baptist. Michaelmas was a more usual time for a fair than St. Thomas's Day, the weather being better then, but the village had always favoured St. Thomas, and St. Thomas had always favoured the village with excellent weather. St. John the Baptist was less reliable, for it had been known to pelt with rain at midsummer, but St. Thomas never failed.

Will arrived home from school the day before the fair in the wildest spirits. He had grown and broadened out and to Froniga's sorrow there were no longer any gaps in his smile. He had his full complement of adult teeth, strong and white. His face was round and red, and rough as a nutmeg grater after the frosts, the hard water of Oxfordshire and not drying it properly. He permitted himself to be briefly kissed by his mother but not by Froniga or Jenny. If his breeching had made him technically a man a term at boarding-school had brought him very much nearer one in actual fact. He was full of strange oaths, which he was able to use before Margaret and Jenny because they did not understand them. He did not use them before Froniga because he feared she might, and he had not yet forgotten the feel of her hand against his stern. His clothes were in a shocking state and he had a black eye. There was a high watermark round his neck where he had not persevered with his ablutions in cold weather. Amongst his assorted luggage were a couple of white mice in a cage, the skin of a snake and a shepherd's crown, this latter object being a fossilised sea-urchin found by himself in the soil of Oxfordshire. Froniga perceived that the collecting craze was now upon him and Margaret had her sympathy. After the supper that had welcomed him home he became suddenly very sleepy and went off with the mice to put himself and them to bed in his father's dressing-room. He closed the door behind him with such masculine finality that no one had the temerity to go in and suggest that he should wash. Jenny and Maria went to bed as usual in the big bed by themselves, and it was a long time before Jenny fell asleep.

She woke up in the early morning, while it was still dark, to find herself being roughly pushed from the centre of the bed. She moved over, for she knew who it was. An unseen figure, sturdy and small, climbed in and lay down beside her. Maria wedged herself between them as of old and they pulled the bedclothes up to their chins.

"I was cold," said Will briefly.

Jenny stretched out her warm feet and touched his cold ones, and their feet folded together. In the old days they would have held hands, but they did not do that now. Nevertheless, Jenny was wildly happy. However offhand he might be with her in the day-time, however firmly he might close his door at night, underneath their outward estrangement there was still a unity. When he went away to school she had learned the lesson of the essential loneliness of human beings, now she was learning the lesson of their companionship in loneliness. Things had happened to him at school about which he could not tell her, and did not want to tell anybody. She could not tell him about the third person of whom the painter had told her, and whom she had found; he would not have understood. Nor could she tell him how she saw the painter's face in her dreams, and would never forget it, for he would have laughed at her. But they could lie together like this, their incommunicable experiences a weight upon their hearts, and know the comfort that comes from the contact of one body with another. At first Jenny's feet became as cold as Will's, and then all four feet slowly grew warm. The glow passed all over their bodies and was like the physical expression of the love between them.

"It's the day of the fair," whispered Jenny. "Did you know?"

"Course I knew!" said Will scornfully. "It wasn't too dark to see the booths on the common as I came home. And why do you think I got leave to come home a day early? To see you?"

Jenny laughed. "There's to be grand things, Biddy says. There's to be *Bel and the Dragon*, a giant, and a man who draws teeth."

"I hope there'll be good wrestling," said Will. "Are the gypsies here?"

"They came two days ago," said Jenny.

"Good," said Will. "Then there'll be good wrestling, with people killed. What's that striking? Six?"

And with that he bounded from the bed and left her. It would be as much as his new-found manhood was worth to be found by his mother or Biddy curled up in his sister's bed because he was cold.

The morning dawned clear and frosty, ideal weather for the Christmas fair. Margaret did not attend fairs, for her sensibilities were too delicate for such boisterous occasions, and she did not like the children going, but Robert allowed it and so she could not stop them. Biddy was to take the children after an early dinner and Froniga would meet them there. The little maids would go later in the day.

Under a brilliant midday sun the party set out, Biddy and Jenny with baskets on their arms so that they could buy good things for Christmas. Biddy had her voluminous skirts looped up out of harm's way and wore her russet cloak and hood. Jenny in a cloak and hood of kingfisher blue, walked beside her. Will strutted on ahead, magnificent in his dark green breeching suit with his sword at his side. He was my Lord of Essex, protecting them from the wolves in the undergrowth and a surprise attack by Rupert's cavalry. However, he had soon left them behind, for Biddy felt her bulk upon the hills, both going down and going up, but particularly going up, and Jenny was far too kind-hearted to let her puff and pant alone. As they toiled up the last steep slope to the common, Will being out of sight, they could hear the joyous noises of the fair, the shouts of the hucksters, the exciting brazen call of a trumpet, the rattle of a drum and the subdued roar of a large crowd of people all enjoying themselves. Biddy made a final effort and they came to the top of the hill, and there was the fair spread out before them in all its glory. Jenny gave a sigh of delight. Christmas had begun.

All round the edge of the common were hay-wains from neighbouring villages which had brought family parties, grandparents, mothers and fathers and children, three or four families all crowded together to see the glory of the fair. Then there were gypsy wagons and the carts that had brought the goods and wares of the showmen. In summer they were often decorated with bunches of flowers, but now they were twined about with greenery and bunches of holly and mistletoe. Behind them the horses were tethered, quietly cropping the grass, and just within the hollow square formed by the wagons were the booths, rough planks placed on barrels and piled high with such bright wealth that it made the heart glow and the mouth water, and the head reel with calculations. Some of the booths displayed ribbons and handkerchiefs, embroidered gloves and belts, rosettes for shoes, strings of glass beads and boxes of pins. Then there were wonderful things to eat, candied and dried fruit, gilded gingerbread, marchpane, nuts and apples for the Christmas kissing rings. There were dolls cunningly carved from wood, painted and dangled on strings, toy trumpets, small chiming bells, knives and nails, plaited rush baskets, babies' caps and collars, and innumerable other things that one had not known one wanted until one saw them, but at sight of which life seemed suddenly incomplete. At strategic points small platforms had been erected. One of them belonged to the wonderful man who drew teeth, another to the juggler who tossed up myriads of little coloured balls into the air and never let a single one drop, and one of them was a little stage upon which would presently be enacted the story of *Bel and the Dragon*. Every now and then people would be summoned by trumpet or tuck of drum to one platform or another to see the performance. Exciting characters mingled with the crowd, the fiddler ready to play for any who wished to dance, a dwarf, a giant with three eyes who said to be the finest wrestler in the world, and the gypsies.

The gypsies came into their own on fair day. On ordinary days they were tolerated because the squire commanded it, but on fair days they were almost welcomed. Their wild sparkling looks and gaudy rags added their own bright notes of shifting colour to the brilliant scene. The gypsy men were fine wrestlers, and for coins flung to them they would wrestle fiercely with each other, or with any ruffian who would take them on. If a real fight developed, all the better; there were few people who would not travel miles to see a gypsy fight. The gypsy women told fortunes, sold spells and charms and did a fine trade in their elder-wood skewers and pegs. Yoben, known to the village as Bartholoways the Tinker, was seated under one of the great lime trees at the further end of the common, not far from the inn door. Many housewives, knowing he would be there, had brought their pots and pans for him to mend, for no one in all the countryside could make an old pan into a new one as Bartholoways could do, and watching him do it was one of the attractions of the fair. Another attraction was old Piramus. As he lounged through the crowd, his great head sunk between his shoulders, leisurely yet with a menacing power in his slow movements, the timid shrank away and the not so timid moved to get a nearer view of him. If they were women he leered at them; if they were men the savage contempt in his eyes infuriated them; and yet they would move to where they could look at him again. It was known that his velvet doublet had been dragged from the corpse of a man he had murdered, and it was rumoured that the buttons on it, bright discs that winked in the sun, were not brass but gold pieces taken from the pockets of the same victim. It was also rumoured that his horse was shod with silver. It was known that he used to lash his wife to a cartwheel and beat her till she fainted, and that in his youth no man had ever been able to stand up against him in a fight and live. It was always hoped that he would one day fight again. As the hours passed at a fair and he became increasingly drunk hopes always rose, for Piramus in his cups was never morose or maudlin, but magnificently mad, as a bull is mad when it paws the ground before a charge, or a tiger crouching to spring. But he never did charge, he never did spring. The fury would rise in him to the point of murder and then die away. He was old. Just when hopes were raised to fever point it would be seen that he was there no longer.

He had a rival today in the giant, a black-bearded bully who overtopped him by a good three inches. The giant was horrible. The third eye in the middle of his forehead had a ghastly glitter, his girth was tremendous, his arms and legs were like branches of trees. He had red lips in his black beard and long pointed teeth like an animal's. Jenny shuddered when she saw him for he reminded her of that terrible man who had come leaping down upon her and Will in the wood; and then had turned into Mr. Loggin the painter. This man was obviously not going to turn into anything at all agreeable and she looked the other way.

Under the lime trees by the inn, and close to Yoben, stood a group of men who wanted employment. They all carried something to tell prospective employers what their trade was. Carters carried a whip, labourers a shovel, woodmen a billhook and shepherds a crook. Usually there was a long line of them, and farmers in need of labour looked them over as though they were cattle, choosing the sturdiest, but today there were very few because so many men were away at the war. The smallness of that group was the only thing in the whole gay scene to remind anyone that England was at war, and few of them remembered. They had learned to live for the day. When pleasure came their way they took it to themselves with riotous enjoyment and gave no thought to what tomorrow might bring.

Jenny and Biddy soon found Froniga. Will had found her already. In the past she had always attended fairs in her green gown and had been almost as striking a figure as Piramus himself, but Jenny thought she looked just as lovely now in her gown and cloak and hood of grey; they seemed to make her cheeks rosier and her eyes more softly and deeply dark.

"If you'll keep an eye to the children, Mistress Froniga, I have purchases to make for the mistress," said Biddy, half-winking an eye. Will and Jenny, tingling with pleasure, knew what she meant. Secret things were to be bought, things they would not know about till Christmas morning.

"You go that way, Biddy," said Froniga, "and we'll go this way."

The three turned their backs on the booths and Will pulled at Froniga's hand.

"Cousin Froniga, Master Pippin is going to pull out teeth! Quick!"

He hurried them over the grass to a raised platform near the lime trees and was able to push them into an excellent position in the front row. A little boy was sitting on the edge of the platform beating a drum, and the fiddler was standing on the platform tuning his fiddle. For Master Pippin liked to draw teeth to music; it seemed to make more of an art of it. He himself stood beaming down upon the assembled crowd. He was a large man with a jovial round face, a bald head and a small red beard that stuck out at a most attractive angle. He was toothless and liked to tell his patients, before he started on them, how he had drawn them all himself and felt no pain whatever. Master Pippin looked, and was, a happy man, as well he might be, for it is given to few to relieve pain and give entertainment at the same moment, and that to music and tuck of drum. Moreover his stock in trade was small, a stool for the patient, a wooden bowl for the blood and a pair of pincers for himself, and with these he travelled the lanes of a lovely land, from village to village and from fair to fair, always sure of employment, for if there is one thing in this world that can be relied upon it is the decay of teeth.

"Step up! Step up!" he cried above the rattle of the

drumsticks, in a voice that literally rang with reassurance. "Step up! All over in the twinkling of an eye. No pain. Took out all me own with never a twinge. See now, good people!" He opened his own enormous mouth and showed its cavernous and blessed bareness. "Step up! Step up! You there, sir? That's the style! Sit here, sir, where they can see you. Give 'em confidence. You'll feel nothing. Never a twinge. Strike up, Jack Fiddler! Strike up!"

A raw-boned boy was sitting on the stool clutching his knees, his eyes round with terror and the sweat pouring off him. The Haslewood children saw with a shock of sympathetic dismay that it was Tom Fettipace, their groom. It was obvious that nothing but the pain he had been enduring would have driven him to this, and now his frantic eyes looked round for some way of escape. Better the pain than this. Now it was come upon him he would rather have had the pain. Should he make a bolt for it? The crowd endeavoured to cheer him up with catcalls, groans and hoots.

Will was entranced. Jenny could not take her eyes from Tom's terrified face. She felt sick and cold and her nails bit into her palms as she clenched her hands. Froniga had forgotten both children, for she treated toothache herself, and when her professional interests were engaged she forgot everything. While the fiddler struck up a merry jig Master Pippin twisted Tom's head back in a manner that caused his mouth to fly open as though a spring had been touched, glared into the cavity for one moment, then inserted his pincers and withdrew the tooth, all at such speed that it did cross Froniga's mind to wonder if it was the right tooth. But right or wrong it was out. Master Pippin was brandishing it triumphantly and Tom was happily spitting blood into the basin. Presently he was struggling down from the platform weak but triumphant, cheered to the echo as the hero of the hour, and Master Pippin was calling for the next man up.

After two more extractions Jenny whispered, "I don't think I like it very much."

Froniga looked down at her white face and was stricken with remorse. What had she been thinking of to let a little girl witness this? Only hardness of heart or professional interest made such sights a pleasure and Jenny was possessed of neither. But Master Pippin was such a marvellous practitioner that she did not want to go away herself yet, and nor did Will.

"Do you see the tinker working over there under the lime trees?" she asked Jenny.

"Yes," whispered Jenny.

"He's a good man. Go to him and ask him to look after you till I fetch you. Tell him I sent you."

"Yes," whispered Jenny, and ran off, while Froniga and Will settled happily back to watch the fascinating Master Pippin until the last tooth.

2

Yoben, sitting beside his brazier, was happy as he worked. He never spoke to Froniga in public but he knew she was there and her nearness gave him the peace it always did. And he enjoyed mending pots and pans. He had not always been good with his hands but he had taken infinite pains to learn his craft perfectly, and also to learn the tinker's Shelta. That he now spoke so well that he could say with Shakespeare's Prince Hal, "I can drink with any tinker in his own language." He was humming a tune as he tapped and hammered and he did not hear her light footsteps approaching him.

"Good-day, sir."

He looked up and saw her, and said, "Good-day, Persephone. Spring has come early."

He thought, "An adorable child. A frail child, and yet strong. She will never be at the mercy of the sins of others; they will break against her sturdy spirit and recoil away." The piece of work he was doing was delicate and he could not for the moment put it down, but over it he looked into her tranquil eyes and smiled, and she smiled back fearlessly, her hands held out to his warm brazier. The small spread fingers were edged with rosy light, and presently she sat back on her heels, so that her face too was rosy within its blue hood.

"My name is Jenny," she said. "Cousin Froniga sent me to you for you to look after me. She is watching Master Pippin, but I do not like to see teeth drawn."

He had thought she was Jenny, for she had Froniga's serene charm. He wondered from what source it came. From all he had heard of Squire Haslewood and his wife they were distinguished chiefly by their ordinariness. Somewhere in the stream of heredity there had come in a freshet of pure gold.

"Nor do I like to see teeth drawn," he said. "Will you sit

down here by me and watch a Romany tinker at work instead? I will take care of you."

She smiled and sat down beside him and they talked of white mice, of the migratory birds who had gone away to the moon, of gilded gingerbread, of worms and their habits and the price of tea. They could have talked to each other for ever upon these subjects of mutual interest, so great was their mutual liking for each other, but a baleful shadow fell upon them. Piramus was stalking by towards the inn, followed by a group of village men and the giant with three eyes; there was a pinch of frost beneath the sun and fiery liquid in the veins would not come amiss. Jenny moved close to Yoben, for she was scared of Piramus and the giant.

"Has he really got three eyes or is one stuck on?"she asked.

"I cannot tell you," said Yoben. "But we will know for certain when the wrestling starts. If it's a false eye it will then fall out. If it's a real one it will stay in."

"I shan't be here for the wrestling," said Jenny. "They'll all be drunk by the time the wrestling starts, and Biddy and I go home when they start to be drunk. I don't like seeing people drunk. Will does. Will is going to stay for the wrestling with Cousin Froniga to look after him. I'll tell them to watch the giant's eye. Do you like unicorns?"

"That again I cannot tell you," said Yoben. "To meet a unicorn is a great privilege and one of which I have not yet been worthy."

"We've one in our family," said Jenny. "Did you know?"

"No, I did not," said Yoben. "Will you tell me about him?"

Jenny was happy again. She looked up at him and laid her hand upon his knee to command his undivided attention. He set aside his work that she might have it. The occasion was momentous. He put in many hours telling stories to Meriful, Dinki and Cinderella but this was the first time that a child had offered to tell a story to him. And he believed he was about to discover the source of that freshet of pure gold.

"Listen," said Jenny. "Once upon a time . . ."

3

Fair day was the only time that Meriful, Dinki and Cinderella chose the company of their mother rather than that of Madona or Yoben. Madona no longer attended fairs, for in her old age she had wearied of them, and though Yoben attended them he sat always in one place, mending pots and pans that were brought to him, and to stay with him was far too dull. But Alamina went everywhere about the fair, telling fortunes and selling pegs and skewers and charms, and the children went with her, clinging to her skirts, assured both of seeing the sights and not being scolded or banged on the head. Alamina had a honied tongue upon fair day. The presence of her sweet little children enabled her to sell more of her wares than she would have done without them, and her excellent histrionic display of mother love caused many to trust her fortune-telling who might not otherwise have done so. They thought her a good, loving woman who would not deceive him.

"There now, sweet lady," said Alamina to Biddy, bestowing the pegs that Biddy had just bought in her basket. "No west wind will snatch the washing from the line with Alamina's pegs holding it firm. Made of elder-wood, they are—fairy wood, as all know—and cunningly made by my poor dear husband, may the great God rest his soul."

Her voice broke, but she straightened herself bravely. With one hand she caressed the curls of little Cinderella, who was leaning against her with her thumb in her mouth and gazing up at Biddy, and with the other she removed a tear from the corner of one eye with her apron. It was a real tear, as Biddy perceived, large and lustrous as the eye from which it fell so pathetically. Alamina was so good an actress that her body was at all times under the control of her art.

"Ah dear!" said Biddy sympathetically. "And three little ones. Ah dear!"

"And another little one, my baby, at home with his grannie," said Alamina with sweet patience. "But they are good children. They are my jewels. And this one," and here she laid her hand gently on Meriful's head, "my eldest, my dear *tschavo*, is as a father to the little ones. If I've lost my *rom* I've my *tschavo*."

She was in a fair way to break down altogether, and Meriful gave Biddy a wistful little smile, pleading indulgence for his mother's weakness. Dinki's baby mouth trembled a little and his lovely eyes brimmed with unshed tears. Both boys had inherited some of their mother's genius.

"*Rawni*," said Meriful, "will you not let our mother cross your palm with silver and tell your fortune? I see in your face, kind lady, that your fortune will be good."

Alamina raised her bent head, wiped her eyes on the back of her hand and then slipped it light as a feather under Biddy's. Kind Biddy could feel the tears upon it and grieved for the poor girl. Four pairs of expectant eyes were fixed upon her, confusing her with their dark brilliance. Alamina's other hand, slightly cupped, was presented to her notice. Without meaning to do any such thing, because she could have put her last silver piece to better use, Biddy dropped it in the cupped palm. Quick as lightning her hand was crossed with it and it disappeared from sight. In an atmosphere so tense that it made her heart beat faster she spread her plump palm for inspection.

Alamina bent her head, began to speak and then stopped, her lips parted. She stooped a little lower and her leaf-like hand began to tremble under Biddy's. She gave a stifled cry and put her free hand to her lips.

"What now?" asked Biddy in a panic. "What is it, girl? What is it?" A slight perspiration broke out on her forehead. "What do you see, girl? Is it misfortune that you see? Ah, dearie me, what was I thinking of? My old mother used to say, if you turn your eyes towards tomorrow's darkness you will only stumble in today's light. But now I have done it and I'll not rest till I know the worst."

Alamina raised her head. Her cheeks were pink and her eyes like stars. "There's no worst," she said.

"No worst?" asked Biddy.

"No. My *tschavo* was right. It is good beyond all dreams. But not here, my dearie, not here."

She gripped Biddy's wrist and looked about her, then, pulling Biddy with her, glided between two booths and through the gorse-bushes beyond, where no one could see or hear. Then she bent over Biddy's hand again, panting with eagerness. Biddy herself was extremely short of breath and the children's eyes were like stars as they craned to see. Presently Alamina looked up.

"Did you know it was down there under the house, deep down waiting?" she asked, and her bright eyes seemed to pierce right to the back of Biddy's head.

"What?" gasped Biddy.

"The brightness and the gold," whispered Alamina. "It was hid, was it not?"

"How do you know that?" gasped Biddy. "Yes, they say the old sea captain hid it. Gold from El Dorado. But the children and I have looked for it and not found it, and the Squire he's always said it's only a tale."

"El Dorado," whispered Alamina, her lovely voice making music of the name. "Gold from El Dorado. Magic gold. Under the house. For you."

"How can I go digging in the cellars?" asked Biddy.

One of Alamina's hands was still holding her hand and now the other was laid on her shoulder, while the gypsy's marvellous eyes shone into hers. "Did you never hear that gold brings gold, dearie?" she asked.

"Heard it and know it," said Biddy grimly. "Always the rich gets more."

"And it's you, dearie, are to be rich now," said Alamina, and her joy in Biddy's good fortune was like starlight over her face. "Let me in tonight when the moon's full and the young maids are gone to their beds. You've your wages saved?"

Biddy gulped and nodded. She had her savings in a stocking under her mattress.

"Then tie your treasure in a handkerchief and have it ready when I come to you, and I'll show you how to bring the gold of El Dorado to it. You're treasure is nothing, I know, just a few coins, but if you give all it will bring all. That's what the good book says. There's magic words to be said, but I know them, and I'll say them for you. The magic is good and the blessing of God is upon it. *O boro Duvel*, sanctified in heaven and upon the earth, loves to reward the poor. You trust me, dearie? There, I see that you do. I'll ask nothing for myself but one gold piece for my trouble. Tonight, my dearie, after the moon is full."

She was gone and the children with her. They vanished so swiftly that it seemed as though the gorse-bushes had swallowed them. Dizzy and confused, hardly knowing if she were asleep or awake, but with a heart drumming with excitement, Biddy went to look for Froniga and the children.

4

She found them before the puppet show of *Bel and the Dragon*. The children had never seen living actors on a real stage, but to them these carved and painted puppets were absolutely alive. From the moment when Master Will Harrier dived behind the narrow wooden tower covered in cloth that supported the puppet stage, until the moment when he emerged again, they forgot about him. In their minds he had nothing to do with the thrilling characters whose adventures enthralled them, and their varied voices, some so sharp and shrill, some so thrilling and deep, and the lion's fearful roar, were the character's own voices, and had no connection with Master Will mopping his red face and clearing his excoriated throat at the end of the performance. Froniga was almost as thrilled as the children, and Biddy would have been if her head had not been full of the gold of El Dorado. And indeed the story of *Bel and the Dragon,* though slightly confusing, was packed with dramatic situations, from the moment when the rising curtain displayed Sirus King of Persia bowing before the golden idol Bel and the brass dragon, while Daniel peeped round the corner and laughed at him, until the final curtain, when all the enemies of Daniel were thrown to the lions. Will roared with delight when the dragon burst asunder, but Jenny liked it best when the Angel of the Lord took Daniel by the hair of his head and through the vehemency of his spirit set him in Babylon over the den. The Angel of the Lord, with hair of tow and spangled wings, was her favourite character. Froniga loved the humble kind old Habbacuc who made pottage and broke bread in a bowl and would have taken it to the reapers in the field, had not the Angel of the Lord picked him up by the hair of his head and made him take it to Daniel instead. What wonderful times to live in, thought Froniga, and lost herself in a happy vision of the Angel of the Lord with King Charles dangling from one hand and John Pym from the other, carrying them away to where they would no more trouble the land. She came to herself to hear Master Will Harrier's voice pealing up to the skies in Daniel's final shout of triumph, "Thou hast remembered me, O God; neither hast Thou forsaken them that seek Thee and love Thee."

Master Will Harrier came out from behind his little theatre, mopping his forehead and clearing his throat in the most painful manner, coins showered into the hat he held out with a shaking hand (for he was always wrecked by his own genius), and the performance was over.

"It was lovely!" said Jenny with a deep sigh. "The Angel of the Lord was beautiful!"

"The dragon burst better than ever," said Will. "Cousin Froniga, I want to see the wrestling."

Froniga stifled a sigh. Tooth-drawing engaged her

professional interest, but there was nothing in wrestling that appealed to her. But Will was growing up in a brutal world and she thought it as well that he should watch wrestling, learn the right methods of attack and defence and take a good look at blood and courage.

"Biddy," she said, "Jenny has not made her own purchases yet. Will you help her and then take her home? It's growing colder. Master Will and I will look after each other. Are you all right, Biddy?" she added sharply, for Biddy was looking extraordinarily odd.

Biddy hastily brought her abstracted gaze back from the middle distance. "Yes, Mistress Froniga, to be sure. It's getting colder, as you say. Come along, my dearie; we've left your mother too long alone." And she hurried off with Jenny's hand in hers.

"There!" said Will with satisfaction as he and Froniga made their way to the far end of the common, where the ring was. "Now they've gone we can enjoy ourselves." He looked up at her with a wicked conspiratorial gleam in his eye, as one man to another. This, she realised, was his new look, masculine and assured. Then he seemed to realise that Froniga, though in her strength she seemed a man, was not one. "I'll take care of you," he said. "You needn't be nervous."

"Thank you," said Froniga meekly. "Will, your neck is very dirty."

Her remark was not prompted by a wish to make him a child again but by consternation. She was very much in advance of her time in the value she put on cleanliness.

"I know it is," said Will. "I haven't had time to wash it yet. I've had a great deal to do since I came home."

"You must wash it, Will," said Froniga. "And behind your ears too. You might get scrofula."

"What's scrofula?" asked Will.

"Ulcers round your neck and behind your ears. It's called the King's Evil because the only certain cure, if borage and marigold fail, is for the King to touch it. And now we are at war it's not very easy to go to the King. So you must be careful, Will."

"Does it come from a dirty neck?" asked Will.

In the practice of her healing art, and in the advice which she gave, Froniga always tried to be strictly truthful. "Apothecaries do not always agree as to its cause," she said carefully, "but it's my own opinion that the disease is contracted through neglect of soap and water."

Will said, with an acuteness which surprised her, "Then you'd expect almost everyone to have it, wouldn't you?"

They had reached the wrestling, which had started some time ago. A big crowd had gathered round the ring, but way was made for them and they were passed through to the front. That Froniga should come virtually unprotected into this rough crowd astonished no one, for they were used to her vagaries and admired her courage. All who knew her respected her, and though some feared her many more had had their fear swallowed up in gratitude for what she had done for them. "Stand here, mistress," said a stout old carter enthusiastically. "You stand here with the young master, right up here against the rope, and there won't be no one what gets a better view than what you do."

Froniga drew her cloak about her, for it was nearing sunset and the warmth of the day had gone. The atmosphere about her was tense and angry, for no one, neither village man nor gypsy, could get the better of the giant. He was resting now, sitting on an upturned barrel with his hands on his knees, having his cuts and bruises attended to, but the light of battle was still in the one eye left him (the one in his forehead had fallen out and the other was closed up) and there was a confident and maddening smile on the cruel red mouth in his black beard. He sat facing the west and the muscles in his huge bare arms and legs shone in the golden glow like twisted columns of bronze.

"He's like Bel, isn't he?" Will whispered to Froniga.

Now and then he flung back his head and laughed, and then a flow of taunts would come from him as he watched the two men now in the ring, a stalwart gypsy and a young blacksmith from Highmoor, a savage Celt who was fighting with a deadly intensity that was telling hard on the fire and valour of the gypsy. The village men hated the Highmoor men upon all days except fair-day, and then they banded together as one man against the gypsies. But today the simplicity of this state of things was upset by the fact that far greater than the hatred of countryman for gypsy, or of gypsy for countryman, was the hatred of both for the giant. He was a devil, and he had played a few dirty tricks that no decent man would stoop to. Several men were already lying on the edge of the crowd, inert mounds of bruised and torn flesh, too battered for even hatred to get them on their legs again, and the giant was scarcely dented. But, sensing the feeling of the crowd, Froniga knew their blood was up. If they had to go on fighting by the light of torches they would go on until the giant was down. Most of the men in the crowd were already drunk and Froniga wished she had not brought Will to this scene. She had not known it would be as revolting as this; nor would it have been but for the laughing man on the barrel. The sense of corruption that was stifling her seemed to come from him. She looked away from him to the panting, struggling men in the ring but she could not bear to look at them either, for in them the two parts of her being seemed to be striving and the fight rent her.

"Will, let's go," she said, but when she looked down at Will she saw that he had not heard her, and the expression of ecstasy on his face was that of a cherub in heaven. She looked to her left and saw Piramus towering above the rest of the crowd, shouting encouragement to the young gypsy, drunk but magnificent. She found that her eyes were clinging to him in desperation, as though he only could put an end to the mounting terror of this scene. She almost called out to him, "Piramus! Piramus! Stop it in the name of God!" There was a shout and the young gypsy was down. He tried to get up again but rolled over and they picked him up and carried him away. The giant jumped to his feet and lurched forward into the ring.

"The last of the gypsies?" he asked tauntingly. "The last of the Herons? None of them left with the guts to stand up against the gorgios?"

And then his opinion of all gypsies, but especially of Herons, flowed from him in a stream of profanity that was like lava, it was so even, smooth and deathly. It seemed to Froniga to flow round them all, isolating them. She could not have moved now if she would.

The smooth ugly voice stopped at last and she was aware of a change in the atmosphere. There was a huge quietness holding them all. The noise of the rest of the fair seemed to come from a great distance. She felt through all her sensitive being that awareness that greets the breaking through into normal life of what to those still in the body seems strange and terrifying. But to her it was not terrifying. Though the awareness about her was that of fear, her own was warm and glowing. In the last light streaming from the west she saw two giants on the green grass, both of them bathed in gold, Bel and Piramus. The silence had ended now in protest and dismay. Piramus was old, he was drunk, the light was going. That gold would dazzle the eyes. Voices cried to Bel the giant to have mercy on the old man, they cried to Piramus to stop being a fool and come away. But Piramus, pulling off his velvet doublet, took no notice. There was a half-smile on his wicked old face, and a look of exultation. There was grandeur in his bearing. If he had been drunk he seemed so no longer. Something, the exultation or the gold that clothed him, had made a strong and sober man of him. It was Bel who seemed now not quite certain of himself as he drew in his fists and crouched.

For years afterwards men talked of that fight. They would discuss it on winter nights, when smoking their clay pipes before the inn fire, or on long light summer evenings riding home on the top of the great wains piled high with hay. It was to them as great a fight as Edgehill, and greater than those other fights of the civil war that had taken place in foreign parts, outside the borders of their own country. After that fight not even Alamina could dim for long the lustre that shone about the name of Heron, and after that fight Bel the giant was never again able to show his face at the fair. For he need not have put out all his cunning and strength in the way that he did, he need not have fought to kill. Though in justice to Bel it had to be said that in the first round he needed his strength and cunning. Piramus had been a great fighter in his youth and he had not forgotten the way of it, and now every ounce of strength he had, all his courage, all the twisted good in him, were channelled into retrieving the honour of his people. He did not care if he died. Death with honour was a great good. It was a great good when a man could die fighting, not panting out his last breath among a crowd of wailing women or pushed off the ladder by the hangman and left choking at the end of a rope. He fought with chivalry and skill as well as courage, and he kept the rules even when his strength was failing him at last and the tide was turning against him. It was Bel who, maddened by the old man's tenacity, and by the streaming golden light which seemed beating in on his brain, did not in the end care what he did if only he could get him down. Yet Piramus did not die of the foul blow which felled him, he died because his old heart failed. He died in the very act of getting up again.

Froniga knew he was dead or dying, knew it by the icy coldness that always gripped her body at the approach of death, and she was the first to duck under the rope and run to him. Kneeling beside him, looking down at the grim triumph on his face, she wanted to laugh and cheer, for the same triumph was in her. Men feared death, and well they might, for to die was to fall into an abyss of which nothing could be known except its stark strangeness, and some deaths she had seen, degrading deaths, had filled her with fear and revulsion, but every now and then came a death of peace and serenity, or of resounding victory like this one, and Azrael was seen for what he was, mighty but merciful, terrible but righteous. When the quietness of his presence had held them all a short while ago she had done right to glow. She was trembling now only because it was a part of her healing gift to recognise death by this strange coldness.

But her shivering was misunderstood. A man came pushing through the crowd to her, helped her to her feet and with an arm round her made way for her with vigorous blows of his free arm. It was Yoben. He took her away and presently she found herself on an almost deserted patch of the common, for at news of a death everyone had gone flocking to the scene. Yoben was on one side of her and a round-eyed Will on the other, and she herself now was the steadiest of the three. The sun had sunk below the woods and in the west the glory of its setting glowed like fire along the horizon. The frost had already made the grass crisp underfoot and Froniga felt its sharp invigorating touch as warmth came back to her body. When the light went off the west it would be a night of moon and stars.

"Did you see the fight, Yoben?" she asked.

"Yes," said Yoben. "I don't watch fights as a rule, but I knew I had to watch this one. I climbed to the lowest branch of that lime tree there and saw it from start to finish."

"Then go straight to Madona and tell her how great a death it was," said Froniga. "Go quickly, Yoben, before any of the others can reach her with their wailing and lamenting. You saw it and you know. And, Yoben, try to persuade Madona to bury him in Flowercote Wood near the spring. There is so much laughter there."

"I must take you home before I do any of these things," said Yoben. "Madona will be expecting this. The cry of the death-hawk was heard over the camp last night."

"I heard it too," said Froniga. "Yoben, Will is taking me home. He will take care of me."

Twenty minutes later, having taken Froniga home, kindled her fire for her and drawn her curtains, Will trotted back to the manor in the afterglow, under the first stars. He trotted fast, for if he had not been puffed up with pride and grandeur he might have been scared of the shadows under the trees. As it was he was not exactly scared, only pleasantly titillated by a kind of creeping sensation between his shoulder-blades. But he was not afraid. His sword was at his side and he was prepared to run Rupert through at any moment. Honours were thick upon him. He had taken Cousin Froniga home and looked after her there. He had gone to the fair in manly garb, breeches, sword and all. He had seen a wrestling match. But best of all he had seen a man die. Now he was grown-up. Nevertheless, when he saw the lights of home he bolted for them like a rabbit.

CHAPTER VI

THE GREAT TRICK

A soft tap came at the kitchen window. Biddy started up, suffering from such violent palpitations that she felt she had a yaffingale inside her, knocking against the cage of her ribs. An owl screeched eerily and she thought she would have died. Nevertheless her failing legs carried her to the back door and her fumbling fingers turned the key and lifted the latch. She opened the door and saw Alamina standing wraithlike in the moonlight, a ragged shawl over her head, her eyes glittering in her white face. The moonlight seemed to have drained her of colour so that she looked more like a spirit than a woman. Then she stepped into the firelight and candlelight of the kitchen and the warm colour flowed back into her lips and cheeks, into the dark crimson of her skirt and the green-and-orange diklo that she wore on her head under her ragged tawny shawl. "Now then, my dearie," she whispered quickly and urgently. "Is all ready? Have you the silver and gold?"

Biddy nodded, still too breathless to speak, and laid her hand upon her bosom, where inside her bodice she had placed the old stocking with the savings of all her working years. Like all women, she had dreamed of a home of her own in her old age and now, if she could bring to this gold the gold of El Dorado hidden in the house, her goal was in sight. She did not think she was being dishonest. Surely she, who had toiled for years in this house, was more deserving of its gold than another? And in trusting to Alamina's spells she was not more credulous than other countrywomen of her time. She believed in magic and she believed that gypsies had miraculous powers that were denied to other folk. Looking at Alamina she believed it more than ever, for the girl was obviously transported beyond herself. That strange glitter was still in her eyes and her face was rapt.

And indeed Alamina was not acting now. She was entirely fey. She was about to continue the *hokkani boro*, the great trick, called by some the great secret, brought by the Romany people from the East and having for them an almost religious significance. It had three parts : the first was to *pen dukkerin*, or to tell the fortune; the second was to *lel dūdihabin*, or to take lightning, to take away the property; the third was to *chiv o manzin apré lāti*, or put the oath upon the victim. Alamina had already told the fortune, but now, tonight and tomorrow morning, the more difficult part of the *hokkani boro* was before her.

"The gold is in the deeps of the house," she said to Biddy. "Is there some place there in the deeps where your own treasure can lie undisturbed? It must lie there three weeks, dearie, bringing other gold to it, and no eyes must rest upon it, not even your own."

Biddy swallowed and managed to speak. "The far end of the cellar," she whispered. "No one sets foot there."

"Then bring a candle and come quickly," said Alamina.

But Biddy's hand trembled so much that it was the gypsy who had to carry the candle as they went down the stone steps which led from the kitchen to the cellar. They made their way past the barrels of home-brewed wine and metheglyn, and down a few more steps to a deeper part of the cellar that had not been used since old Walter Haslewood had died. Cobwebs hung in all the corners and the air was thick with the smell of fungus and damp. "Here's the place, dearie," whispered Alamina, and putting the candlestick on the floor she knelt down, motioning Biddy to kneel before her. "Now take your treasure from your bosom."

While Biddy did so Alamina pulled the diklo from her head and tore it dramatically in half; one half she put into her bodice and the other half she wrapped about the bulging stocking. Then she laid the bundle on the floor between herself and Biddy, and with her glittering eyes fixed on Biddy's began to murmur spells in the Romany tongue, her voice rising and falling as though she were chanting. Biddy, looking at Alamina was as mesmerised by her as a bird by a snake. The murmuring stopped abruptly and Alamina said, "I'll come tomorrow, dearie, before dayspring, and before the moon sets and before your little maids come down to work. I'll be here at five of the clock and we'll see how the charm is working."

"Could it fail?" asked Biddy.

"Only if the gold of El Dorado is not here," said Alamina, "but it's here. I saw it in your hand." She picked up the candle and led the way up the steps. "Tomorrow, dearie, you must bring your Bible with you. That's part of the charm. You have a Bible?"

"There's one in the house," faltered Biddy. "I can lay my hands on it."

"Then do so," said Alamina. She put the candlestick down on the kitchen table, glided to the door and opened it. "Sleep well, my dearie, and three weeks from today you will be the richest woman in the village. You'll be richer than your master. You'll have a satin petticoat, dearie, and a sable muff."

She slipped out of the door and vanished in the moonlight. Biddy locked the door behind her and crept up to bed. But though she took off her skirt and bodice and lay down she did not sleep. She lay watching the moonlight moving across the floor, listening to the rising wind and turning her hour-glass. When she judged it was half-past four she put on her skirt and bodice again, lit her candle, crept downstairs to the parlour and took the family Bible from the carved oak Bible case that stood against the wall. Then she went to the kitchen. There was still warmth and a rosy glow within the ashes of the fire. She put on fresh wood and a few pieces of the precious sea-coal and soon it was alight. But in spite of the warmth she was shivering as she sat waiting for Alamina. She was terrified that she might not come; or come too late when the little maids were already downstairs. But at five o'clock Alamina tapped on the window. She knew better than to be late. She allowed only a few hours of eerie darkness between one visit and another. No daylight hours, for daylight and the routine of ordinary living were apt to foster second thoughts.

Alamina looked haggard and pale for she had been up all night lamenting the death of Piramus. Not that she cared the hoot of an owl for Piramus, who had beaten her often and thoroughly, but to wail for the dead gave her a sensuous enjoyment almost equal to the pleasure of sexual love, or of the *hokkani boro*. Her eyes looked bright and feverish, the lids swollen with weeping, and her hair hung about her like the sweeping curtains of a dark storm. She was a wild elemental creature as she swept into the kitchen on a gust of wind, closed the door against it, gripped Biddy's wrist in an ice-cold hand and pulled her, the Bible gripped under her arm, towards the cellar door.

"The candle!" gasped Biddy, dragging her hand away to pick it up. "You'd have gone down in the dark!"

"The dark!" whispered Alamina, her breath caught by a sob. "He's in the dark, Piramus, the father of my soul. He'll lie in the dark for ever, the dust in his eyes. And the gold is in the dark. The sweet, sweet gold. We come all to the dark and the nibbling of the blind worms."

They were going down the cellar stairs and at mention of worms Biddy nearly dropped the candle. Alamina snatched it from her and led the way, holding it aloft, walking now with grace and dignity, for they were approaching the heart of the great trick and she was as a prophetess inspired.

They knelt one on each side of the poor little bundle of treasure, and Alamina murmured a few strange words as she bent and laid her thin brown hands on the bundle. Then slowly she raised herself, her lips parted in joy, her eyes brimming with tears of delight for Biddy. "The magic has worked," she whispered. "The power is within the gold, drawing the hidden gold to it." She held her hands out to Biddy palm upwards and said solemnly, "Dearie, lay the good Book in my hands." Biddy did so and with the tears of joy trickling down her cheeks Alamina said, "Lay your hands on the Book and swear this oath after me. Swear, Biddy, on the Book."

And Biddy swore on the Book that she would not look at the bundle, touch it or speak of it for three weeks.

"There, my dearie," said Alamina gently, giving the Bible back into her hands and smiling sweetly into her eyes. "Keep your oath and you will be a rich woman. Come in three weeks and you will find the gold of El Dorado. Now we'll go. There now, take the candle and lead on."

Moving like a sleep-walker Biddy did so. Quick as lightning Alamina took a bundle of fir-cones wrapped in the other half of the diklo from her bodice and put it in the place of Biddy's treasure, which she placed between her warm breasts where the cones had been. When Biddy glanced back once over her shoulder she saw no change in the bundle on the floor. Alamina followed Biddy up the stairs. In the firelit kitchen they kissed each other gently, like mother and daughter, and then Alamina went out into the wind and vanished.

CHAPTER VII

A WITCH HUNT

I

The wind that night kept Froniga awake. The triumph she had felt in the calm golden sunset left her as she lay listening to the wind rushing over the roof, feeling the chill of it blowing in through the ill-fitting window. The weather had changed quickly. The wind had veered round from east to north and now to north-west. It was not a good wind but a wind with a scream in it such as she hated. It might perhaps bring snow for Christmas, and the children loved snow, but between now and Christmas she knew there would be disaster. The death of Piramus had opened the door to violence and anger and things would go badly until the anger had spent itself. It was her belief that at every death the escaping spirit, poised for a moment in the doorway between life and death, drew to itself from the world beyond that which it was. Sometimes at the deathbeds of the meek she had felt the airs of paradise and breathed the scent of flowers before the door was shut again. But Piramus had been no saint. His courage might have sent him through on the blast of a trumpet to his purgation, but something of hell would have to be wrestled with for a few days after his passing. She wished she did not know this. It was part of the price that she had to pay for her great gifts that she knew too much.

She went through the next day in a state of mind as grey and leaden as the day; and in the evening she was further saddened because Yoben came to say goodbye to her. The grim ritual of a Romany funeral was something he loathed and from which he always escaped if he could, and this time he was taking Madona and the children with him in one of the wagons. Madona was grieving at the death of her husband, for brutal though he had been he was part of her life and she did not want to witness the great burning. They would travel to the next camping place, where the rest of the tribe would join them after the funeral. "For we cannot stay here," said Yoben. "Alamina has been practising the *hokkani boro*."

"On whom?" asked Froniga sharply.

"I never ask on whom," said Yoben wearily. "I hate the great trick only a little less than a funeral."

After he had gone she passed another restless night and dreary morning and at dusk of the second day after the fair she stood at the window looking out. Dark clouds scudded before the bitter wind and in the gloom beauty had vanished from the earth. Then in the distance she saw the glow of fire. She knew what it was : the funeral pyre, the fiery climax of the long-drawn-out drama of a Romany death. She had been following it in her mind ever since Yoben had left her to go to Madona. There would have been no proper sleep for any of the tribe either that night or the night after, for gypsies do not lie down on their beds while a corpse lies unburied. They would have sat round the fire both nights mourning for the dead man. Sometimes one or another would have fallen into a brief doze, and that was forgiven provided at least three stayed awake to keep Piramus company. For that was the law. Reverence for the dead formed the major part of their religion, but there was also fear of the dead. Until they had got Piramus safe underground his spirit was still with them, and Froniga guessed that they feared him more in death than they had in life. She wished she could have sat with them, mourning around the fire, huddled in her cloak against the wind. She wished she could have helped Madona lay out the dead. Piramus would have been arrayed in his best clothes, in all possible magnificence, and with him in the coffin that the men of the tribe had made they would have placed a hammer, a candle and two coins. Thus he would have light along the dark ways of the dead, the means of battering against doors closed to him, even the means of bribery if necessary. This morning he had been buried, she hoped and believed, in Flowercote Wood, for no Romany was ever buried in a churchyard : they liked to be buried in wild and lonely places. Water had been sprinkled on the coffin, and earth thrown on it, and after the grave had been filled in libations of ale had been poured upon it. Now all that Piramus had possessed was being burned—his tent, his wagon, his bedding, his clothes and his stick. All that could not be burned, such as crockery and cooking-pots, had been smashed to pieces and buried. Not one of his possessions must be left, or they would not be free of his ghost. It would haunt them so long as there remained one thing that he had used, about which it could creep possessively.

Suddenly Froniga remembered something else. Animals were also destroyed, and Piramus had owned the white pony who had galloped across the field in the moonlight and whom she had mistaken for the unicorn, and who had been cropping the grass on the other side of her garden hedge on the morning when she had been thinking of the wholesomeness and delightfulness of the creatures. Generally the dogs and horses of the dead were killed humanely, but she had heard stories of their being bound and flung alive on the funeral pyre. Madona and Yoben were not there to speak up for Baw, who had pulled the royal wagon of Piramus and Madona. Froniga was not a woman who ever hesitated. If she wanted to do a thing it was her custom to do it upon the instant, no matter how mad or how dangerous. She seized her cloak and her purse and in a matter of minutes she was running with the wind over the heath, and as she ran the flames of the great pyre leaped higher. The wind caught them and they streamed away like banners into the dusk.

She ran down the slope of the field to the hollow where the camp was pitched. She could hear the roar of the fire now and see the dark figures moving about it. She saw a white creature, white as her Pen, rearing up, and heard his scream of terror. She had never heard a horse scream before and the sound was to her more terrible than the scream of a man would have been. Men often deserved what they endured at each other's hands, but animals, as she had thought on that morning that seemed so long ago, were without sin and yet were tortured by the sin of man.

Baw filled Froniga's whole vision, her mind and heart. She ran as fast as she could and reached him. She seized his bridle with her left hand and with her right balled into a fist struck first one man and then another straight between the eyes. She looked wild and dishevelled as a madwoman now, her hair on her shoulders and her eyes blazing. She cursed and swore, as she had heard her father do when he was drunk, but had never expected to do herself. Her respectable gorgio relatives would have died of shame could they have seen and heard her. It was the mercy of heaven that Yoben was not there. Her Romany relatives fell back from her in numinous dread, for they thought her possessed. She took the purse out of her pocket and threw it at the feet of Piramus's nephew, Logan Heron, whom she judged now to be the head of the family. The silver pieces rolled out in the grass. "Take that for Baw!" she shouted at him, and swinging round she flung herself across Baw's back and scrambled up. He had no saddle, but her father had taught her to ride bareback. He reared again, but her power over animals was very great and in a moment or two she had mastered him. "Go on now, Baw!" she said to him, kicking her heels against his sides. "Run now! Run like the wind!"

But as she rode forward there was a confused shouting behind her. "*Chovihan!* She's a witch, burn her! She killed Piramus. She and the black witch down by the wood. She went to the house of the black witch. Logan saw her. They bewitched Piramus and in the hour of victory he fell. Burn them! *Chovihan!*"

Froniga rode for her life, pursued by the hatred of her people. She knew they were pursuing her, some on foot, and some of the men on horseback, for she heard the pounding of hoofs behind her. She did not look back, for only cowards look back. But she did not want to be burnt with Baw. The love of life was hot in her and she would save herself and the pony if she could, and if not she would not give her enemies the satisfaction of seeing her waver or blench. They should have no power over her. If she died without fear they would get no pleasure from her death. She hated them now as much as they hated her, and hatred sustained her and passed from her body to that of Baw, so that he galloped as mad with rage and excitement as she was herself. But he had more sense than she. Beside herself as she was, she had no sense of direction as she urged him forward, and no longer knew where home was, though she supposed they were going home. But Baw knew better than to gallop uphill towards her cottage; instead he headed towards the village and the church. His choice saved them. Had they ridden home the rising ground would have checked their speed and the men behind would have caught them, but straight on towards the village there was nothing to stop Baw and he was the fastest of the gypsy ponies.

As she came out of the fields into the lane by the church, Froniga knew she had outdistanced her pursuers. It was nearly dark now, but to her left she could see the squat comfortable shape of the little parsonage. She longed to go in and find safety with the old man within, but Parson Hawthyn had no stable. There might be safety for herself, but there would be no safety for Baw. She rode on, so tired now that she had little idea where she was going, save only that she was seeking safety for Baw. It was not until the beech-woods closed about her that she realised that his instinct of hers was taking them to the manor, and her heart lifted. She could see the warm safe locked stable, the candle-lit parlour and Margaret and the children tying up the Christmas presents by the fire. She would stay the night at the manor and not go back to her lonely cottage. Her rage and courage were spent now and she was cold, shivering and miserable. And Baw was in much the same case. He stumbled as he strained on through the dark and when they came to the rising ground he nearly fell. She pulled him in to a walk, patting his neck, feeling his coat rough and clammy with sweat. "We're nearly home, Baw," she said. "Just a little further and we'll be home."

They toiled slowly up the hill, but when they came out on the stretch of common before the manor-house the wind revived them, and Froniga found herself able to think a little. "It's dark now," she thought. "Tom will have locked the stable and gone home. I must ask Biddy for the key and look after Baw myself." Then the road turned and she saw the manor, with the stable behind it, and inside the stable there was light. "Tomorrow will be Christmas Eve," she thought stupidly. "That's why there's light in the stable."

A rough cart track led round behind the manor to the stable and this she followed. She slipped off Baw's back so weary that she nearly fell when her feet reached the ground, then pushed open the stable door and went in, leading Baw. A cheery sound of whistling greeted her, and there inside was tow-headed Tom rubbing down Robert's mare Diamond, with Will's Pal and his own Noah beside them. A lantern hung from a hook in the ceiling and its light shone down upon a scene of warm and comfortable safety. Diamond was very weary, but gladness to be home was in every line of her body and her nose was lowered thankfully into her manger. Pal and Noah looked round and whinnied in welcome. Diamond took her nose from her manger, looked over her shoulder and whinnied too. Baw answered them, then coming forward over the cobbles, he pressed in between Pal and Noah and they not only suffered him to do so but gently touched noses with him.

Froniga and Tom stared in amazement, for they had never before seen horses welcome a stranger so gladly.

"It appears that he's come home," said Froniga. "It's his own stable in which he's apparently expected. Tom, give him to Mistress Jenny in the morning with my love and tell her his name is Baw."

Then her legs gave way beneath her and she sank down on Diamond's saddle against the wall.

"Mistress Froniga!" gasped Tom, wide-eyed and crimson with dismay as he looked at her tumbled hair and ashen face. "Be ee poorly?"

"No, Tom," she said, "but I've just saved Baw from being burned on Piramus Heron's pyre." And then she thought with shuddering horror, "and myself too. They were so mad that I believe they would have done what they said. They are elemental under the skin and so am I." She believed she was shuddering at herself as much as at them. It was fearful to her to think that the surface of things could so split open and show such savagery down below. Tom gazed at her with amazed embarrassment. "Lemme fetch Biddy, mistress," he begged.

"No, Tom," said Froniga. "Fetch no one. Get me a drink of water from the well."

Tom fetched water from the well in the stable yard in his own leather bottle. When he returned she had gathered back her hair, pulled the hood of her cloak over her head and was looking more like herself. She drank some water and her strength began to come back. "Diamond!" she exclaimed. "What's Diamond doing here?"

"Squire's home, mistress," said Tom. "Come home sudden like. His wound healed better than was expected and he's home for Christmas. The war be at a standstill just now, so Squire's home."

Froniga should have felt happy, but instead she felt intensely anxious. She got up, steadying herself with her hand against the wall. "Shall I help you to the house?" he asked.

"No, Tom. I am rested. I am going home." He clacked his tongue in dismay, then saw that she was looking more like the Mistress Froniga whom he knew and feared a little, so strong was she and at times so stern. She was stern now, commanding him from her great height. "Say only that I have bought Baw from the gypsies for Mistress Jenny," she said. "Do not speak of the fire, for she knows nothing of such things. Take care of him, groom him well and let her see him in the morning."

She patted the three ponies and Diamond, smiled at Tom and went out into the windy darkness. She feared to go home, but she was not going to intrude upon the first night of Robert's homecoming. Robert and the children would welcome her, but the feelings of poor Margaret deserved consideration. And she dreaded Robert. For some inexplicable reason she feared the man from whom she had parted with such love, and wished he had not come home.

As she walked her courage returned. She was a woman so naturally valiant that no weakness could master her for long. Presently she was walking through the beech-woods, where the dark leafless trees roared over her head in the wind, resolutely subduing a tendency to hurry and forcing her mind to think calmly of what had happened. She must face it. *Chovihan!* It had been a witch hunt. She who lived only to do good to others had been branded as a witch by her mother's people and nearly hunted to death. They had cried out that they would burn her and the other. Suddenly her heart nearly stopped. She stood still breathless, then began to run. Then she got control of herself and checked her speed. No good to run, for she would only exhaust herself. She would get there quicker if she merely walked fast and steadily. It appalled her that in her haste to preserve her own life she had forgotten the other. She was now, she was sure, too late, but too late or not she must go to the inn and get help and then go to Mother Skipton's cottage and see what had become of her, and if she could not get help she must go alone.

When she reached the windy height of the other common the moon struggled out for a few minutes, and now by its light she did run. When she reached the linden trees near the inn she stopped, leaning against one of the great trunks to get her breath; from here she could get a glimpse of her cottage and to her astonishment she saw a light in the little kitchen window beside the back door. She had left her fire nearly out, but in any case it was not the flicker of firelight but the steady gleam of the candles that she saw. Someone was there and the square of light gave her reassurance. She did not go to the inn, but walked on quietly down the lane to her own home.

2

If Froniga had gone to the parsonage she would not have found Parson Hawthyn there, for he had gone to Henley to have his hair and beard cut and trimmed by Master Isard. After that he visited an old friend in the town, a green fingered man, and from his house and sheltered old garden had been given a few treasures for the altar of his church on Christmas Day: sprigs of scented geranium, Christmas roses and a few violets. As he walked home through the dusk, up Pack and Prime lane, he was holding these treasures carefully, rejoicing in them. The hair-cut had cost him coins he could ill afford, but it had been worth it to have the Christmas roses and the violets. Also he had wished to be particularly trim and tidy this Christmas. He wished to honour God in every way possible. He wanted the church to look gay and beautiful as it had never looked before, the services to be memorable with prayers and hymns that were wholehearted in God's praise. He wanted his people to remember this Christmas for he thought the time was coming when they might no longer be able to worship God in the way he had taught them, and which was natural to them, the way of beauty and gaiety of heart that was akin to the world about them, where birds sang and flowers and stars bloomed and shone, the way that he believed was God's way, who had made all things bright and fair. For Parson Hawthyn was not very optimistic about the future. He believed the King would fight great battles yet, would be victorious for a while, but he feared that the darkness that confronted him was like that of a mounting storm that will not pass until it has broken. Then it would pass, as all things pass, but that time might be a long way ahead, and Parson Hawthyn did not suppose he would live to see it. But the times ahead were none of his business. His business was this Christmas that had been so miraculously given to him. By next Christmas, Robert, the patron of his living, might have driven him out of his church, but this Christmas, by God's mercy, Robert was not here. For that, as he trudged along Pack and Prime lane, leaning on his stick, he gave thanks, speaking aloud as was his custom, and singing a little in his cracked voice.

But presently he ceased singing, for the way was miry and rough and he was tired. In his younger days, before the rheumatism got hold of him, the walk to Henley, four miles there and four miles back, had been nothing to him, but now it seemed long. And darkness was coming down quicker than he liked with a few flakes of snow in the wind. Ahead of him, as he walked, there was a glow in the sky. He knew what it was, for he had heard of Piramus Heron and his mighty death. Outlined against the glow was a rickety chimney and he knew what that was too, and he never saw it without a stab of reproach. Several times in past years he had gone to see Mother Skipton. Each time she had let him in politely enough, dusted a chair for him and bade him sit down. Then she had stood before him while stumblingly he had tried to talk to her, a half-smile on her lips and her eyes veiled. Whether she had ever listened to what he had to say he had no idea, for she had never made any comment beyond that contemptuous smile and that glance turned inward, as it seemed, to her own darkness. Sitting in her cottage he had suffered a helpless misery. He had felt that he was trying to crawl up a surface of cold marble with no handhold anywhere, nothing to hold on to, nothing to which he could appeal, and in the sickening evil of the place any small good that was his had seemed to drain away. He had never left her without wondering if he had built his life, after all, only upon a nothingness, and so he had ceased to visit her, although he had never ceased to pray for her. But he could never see her cottage without a sense of shame. His faith was weak indeed if it could be stifled by the evil of one poor frail woman.

As his fatigue grew, depression grew with it. What a wicked country was this England, even now in the ending for this year of grace 1642. Though it would be hard to find a man or woman without faith of some sort, the faith of so many was twisted to evil. Though the gypsies acknowledged the boro Duvel, and Christ who had ridden on a donkey and was therefore one of them, that fire there was a heathen fire, for their true religion was fear of the dead, and from their fear grew much cruelty. And were the fanatical among the Puritans much better? Their God was the tribal God of the Israelites and they had forgotten the mercy of Christ. And for that matter so had many men and women who acknowledged a like faith with himself, for what had the tortures of Tyburn, the block, the gallows and the pillory to do with Christ? He stumbled over a stone and almost fell. Under the lowering sky with its dark and phantom clouds the evil of the world seemed crushing him into the earth.

There was a cry of terror. He stood still, his breath choking him and his mouth dry. Was it the wind? No, not the wind, or his body would not so echo the fear. It had been a woman's cry, and it had come from his left. Somehow, clutching at the hedge above him with the crook of his stick, he managed to scramble up the bank and push through the bushes. Flying through the dusk of the field he could see dark shadows, the dark forms of men, and they were hunting silently, their silence far more deadly than baying hounds would have been. Their quarry was ahead of them. He could see a gleam of streaming white as of a banner or scarf, but no more, she ran so fast, as fast as a white hare before the hounds. She was making for the wood that lay beyond the fields, the leafless branches roaring in the wind as though it were a bitter sea that beat upon their dark shore. But she would not find safety there. The men who pursued her were men of the woods and could see in them with the eyes of a cat.

The strength of his youth returned to Parson Hawthyn. The witch hunt was running parallel with the lane and not far from it. He had only a short distance to run before he had come between the woman and her pursuers, and just at that moment she caught her foot in a tuft of grass and fell. By that fall she saved herself, for in a moment Parson Hawthyn had reached her and was standing over her brandishing his stick.

He was a comical knight errant with his sparrow-like figure, crimson face and jutting white beard. He had lost his hat and his priestly white bands were all awry. He was almost as much beside himself with indignation as Froniga had been, but he did not swear, for the depths of him had been purged of their mirk long ago. What welled up from them now was a white-hot flame of anger that was terrifying by reason of its very purity. If the prayer of a righteous man availeth much, so does his anger. It built a wall about the old man and the prostrate woman, and the hunters halted.

"I forbid you to touch this woman," said Parson Hawthyn, brandishing his stick, his voice ringing out powerfully. "And you cannot touch her without killing me first, and I am a *rashai*. You know what will happen if you kill a *rashai*; you will yourselves die and your souls will lie for ever deep in hell."

They could tell that he was a *rashai* by his garments, and a few among them knew him by sight. They had a superstitious fear of parsons. Even to see one was unlucky, to kill one was worse. They drew back a little, as dogs will do when haunted by fear. First one and then another slunk away into the shadows. In a few moments there was no one left but the parson and the witch. "I think that is all, my daughter," he said. "But you cannot stay alone in your cottage tonight. You must come with me to the village."

He helped her to her feet. He could see that her face was ashen and that she could not control the trembling of her jaw. Her eyes stared towards the glow of fire in the distance and he could imagine what the dread of fire was to a witch. The white thing that he had seen was her apron. It had been torn in her fall and she pulled at it with a sort of fretful anger, as though realising it had increased her danger. It came away in her hand and she dropped in on the ground.

"I was at the well," she said. "If they had got me in the cottage I could not have escaped." She began to shiver and he took her arm and held it.

"Mistress Skipton," he said sternly, "if you cannot control your trembling I cannot take you to safety. Your will has always been strong for evil, use it now for good. For life is good and you will win life if you will do as I bid you. Come now."

He helped her across the field and they struggled through the hedge together and down the bank into the lane. They stumbled along it, helping each other, for Parson Hawthyn was now once again feeling his rheumatic knees and fatigue. They might both have found progress impossible had it not been for the help of his stick. As they walked he wondered where to take the woman. Though he knew that many of his parishioners secretly made use of her and her spells he did not suppose that any of them would welcome a witch for the night, and he had no room in his own house in which to put her even if she could have walked so far. Then he thought of Froniga. Hers was the first cottage they would reach in the lane, and she was strong and courageous. Moreover he thought in his ignorance that Froniga, being herself half a gypsy, would be in favour with her mother's people and anyone whom she protected would be safe from them.

"Mistress Skipton, I am taking you to Mistress Froniga Haslewood," he said. "Of all of us in the village I think she is best able to protect you."

The witch made no answer. He could not know her state of mind, but he guessed she was a creature thrown out of her element and stunned by shock. Her element of evil had been as familiar to her as is its lair to a beast. He wondered if she would be able to make the effort to stay out of it and so to save herself, or whether beast-like she would crawl back to it again.

They came to Froniga's cottage and to his dismay he saw that the windows were dark. If she had gone to spend Christmas at the manor then he did not know what to do, but if she was out attending some sick person then she had probably left her back door unlocked, according to her careless and dangerous custom. They dragged themselves round to the back door, he lifted the latch and to his relief the door opened. In the warm fragrant little room inside a faint glow still came from the fire, and also from that other fire beyond the east window. He put Mother Skipton in Froniga's chair with her back to it and quickly pulled the curtain, threw fresh dry wood and fir-cones on the fire and lit the candles. Then he looked round anxiously. He knew he should give Mother Skipton some hot drink to revive her but he did not know how to come by it.

"Heat me a little hot milk over the fire," said Mother Skipton in a voice faint and dry as the rustle of dead leaves. "She keeps her saucepans there, hanging from those hooks. The milk is in the blue jug on the dresser."

"I see that you've been here before," said Parson Hawthyn, as he did her bidding.

"No," she said, "but I have looked through the window. I have looked through it many times to increase my hatred of her. I have seen her with her witch's hair lying on her shoulders in the arms of her gypsy lover. You have desired to save me from evil. You should look nearer home."

Parson Hawthyn, kneeling on the hearth to warm her milk, steadied himself with his hand against the wall. He looked at her. The words had been venomous, but her eyes were blank and unseeing. If the venom had been in her eyes too he would have given up all hope of her. As it was he felt wretched enough. He had heard of the taming of wild beasts, but he had never heard of a tame adder. He gave the woman the cup of hot milk and turned to warm his hands at the fire, trying not to see that picture of Froniga that her words had conjured up in his mind. Presently they drew up their chairs to the fire and sat in silence. Mother Skipton, when she had finished her milk, sat with her eyes shut and without movement. The old man tried to pray, but he was too tired and confused, and before his eyes if he closed them was always that picture of Froniga.

There was a quick step outside, the latch lifted and there she was. She saw Mother Skipton and joy and relief banished the white weariness from her face. Her cheeks and her eyes glowed with the joy, and the generosity of it wiped the other image of her out of Parson Hawthyn's mind and he never thought of it again.

Froniga went to Mother Skipton and put her hand on her shoulder. "Thank heaven you are safe," she said, and then turned to Parson Hawthyn. "Did you find her?"

"Yes," he said, reaching for his stick and getting to his feet. "She has been in great danger from the Romany people, but she has escaped by the mercy of God. Look after her, Froniga, I must go home." He limped to the door and she went with him in concern, for she did not think he looked able to walk home. "Stay here and rest a little longer," she begged.

He drew her outside the door and closed it. "Your concern is not with me, but with that poor woman," he said. "Keep her with you now, and after Christmas we will consult together on her behalf. I put a heavy burden upon you, but you are strong. Do not let her go back to her cottage. If she did so it would be like—"

"A dog returning to its vomit," interrupted Froniga. "I know. I've been there. I'll do my best. Have you lost something?"

"I had a bunch of flowers and leaves," he said sadly. "They gave it to me in Henley for the church. Well, of course, I dropped it. I cannot go back."

"There are even now many fair things in my garden," said Froniga warmly. "I'll bring all I can find to the church in the morning."

"I will be glad of them. Good night, Froniga."

He trudged away into the windy darkness. Froniga went back to the silent woman in the chair. "Do not speak of it tonight," she said. "Come to bed. I will make up a potion of herbs for you and you will sleep. Trust yourself to me."

Mother Skipton, in indifferent silence, did all that Froniga told her to do. She lay down in Froniga's bed, drank the soporific draught that she was given and presently slept. Froniga lay down on the truckle-bed in the next room, but she did not sleep for many hours. She was no longer afraid for she judged that the intervention of Parson Hawthyn had protected both herself and Mother Skipton, but she dreaded the morrow. Evil had been drawn upon them by Piramus's passing. Fire still glimmered faintly beyond her window. From sheer weariness she slept at last, and when she woke she saw to her dismay that the dayspring had come. She went to her window and looked out. The wind was still blowing and in the east the grey clouds were laced by flame, but below them on the earth there was no flame. Piramus's funeral pyre had died out into grey ash and the Romany wagons had gone. Fearing justice and perhaps a too early exposure of the great trick the gypsies had all vanished in the night. Impetuously eager to tell Mother Skipton the good news, Froniga opened the door of the next room and went in. The bed was very neatly made. Mother Skipton had also vanished.

CHAPTER VIII

CHRISTMAS EVE

I

Jenny woke up and it was the dayspring. Christmas Eve! She fell out of bed and ran to the window. No, there was no snow. For a moment she was sad, but on opening the window a crack she felt the icy dampness in the wind and cheered up. It might yet snow. Her heart glowed at the thought of the Christmas bells ringing out over the sparkling whiteness, the hymns in church, the presents, the kissing ring and the Christmas goose. And her father was at home. Since he went away she had learned to play very prettily upon the virginal, and she had learned now to read more than "a little". On the wonderful day when Tobias Shakerley the postman had come just before the fair he had brought her a parcel from Oxford. Inside it was a book of fairy tales and on the fly-leaf was written, "For Mistress Jenny Haslewood from her devoted servant John Loggin the painter. Do not forget to read about Beauty and the Beast." To have a book of her own was to Jenny a thing so marvellous that she had not yet quite grasped the marvel. But helped by Froniga she had read *Beauty and the Beast* and grasped the meaning of that very well indeed. Tomorrow she would show the book to her father and she would play to him upon the virginal.

At the thought of her father a slight chill fell upon her glowing heart. He had come back last night, but he had seemed different, not the same father whom she and Will had run to meet at his last homecoming. He had seemed stern and remote. But he had been glad to be home, and he had kept looking at her and Will with a sort of appeal that she could not understand. As she washed and dressed she thought perhaps she did not love him enough. She loved her mother and Will much more. Suddenly she wanted to love him more than she did, and she brushed her hair in a tearing hurry and ran downstairs with Maria at her heels. Her father always got up earlier than anyone else except Biddy and the maids and perhaps he would be downstairs already. The door of the dining-parlour was slightly open and there was firelight showing through it. She flew across the hall, pushed the door open and went in.

Her father was sitting by the fire with a black book in his hands. "Father!" she cried joyously, and he jumped up, gladness flooding over his face and his arms held out. She would have run into them had it not been for Maria suddenly getting tangled up in her legs. She remembered how her father disliked Maria and had wanted her to be dead. In a panic lest he should still want it she pushed Maria out into the hall and shut the door on her. When she turned to Robert again her joy was dimmed and she looked at him with a shadow of fear. His gladness was gone too. He looked much older. "Jenny, let Maria come in," he said. "I'd like her to come in." But Jenny was not taking any chances. "She can go to the kitchen," she said, and going to him, for his hand was held out to her, she dropped a demure curtsey and kissed him sedately on the cheek.

He sat down and took her on his knee and he thought. "I'll win them this Christmas. Please God I'll win them this Christmas." And then tried to talk to her, but he found it difficult to know what to say. Though he had been away from home only a few months it seemed years. He had endured much both in body and mind, and in his spirit had suffered a sort of death and been re-born again to a new way of life, but his home was as it had been and he felt a stranger in it. Last night in bed he had tried to explain his new thoughts to Margaret, but she had not understood and in the end had lain weeping in his arms. She had soon fallen asleep, for crying always made her sleep, but he had lain awake for most of the night. What could he say to his daughter, to this beloved little girl with her air of remoteness and her large dark eyes?

He looked from her to her portrait hanging on the wall beside Will's and he felt a rush of anger. It was exactly like her, it was painted with skill and understanding, but that only increased his hatred of the man who had painted it, the spy who had accepted his hospitality and then sucked valuable information out of the credulous fool he had been. And then had spared his life. He could not think of that moment of recognition between them without hatred and a prayer to the Lord God of Battles that he might have vengeance. That swerving aside of the more valiant soldier, the one who had attacked and not fled, the dropping of the sword and the flicker of contempt that he thought he had seen in the eyes, was something he brooded on ceaselessly. It seemed to him an insult, as though the man had recognised his worthlessness. He was now worthless no longer, but one of the Lord's chosen people, eaten up with zeal for his service, but there was one thing he could not yield to God, and that was the right to be the Lord's instrument in the taking of revenge. He prayed that he might not bear the sword in vain, but might be "the minister of God, a revenger to execute wrath upon him that doeth evil".

And still he had said no word to his daughter. He was just going to try and tell her that he loved her when Margaret, Will and breakfast entered together and his chance was gone. They gathered round the table and Robert repeated the very long grace before meat now used by the Lord's chosen. It was new to his family and seemed to have a depressing effect upon them, as they watched the food growing cold. They did not speak much during the meal, and when Robert had repeated the longer grace after meat, and announced his intention of riding round his estate with his bailiff, no one protested. He had hoped they would, with an insistence not to be denied, for he was feeling ill and exhausted after the journey yesterday and would have liked to sit quietly in the parlour with Margaret, and have the children come and chatter to him as other children chattered to their fathers, but as they did not protest he could not let weariness divert him from his duty. That was part of the new discipline. He called for Diamond and rode away into the bitter wind while Margaret watched him from the window, and began to cry again because she knew he was not fit to go out. Jenny ran to comfort her and Will went hurriedly off to the stable, as was his habit when the women wept.

In ten minutes he had come dashing back again shouting, his cheeks flaming with excitement. "Mother! Jenny! There's a new pony! Cousin Froniga bought him from the gypsies for Jenny. He's all white and belonged to Piramus the gypsy that I saw die. His name is Baw the Comrade. Come quick! Tom's brought him to the door. Come *on*, I say!"

He dashed out again, and Margaret and Jenny followed him to the front door. There stood Tom, grinning from ear to ear and holding a snow-white pony. He had put a light side-saddle, that Margaret had once used, on Baw's back and groomed him so well that he shone as though he stood there bathed in moonlight. He seemed a magical beast.

"A unicorn!" said Jenny, and she came forward a few paces,

her face white with incredulous joy. "For Will," she whispered.

"For you, Mistress Jenny," Tom insisted. "He's all yourn."

Baw turned his head, looked at Jenny and whinnied. She did not rush him, but yet her feet scarcely seemed to touch the ground as she moved. He put his muzzle in her left hand while with her right she caressed him. Her face was now as rosy as it had been white and her eyes shone. She and Baw were alone together. There was no one else. It was spring and about them rustled the leafy gold and green of the wood. Tom broke the enchanted silence. "'Tis your little horse, 'tis Baw," he said. "The pony Mistress Froniga bought for ee. Your Christmas gift, I was to say. He's just so gentle as a white dove. Will ee get your cloak and come riding, Mistress Jenny? Mistress Haslewood, I'll take take good care of Mistress Jenny."

Jenny flew into the house, but ran back again to ask, "May I, Mother?" but she barely waited for her mother's permission before she was off again. Will meanwhile ran to the stable to saddle Pal with no permission at all. Margaret, abandoned by both husband and children, went back to the parlour and shut the door, but this time she was too angry for tears. That Froniga should have taken it upon herself to give a pony to Jenny, and a gypsy pony too, without asking permission of the children's own mother, and with intent to take her child's love from her, was bad enough, but that it should have been Froniga who had brought that look of joy to Jenny's face was infinitely worse. And Froniga always spent Christmas Day with them. How was she to get through Christmas Day eaten up by this hatred of Froniga?

Jenny and Will and Tom trotted towards the wood on their ponies and they did not know that the day was grey and dark and the wind cold. For all they knew it might have been spring; and so it was spring, the mid-winter spring of Christmas that burgeons in all hearts that are without hatred and self-reproach. Their cheeks glowed and their eyes shone, and their ponies, white and dapple grey and chestnut, shared their joy.

They rode under the archway of beech boughs, where Robert had seen his children standing, and down into the wood, Jenny leading them. She rode well, as well as Will, though she had had so little practice, and already there was love between herself and Baw. "We belong to each other, Baw," she thought. "The hollow on your back was made for me and I was made for the hollow on your back, and I wish Cousin Froniga could see me now."

And Baw thought. "I drew the wagon of a king, and though it was heavy I was proud to draw it along the roads of the world, but I did not want to draw it down the paths of the dead, for I am a white pony and I do not love the dark, and so I am glad to carry this maiden, for she is light as a feather and young as the morning and she too is a princess. And that was a queen who rode on my back last night, and I would like to thank her, for she rode me away from the burning and renewed my youth with the youth of this royal child."

And Jenny, looking back over her shoulder at the two boys, called, "I'm going to Cousin Froniga's cottage." But when they rode up on to the common, Baw did not go straight on to the cottage, but swerved away to the right along the lane that led to the church, and he cantered so fast that Tom and Will had to urge on Pal and Noah lest they be left behind.

2

Froniga pillaged her garden and the hedgerows of the lane, and then, laden with holly, ivy, Christmas roses and rosemary, she walked quickly to the church. At the churchyard gate she met Parson Hawthyn, cheerful but hobbling painfully upon his stick. "I climbed hedges like a ten-year-old yesterday," he said with a chuckle, "but this morning I know my age. Thank you, Froniga; that's a fine big Christmas posy. Is that poor woman still with you?"

"No," said Froniga. "When I got up this morning I found the gypsies had gone and so had she."

"Not back to her cottage?" asked Parson Hawthyn in distress.

"I'm afraid so," said Froniga. "When she saw the gypsies had gone she would have known she would be safe there. What can we do now?"

"Nothing at this moment," said Parson Hawthyn. "This is not her moment, but the children's. Look there."

She looked where he pointed and laughed, for the grey gloom of the day had parted and had let through colour and delight. A little figure in a cloak and hood of kingfisher blue, riding a white pony, was flying towards them. Just behind came a dapple grey bearing a boy in elfin green, and beside him Tom's face shone ruddy as a lantern, and his clothes, like his pony, were chestnut brown. The sound of the ponies' hoofs had been heard and more children came running out of the cottages on either side of the lane, all rosy-cheeked with pleasure and carrying holly and branches of fir, for Parson Hawthyn had summoned all his pupils to decorate the church. They were a few moments before the appointed time, but the sound of the cantering hoofs, and then the sight of Mistress Jenny riding a new pony, had brought them all flying along like a flock of birds. Froniga thought with a sudden ache of the gypsy children, and her thoughts seemed to bring them winging in from the east to join the others. Then Baw came to a standstill beside her, his head against her shoulder, his nose pushing into her hand, and Jenny slipped off his back into her arms.

Presently, when the ecstatic thank yous had been said, and all the children had patted Baw and Pal and the bolder ones had been sat on their backs and given rides, the ponies were left in Tom's care and Parson Hawthyn and Froniga led the children into the church. Both knew better than to try and use the children as their helpers; that way madness lay. They told the children what had to be done and left them free to do it as they liked, as was in any case their right upon their own festival. They themselves sat down filled with that sublime indifference to results which distinguishes the truly great after right action has been taken.

The results were good, if unusual, and if some of the holly and greenery were put in surprising places, the children did not forget the little lady and her unicorn upon the tomb. The lady had holly on her pillow and the unicorn a wreath of ivy about his neck. Parson Hawthyn had felt that the Virgin's arms could not be empty on Christmas Day, and he had carved and painted a new baby, even more beautiful than the one Cinderella had stolen. On top of a flat tomb he had made a stable with a thatched roof, and filled it with hay, and set the Virgin and Child within it, and he had carved figures of the shepherds and the animals to stand around them. The children were thrilled with this and they put the brightest bunches of holly within the stable. By common consent of the children, Jenny was left to arrange the flowers on the altar. Two of the big boys fetched her some water from the spring in the wood and with stars in her eyes she arranged the Christmas roses and rosemary with sprigs of holly, in two pewter pots and put them one on each side of the silver cross.

It was one of those hours in which pure joy, strong as an encircling wall, shuts out past and future as completely as intense pain can do, giving to time the quality of eternity. Neither Parson Hawthyn nor Froniga ever forgot it. The old man felt the weight of his griefs and worries fall from him. Even his body felt less heavy with age and pain. He was conscious of unseen presences within the church and warmed himself in their gaiety. He had a foretaste of paradise, and realised for the first time how full of laughter the place must be. Froniga lost herself in a dream, for to have children all about her within a wall of safety had always been the best of her dreams. Outside the bleak and drifting clouds parted for a moment and the church was filled with sunshine.

3

Robert had ridden round his estate with his bailiff, and the new zeal that was in him had caused him to find a good deal of fault with what he saw, to the consternation of poor Master Bellows, who until now had always found the squire an easy-going and good-humoured man. Then he had visited the old sexton and the bell-ringer and told them that there was to be no ringing of the bells on Christmas morning, and no music of flutes and viols in the gallery. Bell-ringing, whistlings and scrapings were popish practices and were to be discontinued for the future. Turning his back on their incredulous dismay, he glanced with brief longing in the direction of Froniga's cottage and then turned his back on that too. His love for his cousin was a sin in the eyes of God, and must be mortified. She would spend Christmas Day with them tomorrow, as she always did, but he must give her to understand that kisses and soft words were ended between them. Having decided this, he turned thankfully homeward. It would be good to get indoors out of the bitter wind and sit with Margaret before the fire.

But half way across the common the question that had been knocking at the back of his mind ever since he had come home last night, and which he had been trying to forget, thrust itself forward. Had Parson Hawthyn obeyed him? Had the popish images been removed from the church? Was it or was it not his duty to go and see? He did not want to go? He was shivering with cold and his head was aching. He wanted to get home, and he did not want to quarrel with the old man he loved. He had so longed for this Christmas with his children, that he might truly get to know them and win their love. He wanted no shadow to fall upon it. Surely he had done his full duty in writing that letter. Had he? No! Not so did the Lord's servants perform His will. He dragged at the reins, trying to pull Diamond away to the left, away from the road home. Diamond resisted, for she was as anxious to get home as her master was, and the sudden wrench on her mouth was not the sort of treatment to which she was accustomed. The obstinacy in his horse hardened Robert's purpose, and he spurred her along the road to the church, brutal to her because he was being brutal to himself. He lashed himself with savage contempt as he rode. Did he call himself the Lord's servant and then propose to put his own comfort and convenience before the Lord's work? He was an unprofitable servant, and if consolation was not granted to him, as it was to others of the Lord's people, if he was left hungry in outer darkness, it was not to be wondered at. "Give me strength, O Lord," he prayed, "give me the strength to do your will today though it slay my heart. 'Though He slay me yet will I trust in Him.' You have given me strength in battle, give me strength in this thing also."

As though in answer to his prayer, the dark clouds parted above him and the light streamed down. His heart lifted a little. It might be that if he could do the Lord's will in this hard thing he would know consolation.

It so happened that Tom and the ponies had betaken themselves to the far side of a haystack, to keep out of the wind, and Robert did not see them as he dismounted and tied Diamond to the churchyard gate. He walked slowly up the path to the church porch. His heart felt like a stone, it was so heavy, and the hammer-strokes of pain beat so ceaselessly on his temples that he felt bewildered and unsure of himself, "Lord, give me strength," he prayed again, and pushed the door open.

For a moment, with the sound of the children's voices in his ears and the colour and sunlight dazzling his eyes, he did not believe what he saw. This was some feverish dream. He shut his eyes for a moment, for the sunlight on the silver cross was blinding, but when he opened them it was still there, and so were the popish images decked out in gaudy berries and greenery. And Parson Hawthyn was sitting smiling on a bench, and beside him, smiling too, was Froniga. At sight of her glowing beauty a surge of hot passion went through him, and then came anger, such tearing anger as he had never known. Something seemed to break in his aching head and all power of control left him. All that was in him came surging out: his cruelty, his zeal and new-found strength, his suppressed and wounded love, and his anger. Like an avenging angel he went with powerful strides to the altar and took the cross from it, and tossed the flowers upon the ground. He carried the cross to the door and flung it outside. Then he took the stable and all the little figures in it, and the straw, and tossed them out into the churchyard too. He came back and shouted to the terrified children to bring out the greenery and garlands and the rest of the images that were defiling God's house, and reaching up he himself swept a row of little birds from a window-sill and hurled them through the door. He went to the screen and kicked the painted figures of the saints, soiling the soft colours of their robes. His eyes blazed, but his face was white as paper.

Parson Hawthyn and Froniga stood together, the old man trembling, Froniga frozen, and looked at him as though he were a stranger. Some of the children, huddled against them in fear, began to cry. Courage and control came back to Parson Hawthyn. "Don't cry," he said to the children. "There must be neither tears nor strife on Christmas Eve. We have had a happy hour. Do what the squire tells you. Take the fir branches and the little figures outside." Then, as a few of the older boys obeyed him, he turned round upon Robert and said sternly, "Robert, bring back the cross. The rest is of no importance, but the cross must come back to the altar."

But Robert did not look at him; indeed, he did not hear him. With his arms full of fir branches and holly he strode out into the churchyard and gathering everything together in a heap he took his tinder box from his pocket and set fire to the dry hay and branches. Then he strode back to the church again. In the porch he was halted, as hands caught and held him.

"Are you mad, Robert?" asked Froniga. The shock had seemed to turn her to stone, but now that it had passed she was so angry that her fingers bit cruelly into Robert's arms. Yet her voice was cold and it pierced him. He had not heard Parson Hawthyn, but he heard her, though her voice seemed to him to come from a great distance. His arms, that had been struggling against her grip, were suddenly still, his eyes met hers and a childish bewilderment came into them. Pity was mixed with her anger. "You don't know what you are doing," she said more gently. "Think what you are doing and stop behaving like a madman."

She took her hands from his arms and ran back into the church, for she could see Parson Hawthyn groping to pick up the scattered flowers before the altar, and he appeared to be groping sightlessly. Her wide skirts and her cloak had hidden the two children behind her. Robert, now that her hands no longer held him, felt suddenly lost and unsteady. His eyes, that had been looking into hers, looked still where she had been, but it was a full minute before he saw Jenny and Will standing huddled in the corner of the porch, two small forlorn figures holding hands and looking at him. Will's mouth was open and his eyes were round as an owl's. When they met those of his father they dropped. In a flash Robert saw Will's face when he had brought him his sword and they had smiled at each other, and then again he saw Will's face now, with the mouth so stupidly open and his eyes looking on the ground. And then it was Jenny's face that he saw, white and cold. Her lips were closed tightly and her eyes stared at him with no recognition in them. "Jenny," he whispered and held out his hand to her. She did not shrink away, but there was still no recognition. Though it was only for a couple of minutes, it seemed to Robert that he stood there for an eternity looking at his children. It did not seem to him possible that the Lord could have let them be there, could have let this happen. The Lord had forsaken him.

A boy was pulling at his sleeve and trying to tell him something. Other boys were running in and shouting, and the children who were still in the church were running out and falling over each other in the porch. Outside he could hear cries and the crackle of flames. Froniga had taken hold of his other arm and was pulling him out into the churchyard. He heard her crying out, "Jenny, keep the little children in the church." And then he was running with her down the path towards the churchyard gate, where Tom was already unfastening the terrified Diamond and taking her to a place of safety with the ponies.

It had not rained for some while and the bonfire he had kindled had soon taken hold of the dry hay and branches, and then the little wooden figures. The wind had caught up the flames into long streamers of fire and the flying sparks had blown on to the dry thatch of the parsonage, and it was blazing. Men from a nearby farm and women from the cottages came running, and in a few moments they had formed a chain of buckets from the nearest well and were working with a will. But it was hopeless. The little cottage was built mostly of wood and it burned like a torch. The flames leapt up against the dark driven clouds and streamed away with them before the wind. There were only fields south-east of the parsonage and the wonderful mercy of that morning was that no other home was destroyed and no one was hurt except Robert, who went into the blazing cottage to try and pull out some of Parson Hawthyn's belongings. He rescued no more than the old man's table and chair, and a plate with flowers upon it that he thought might be a special treasure, before he was seized and dragged away. "Do not risk your life, Robert," said Froniga sternly. "You cannot undo what you have done by burning yourself as well as the house. Look at your hands!"

He had burned them badly, but he felt no pain, and he had felt no fear when he went into the burning house. He had felt nothing but the longing to die there in the flames, that he might not again have to face his children or Parson Hawthyn. The Lord had forsaken him and he was in hell. Why could he not be allowed the flames of hell? Instead of that he found a kindly crowd about him. Someone had fetched salves and linen from the farm and Froniga was binding his hands. The little house was now a smoking ruin and Parson Hawthyn was thanking him courteously for saving his treasures. "That plate was my most valued possession," he said, smiling at Robert. "And the chair and table I valued greatly." None can lie more convincingly than the saints, when they feel that once in a while a lie is called for. The happy smile on the old man's face was no indication of the misery that was in his heart. Though he kept smiling, and saying to those about him the things he ought to say, his personal bereavement was just now very bitter. He did not mind in the least that the cottage had gone, and for the moment he had forgotten all that had happened in the church, but his books were burnt, including the book that had had "Charles. R." written on the fly-leaf. He did not know how he was to bear it. If only Robert had thought to pull out his books.

For the villagers and most of the children pleasurable excitement had now taken the place of alarm. They were used to fires, for with homes built so largely of wood and thatch they were a common occurrence, but what they were not used to was the squire taking leave of his senses. This was something quite new. The tenor of life's course had been delightfully interrupted. This was better than the war, for the war was at a distance, but the squire going mad was under their very eyes. It was obvious from the looks of him that he was mad, so they felt little indignation at what he had done. It was on a par with old Sam Tidmarsh flinging all the mugs of ale out of the inn when he was drunk. They all wanted to help Robert to his horse, and lift Jenny up in front of him that she might take the reins that he could not hold with his burned hands, so that Diamond could take him home. Froniga mounted Baw, for she was going with them. Margaret would never be able to care properly for Robert, or for the children in the state of bewilderment and shock that they were in. It was hard on Margaret, but she must go.

"You must come too, sir," she said to Parson Hawthyn. "You must come to the manor."

Robert was sitting his horse staring at the ruins of the parsonage, and now he looked down at the old man standing by his stirrup. "Let me make that much reparation," he said hoarsely.

Parson Hawthyn smiled at him. "It's not out of bitterness that I refuse," he said, "but because there is another house in my parish where I think it is my duty to go." He paused, drew nearer and said, "Robert, do not take this to heart. You did what you conceived to be your duty, and from the darkness that is our honest conception of light God in His mercy always brings some good."

Robert did not hear a word, but he was aware of the old man's forgiveness and was crushed by it. He bowed his head and sat inert upon his horse. Jenny took charge, turning Diamond round and heading courageously for home, with Froniga, Will and Tom riding after her. Parson Hawthyn watched them go pitifully, then turned to his parishioners.

"The services will be as usual tomorrow," he said briskly. "And the bells will be rung."

"Squire said no bells," a man called out.

"The bells will be rung," repeated Parson Hawthyn. "And

every man, woman and child in this parish will come to church. Will one of you be so good as to take charge of the table and chair that the squire risked his life to save for me? Later I will send for them to my lodging. Good-day, good people, good-day. A happy Christmas to you all." Wrapped in his cloak, leaning on his stick and carrying his plate, he limped at a good pace down the lane, a sparrow-like figure of immense if comical dignity. No one followed him, for they knew he did not want to be followed. Instead they went into the church and restored what order they could to the desolation there.

Parson Hawthyn trudged across the common and turned down the lane past Froniga's cottage. His lips moved as he walked. Did he remember it? It had been in the book that was burnt.

> "I'll take Thy way; for sure Thy way is best:
> Stretch or contract me Thy poor debtor:
> This is but tuning of my breast,
> To make the music better.
>
> "Whether I fly with angels, fall with dust,
> Thy hands made both and I am there:
> Thy power and love, my love and trust
> Make one place everywhere."

How long would he remember it? He had learned a great deal by heart out of his precious books, but his memory sometimes failed now in his old age. Ah, that was the hardest thing to relinquish! Vigour of mind. The material things were not hard to give up, but memory, intellect, even perhaps at last the power to pray, that had been symbolised by the books upon his shelves, from these it would be hard to part. Being human, he was feeling slightly sorry for himself at the moment and he found himself praying that he might never part from them, that he might die before that final stripping. Then, as he turned north at the corner of the lane and the cold wind struck him, he remembered the season. Christmas Eve. The Child in the manger had not only stripped Himself of the glory of heaven, but of His wisdom too. The doing of the will of God had caused Him to lie there possessing neither memory, intellect nor the power to pray.

Parson Hawthyn was ashamed. How unctuously he had

preached to the young painter about the will of God! At that time he had been experiencing only its more gentle pressure, he had not fought against it as he was fighting now against this bitter wind. Every step forward now was exhausting him, and not only because of the wind, but because of his own desperate inner reluctance. To go to that evil house and live there pressed upon night and day by that woman's wickedness. He groaned as he bent forward into the wind and then stopped altogether, so overwhelming was the temptation to turn back. Surely he was guilty of presumption in going on? What could he, a weak sinner, do against that evil? He would be embedded in it like a fly in treacle, helpless. He would himself be lost. Yet she was in physical as well as spiritual danger. His presence in her house would at least give her physical protection. That he might have a little rest from his conflict with the wind, he turned round. Facing south it seemed almost balmy, and there was a line of light in the sky behind the village and the church. Unconsciously he took a few steps back towards the light, and then stopped, checked by the very ease of what he was doing. Ease and the will of God were seldom synonymous. He turned round again and struggled on, and found it had begun to snow.

By the time he reached Mother Skipton's cottage a thin white blanket had been spread over the unsavoury garden, but by this time he was too tired to notice anything. He was entirely taken up with trying to keep upon his feet. He got to the door and knocked upon it. Then stood leaning upon his stick trying to get his breath. The door opened, and still he had not got it. "My house—" was all he managed to say.

"It's burnt," said Mother Skipton. "I saw the flames."

She took him by the arm and led him into the cottage and dusted a chair for him. She took his cloak and shook the snow off it at the door, then closed the door and came back to him. She stood before him, her hands folded, smiling. Presently he got his breath back and said to her, "My daughter, I come to you as a suppliant. Could you give me lodging? You have a room to spare, I know, and I can pay whatever is right." He paused. "I ask you in the name of God."

He waited, aware of the struggle that was going on in her. He gave no sign of his own anxiety as he waited for her answer. His reluctance to be here was now a thing of the past. If she yielded to that plea he believed she might be saved.

She spoke at last, her voice low and hoarse. "You saved my life. You may lodge here."

"In the name of God," he said. "Repeat it after me, in the name of God."

She was silent.

"In the name of God," he repeated.

She struggled again and then gave in. "In the name of God," she said, and suddenly reached breaking point. Her arms upon the table, her face hidden, she wept long and wildly. When at last she lifted her head she found herself looking at a china plate brightly patterned with roses and forget-me-nots. It seemed to glow and sparkle in the dark room.

"I brought it for you," said Parson Hawthyn cheerfully. "And surely it's long past dinnertime?"

She took it up and began to laugh.

CHAPTER IX

CHRISTMAS DAY

I

"Robert, you have fever and cannot possibly go to church," said Froniga firmly.

"If I do not go there will be no service," said Robert. "Parson Hawthyn has left the parish. The church being now cleansed of idolatry I must myself preach the word of the Lord and pray with my people."

"How do you know that Parson Hawthyn has left the parish?" asked Froniga.

"Biddy tells me he was seen walking to Henley," said Robert. "I am glad he had the wisdom to realise that his time here is over. You may argue as you like, Froniga, but I am going to church, and you, Margaret and the children are coming with me."

Margaret, sitting on her day bed, sighed and wiped her eyes. Jenny and Will sat stiffly on the edges of their chairs. Outside a slight fall of snow had spread a perfect white coverlet over the world, and the sun was shining brightly in a cloudless blue sky, but it was not Christmas Day. It couldn't be. Christmas Day had always been the happiest day in the year, and this was a miserable day, so it couldn't be Christmas. Yet the parlour was decorated with fir and holly and there was a little pile of presents waiting to be opened when they should come back from church. Jenny thought that if she heard the bells ringing she might feel less miserable. Perhaps outside the tightly closed windows they were ringing.

"Are the bells ringing yet?" she whispered.

"There will be no bells," said Robert. "Bell-ringing is a popish custom and I have forbidden it."

There was silence in the room. Froniga looked at Robert as they stood together before the hearth. He had become much thinner since his last visit home. His face had lost its roundness and the bones showed clearly, giving it a new look of maturity, and though the tight line of his mouth was obstinate rather than strong it called forth her respect. The old Robert, in pain and fever, would have taken to his bed and stayed there, thankful for a valid excuse for keeping away from a difficult situation. The new Robert intended to face the situation. She looked into his eyes, feverishly and fanatically bright in their dark hollows, and had never loved him so much. Forgetting Margaret and the children, she put her hand on his shoulder and said gently, "You must do as you wish, Robert."

He recoiled from her hand as though she had struck him. "Woman, you forget yourself," he said harshly. "Margaret and Jenny, put your cloaks on."

Jenny was coming downstairs in her cloak when she heard the bells. She stopped instantly, put up her hand and laid it on the curved neck of the unicorn, for the bells had begun when she reached the stair beside him. His neck was warm, for the sun was pouring through the east window behind him and spilling down the stairs in pools of light. A moment before she had been shivering, but now she was suddenly warm. The bells seemed ringing in the walls of the house, they seemed ringing in her own body. It was Christmas. It was the happiest day in the year. Nothing that happened to people could prevent Christmas being the happiest day of the year. It was a fact. She ran quickly downstairs, taking the last two at a jump. In the hall Will was sitting on the floor putting on his boots. She pulled him to his feet and whirled him round. "It's Christmas Day, Will!" she cried. "It's Christmas and the bells are ringing!"

Well wrapped up against the cold, and carrying posies of herbs to counteract the aroma of any neighbours in church who might wash less frequently than they did themselves, the Haslewood family walked through the beech-wood, and behind them at a respectful distance came Biddy and the two little maids, also carrying posies. Robert walked in sombre silence and Margaret walked beside him, her hand in his arm. She felt more cheerful now, for when they had come out of the house Robert had very deliberately turned his back upon Froniga, who was now walking behind with the children, and offered his arm to his wife. He had even smiled at her, a wintry sort of smile, but one intended for her alone. She held his arm tightly, feeling that she was supporting and helping him. Now and then she fancied that he pressed her hand against his side. If it was only a fancy it made her happy.

There was joy in Froniga's heart as she came behind with Jenny and Will, for through the whole of her sensitive being she was aware of blessedness. It was the same sort of awareness that came to her sometimes on a winter's night in the middle of a storm. She would go to her window, draw back the curtains and see that the driving clouds had parted as though a hand had drawn them aside like a curtain, and in a pool of tranquil sky she would see a few stars gleaming. The storm was not over, it would rage on until it had blown itself out, but the depth of mercy beyond had shown itself. That pool of sky held all the springtimes of the world. And so it was with the storms that men in their wickedness chose to let loose upon the world. They must spend themselves. But now and then, through them and in spite of them, mercy shone, imposing some pattern upon the flux of things. Froniga knew now, as the children had known for some while, that this was to be a happy Christmas.

Jenny and Will upon either side of her went along as though they had wings upon their feet. Unable to walk fast because of their parents, slow progress, their exuberance expressed itself in sudden upward leaps or dartings sideways, like birds in spring. The snow was thinly spread, crisp and sparkling, and the pattern of their small feet made upon it only a delicate tracery. In the wood the shadows were violet and azure about the trunks of the trees, and far overhead the frosted branches made a silvery filigree against the brilliant blue of the sky. The music of the bells, upon which no one had made any comment, seemed now to be ringing through the aisles of the wood and raining down upon them from the sky. Froniga realised with amusement that this year they were being rung for a longer period than was usual, and with greater vigour and beauty.

When they reached the common they saw other family groups making their way to the church. From every cottage and farm they were coming out in their gay best clothes, that were kept for most of the year in presses and chests and brought out only on fair days and festivals. The gowns of blue and apricot, the red and green cloaks, made each family look like a flower-garden in bloom upon the sparkling snow. Froniga had never seen so many churchgoers. Never mind what brings them, she thought, curiosity or anger, pride or pity, the pattern will be imposed on us all once we are there.

With the bells ringing out over their heads they passed the

ruins of the little parsonage, and Robert forced himself to turn his head and look at them steadily. Then they went on through the churchyard, where the snow had hidden the remains of yesterday's bonfire. Robert found himself oddly thankful for that. The ashes of Parson Hawthyn's little figures, and the blackened cross, would have made him even more wretched than the sight of the parsonage, for that destruction he had intended and the other he had not. Yet he was ashamed of his softness that could still desire so passionately the esteem and love of those about him, and hate to hurt their feelings. Did that great man of God, Colonel Cromwell, consider feelings? No! Whenever idolatry confronted him he was an avenging sword in the hand of the Lord. Would Colonel Cromwell's heart have failed within him at the thought of standing up before a hostile congregation, whose papistical priest he had driven away, and proclaiming the word of the Lord in his stead? No. His voice would have been as a brazen trumpet, and his words winged fire. Removing his hat as he came to the porch, Robert closed his eyes and prayed for strength.

He opened them and found himself looking into the bright eyes of Parson Hawthyn, and thought with a sense of shock and confusion that no one in the world had such piercing, farseeing blue eyes, excepting only Colonel Cromwell himself. He paused, clearing his throat, trying to find the courage to tell the old man he was not to take the service today, and found that he was trembling. "A happy Christmas to you, sir," said Parson Hawthyn loudly and cheerfully, before he could speak, "And to you, madam, and to you, mistress, and to Jenny and Will. Peace to you all." His voice dropped. "Peace to you, Robert. The peace of God." His voice rose again, ringing out cheerfully. "A happy Christmas to you, Sam Tidmarsh. And to you, Mistress Wilkins. A happy Christmas to you all."

There was such a press of people behind them that Robert was forced to move forward. Stumbling a little, his head aching from the clanging of the bells, he let Margaret lead him to their accustomed seat and sat down, covering his face with his hat.

When at the conclusion of his prayer he removed his hat he found that Jenny was upon his other side. She looked up at him and smiled, but it was a careful smile with a pitying tenderness in it, the kind of smile she might have given an afflicted stranger she was passing in the street, and it hurt him unbearably, when he remembered the hopes he had placed upon this Christmas. He looked across his wife to Will upon her other side, and then to Froniga. Margaret and Froniga were looking at him with anxiety, and when he smiled at them their answering smiles were those of intense relief. Why? He looked round the church and saw why. The cross, tarnished and battered but intact, was back upon the altar. The flowers that he had flung on the ground had been rearranged in their pots upon either side of it. Fresh greenery and holly, exquisitely arranged, decorated the pulpit and the screen and the tomb of his grandmother. Except for the loss of the little figures everything was almost as it had been, and in his bewildered state he had noticed nothing when he had come in. It was his absence of protest that was causing such relief to his family. He felt not anger, but sorrow. Who had done this to him? Who had rendered null and void all he had tried to do for the Lord? Parson Hawthyn had himself perhaps found the cross and put it back, but the beauty of the green garlands was beyond the old man's powers. He looked at Froniga, who smiled and bent her head. The bells stopped and behind him the viols and flutes in the gallery, whose music he had forbidden, led the congregation triumphantly into the first hymn. As the surge of singing rose about him, louder and more triumphant than he had ever heard it on Christmas Day, Robert gave up the struggle. He was defeated. Physical weakness and family love had him in chains.

Yet as the service went on he was aware of freedom. He felt curiously untrammelled, as though he looked down upon his body from above it, as though he were dead and had left its weakness and pain behind him. He was scarcely aware of the details of the familiar service going on around him, but he was intensely aware of the ascension of prayer and praise; and not from this place only, but from every diverse place in every diverse circumstance wherein upon this day men prayed and gave thanks. It lifted him free of the limitations of the body and then free of the limitations of the mind too. When it reaches the blue illimitable air, the fire from many divided hearths loses itself in the one sunshine. For the space of a couple of minutes Robert also lost himself.

With extraordinary gentleness, as though upon wings, he sank down again to awareness of his surroundings. He had been carried down on the words of a prayer. Parson Hawthyn's voice was always beautiful, but today it had a burning sincerity which made each word seem living as well as lovely.

"Bless, O gracious Father, Thine holy Catholic Church. Fill it with truth and grace. Where it is corrupt, purge it; where it is in error direct it; where it is superstitious rectify it; where it is amiss reform it; where it is right strengthen and confirm it; where it is divided and rent asunder heal the branches of it. O Thou holy one of Israel."

Robert had said a loud amen before he remembered that Archbishop Laud had written that prayer. Though he was once more imprisoned within his painful body and his narrow mind, he felt no more than a passing embarrassment. Whoever had written them, the words were good. Misguided men did occasionally escape into truth. He knew that now, for he had just done it himself.

The concourse of viols and flutes in the gallery played the air of another hymn. They sounded like thrushes in spring. Then the congregation got to its feet and sang with such full-throated heartiness that the viols had to uplift their music to the utmost, like a stormcock who sings against the wind and rain. When the hymn was over Parson Hawthyn was seen to be in the pulpit.

The congregation was tingling with expectation. What would he say? This was the first Christmas of the war. A great battle had been fought and there would be more to come. The future was dark with suffering and disaster. Not only the church but the country was "divided and rent asunder". Even their own village had been rent with differences between squire and parson. And now the squire was in the congregation and the parson in the pulpit. What would the parson say?

"Good people," said Parson Hawthyn, "I am not going to speak to you today in my own words, because I believe that in times of conflict and emotion men often speak words that after they are sorry for. Therefore the sermon I shall preach to you will not be my own but that of another. Good people, eighteen years ago today, just a few weeks before I came to be the vicar of this parish, I was in St. Paul's Cathedral, and I heard Dean John Donne preach upon the mercy of God. I was able afterwards to write the sermon down but, alas, I cannot read it all to you because the book in which I wrote it has been accidentally destroyed. And so now I can only repeat to you that portion of it which I learned by heart and which my poor memory has retained. It will take but a few minutes, and will be the shortest sermon I have ever preached to you, but I bid you listen carefully, for in all the sorrow and conflict of our day there is one thing, and one thing only, which never fails us, and that is the mercy of God. And so, good people, 'we will speak of that which is older than our beginning, and shall overlive our end, the mercy of God. Nay, to say that mercy was first is but to post-date mercy; to prefer mercy but so is to diminish mercy. The names of first or last derogate from it, for first and last are but rags of time, and His mercy hath no relation to time, no limitation in time. It is not first nor last, but eternal, everlasting. Let the devil make me so far desperate as to conceive a time when there was no mercy, and he hath made me so far an atheist as to conceive a time when there was no God. As long as there hath been love, and God is love, there hath been mercy. And mercy, in the practice and in the effect, began not at the helping of man when he was fallen and become miserable, but at the making of man, when man was nothing. . . . God . . . brought light out of darkness, not out of a lesser light. He can bring thy summer out of winter, though thou have no spring. Though in the ways of fortune, or misunderstanding, or conscience, thou have been benighted till now, wintered and frozen, cloudy and eclipsed, damp and benumbed, smothered and stupefied till now, now God comes to thee, not as in the dawning of the day, not as in the bud of the spring, but as the sun at noon, to banish all shadows; as the sheaves in harvest, to fill all penuries. All occasions invite His mercies, and all times are His seasons. . . . God goes forward in His own ways, and proceeds as He began, in mercy. One of the most convenient hieroglyphics of God is a circle, and a circle is endless. Whom God loves He loves to the end; and not only to their own end, to their death, but to His end; and His end is, that He might love them still.' "

A few minutes later the congregation filed out into the sunshine, which might have been that of summer. "He can bring thy summer out of winter though thou have no spring," thought Froniga. She looked towards the trees of Flowercote Wood beyond the churchyard wall, marvelling at the wonderful colour of the bare branches and the depth of the blue shadows within the wood. A single track of delicate footprints patterned the snow from the churchyard porch to the stile which led into the wood, and each footprint brimmed with azure. A woman's figure was disappearing like a shadow within the wood. Someone who had perhaps been listening in the porch had made haste to slip away before she could be seen, but Froniga knew who she was.

2

Robert had very little idea how he got home, or what happened when he got there, but he woke up to find himself lying in the big four-poster with the window curtains drawn and a log fire burning on the hearth. He felt extraordinarily refreshed, and vaguely remembered Froniga bending over him with a commanding look in her eye and a steaming cup of camomile tea in her hands. He had drunk it, he supposed, though he hated camomile, and it must have worked magic on him, for he had obviously slept for hours. Through a chink in the window curtains he could see the frosty stars. His head was no longer aching and the fever seemed to have ebbed in his body; there must have been something else beside camomile in the potion which he had drunk. His hands felt less painful, for Froniga had treated them with ointment made from Lady's bed-straw; an invaluable herb for the stopping of nose-bleeding and the healing of burns. He felt a sense of deep consolation. There was yesterday and there was tomorrow, but neither intruded upon this day of mercy. The Lord had granted him consolation, not in victory but in defeat. He looked at the gilliflowers and roses embroidered on the green bed-curtains. It was summer in Froniga's garden and the music he heard was the thrushes and blackbirds singing in the apple trees. The children were in the garden too: he could hear their voices. Rousing himself, for he had been nearly asleep again, he realised that someone was playing the virginal downstairs and the children were laughing and singing. The stab of pain that he felt was not because he was not with them but because if he had been with them he would have spoilt their joy. The hard path of God's will had brought him now to a strange place; where he could thank God that his family had been able to forget him. He dozed again, then roused at the gentle lifting of the latch of his door. Someone came across the room as quietly as a mouse and stood beside his bed, shielding the flame of the candle she held in her hand so that the light should not shine in his eyes. She smiled at him, her eyes soft and bright in the candlelight. "Jenny," he said. Seeing him better she glowed with satisfaction. Her fear and restraint had gone, but their father-and-child relationship was not back again where it had been. It was reversed. Robert as well as Margaret had because of his inexplicable behaviour become her child. She looked very mature as she said with great kindness, "I'd not forgotten you; did you think I'd forgotten you?"

"I hoped you had," he said.

"We'd none of us forgotten you," said Jenny with gentle indignation. "Of course we hadn't. But it was good for you to sleep. Did you wake up in time to hear me playing the virginal?"

"Yes," said Robert.

"I was playing it for you," said Jenny. "Even if you didn't hear me, it was for you. Now you're awake shall I read to you?"

Robert said he would like that, and she fetched a stool and sat upon it, with her candle beside her upon another stool. She opened her book and laid it on her lap.

"What is your book, Jenny?" he asked.

"It's a book of fairy tales I had as a Christmas present. Cousin Froniga has been teaching me to read aloud. I'll read you the one called *Beauty and the Beast*."

The mercy of God, which had taken possession of this day, prevented Robert asking who had given her the book; he supposed that Froniga had given it to her. He said humbly, "I could not read aloud at your age. I'm not so clever as you are."

"Now listen," said Jenny. "It's a nice story."

Robert paid little attention to the story; though he did grasp the truth it held like the kernel in the nut; the truth of a friend held within the pelt of an enemy. What he paid attention to was Jenny. He adored her. As soon as he was on his feet again he must go back to the army, but next time he came home he would win her. Next time he would discover his wife and his children, know them and love them as never before.

CHAPTER X

CANDLEMAS

I

After Christmas bitter cold and an outbreak of the plague clamped down upon the country. The time seemed long. It did not seem possible that spring would ever come.

Froniga and Parson Hawthyn, who had the sick to look after, had never worked so hard. Froniga was so strong that struggling through fearful weather to bring her skill to the sick in outlying cottages held no terrors for her and did her no harm. It appeared to hold no terrors for Parson Hawthyn either, but he aged five years in as many weeks and he grew very thin. People shook their heads and wondered how he fared in his present lodging. Did Mother Skipton give him enough to eat? Was there any warmth to be had in his room under the rotting thatch? How was his rheumatism faring in the awful dampness of the place? No one dared to ask him these questions and he gave no information. Mother Skipton herself was never seen and no one went to consult her these days, partly because of the weather, partly because it would have been an embarrassment to ask her to cast her evil eye on a neighbour's pigs, or to make a wax image of a rival in love and stick thorns into it, with the Parson in the room above hearing every word through the cracks in the floor. But curiosity was rife. What was the black witch doing to the old man that he looked so aged and so ill, and what was he doing to her?

Froniga was so happy these wintry days, that she felt her joy would never leave her. She knew she had no right to be happy, with the country at war and sickness and sorrow all round her, but she had long ago accepted the fact that happiness is like swallows in spring. It may come and nest under your eaves or it may not. You cannot command it. When you expect to be happy you are not, when you don't expect to be happy there is suddenly Easter in your soul, though it be midwinter. Something, you do not know what, has broken the seal upon that door in the depth of your being that opens upon eternity. It is not yet time for you yourself to go out of it, but what is beyond comes in and passes into you and through you.

Through all these days Froniga was proudly aware of herself as a channel of power. When she was nursing the sick her body sometimes trembled and glowed with the power that was passing through her. When she was questioned she would say that it was not her own, but she felt such an intense delight in her own ability to be so used that her ability and the power tended in her secret thoughts to become one and her own. She moved as a queen, glowing and happy. The sick would cling to her hands and beg her not to leave them, and she would stay with them often for whole nights together. Very often Parson Hawthyn would be kneeling on the other side of the bed. The dying (and there were some who died, in spite of all that Froniga could do) would turn their faces towards him as he prayed for them, but they did not let go of Froniga's hand. No one died in fear. A great bond of sympathy was forged between Froniga and the old man. Froniga did not know what had opened the door in her, one never knew, but she could wonder. She thought it might have been the sermon upon the mercy of God. Something had broken in her when she heard it. Quite unconsciously she was making little use of her spells these days but was relying almost wholly upon the healing properties of the herbs she used, and upon the power that flowed through her. Parson Hawthyn noticed this and was able to take a little comfort. For in his soul there was no Easter. He was so saturated with evil, so stifled by it, that he felt as though he had sunk in some foul bog that had closed over his head. For the first time in his life his faith had almost failed him. Weak and desiccated it bent to the wind of evil, as the poor withered plants in the garden rattled and shook in the north wind. In what he suffered, as in all true suffering and true joy, there was the quality of eternity. He could not believe it would ever end.

Whenever she returned to it Froniga found fresh delight in her home. When she got up on fine mornings she would find her window covered with frost flowers, with behind them the fires of the rising sun. She could not see the sun, she could only see the flames that seemed sparkling and crackling just behind her window, and she would stretch out her arms and laugh with joy. The fire on her hearth had never seemed to burn so merrily. The apple logs had blue and yellow flames, the cherry logs smelt like flowers and the burning fir-cones were edged with the same colour that had sparkled behind the frost flowers on her window. She would kneel before the hearth, warming her hands and singing, and Pen, her white cat, would weave round and round her purring and vibrating. But Pen was not so white as the snowflakes that fell outside her window, sometimes singly, like the feathers of a white swan that had passed over-head, sometimes in dense masses of falling light. Her room too was then so full of light that the flames on the hearth paled, and did not come into their own again until dark came and she drew the curtains, and sat with her spinning-wheel before the fire. She delighted both in weaving and spinning, but especially in spinning. The whirr of the wheel, the rhythmic movement of her foot upon the treadle, the thin fine strand of white wool passing lightly through her fingers and winding itself upon the distaff, were an enchantment to her. Sometimes the firelight would illumine the strand of her wool and then she would think of the gypsy girl who had tried, and failed, to save her lover's life by spinning and weaving, and of the cobwebs bright with tears that she spreads upon the bushes to this day.

She had been spinning when Robert came to say goodbye to her, and again when Yoben came. Robert had gone back to his regiment as soon as his hands had healed, and before the cold weather had taken its full grip. The first snow had thawed and the thrushes were singing on the morning when he lifted the latch and walked in.

"I have come to say goodbye, Froniga," he said bleakly.

She took her foot from the treadle, stilled her wheel and stood up. She smiled only politely and made no move, since he now regarded her as a temptation of the devil, but she could not prevent her eyes looking straight into his. They were full of unhappiness, but she saw herself in their pupils. His hands were behind his back, but she knew how they shook with the intensity of his longing and his control. She was well aware that at no moment of their lives had he loved her so much. The new strength in him was increasing his power of love. Was the love in him burning out his cruelty? Had that destruction in the church been a last venting of poison? She could not know and nor could he. Only the potter understands what he is doing with the clay.

"Goodbye, Robert," she said cheerfully. "I will look after Margaret and the children. Though really I hardly think I am necessary now that Jenny has become so grown-up and motherly."

At the mention of Jenny he smiled. Impulsively he took one hand from behind his back and slipped it within his doublet. She knew that he was going to take something out and show it to her. Then he checked himself, the smile died and his rigid control came back. There was nothing in his hand when he withdrew it from his doublet. He lifted her right hand and kissed it formally. "Goodbye, Froniga," he said, and went away.

She stood listening to the sound of his horse's hoofs in the lane, and she reproached herself for the brevity and coldness of the goodbye. She should have made him stay a little longer. She should have managed, somehow, to make him happier. "Never mind," she thought, "it is goodbye only for a little while. I will make things right again next time he comes."

Yoben had come later, on an evening of frost and stars, yet dark, for it was moonless. She had set aside her spinning-wheel and without a word gone straight into his arms. They had stayed thus for a few minutes without moving, for it seemed long to them since they had seen each other. Their shadow, cast on the wall by the firelight, was the shadow of one being, not two.

She had known he was coming and the meal was ready: the hot soup flavoured with herbs, the bread and cheese and wrinkled apples. As they ate he told her of Madona and the children. They were well, but life was now desperately hard for the gypsies, wandering from place to place in the bitter cold, afraid to stay anywhere long and afraid as yet to return to the one place where they were safe. Alamina had become most unpopular. The gold and silver that she had stolen were not enough to make up for even temporary banishment by Flowercote Wood.

"Upon whom did Alamina practise the *hokkani boro*?" asked Yoben. "She would not tell us."

"Upon Biddy, the housekeeper at the manor."

"I am sorry. Poor Biddy."

"It was poor Margaret. When Biddy found she had been tricked she took to her bed with a crisis of the nerves. I cured her with conserve of cowslips (excellent for nerves) but it took a fortnight. She is happy now. She has received much sympathy and a gift of money from Margaret. Yoben, where were you for Christmas?"

"Not far from Edgehill. It was a cold Christmas and there were wild tales told. No one will cross that battlefield after dark. Shepherds said that at midnight on Christmas Eve they heard the clash of arms and the shouting of men and saw troops of spectres fighting in the clouds. One of the spectres, they vowed, was Sir Edmund Verney. News of the apparition was sent to the King at Oxford and he sent officers to enquire into the matter. The figure they described was certainly that of Sir Edmund Verney."

"You believe these things, Yoben?"

"I neither believe nor disbelieve. Yet that shepherds on Christmas Eve should have even fancied they saw not angels in the clouds but men fighting is to me a bad omen. The spring will bring no peace."

"I found Piramus's grave," said Froniga, to change the subject. "I am glad you buried him in the happy wood. When the spring comes I will plant marjoram on his grave that he may rest in peace."

Yoben laughed. "The Greeks did the same," he said. "What a pagan you are, Froniga! And what a pity it is that poor Piramus must wait for his peace until it is the right season for planting marjoram."

Froniga laughed too, for she never minded Yoben's occasional mockery. Yet as they got up from the table she said to him, "When you talk about yourself, Yoben, you tell me only trivial things. I tell you of my beliefs, and they seem strange to you, but perhaps if you told me yours they would seem to me stranger still."

The laughter went out of Yoben's eyes. "Perhaps they would," he said shortly. "And now I must go."

"But you have hardly come!" she cried in distress. "Where will you sleep the night?"

"At Greenland House," he said, looking at her steadily.

It was one of the few Royalist houses in the neighbourhood. She bowed her head but she asked only, "When shall I see you again, Yoben?"

"I do not know, Froniga. Perhaps not for some while. But I shall see you again. I am sure of it."

"Yes," she said. "I am sure too. If I were not sure I could not let you go."

Again their shadows came together on the wall and again they parted. She went with him to the door and watched him tramp away, his old cloak wrapped about him, his head bent against the wind. It was so dark that she soon lost him. She locked her door, came back to the fire and threw more logs upon it. Then she sat in her chair and wept. That was the only night in all those cold weeks when the spring of joy died down in her. And yet she knew she would see him again.

2

Froniga might call herself a Puritan, but the old religious customs, if they had anything to do with flowers, died hard in her, and on Candlemas day she went out to see if she could find any snowdrops, as her paternal grandmother and all her ancestresses had done for generations past. According to tradition the first snowdrops open on the second of February in memory of the Purification of our Lady and the Presentation of the Child Jesus in the temple, and in the days of faith were strewn upon every altar as emblems of purity.

"I'll find none this year," thought Froniga, as she wrapped her cloak about her and went into the garden. A partial thaw had melted most of the snow, but now it was bitterly cold again and wreaths of it still lay on the ground waiting for more snow to come and fetch it away. About the trunks of the apple trees, where the ground was mossy between the roots, the snowdrops always grew thickly in the spring, but now there were only leaves to be seen, there were no flowers. She went down to the far end of the orchard and pushed her way through the bushes to a sheltered dell in the copse beyond. Here she always found the first primroses and here she had planted snowdrop bulbs. She went down on her knees and searched among the wet leaves, and to her joy she found a few that were showing a little white. They had not yet learned humility and bent their heads, but they were standing stiffly and uncompromisingly upright. They were shaped like spears, and like spears they would stand until their enemy the frost had relented a little and the warm air persuaded them to open their petals and bow to the sun. But Froniga thought that in her sitting-room they might mistake her fire for the sun, and she picked them and carried them indoors and put them in a bowl upon the hearth beside the white cat Pen.

As she went about her work that day, visiting the sick in the village, she wondered if Parson Hawthyn had found any snowdrops to put on the altar in the church. They usually grew thickly in the churchyard, and that was something he had never failed to do. Finding herself, at dusk, near the church, she went in to see. There were no flowers upon the altar and the candles, new ones, had not been lit that day. The icy coldness of the church struck at her heart as well as her body and she found she was shivering. She remembered that several times today she had shivered, as though with fear, though she herself was perfectly well. "Nonsense," she said to herself; "he put no snowdrops on the altar because there are none. And now he has to pay Mother Skipton for his lodging he cannot afford to light candles except on Sundays; no, not even on Candlemas day." Yet she almost ran from the church to the sheltered place under the churchyard wall where the best snowdrops grew. They were more advanced than her own. Among a whole regiment of sturdy green-and-white spears were two that had bent their heads. She picked them, the proud and the humble together, carried them into the church and strewed them on the altar. Then she took the tinderbox that was kept in the church and recklessly lit the candles. They would burn out during the night, but she had plenty at home and she would come with fresh ones in the morning. The same deep inherited instinct that had made her look for the snowdrops this morning had made her light the candles now. She had time to say only the briefest prayer for the life of Parson Hawthyn, she had not time even to kneel while she said it, but while the candle-flames lasted it would burn on in the presence of God.

She ran home and fed the cat. No matter who was dying, she never forgot Pen. She was not ashamed of loving animals so much, but sometimes she was a little ashamed of loving human beings so little in comparison. She did not feed herself; there was no time for that. Then she packed her basket with the remedies she might need. Her foresight knew now that the old man was very ill, but she did not know what was the matter with him. It might be the plague, and she put angelica in the basket, for it was invaluable for the plague as well as for flatulence, whether the patient chewed the root or drank the distilled water of the herb. It was called after the angel who had revealed its healing properties to a holy monk in a vision. Or perhaps Parson Hawthyn's heart had failed with so much tramping about the countryside, and she packed a bottle of her heart cordial compounded of borage, bugloss, calamint, hart's-tongue, red mint, violets, marigolds, saffron and sugar boiled in white wine. In any case she knew he had fever and she packed a bottle of elder-flower water. To ease pain she had a bottle of borage flowers steeped in the oil of sweet almonds. The herbalist Thomas Hill had been a great believer in this latter remedy. "The flowers of borage," he had written, "steeped for a time in the oil of sweet almonds, and after the wringing forth of this, tenderly applied to the stomach, and region of the heart, do marvellously comfort the weak patient." Then she ran upstairs, took the blankets from her bed and fastened them into a bundle, with strips of material for poulticing inside it. She poured broth that she had made into a leather bottle and put that too in the basket. She had just put her cloak about her when she saw the snowdrops in their bowl upon the hearth and picked them up with a cry of joy. They had opened right out in the warmth, showing their golden hearts within the delicate veinings of pure green. She looked hungrily at the splash of green, shaped like a new moon, upon the outer side of the inner petals. When she saw the new moon she always knew that, whatever the weather, spring would not fail to come. She twisted some thread from her spinning-wheel round the little bunch and dropped it in the basket, lit her lantern and went quickly to the door.

Halfway to the cottage, walking as fast as she could over the frozen ruts of the lane, she saw another lantern coming towards her. She knew who it was and quickened her pace still more, and at the bend of the lane the two women met.

"I was coming to fetch you," said Mother Skipton. "Parson Hawthyn has been very ill for three days now."

"Then why did you not fetch me three days ago?" demanded Froniga, hurrying on in breathless anger.

Mother Skipton gave no answer, but looked at Froniga with hatred. Froniga felt a gust of joy within her, for Mother Skipton was jealous of her. She loved Parson Hawthyn enough to be jealous of the other woman's healing power. And now that her own had failed she loved him enough to fetch Froniga rather than let him die. The woman from whom Froniga had endeavoured to borrow a skull four months ago had been incapable even of jealous love.

"What is it, and what remedies have you tried?" asked Froniga.

"It is fever, but not the plague. I think he will die tonight.

He would have none of my remedies, except a little camomile tea. But unknown to him, secretly, I have practised every healing art known to me. I have practised arts that I have never known to fail. Yet they have failed."

"If you mean that you have invoked the powers of evil, and in particular that evil spirit who possesses you, to prolong the life of a man who inch by inch is forcing your evil out of you, of course you have failed," said Froniga impatiently. "What did you expect?"

They had reached the cottage and went in. It was bitterly cold. There was a wood fire burning, but it was smoky and sullen and the wind was blowing the smoke back into the room. Near the ill-fitting door the damp that had seeped up into the hollows of the earth floor had formed a film of ice. Near the fire it was an evil-smelling scum. Owing to the weather the jackdaw had been brought indoors and squawked raucously from his cage. The horrible little room stank more than ever of bitter poverty, but Froniga found that she could draw her breath more easily than she had before. The evil was less stifling. Mother Skipton lit a guttering candle, handed it to Froniga and opened a door in the wall. "Go up alone," she said curtly. "There is no more I can do. If you fail now, yours is the shame."

"Heat me some hot water, please," said Froniga. Then she climbed up the steep stairs that came up directly into the garret, hardly bigger than a cupboard, where Parson Hawthyn had lived and slept all these last weeks. He had been lying in the dark until she came to him. She held up her candle and looked about her in horror. The rotting thatch had been stuffed with rags in places, but even so much water must have dripped through in wet weather. The floorboards were rotting too and smoke from the fire below came up through the holes. Fungus grew in the corners of the room. It was almost as cold as it was outside, and the crazy little cottage shook in the wind as though it would fall to pieces. Parson Hawthyn had lived in poverty and austerity in his parsonage, but he had had the modicum of comfort that preserves life. No old man of gentle birth and upbringing could have been expected to live through such a winter in conditions such as these, and he had been working beyond his strength in caring for his people and had been fighting a spiritual battle in this place. One glance at the old man told her he was near death. He lay on a low wretched bed, covered with his cloak. The fever had abated, she thought, but his pulse was feeble and his skin cold and clammy to her touch. Though his eyes were open he did not answer when she spoke to him. He may have known she was there, she felt that he did know, but the power of communication with those about him had left him. Froniga wrapped him in the blankets she had brought, and then knelt beside him chafing his cold hands with hers that were nearly as cold. For she felt hopeless. This was the bitterness of death, these hours when a soul drifted in loneliness, beyond the power of help in this world and not yet received into the other. Froniga felt near to weeping, for she had come too late.

Then she realised that her cold hands were beginning to glow and that within her there was that springing joy. Through her warm hands she and the old man seemed fused into one. Something that still lived intensely in Parson Hawthyn had communicated with the same thing in her. His delight in the service of his fellow men and her delight in life and all creatures, though the one was purged of self-will and the other was not, were akin. Fundamentally what they both adored was God, and now their love was burning so strongly within them that flame was lit from flame. Froniga began to understand something of a love like Parson Hawthyn's. Through the past weeks she had exulted to feel herself the instrument of love, had glowed in her own usefulness, but now she felt shame at the memory of her pride. Not in her manner would the old man have offered himself, his life or, if that failed, his death, for the woman downstairs, and if she was to save him now, it must be in his manner and not in her own. She must put aside her pride in her power, her wish to succeed where the other woman had failed, put aside even her selfish longing that he should live, merely because she would miss him if he died. She must use this strong love that was being kindled in her in the way that love willed. His hands were growing warm now in her own but it was he, almost at the point of death, who was the channel and not herself. With a strange, strong, desperate effort she tried to free herself from herself and offered what she had dragged away. Then she took her hands from Parson Hawthyn's and got up. She had been kneeling by him for only a few minutes, yet it had seemed long. Her knees were shaking and she looked like an old woman. She went quietly out of the room and felt her way down the rickety stairs.

"I think he will rally," she said.

"An apothecary would say it was impossible," said Mother Skipton, "but no doubt your spells are more potent than my own."

There was venom in her tone, but she had heated the water. Froniga took the remedies she had brought from her basket and showed them to Mother Skipton. "I used no spells, but I brought these," she said gently. "Would you like to use them?"

"*I* use them?" asked Mother Skipton sharply.

"I have come here only to help you," said Froniga. "I will not go to Parson Hawthyn's room again unless you need me. Since he has offered himself, in life or death, to serve you, he would prefer that you, not I, should serve him."

"I know these remedies," said Mother Skipton. "And I know how to use them. I was a herbalist once, and in my youth I did much nursing of the sick. But what use is anything without warmth? I am nearly at the end of my wood, and it is damp."

"I have dry wood and sea-coal at home," said Froniga. "I'll go to the inn for help and the men shall bring it down to you. A good fire here, and the door to the stairs left open, and the heat rising through the cracks in the floor will warm the room above."

She went out into the dark again and did what she had said she would do. The men carried the wood and the sea-coal and she carried all she had been able to lay her hands on in her cottage that would help either Mother Skipton or the sick man. All the night she stayed humbly in the kitchen, keeping the fire burning, heating broth for Mother Skipton when she came downstairs, looking after her in all the ways she could. And, astonishingly, Parson Hawthyn lived through the night and rallied. The next day she went home for a little while, to look after her cottage and Pen, but she came back and sat with him for some hours while Mother Skipton slept. He was sleeping too and did not know that she was with him. As soon as he showed signs of waking she fetched Mother Skipton. That night she came downstairs and said to Froniga, "He is sleeping again and he will live."

"Are you sorry or glad?" asked Froniga.

"How can you ask such a question?" demanded Mother Skipton indignantly. "He saved my life."

"And if he gets well you will have to let him do it again," said Froniga. "Do you want that?"

"I don't know what you mean," said Mother Skipton curtly.

They were sitting together by the fire now, talking in low voices so as not to disturb the sick man. Above them on the mantelshelf the bunch of snowdrops, that Froniga had put in water in a cracked cup, shone as though it had light within itself.

"Yes, you do," said Froniga. "He will not be content with having saved the life of your body unless he can save the life of your spirit too, and you have lived with him long enough to know how immensely precious yours is in his sight. If he is to go on living in the body merely to watch the death of your spirit, it would have been less cruel to let him die."

There was a long silence, and then Mother Skipton said in cold misery, "It is too late."

"Why did you come to the church on Christmas Day?" asked Froniga.

"How do you know I did that?" demanded Mother Skipton.

"I saw you going away," said Froniga. "And I will tell you why you were there. You came because Parson Hawthyn had woken in you a longing for the days when you had not yet chosen evil for your good. If it had been too late you would not have been capable of longing."

"You do not know what you are talking about," said Mother Skipton. "If souls in hell were incapable of longing they would not be in hell. That *is* hell—longing for what you've thrown away and can never get back. I was a woman who wanted power. Through what stages I passed from white to black witchcraft I need not tell you, but they were all governed by the passion to possess power over the bodies and souls of men. At last, I liked to kill. But power is a devil who turns round on you at last. You possess it, then it turns and possesses you. Then power becomes powerlessness. I am far too tired now to change my way of life."

Her words had come in a sudden quick strange burst of speech, but now her voice died away into an exhausted silence. The dull hopelessness of her despair made Froniga feel cold and sick. The night pressed upon her and the squalor of the room where they sat. She was sinking herself into the other woman's powerlessness. Then, as though she were dragging herself up out of some morass of mud, she roused herself and said, "I believe I can guess what you heard when you knelt in the porch, listening by the crack of the door. 'Though thou has been benighted till now, wintered and frozen, clouded and eclipsed, damp and benumbed, smothered and stupefied till now, now God comes to thee.' You heard that. Can't you believe it?"

"You talk nonsense," said Mother Skipton. "The old man talks nonsense. God does not come to lost souls."

"He has come," said Froniga. "In His servant, the old man. He has come. Can you not just do what the old man tells you to do? Not for your own sake, but for his in sheer gratitude. Is that so hard? I could help you. I know one thing he has told you to do and that you have not done. I'll do it for you. When you go upstairs give me the key of that cupboard there and I will open it, take away all that is in it and destroy it."

All Mother Skipton's lethargy and powerlessness left her. She was on her feet in an instant, her eyes blazing, her face twisted into snarling lines, her thin fingers curving like claws. It was as though something within her were suddenly awake and shaping her body to its will. Froniga had never felt so sickened and so terrified. She had managed to get to her feet too, but she could not escape, though involuntarily she put up her hands to protect her throat as the other woman sprang at her. Then abruptly her fear vanished and her hands flew out from her throat and clasped the clawing hands of the other woman, holding them firmly. Mother Skipton struggled fiercely for a moment and then went limp. It seemed to Froniga that only their hands locked together kept her on her feet. Froniga looked dazedly at their clasped hands. It was not she who had acted with such lightning quickness but the love within her to which she had yielded herself. She seemed to be leaning wearily against its strength, with the other woman drawn away from what had possessed her and into her own being, as though she and her sister were one.

Upstairs there was a weak and bewildered cry, like a child's. The old man had awakened and did not know where he was. Froniga gently withdrew her hands. Mother Skipton took the key that hung from her waist and dropped it on the floor. Then she turned without a word and went to him.

Froniga shut the door at the bottom of the stairs and unlocked the cupboard. The sickly stench that she remembered flowed out of it, nearly choking her, and her terror returned. Yet she did what she had to do. She took off her big apron and spread it on the floor, and she began to take the things that were in the cupboard out of it and put them on her apron. Her limbs felt as heavy as lead and her fingers were cold and fumbling so that she moved with fearful slowness. The evil that oppressed her, that was here with her in this room, pressed upon her as a great wind does in a nightmare. She felt that she was giving ground, not gaining it, and she was in an agony that Mother Skipton might come downstairs again before she had finished. Yet she continued to take the things out of the cupboard : the skull of a child, another skull, the mandrake root, the phials that contained she knew not what, though some she thought held blood, and others poisons, wax images cruelly pierced with long thorns, and some mildewed old books. She had taken them all out at last and then, with some confused remembrance of the room in the Bible that had been cleansed of the evil spirit but left empty, she put the snowdrops in the open cupboard in their place. Then she tied the evil things up in her apron, put on her cloak and dragged the heavy bundle to her shoulders, holding it by the strong linen straps of her apron. She went to the door, opened it and went out. It was long past midnight, but there was a moon, so that she could see her way. She dragged herself through the garden and out into the lane. In the fresh cold air her terror was a little less, but the weight on her back seemed to grow greater with every step she took. The sweat streamed off her and she gasped as she struggled slowly on, bent over like an old woman. Again she felt that she was giving ground, not gaining it. The conviction came to her that soon she would fall and lie with her face against the frozen ruts of the lane, and that the thing on her back would crush her face in, and break her back, and she would die. And presently, believing this, she did fall. She tripped over a stone and fell headlong, and the bundle rolled off her back and burst open.

She picked herself up, with grazed hands and knees but no other injury, and looked at the things lying in the bright moonlight at her feet. They looked completely ordinary. The phials had broken and the liquids they had contained were running away into the ruts of the lane. The blood ran slowly and thickly, but it was only the blood of a black hen. The skulls looked like grey stones in the moonlight. For the rest she saw only some lumps of wax, the root of a plant and some old books with torn pages. Within the books, Froniga knew, were invocations of evil, Satanic prayers, perhaps even the words of the Black Mass, but unless the words were actually read or spoken they were lifeless, no more than black marks on paper. All her terror fell from her. She gathered everything together, being careful to leave no broken glass to hurt the feet of wild creatures, fastened up her bundle again, lifted it easily and walked on.

But she was immensely surprised at what had happened and her tired mind fumbled at the problem. She thought to herself that men and women, reaching out beyond the confines of the physical world, whether to good or evil, do so by means of symbols and ceremonies, as children reach out to adult life by means of toys and games, making of them a bridge between one world and another. The little girl's wooden doll, symbol of her future maternity, is alive to her as she cuddles it. She does not feel hard wood against her cheek but warm soft flesh. "Until she drops it," thought Froniga, "as I dropped those things just now, and hears the hard wood clang on the floor. Then she knows that only her own mind made the baby's cheek so soft. Yet when she cuddled the babe she did most truly possess what she longed for."

She came to her cottage, and Pen welcomed her. She put the bundle down by the hearth and with no sense of fear she left it there while she pulled the curtains and lit the fire. Then she sorted out the contents of the bundle. The skulls and broken bottles she set aside, to be buried at the bottom of the garden tomorrow. The wax images she put in an old iron cooking-pot to be melted down before the fire. She was so without fear of them now that she thought she would make rosemary-scented candles of them later on. One little image reminded her of someone, though she did not know of whom. She held it in her hands, looking at it, and then with a final flare-up of panic she pulled the thorns out of it and broke it to pieces in her hands before she threw it in the pot. Then she burned the mandrake root and then, without looking at them, she burned the books. If there was a part of her mind that half expected evil-smelling smoke and writhen flames from the burning, it did not get what it expected. The books burned quietly and fell into black dead ash. She was so tired that she could hardly drag herself upstairs to bed, but once she was there she slept soundly and happily.

PART THREE

CHAPTER I

THE KING'S EVIL

I

February passed into March and the long hard winter was over, but all over England joy in the coming spring was tempered by the thought of the renewed fighting it would bring. In London, in the bright March sunshine, men and boys turned out in their thousands to construct fieldworks and entrenchments, in case the King should make another attempt upon the capital.

Charles and Rupert were planning the attempt. They were at work turning the plain of the upper Thames into a fortified area, Oxford at its centre within a ring of garrisoned points, with access to the lower Thames by way of Reading. They hoped that from this great base, from Cornwall and from York, three armies would eventually march upon London. Essex made no attempt to interfere with them, and no attempt, as yet, to recapture the isolated Royalist outpost of Reading. This summer, the King hoped and prayed, would end the war.

Across the Chiltern heathlands the March winds blew keenly, with squalls of cold rain from inky clouds and sudden gleams of brilliant sunshine. The first cadences of birdsong were crystal clear in the cold air, a faint haze of warm colour stole over the woods, where the buds were swelling, and there were more and more snowdrops in Froniga's orchard. The spring ploughing began and the gulls that had come up the Thames fluttered in white clouds behind the horses. Froniga's life passed quietly, for the sick people were getting well and there were fewer demands upon her. Parson Hawthyn was well again, though more bent and frail than he had been. He was lodging now at a farm near the church, for Mother Skipton had gone to be housekeeper to an old couple whom he knew in Oxford, and her jackdaw had been set free in Flowercote Wood. She had written to him and to Froniga and told them that though she still struggled and suffered, tormented by the thought of the evil she had done and taught living on and working havoc in ways she would never know, yet she had hope. The old couple had need of her skill in nursing and there was a patch of garden where she meant to grow rosemary, rue and costmary, and all the flowers that are the colour of sunshine. In the city of towers and spires there was music of bells and birdsong and all the gay traffic of the Court, and though it all seemed far away from her, yet she was aware of it. She went shopping with a basket on her arm and people looked at her as though she was one of them.

As the weather improved, Froniga's quiet days were enlivened by visits from Jenny, who rode over on Baw with Tom as escort. Toasting their feet at the fire they sat together reading, sewing or spinning, pausing sometimes to look out of the window and laugh for joy at the sight of a great rainbow encircling the woods, or listening entranced to a robin singing between the showers. Sometimes Froniga read Shakespeare to Jenny while she sewed her sampler and sometimes Jenny read fairy tales to Froniga while she spun her wool, and they talked of Mr. John Loggin. For some reason that was not clear to her, Froniga knew it was important that they should do so, and Jenny told her one day what Mr. Loggin had said about looking at something and forgetting yourself and then finding that someone had come alive between the two of you, making the three of you one.

"That's love," said Froniga.

"But he's a person," said Jenny with conviction.

"Love is a person," said Froniga with equal conviction. "And to be made one with the object of your love, and with love, the eyes of your body are not always necessary. The spirit has its own sight, you know, and distance makes no difference to your spirit."

"I don't see with my spirit," said Jenny. "I remember. I remember Will and Father and Mr. John Loggin."

"Memory is the spirit-sight I spoke of," said Froniga. "But memory, like bodily sight, is blindness without love."

March passed into April, with warm days and a haze of green over the trees, and one morning Jenny came to Froniga, riding fast on Baw, and said, "Cousin Froniga, come at once. Will has come home and he's ill."

"What's the matter with him?" asked Froniga, though she thought she knew, for she had woken up that morning with pain in her neck and ears.

"Dreadful ulcers."

"The King's evil," said Froniga. "I've feared that for Will; he so hates soap and water. When did he come home?"

"Three days ago," said Jenny. "Mother sent for the apothecary from Henley and he put on poultices and gave Will a horrible black draught to drink, but it hasn't done any good."

"The poultices and draughts of Master Buckthorn never do any good," said Froniga with withering scorn. "When will your mother learn that! Did she send you to fetch me?"

"No, I came myself," said Jenny. "Cousin Froniga, don't stand there arguing! Come at once. Will's been crying all night. It *hurts* him, I tell you."

"Steady, Jenny," said Froniga. "It won't hurt him much longer. Borage and marigold will soon cure him. Have you ever known my herbs to fail?"

"No," said Jenny, "but be quick, Cousin Froniga, be *quick*!"

Her face was white and tense, her eyes dark and angry and deeply shadowed. Froniga knew that she had been awake most of the night and that Will's ulcers were hurting her almost as much as they were hurting him; though not as much, for Froniga did not subscribe to the sentimental view that those who love the sufferer suffer more than he does himself. She knew too much about suffering to believe any such nonsense. Nevertheless, Jenny was very miserable, and Froniga gave her a spoonful of melrosette to pull her together. Then she took the herbs and salves she needed from her cupboard with a confident air. But in her heart she did not feel her usual self-confidence. Scrofula was a very obstinate complaint.

At the front door Margaret flung herself weeping into Froniga's arms. When Froniga was not there jealousy made her feel that she would rather die than send for her, but when she was there her weakness collapsed thankfully on Froniga's strength. "Poor, poor Will!" she sobbed. "They say scrofula is the result of evil living. Froniga, what will people think?"

"Who cares what they think!" said Froniga scornfully. "And as for what they say, it's nonsense, for the Haslewoods have never lived evilly. As for your family, of course, I lack information, but I maintain that scrofula is an infection due to dirt, and nothing else, and we shall soon cure it."

Then she relented, kissed Margaret briefly, told Jenny to look after her, and went upstairs to her patient. Will was sitting up in his mother's big bed, swathed in bandages. He looked a pathetic sight, but he had stopped crying and managed a watery smile when Froniga came in. Maria was beside him, ears drooping, the picture of dejection, but she managed a quirk of the tail.

"You're a brave boy, Will," said Froniga, "and you'll soon be well. Brave people always get well sooner than cowards, because courage is a good thrower-out of impurities in the body. And so is marigold, and I'm going to give you a drink made from it, and then I'm going to take off those poultices and give you fresh ones. It will hurt, but I know you won't cry any more because that would distress your mother."

"It's my own fault," said Will sadly. "All through that cold weather I didn't wash once. If I get well, Cousin Froniga, I'll never not wash again."

"That's a good boy," said Froniga, and set to work on him.

But the days passed and Will did not get much better. Her herbs having so mysteriously failed, Froniga took to her white spells again, invoking all the good spirits to come to her aid, but they failed her too. Parson Hawthyn came every day and cracked jokes with Will, and prayed for him ceaselessly, but in the unfolding pattern of things his prayers were not immediately answered. Jenny read to Will and told him stories and never left him unless she was made to. Margaret cried. Biddy and the little maids also cried. Will grew daily in courage and patience; and the Earl of Essex suddenly awoke from his habitual lethargy and marched on Reading. The household at the manor was scarcely interested. Will mattered to them far more than the fate of Reading. When they heard that the King himself was advancing to the relief of Reading they still did not care. On the twenty-fourth of April the King's inadequate force was repulsed, and Essex captured Reading, but the news brought them no joy, for Will was worse. And then, after dark, Parson Hawthyn came to the manor for the second time that day, knocked at the door and asked for Froniga. She ran down to him, saw him standing there in the moonlight and reproached him. "Twice in one day is too much walking for you," she said.

"Froniga, our gracious King lies this night at Nettlebed."

She looked at him at first without comprehension, so tired and numbed was her mind, and then she was shaken by such joy that the world turned upside down about her.

"Where?" she whispered.

"At the inn," said Parson Hawthyn. "One of the farm men was at Nettlebed today and has just brought the news. Froniga, His Majesty touches for the King's evil at Michaelmas and Easter, and Easter is only just past."

"I'll take Will now," she said impetuously.

"It is late, Froniga. By the time you get there, His Majesty will have gone to rest. Go early in the morning."

"Will he trouble himself?" asked Froniga, disturbed by second thoughts. "They say he is a hard and cruel man."

"They lie," said Parson Hawthyn fiercely.

"How shall I come to him?"

"Your own wit must teach you. And now good night, my daughter, and God be with you."

He limped away into the moonlight and Froniga ran to find Margaret.

2

At five o'clock the next morning Froniga and Will were ready to start. Will was to ride his pony and Froniga to walk beside him. Margaret and Jenny came down to see them off. Jenny would have given everything she possessed to go too, but she had to stay and keep Margaret company. Biddy had not been told of the adventure. So convinced was she that the Bloody Tyrant killed and ate little children that her state of mind would have been pitiable had she known where Will was going.

"He'll be dead before you get him there," Margaret whispered to Froniga with a stifled sob as Will was settled on his pony.

"Don't talk nonsense, Margaret," said Froniga.

"I'm feeling very well," said Will stoutly. "Now, Mother, don't fuss. Goodbye, Mother. Goodbye, Jenny."

He waved cheerily, but when they reached the beech-wood and were hidden from sight he relaxed with a sigh of relief. "Women can be a burden to a man," he said, forgetting, as people so often did, that Froniga was a member of the weaker sex.

She carefully kept all anxiety out of the glance she gave him. He certainly looked a yellow-faced, puny little goblin of a creature and four miles was a long way for him to have to ride after his days and nights of pain, but she had given him a strong reviving herbal draught before they started and certainty that he was going to be cured had put new life into him. He kept his back straight and his shoulders braced and he insisted upon wearing his little sword. She was proud of him.

"Shall I be well the moment the King touches me?" he asked.

"You will begin to get well as soon as he touches you," said Froniga, keeping on the safe side. "It may be a little while before you are completely well, but you won't mind that because you will know that recovery is certain. The King's touch never fails."

"You've got a green gown on!" said Will, startled.

"My grey one was dirty," said Froniga. "And I wanted to look as gay as possible on this happy day."

In reality she had abandoned her Puritan dress because she was afraid the King's servants would not let a rebel woman into his presence. She wore her grey cloak, but she had let the hood fall back and the sun shone on the gleaming coils of black hair.

"You look pretty, Cousin Froniga," said Will shyly.

They came up on to the common, where a cool life-giving wind was blowing out of the south-west. Far up in the sky a lark was singing and the few clouds that were sailing across the great dome of blue were saffron and gold, for it was still very early. They crossed the common and came to the rough road that wound through the fields and beech-woods to Nettlebed. The banks were green with moss and starred with primroses and tall cherry trees in bloom were like fountains in the blue air. From the russet floor of the woods the tall beech trunks rose smooth and silver and above them the first platforms of pale green leaves were edged with gold where the sun touched them. It was still in the woods and they no longer felt the wind. The birdsong rang and echoed. Froniga forgot her anxiety and Will his pain. They heard yaffingales laughing and they heard the cuckoo. Then they came to a small green field that was almost a carpet of primroses, set about with blackthorn blossom, and here they stopped and rested, sitting on Froniga's cloak, and Will fell asleep within the circle of her arm. When he woke up she gave him a little saffron cake from the small willow basket she had brought with her, for saffron, as well as marigold, has a very good effect upon the spirits. The great Francis Bacon himself had said of saffron, "It maketh the English lively."

When they came near Nettlebed they found it an armed

camp. Cavalry horses were picketed on the common, camp fires were already lit and men were moving about them. Pausing cautiously within the shelter of the trees they could see sentries on guard. Will was shaking with excitement but Froniga felt a tremor of fear and discouragement. What was in reality a small force seemed to her a vast army, and soon it would be on the move, marching back to Oxford. If she did not get to the King quickly it would be too late, but she was not likely to reach him through the ranks of his men. Yet if she went round she would lose precious time, and when she reached the inn she might find that too surrounded by troops. For a moment she felt hopeless. It was not an easy thing to come into the presence of a king. Then her resolution hardened and taking Pal's bridle she led him back into the wood.

"Aren't we going on?" asked Will.

"We're going round," said Froniga.

Making a circuit through the fields and woods they made their way towards the garden at the back of the inn, but it took them longer than Froniga had expected and though no more troops barred their way she was anxious. She had been to the inn before and she knew that in the thick yew hedge that surrounded the garden and bowling green there was a gate opening on the field beyond. She moved very cautiously along the yew hedge, leading the pony and looking for it. The hedge was so thick that she could not see through it, but to her relief she could hear men's laughter on the other side, voices and the click of bowls. There was a sudden exclamation and her arm was tightly gripped. She had come to the gate and walked straight into the sentry. Instantly all her courage came back to her and her mind grew composed and quiet.

"Sir," she said in her clear ringing voice, "I would see the King."

"Would you indeed, my dear," said the sentry insolently, his eyes roving in appreciation from her white neck to her trim waist. "Not today, I am afraid." And though his eyes lost none of their ardour his hand gripped her arm more harshly. Dropping the pony's bridle and exerting all her strength she twisted out of his grip and leaned over the gate. "Sirs!" she cried. "Will you help me?"

The half-dozen young men in the garden had heard her first cry, as she had intended they should, and were already strolling towards the gate in search of amusement. The King's horse had cast a shoe and they were delayed. The bright sun glinted on their shining cuirasses, crossed from shoulder to hip by the Royalist blue scarves, on their smoothly combed lovelocks and cheerful young faces. If they had suffered a reverse yesterday it seemed to have left no mark on them, and an attractive woman was just what they were needing to while away the time until the King was ready. They exclaimed at her beauty, they asked if she had mushrooms to sell, and what was the matter with her little boy?

"The King's evil," said Froniga, "and I have no time to dally with you, sirs. Will you please bring me to the King that he may cure my child?"

They laughed and told her the King had no time for such nonsense in the middle of a war. Had she any mushrooms in that basket? Her eyes went from face to face and saw a man she knew. It was Francis, gazing at her in careless, insolent admiration, hands on hips, without a sign of recognition on his face. For a moment she felt hotly angry, though she too gave no sign of recognition, for if he was not going to recognise her, she was not going to recognise him. Then he came a few steps forward and she saw his eyes, twinkling with fun and kindness. "Why should she not come to the King?" he demanded. "It will make a diversion for him. He likes a pretty woman as much as any man." He opened the gate. "Come now, my dear. Can the boy walk? Then let him get down and we'll tie your pony to the gate."

"Don't say a word, Will!" whispered Froniga as she lifted him to the ground. But Will was now so tired and so scared that she doubted if he recognised Mr. John Loggin in this shining cavalier. Not even when he staggered from weakness, and Francis picked him up in his arms, did he dare to lift his eyes, though afterwards it was a matter of great pride with him that one of the King's officers had carried him the length of the bowling green and into the inn, and down the passage to a door where a sentry stood on guard. The sentry saluted, Will was set on his feet and Francis knocked on the door. A voice said, "Enter," and they went in.

Will remembered very little, afterwards, of what he saw or what happened to him, though for the rest of his life his fine imagination enabled him to give vivid and varied accounts of it to anyone who was interested, but for Froniga that brief ten minutes was so stamped upon her memory that she never forgot the smallest detail of it; not even the pattern of the lace on the King's collar or the shape of a little scar on one of his hands. When they came in he was standing by the window reading a letter and he swung round on them with a gesture of irritation, quickly checked. But he was not pleased by the intrusion and his arched eyebrows rose a little higher. He was in no mood to be disturbed. He had been bitterly angered by the apparently treacherous capitulation of Reading, and his own arrival too late and with too inadequate a force to save it.

"What now?" he enquired of Francis coldly.

"Two of Your Majesty's most loving subjects," said Francis with conviction, for if they were not that yet, they soon would be. "They are in need of help which only Your Majesty can give."

Froniga curtseyed, came forward and sank to her knees before the King, pulling Will down to kneel beside her. She looked up into his face and said, "God's blessing upon Your Majesty. Sir, this little boy is grievously ill with the King's evil. I ask you to have pity upon his pain and to lay your hands upon him that he may recover."

The King's heavy-lidded eyes looked wearily down at her. At all moments of the day and night, it seemed to him, he was beset. There were times when he felt like a sick and helpless body covered with leeches; only in his case the blood-sucking brought no relief, only an exhaustion unto death. Then the stern lines of his tired humourless face relaxed a little. The eyelids lifted, showing a gleam of interest in the eyes. He was looking down into a remarkable face. Strong and square, with prominent cheek-bones, it might have been a gypsy's face, but the wonderful dark eyes had not the hard sparkle of a gypsy's. She bore herself as a great lady, but her green gown was shabby and her cloak a peasant's cloak. He glanced briefly at the little boy. He was the usual yellow-faced sick creature, leaning weakly against his mother, eyes goggling in the usual sick entreaty, and dry cracked lips gaping open. There were always so many of them, at Michaelmas and Easter, and Charles dreaded those cracked lips that drained his life. He had thought to escape this year.

"I touch only at stated times in my own palace, as part of a special religious ceremony, and only those may approach me who have complied with certain regulations," he said coldly. "If I were to touch every sick creature who chose to thrust himself into my presence, what time should I have left for matters of more importance?"

"Sir, is anything of more importance than a sick child?" pleaded Froniga. "Were your own children, who died, of no importance to you? And every child in this realm is your child. Are not the King's subjects a sacred trust from God, and does not the love and mercy of God reach us through the love of the King?"

Francis, hitherto despondent in the background, suddenly became jubilant, for unwittingly Froniga had touched upon the King's most cherished belief in himself as King by divine right, a King who should be as God to his people. Then he saw that she was trembling and that her eyes, though they did not leave the King's face, had filled with tears. The sight of such a strong woman trembling and near to weeping was to Francis profoundly moving. He saw that it was so to the King. Charles touched her shoulder lightly and gently.

"Have no fear," he said. "Take your arm from the child and let him kneel straight before me."

Froniga did as she was told, and Will, rising quite unconsciously to the dramatic possibilities of the occasion, knelt as straight as a ramrod, his head up, his eyes fixed adoringly upon the King and his hands folded on his breast. As at his breeching, there was no need now to be anyone. To be himself at this moment was wonderful. To the absolute belief that possessed his mind, to the exclusion of the smallest possibility of doubt, was added an ecstasy of delight in the splendour of what was happening to him. It lifted him up as though on a rising wave. He was at the crest of faith and ecstasy when he felt the King's hands on his head, one on his forehead, one holding his head at the back. They held him lightly but firmly. They were cold at first, then they began to glow and tremble slightly. The warmth spread through Will's whole body, tingling even in his fingers and toes, and where the ulcers were it was like painless fire. The King took his hands from Will's head and put them lightly over the bandages about his neck and Will had the sensation that the painless fire was consuming the pain. The King withdrew his hands, sighed, stepped back and sat down on the great carved chair that stood in the window. Froniga, who had never taken her eyes from his face, saw that beads of sweat stood on his forehead and felt in her own body an echo of the pain that he had taken from the child to himself. She was still trembling, but it was not because of Will. Looking into the King's face, as she had pleaded for the child, she had been aware of the deepening darkness into which he moved. She had for a short while passed into it herself.

The King held out his hand. Francis had come forward to help her, but she did not need his whispered injunctions to know what she had to do. She rose from her knees, curtseyed and kissed the King's hand, but when she tried to speak she could not. Will, however, had now found his tongue and knew exactly what the occasion called for. He bowed deeply, laid his hand upon the hilt of his small sword and said, "I am Your Majesty's most humble, obedient and grateful servant and soldier until I die."

The King smiled and held out his hand to Will too. It gave him a pang of pleasure to feel the child's lips, that had looked so hot and feverish, now cool against his hand. It was over and Francis got them both out of the room with skill and grace.

In the passage there was turmoil, for the King's horse had been shod and all was ready for the return to Oxford. Francis could do no more than bring them to the garden door, smile at them, and go back to his duty. Froniga and Will walked through the garden, slipped through the gate and untied Pal.

They took the same circuitous route, not to get involved with the army, and it was not until they were safely in the cool beech-woods again that Will said, "Cousin Froniga, I'm quite well. May I take off my bandages?"

"From the moment that the King touched you your recovery was certain," said Froniga, "but the ulcers may take a little time to heal."

"It's very silly to wear bandages when you are quite well," said Will.

Froniga looked at him. New strength seemed to have come to him, for he was holding himself upright without effort and riding well. He still looked a wan goblin of a child but she could see from the look in his eyes that the fever had left him. She stopped Pal, told him to dismount, and gently unwound his bandages. She gave an exclamation of incredulous, glad surprise. The discharge from the ulcers had stopped and they were already drying up.

"Why are you surprised?" asked Will. "Didn't you expect it to happen?"

"Yes," said Froniga. "But in this world, Will, where things

are so contrary, when the lovely things you are expecting to happen actually do happen it seems too good to be true."

"You wouldn't think it was too good to be true if you hadn't got the pain any more," said Will. "You'd know it *was* true."

She laughed and helped him back on to his pony and they went on through the cool blue world of ringing birdsong and aspiring trees, two completely happy people.

"Father must fight for the King now," said Will. "It would be very wrong to fight a man who's made me well. He mustn't fight for Parliament any more. Cousin Froniga, why do people say the King is an ogre and a bloody tyrant? He's kind and good and I am going to fight for him. I said I would."

"Look, there's a squirrel!" said Froniga. Mercifully the woods were so full of enchantment, and Will so happy and so fond of the sound of his own voice, that he was content to talk on without much verbal response from her. She walked beside him, almost bathing herself in the music of his voice. It was not actually a musical voice, it was the usual small-boy squeaking croak, but he had been so silent in his pain, and now it was as though after long drought the wells had broken.

CHAPTER II

CHALGROVE FIELD

I

Francis had spent the winter in Oxford with the King. The useless slaughter of Edgehill had left him shocked and saddened, but when fighting started again in the early spring it only consisted of raids into enemy country, exciting and dangerous but soon over, and not too wasteful of human life. He had become one of Rupert's lifeguards and his chief duty just now was bearing the brunt of Rupert's impatience. The Prince was maddened by the loss of Reading and could find no relief for his feelings except in a perpetual harrying of its garrison and a beating up of the Parliamentary quarters round about. And there was another reason for his restlessness. The march of the three Royalist armies on London had been delayed. The army of the West had had great victories, but had not been able to reduce Plymouth. The army of the North was in the same position with Hull behind it still in the hands of Parliament. Neither dared march on London yet and Rupert had to fill up his time as best he could. All through the spring he and his cavalry were perpetually on the move. They would ride out of Oxford soon after midnight and at dawn fall upon the unsuspecting enemy, returning to Oxford the same day with prisoners and booty. The Royalist cause was in the ascendant in Oxfordshire and the morale of the Parliament troops was bad. At Reading the men were dying of plague and only the fact that Hampden was with them kept them from mutiny. The country garrisons were also mutinous, for their pay was in arrears. They lived in terror of seeing plumed hats on the horizon and hearing the yells of the cavaliers. Rupert thought that if he could inveigle them into another battle they might crumble altogether.

He was strolling with Francis in Christ Church meadows one morning in mid June. They walked beneath the wall of Merton College and over it roses were climbing. The trees were in their full glory, massive with foliage but with their green still fresh and cool. The grass in the meadows had grown tall, full of moon-daisies and sorrel. Over their heads, as they walked beneath the roses, bees were humming. Francis was sleepy and at peace, glad that for once in a way they were to have a day of idleness. Rupert yawned cavernously with boredom and frustration. He had never supposed that wars were to be won by strolling beneath roses. Then his tall lounging figure suddenly stiffened into alertness.

"Who's that?" he demanded sharply of Francis. One of his officers was coming towards him with another man walking beside him. The four men met and the stranger was introduced as Colonel Hurry, who had fought for Parliament at Edgehill.

"Indeed?" said Rupert curtly. A muscle twitched in his cheek. He did not like renegades, but in war they must be used, like it or not.

"Sir, I have returned to my true allegiance," said Colonel Hurry, "and can give you information that will be of use to you."

"Not out here," said Rupert, turning abruptly on his heel. "Come to the King's lodgings."

Silently the four men left the roses and the humming bees and turned away into the cool shade of the Christ Church cloisters on their way to see the King.

In the late afternoon of that same day the High Street was dreaming peacefully in golden light. Smoke from the fires that were cooking the citizens' evening meals coiled lazily up above the old red roofs. Cats dozed on window-sills and those who were taking the air strolled with slow pleasure down the quiet street and through the East Gate, pausing on Magdalen bridge, their arms on the parapets, to watch the river winding beneath the willow trees and listen to the music of the water about the piers of the bridge. Over their heads Magdalen tower soared into a tranquil deep blue sky. The rooks in the tall elms in the deer-park were cawing and from all over Oxford, from one tower after another, the hour struck.

It was a charmed hour, very still beneath the sounds of bells and birds and running water. The peace of it possessed the woman with a basket on her arm who had just stopped for a moment upon the bridge. She was on her way home, after gathering river-mint in the water-meadows below, but she always liked to pause beneath Magdalen tower. When she had first come to Oxford in the bitter cold of late February, with evil cast out of her but sick in spirit, empty and dry, and had seen it towering up above the East Gate, it had given her a sudden conviction of the strength and power of good, that hitherto had seemed to her so weak in comparison with the evil she had known. Passing beneath it, she had seemed to pass under a new dominance. She always paused here now, acknowledging allegiance. And today she acknowledged something else, something she had thought impossible. She was refreshed. During the dark years the beauty of the world had been blotted out and since she had come to Oxford she had seen it only from her desert of dryness, like a mirage that she could not reach. Now the beauty of the quiet sky, the bells and the water. came like a runnel of freshness into her arid spirit. Mary Lavenham, who had once called herself Mother Skipton, leaned her arms on the parapet of the bridge and hid her face in her hands. She did not want to be seen crying, but she could not stop. She had not wept since the day Parson Hawthyn had come to ask her for lodging; but that had been in hopelessness, and this was in joy.

The sound of horses' feet clattering on cobbles brought her back to the place where she was. She turned round and found that one of those crowds that gather from nowhere was about her. Dogs were barking and small boys were running along importantly beside the cavalry. She drew back against the parapet to watch them pass, the tears still wet on her cheeks but her face alert with interest; to be interested was in itself a new and blessed phenomenon. This was a larger concentration of troops than had been seen leaving Oxford for some while, it was a small army, and the crowd began to cheer. Prince Rupert rode at the head of his cavalry with his standard-bearer carrying his black standard edged with gold and emblazoned with the arms of the Palatine, his lifeguards behind him. They wore black uniforms now but with their glittering accoutrements and their excited laughing faces they looked the reverse of sombre. Behind the cavalry came a detachment of light infantry. Horses and men passed rank by rank out of the East Gate over the bridge and wound away into the green country. Gradually the sound of the horses' hoofs and the tramping feet died away into silence and the citizens upon the bridge heard the cawing of the rooks again. The bridge seemed empty now, with all those young men gone. They turned homeward, speculating as to what would have happened by this time tomorrow.

The renegade Colonel Hurry had brought exciting news. A convoy of wagons had left London for Thame with twenty-one thousand pounds sterling, the arrears of payment owed to the mutinous Parliament troops, and was reported to be coming up through the Chilterns by way of Wycombe and Chinnor. It was a rich prize, but whether he captured it or not, the expedition would give Rupert the opportunity for penetrating deeply into enemy country and working havoc with the recruiting campaign which Essex from his base at Thame was now carrying on with Hampden's help. Riding and marching all night, taking a roundabout way through the sweet-smelling leafy lanes, beating up several villages and wiping out a regiment of dragoon at Postcombe, they came at dawn to Chinnor and fell upon the garrison, killing some fifty men and taking many more prisoner. Francis did not enjoy this brief, brutal fight. The men they killed were raw young recruits who had seen no fighting yet and it was more of a butchery than a fight. Afterwards Rupert fell into one of his ugly moods and ordered the prisoners to be tied to their horses half-naked and taken to Oxford as an offering to Charles.

Sitting on a grassy bank, binding up a flesh-wound on his arm, Francis found he was hot and tired and full of foreboding. If there was to be more fighting today he had no stomach for it. His attitude towards war had changed completely since he had ridden so confidently towards Edgehill. It seemed he was not much of a soldier after all; not against his own countrymen. The derisive laughter of the men who were maltreating the prisoners revolted him. And how did Rupert imagine they could surprise any convoy if they gave warning of their approach with such an unholy din? The wagons would have escaped into the beech-woods long ago. A trumpet rang out and he remounted and rode back to his duty.

Sending the infantry on ahead to secure the bridge over the Thame at Chislehampton, which they must cross to get back to Oxford, Rupert turned his attention to the convoy of treasure, but, as Francis had expected, his reconnaissance could find no wagons, and he could not waste time looking for them. News of the disaster at Chinnor would soon reach Essex and his army and then they would be hopelessly outnumbered. They must make good their retreat as fast as they could and join up with the infantry at Chislehampton.

They rode on, the larks singing riotously above their heads, but it was not long before they found themselves attacked, not by Essex's army but by small bodies of Parliament cavalry who came riding at them through the fields of standing corn, harrying their rear, retreating, attacking again, like angry bees buzzing at an intruder. Rupert was well aware what they were doing; trying to hamper him, slow him down, keep him from reaching the bridge before Essex could arrive. Their leader, whoever he was, knew his business and had inspired his men with his own pluck. He paid grudging tribute to their courage. He had only to turn on them, with his far larger force, to wipe them out. They were gambling on the time factor. If he stopped to attack them he might reach the bridge too late.

Suddenly, in the black mood he was in this morning, he was maddened by these buzzing bees. "This insolency is not to be borne!" he said violently to those about him. If the enemy leader was a gambler, so was he. He'd teach them a lesson now, and if Essex came down upon him before he could reach the bridge he'd fight the whole rebel army, ten to one. He was still some miles from the bridge, but he sent a messenger to recall his infantry and drew up his cavalry behind a hedge. He was in an unenclosed plain of several acres covered with green corn. It was a good place for a fight and the enemy cavalry, undaunted, were wheeling into formation too. With his standard-bearer beside him, the black-and-gold folds of the standard lifting lazily in the warm wind, he looked along the ranks of his lifeguards, glowing with pride in them. They were ready. His trumpet rang out for the charge. There was a shout from the rebels, and they too charged. Rupert set his horse at the hedge, leapt it and came riding down upon them. The two forces met each other, crashed and reeled, trampling the young green corn beneath the feet of their struggling horses. Overhead the larks continued to sing as they had sung all the morning.

2

Colonel Hampden had spent the night at one of his country houses, his manor at Watlington. He was tired out by many things: by his grief at the recent deaths of his eldest son and his best-loved daughter, by his unsuccessful struggle to induce the cautious Essex to follow up the capture of Reading by an attack on Oxford, by the gruelling task he had had lately at plague-stricken Reading and by the recruiting campaign. Things were not going well just now for the cause of England's liberty, to which he had given all he had and was. There was mutiny and ineptitude. The stream that had seemed so clean at its source was muddied with jealousy, self-seeking and treachery. He had longed for a few hours' quiet and had gone to his manor taking with him only one trooper.

He spent an almost sleepless night, his mind wandering back over the past. He was remembering the great man who had inspired him for this present fight, his friend John Eliot, who had died of his long and merciless imprisonment in the Tower, murdered by the King as surely as though he had lost his head like Strafford. Yet Eliot, at the end, had seemed to forget about politics, what he had been fighting for and what he was dying for. His mind had been filled only with thoughts of the mercy of God. His last letter had been written to Hampden and words from it echoed in Hampden's mind all that night.

> "O! the infinite mercy of our Master, dear friend, how it abounds to us that are unworthy of His service! How broken, how imperfect, how perverse and crooked are our ways in obedience to Him! How exactly straight is the line of His providence unto us, drawn out through all occurrents and particulars to the whole length and measure of our time!"

Towards dawn Hampden slept at last and dreamed he was at Pyrton Manor. It was midsummer and Elizabeth was walking beside him through the garden towards the church that was just beyond the sweetbrier hedge. He could see the tower rising above the trees. Looking down he could see the moss upon the path and Elizabeth's dainty pointed shoes, white and gold, upon the green. Her hand was cool in his and she carried a posy of white roses. It was their wedding day. The bells pealed over their heads, crying out, "The whole length and measure of our time! The whole length and measure of our time!" and he awoke abruptly. For a few minutes he lay still, remembering that it only wanted six days to the anniversary of that wedding day. But Elizabeth was dead. John Eliot was dead. The grief for both that had never healed overwhelmed him again, together with his later grief for young John and the young Elizabeth, his son and daughter.

Through the crack of the drawn curtains the brilliant sunshine came like a sword, and the larks were singing. He could hear his trooper whistling as he groomed the horses. He longed desperately to go back into the dream, but it was sun-up and another day. He got out of bed, went to the window, pulled back the curtains and looked out at the scene below him; distant beech-covered hills hazy in a mist foretelling heat, cattle grazing in the pastures and cornfields freshly green. . . . A lovely land. . . . He leaned at the window, drinking in the beauty of what he saw. At the beginning he, like Charles, had had his dream. . . . The perfect England. . . . They had differed in the way to find perfection, through freedom or autocracy, but it had been much the same dream. And now England was rent by their conflicting dreams, and the dreams themselves were foundering. Yet it occurred to Hampden, as he breathed in the cool air, honey-scented with roses and hay, that he would rather die for a broken dream than for no dream at all. He did not usually indulge such fancies, the times were brutal and he had no leisure for sentiment, but personal sorrow had ploughed deep furrows in him and below the surface failure and stress he was oddly aware at this moment of a deep-down freshness, as though dreams that had failed had sunk down and sprung up in the soul, an awareness of God's mercy.

He suddenly leaned out of the window, his hands on the sill, his keen eyes fixed on a distant winding road that came down out of the beech-woods into the valley below. He could see the tiny figures of horsemen riding out of the wood. It was difficult to distinguish them at that distance, in that heat haze, but he could see that they wore armour for the sun glinted upon it in winking points of light. There were more and more of them coming out of the wood; there seemed no end to them. Apart from the bright armour they seemed sombrely dressed, like black ants. It might have been his fancy, but the black rider on the black horse at their head seemed of almost more than human stature. He stared for a second or two and then his mind cleared suddenly into conviction. He shouted for his trooper, turned back into the room and began pulling on his clothes. When his trooper, and the man who was his caretaker in this house, came to him, he was sitting at his writing-table, still half-dressed, writing feverishly.

"Ride with this, as fast as you can, to my Lord of Essex," he told his trooper, handing him the folded paper. "I've no time to write more or to seal it. I've told my Lord that Prince Rupert with a large force of cavalry is riding towards Chislehampton and asked him to send troops to cut off his retreat at the bridge. I'll gather what cavalry I can and hold him in play till my Lord comes." He turned to the second man. "And you, Tom, ride to Captain Haslewood. You know where he is, at Manor Farm with a detachment of my Greencoats. Tell him to get hold of all the men he can and ride for the Chislehampton road and I will overtake him as soon as possible. Then ride to Colonel Gunter. Give him the same message. Now go, both of you. Don't stop to saddle my horse. I'll do that for myself."

He spoke quietly and calmly but with a controlled force that sent both men instantly from the room. He finished dressing, not forgetting even in his hurry to put on the jewel that he always wore hanging round his neck under his doublet, a silver heart with a red cornelian at the centre of it. Engraved round the rim of the jewel were the words, "Against my King I never fight but for my King and Country's right." Then he buckled on his armour, went downstairs and out to the stable, saddled and mounted his horse and rode out into the gleam and shimmer of the June morning. He had an overwhelming impulse to stop his horse and look back at his home, the fine old house, the garden and trim lawns, but he checked it. He must get on. If they could win a victory over the famous lifeguards, if they could capture that hated, almost legendary figure, the Prince, the disconsolate mutinous army would be heartened as by nothing else and Essex would have the courage to forestall the King's march on London by advancing on Oxford. It might mean the end of the war.

3

Robert did not sleep that night either. He lay thinking of Margaret, of Froniga and his children with almost intolerable longing. He had been so near to them all these weeks, both in Reading, where he had been with Colonel Hampden, and now on this recruiting campaign, but he had not dared to go home in case he took infection with him. In Reading he had been in the midst of the plague, and lately he had caught fever from his men. Margaret had written to tell him of Will's illness and recovery (by what means he had recovered she was tactful enough not to tell him) and that had been another reason for not going home. Will after such an illness would be in no state to stand up against infection. But the outbreak of fever in the army had almost spent itself. Soon now he would ask Colonel Hampden for leave and go home. And this time he would win his children. This time he would not fail.

Sleepless, he lay thinking of the past months. The siege of Reading, and then its occupation, had been a nightmare for him. The siege itself was soon over, but then had come the outbreak of plague within the city. It so happened that up till now Robert had been able to avoid the plague. Nor had he bothered to enquire what it was like, for the plague was the sort of thing that happened to other people. He had not known it was this degrading fearful death. Far better to die in battle than to die like this in fever and sore pain, a mass of bleeding sores, filthy, loathsome, perhaps left to gasp out the last hours alone for the fear and repulsion that all men felt for you. He had to some extent conquered his fear of battle, but now he suffered a torment of fear of this fearful thing. At home, had there been plague in the village, enquiries and jelly would have been all that would have been expected of him as a good landlord, but as a good officer it was asked of him that he should go in and out among his men, doing what was possible for their relief and comfort. Colonel Hampden, setting the example, took it for granted that his officers should do the same. He appeared to think nothing of it, either for himself or for them. Nor did most of them think anything of it. If they caught the plague and died, that was the fortune of war, for this pestilence within a captured city was as much war as a charge on the battlefield, and to war they were committed. "Commitment," Robert would say to himself, "*Vestigia nulla retrorsum*. No way back." Day by day he did his duty as well as he could, inhibited and clumsy, hating those he looked after because their revolting condition threatened his own safety, and hating his own hatred as much as he hated them. Each day it seemed impossible to go on, he had to do such violence to himself, and he felt that this violence was killing him as surely as the plague was killing other men. Then quite suddenly, as it seemed to him, he was no longer afraid; or rather he was still afraid but he was doing what he had to do efficiently and with kindliness, his hatred gone. The Lord had had mercy on him. "The kingdom of heaven cometh by violence and the violent take it by force."

Yet if he had thought this victory would bring him happiness he found it was not so; he felt more grief than anything else. The violence he had done to himself had seemed to open some abyss within him and it filled quickly with a burning pity. He loved his men, helpless counters in this game of war. He loved England, torn by the conflicting dreams of those who professed to serve her. He loved his children and he did not know what the future held for them. He had discovered that the choice between self-love or love of something other than self offers no escape from suffering either way, it is merely a choice between two woundings, of the pride or of the heart. Yet, in the language of the Puritans, the Lord had not left him without consolation. That momentary sense of identity with other men that he had known when he had felt the pain of the boy in the pillory, and the fear of the man whom he had met in the inn doorway, had become something more than momentary. Just now it was his habitual state. If it increased that burning pity within him it banished loneliness.

At dawn he got up and dressed himself with the intention of calling upon the name of the Lord, for it was a Sunday. His intensely personal Puritan faith had taught him to be very familiar with the Lord. In some Puritans this familiarity had led to a making of the Lord in a man's own image and a bending of the Lord to human purposes that filled men like Parson Hawthyn with horror and dismay. But Robert was too humbled now to suppose that what he wanted the Lord necessarily wanted too, merely because he was one of the Lord's chosen people. The chosen, he had discovered, could make mistakes. He had made one when he had thrown Parson Hawthyn's little images out of the church at home; that was obvious from the fact that the Lord had put no seal of success upon what he did. He did not know how he had erred, not to be successful. Perhaps he had been less inspired by zeal for the Lord than he had thought; perhaps it was the cruelty in him that had sent up that spurt of destruction. Yet there had been a blessing, in which he had shared. It had been a blessed Christmas for the whole village, and in some ways his brutal behaviour had seemed to contribute to that. The ways of the Lord were indeed hard to understand. . . . He woke up abruptly to the fact that he was not calling upon the name of the Lord at all, but merely ruminating upon his own affairs. . . . This was very apt to happen at such times as he endeavoured to call upon the name of the Lord. He thanked God that he had not died of the plague, or the fever, for he doubted if he were yet in grace, one of the Lord's chosen though he was. If he were to die now he would surely be lost. He needed time for repentance. He groaned within himself, knelt more stiffly upright and endeavoured to turn his mind to the fifty-first psalm. "Have mercy upon me, O God, after Thy great goodness." But here his mind went off again to that Christmas at home and the words he found himself repeating were not the words of the psalm. "His mercy hath no relation to time, no limitation in time. . . . Whom God loves He loves to the end; and not only to their end, to their death, but to His end; and His end is, that He might love them still."

He heard the sound of a horse's hoofs in the yard below his window and a voice urgently calling his name. He scrambled up from his knees and leaned out of the window. "What do you want?" he called.

The freckled country face of a servant of Colonel Hampden's looked up at him. "A message from the Colonel, sir. Prince Rupert's cavalry are not far off, sir, making for Chislehampton. You're to gather all the men you can and ride to the Chislehampton road. The Colonel will overtake you as soon as he can."

He touched his hand to his forehead and rode away. Robert could hear his horse clattering down the lane beyond the farm. For a moment he stood where he was, holding to the window-ledge, his mind paralysed by the fear he had hoped was conquered. It seemed to go over him in wave after wave, as cold and deadly as nausea. To ride with his handful of men to the Chislehampton road, with Hampden overtaking him, or not, as the case might be, and fight, alone, Rupert and his lifeguards. That was what was apparently being asked of him. He could not do it. No man could do it. Hampden had no right to ask such a thing of any man. He opened his mouth and shouted, but did not know if he had made any sound. He could not do it. He fought down the nausea and shouted again, but his face felt stretched and stiff and clammy with sweat and no sound seemed to come. Yet he must have made some noise, for his men came tumbling out of the barn opposite where they had been sleeping. He yelled his orders at them. He picked out several by name and sent them to rouse other men in neighbouring cottages. He took his hands from the window-ledge and it seemed as though he were tearing them away by main force. He put his armour on and tried to buckle it, but his cold and fumbling fingers would not obey his will. He abandoned the armour. He would go as he was. He fastened his orange scarf across his breast, put his pistol in its holster and his sword in its belt and stumbled down the stairs. His servant had his horse waiting at the door. He mounted it and in a matter of minutes was riding down the lane at the head of his troop.

Out in the fields, cantering towards that column of enemy cavalry, so many of them riding at a good pace but yet with a contemptuous lack of hurry, Robert found that he and his troop were not alone. From many directions small bands of horsemen were converging on the Chislehampton road. Robert felt a sudden glow of comradeship and then was shaken by a gust of wild laughter at their predicament. They were like a horde of bees attacking an elephant. There was a thundering of hoofs behind them and a big grey horse overtook them. It was Colonel Hampden. He passed them waving his hat, and rode on to another troop, calling out encouragement and orders. "Attack and withdraw. Then go for them again. Sting them. Sting them. Lord Essex is not far behind us. Keep them back. They must not reach the bridge."

He rode from troop to troop, then came back to Robert and his Greencoats and wheeled alongside. "Robert, may I lead beside you?" His voice was gay and confident and the men cheered. Robert grinned. If his fear was still with him, clutching at his throat and stomach, he was doing what he had to do. Riding beside Hampden through the green corn he felt intensely close to him and remembered where they were. They were at Chalgrove Field, where Hampden had first raised the standard of Parliament and they had all come flocking to join him. As they came closer to the enemy the bond between them seemed to strengthen. He had never felt anything like it before in his life and the last vestige of fear left him.

Now they were near enough to see the magnificent silver-and-black horsemen laughing at them as they rode. "Fire!" said Hampden. They fired their pistols, wheeled back and away, the bullets of the Royalists pattering after them. The other bodies of horse did the same thing and so it went on for some while, an exciting dangerous game that was slowing up the Royalist cavalry. Their laughter turned to anger and suddenly Prince Rupert shouted an order, wheeled round and halted beneath his banner. He had picked a perfect position and was going to fight.

Colonel Hampden, Colonel Gunter and their officers drew up

their men in three bodies to face him. Though their numbers had steadily increased they were still outnumbered and Essex was not yet in sight. What they were doing seemed like an act of suicide, but Essex could not now be far behind them. If they could delay Rupert for just a little longer it would be well worth while losing their lives to do it. A tough courage passed from the leaders to their men.

Colonel Gunter and three troops of cavalry from Thame, with a few dragoons, took the brunt of Rupert's first furious charge and the long rapiers of the lifeguards swept out at them as though they were themselves the standing corn. They were instantly reinforced by the troop of Colonel Neale and General Percy, and again the cavaliers crashed down upon them and the rapiers slashed and hewed. Colonel Gunter fell. It was too fearful to withstand and the men broke and gave ground. Hampden, with the third body of troops, rallied them and led them in a final charge. For just a moment Robert was riding beside Hampden again, then they were separated. Robert, having survived the first shock of the charge, found himself fighting with a few other men who had also survived. From behind the hedge, where Rupert had now posted his infantry, came a rain of bullets. Suddenly there was a groan from the men about them. He glanced round and saw Hampden on his grey horse riding away, leaving them. His head was hanging and his hands were pressed hard against his horse's neck. He looked mortally wounded. Almost all their officers now were killed or captured. The battle was over and Essex and the army had not come. Those who could, fled, those who could not yielded themselves. But into a few there entered a demon of hatred and obstinacy and they fought on. Robert was one of the few. The sight of Hampden had left him emptied of any emotion except a cold and cruel passion for revenge. The tide of the cavaliers was surging now about the few islands of resistance like the incoming sea about the sand-castles that children built upon the sand. Robert fought on with devilish inhuman skill, and all the more agility because he wore no armour. Close to him he saw a huge man on a black horse, and just in front of him the man he hated, the spy who had come into his home. The Lord had delivered him into his hand. The Lord had heard his prayer and granted him vengeance. He felt a wild savage delight and with his whole being gathered up like that of an animal in its last spring he drove his spurs into his almost foundering horse and had at him. A sword flashed out in defence of the Prince and Robert screamed as the steel drove into his chest.

He came back to a vague awareness before he died, numbed by shock and not conscious of pain. He was lying under a hedge with a man kneeling beside him. He had gulped the water that was held for him before he saw the black uniform and the blue scarf crossing the cuirass. With infinite difficulty and very slowly he raised his eyes to the face above him. He saw first the man's infinite sorrow. It was a face of mercy. Then he recognised him, and all of human life that was still left in him was gathered into loathing. His eyes, as Francis looked into them, were full of torturing and tortured hatred. Francis got to his feet and moved away. What was the use of staying here, tormenting the man? Better let him die in peace. But he could not go entirely away. He sat down on a tree-stump a little way off with his head in his hands. Why had this had to happen? Why? Why? He had thought the man was going for the Prince and had acted instinctively, even though he had recognised Robert in the act of killing him. There had been nothing else to do. But why had it had to be Robert? And what had the fool been doing going into a fight without his armour? As soon as he could he forced his way to Robert, picked him up and carried him out of the last confusion of the fight. He had been light to carry, without his armour, and with the sturdiness that Francis remembered in him worn away. And now he was dead. It seemed to Francis that he had been sitting on the tree-stump for so long that he must surely be dead. He went back to where he lay and stood looking down at him. He was not dead yet, though his face was grey and clammy and the bloody froth was on his lips. His eyes were open and staring, but they showed no awareness of anything about him. I can stay, thought Francis, and he knelt down and crossed himself. Robert did not know he was there. He was looking from the depth of a wood to where the trees above him parted to form an archway filled with dazzling blue. His children stood there waiting for him.

Francis stumbled to his feet and then knelt down again. There might be something in the man's pockets that he could restore to his family. He knew the hasty and wholesale burials after a battle. If he did not look now no one would. Shuddering with revulsion and anguish, he searched the body. He found a few letters, one in a childish but beautiful hand that he was sure was Jenny's, and a small bunch of dried herbs. That was all.

He tied them in his handkerchief. Then he took the ring from Robert's finger and put it on one of his own for safe keeping and got to his feet again. He stood looking out over the battlefield. He must have been with Robert longer than he knew, for Rupert and his men were already out of sight and had taken their wounded and the prisoners with them. He saw only the enemy wounded, and the dead of both sides, and the dead horses lying in the trampled corn. He did not know what the time was, but the sun was high in the sky and blazing hot. The wounded lay in its pitiless glare. For how many more years was this going on, and what for? If he had ever known, he had forgotten. He felt too tired to move or think. Somewhere behind him a horse whinnied, calling to him. He remembered he had left his horse in the lane on the other side of the hedge. He was fond of him and was suddenly glad that he and his horse were still alive. He scrambled through the hedge, mounted and rode away.

Rupert and his tired troops rested that night at the bridge and the next morning marched back to Oxford. They were in high spirits, for they had won both the gamble and a victory and yet lost very few men themselves. Francis, in higher favour even than usual with Rupert because of that sword thrust in his defence, rode beside him and did his best to respond to the gay mood that had replaced the black one of yesterday. It was a triumphant homecoming for all who had the heart for it.

CHAPTER III

THE FACE IN THE WATER

I

The golden hour in which Rupert and his men had ridden out of Oxford had been as lovely in Flowercote Wood as it had been there. Froniga and Jenny had been haymaking in the fields, and now, tired and hot, they had come into the wood to get cool. By mutual consent they made their way to the spring and laved their faces in the water. Jenny looked at Froniga, laughing, through the lattice of her spread fingers, the bright drops of water running down her face and hands. She had got sunburnt the last few weeks and there were a few freckles across the bridge of her nose. Her laughter was delightful and seemed to Froniga to be the perfect expression of the joy of this place. She wondered, not for the first time, if Jenny's laugh was like her great-grandmother's. As Jenny grew older she saw a growing likeness in feature to the carving on the tomb in the church. How had Anne come to flower again in her great-granddaughter? Was she re-born in Jenny, or had those two most ordinary men, her son and grandson, transmitted her laughter and grace to this child? No one could solve the mystery of heredity. Suffice it that Anne had lived, and that Jenny lived now, and would live again in some descendant of her own. Perhaps that child might even surpass Anne and Jenny in worth, possessing their sweetness and mirth strengthened by the greatness of another. Many shining streams went to the making of a river.

Jenny was playing with something that she had taken from her pocket, tossing it into the air and catching it again, for she was happy today, but now she paused and seemed to be listening.

"What do you hear, Jenny?" asked Froniga.

"Horses," said Jenny. "Horses trotting and jingling. Don't you hear them?"

"No," said Froniga.

"Nor do I, now," said Jenny. "I expect I just thought I did." And she began to play with her treasure.

"What is it, Jenny?' Froniga asked idly.

"An elf-bolt," said Jenny, and handed it to her.

Froniga loved elf-bolts and she took it with an exclamation of pleasure. She looked for a few moments at the delicate pointed flint, shaped like a leaf, thinking with awe of its long history, then, as Jenny ran off after a butterfly, she sat there holding it in her hands, looking down into the water of the spring. As she looked it seemed to darken and grow still, like a mirror. She bent closer and saw a face looking back at her, as though mirrored in the water, the face of the man she had seen sitting at the great desk. He was looking straight at her this time, and she looked deep into his sorrow. Then his face changed into another, the face of a young man with Jenny's eyes but far more than Jenny's strength. The military uniform he wore looked strange to her, and his bright hair seemed powdered. He looked arrogant, but he was young and the humour of his face told her it would pass. He had a square chin, a little obstinate, and she had seen that chin in another man. His eyes, because they were Jenny's, held her own more intently than the eyes of the older man. She looked more and more deeply into them and began to know the splendour of his death. She leaned closer, longing for full knowledge, and then the familiar warning flashed through her mind. . . . Stop. . . . It needed all her strength of will to drop the elf-bolt on the grass and take her eyes from the water, but she obeyed and got up. She was trembling. Elf-bolts had a dangerous magic. An object that she had held in her hands had never before shown her its future owner, only those who had possessed it in the past; though that fearful little skull had showed her what she might become if she were, one day, to go too far.

"Come, Jenny," she said. "And pick up your elf-bolt. I dropped it. Did Mr. Loggin give it to you?"

"Yes," said Jenny.

They went a little way through the wood, that was green and cool, with shafts of sunlight striking down through the motionless canopy of leaves over their heads. Now and then Jenny darted aside to pick a wild flower or a spray of fern-like moss. Suddenly she gave a cry, half joy and half fear. Froniga, on ahead, turned round. Through an aisle in the wood they could see the green turf beside the well. He stood there lit by a gleam of sun, yet his silvery whiteness was all of moonlight. He was the most delicate and perfect creature, so lightly poised that a breath of wind might have carried him away like gossamer, yet with strength in the arched neck and perfectly moulded body. His mane and tail streamed out on airs so light that they did not stir the leaves about him. The tip of his little horn caught the sunlight in a sparkling point of fire. Then he was gone, and Froniga and Jenny were left staring at the sunlit grass dappled with the pattern of the leaves.

"Jenny," said Froniga, for the child was motionless too long.

Jenny looked up, her face blanched but her eyes so bright that they seemd to have caught some reflection of the vanished brightness. "It's true," she whispered.

"It might have been only the sunlight dazzling our eyes," said Froniga.

Jenny looked at her with a trace of astonished scorn and with shame she answered, "Yes, Jenny, it was the unicorn. Don't tell your mother. Don't tell anyone."

"No," said Jenny.

"It is no use trying to describe the undescribable," said Froniga. "Now I'll take you home, Jenny."

"No," said Jenny. "If we wait we might see him again. Cousin Froniga, I want to see him again. Please, Cousin Froniga!"

"We shall not see him again," said Froniga, and taking Jenny's hand she ran with her out of the wood. She wanted to get out of it, to get as far away as she possibly could, and she was in such a daze of fear and sorrow that they were halfway home before she looked down at Jenny and saw her with the tears running down her face. Did the child know too? But she had always been careful not to tell her. "What is it, Jenny?" she asked.

"He was all made of light," sobbed Jenny. "He was lovely, and he wasn't there for more than a quarter of a minute. I want to see him again. Cousin Froniga, when shall I see him again?"

"I hope you will never see him again," said Froniga, before she could stop herself. She did not want Jenny to have her powers. Just now they seemed be a heavy burden.

"Why not?" sobbed Jenny. "He's our own unicorn."

"Be content with your home, Jenny," said Froniga. "It was made out of the ship. Love the old *Unicorn* timbers that smell so good when the sun warms them. A house is good company, and so is Baw, your flesh-and-blood pony. Isn't the beauty that you can see with your bodily eyes, and touch and hear, enough for you? Flowers, the shapes of things, birds singing. When you have lost your body, that particular way of loving beauty will be lost too. Make the most of it while you have it. Don't stretch out to anything beyond this world excepting only God, who is the love with which you love its beauty and praise Him for it. And love flesh-and-blood people while they are in this world. If you don't make haste to love them while you have them you may find they have gone away. Now you are home. Good night, dear heart."

She kissed Jenny and stood a few moments at the garden gate to wave to her as she ran into the house. Then she went quickly home. She lay sleepless all the short, warm summer night. The waiting was hard and she was glad when the dayspring gave her the excuse to get up. She cleaned the cottage from top to bottom, washed her linen and hung it out to dry. She forced herself to eat a little bread and drink some milk and then she went out to work in the garden. Usually, her hours in the garden sped by like minutes, but this morning they dragged interminably. When the sun was high overhead, and she and Pen went into the shade of the orchard to rest a little, a sudden hope came to her. It was only because she had held the potent elf-bolt in her hands in that particular part of the wood, by the spring that had such power, that she and Jenny had seen the unicorn. That was all. She was a fool. She was suffering for nothing. She would go indoors and do some spinning. The whirr of the wheel always brought her peace.

But today it did not help her. The spinning went badly, for she was always stopping her wheel to listen. She did not know what she expected to hear, but the whirr of the wheel somehow increased her misery, just because she could not hear it. She put her wheel aside and went to her loom, but that too made too much noise. She went to her porch, where the front door stood wide open, and sat down on the little bench within it. The bees were humming in the honeysuckle and the larks singing riotously. The noise they made was as deafening as the whirr of her wheel. Yet she stayed where she was because she was too tired to move anywhere else. She tried to tell herself again that she was suffering for nothing, and she leaned back and shut her eyes. The sensible thing, after her sleepless night, would be to try and sleep a little now. But sleep was impossible because she was so cold, and she was shivering. Was she going to be ill? No, it was not that sort of rigor. She knew what it was. She must pass through it with him, however long the hours, knowing that what she bore was not what he endured but only the shadow of it falling upon her; and that to her was the worst of it.

It passed suddenly, yet gently, with no more sense of shock than when a shadow passes. Her body began to glow again and the sound of the bees, and the larks singing, were no longer hideous to her. Deep within her she felt that fount of joy.

2

Some days later Froniga was in the still-room at the manor mixing a strong concoction of powerful herbs that she earnestly hoped would enable Margaret to pull herself together. Margaret's grief was great, that she acknowledged, but her total dedication to it was now, after days and nights of sobbing into her pillows in a darkened room, getting on Froniga's nerves. Also it was bad for Jenny and Will, especially for Jenny, who seldom left her mother and was getting to look like a wizened old woman.

Will was less miserable than Jenny. For one thing, there was the pleasure of being brought home from school in the middle of the term, for another he was now himself Squire Haslewood, and finally he had been in the High Street at Thame on the Sunday of the battle and had with his own eyes seen the wounded Colonel Hampden lifted from his horse at the house of Master Ezekiel Browne. The bells had been ringing for Evensong as they lifted him down. Will had run as close as he dared and apart from the Colonel's own close friends he had been the last person (so he said) to see Colonel Hampden alive. When he posed before the mirror as The Squire, when he told about Colonel Hampden over and over again, each time with further embellishments, he was much comforted. And he needed comfort, for beneath his self-importance he was very sad. In his bed at night he would think of his father on the day of his breeching, smiling at him over the heads of the silly women and bringing him his sword. Then he would cry a little (but beneath the bedclothes so that no one should hear) and feel very lonely. He and his father had been the only men of the family. Now he was alone with all these women.

Froniga, infusing her herbs, was not too anxious about Will, but very anxious about Jenny if Margaret did not get better soon. Murmuring every spell she knew, she added rosemary for heartache to camomile for sleeplessness, lavender for swooning to lily-of-the-valley for headache, clove gilliflower for strengthening to mugwort for weariness, and then honey, the white of an egg and a little white wine. She felt she could do no more. If this did not make Margaret stop crying and get out of bed nothing would.

She set aside the cordial and began to make another, a little less drastic, for Jenny and herself. It was not often she dosed herself, but she was tired and grieved. As well as her sorrow for Robert's death she was sorry for the death of John Hampden, who was to be buried tomorrow. The news of his death had been brought to them only an hour ago. He had died, Biddy told her, from a pistol ball in his shoulder, and had endured much torment from the surgeon's probings. If she had been there he would not have died. No man should die of a pistol ball in his shoulder. The wound must have become infected and probably all for want of a few cleansing, healing herbs; bugle, milfoil and samile. The needless loss of that life hurt her intolerably. Why, oh, why, would people insist upon putting their faith in these surgeons and apothecaries who had forgotten the wisdom of their fathers, and whose new wisdom was at present such ignorance that it was causing more deaths than the plague? They said that when John Hampden had left the battlefield he had tried to get to Pyrton, where he had been married to his wife Elizabeth, but the enemy blocked his way, and he had turned aside to Thame. That had grieved her too. To wish to die in the place where you have known your greatest happiness is a natural instinct and she was sorry he had not died at Pyrton. And now he was gone, the man who could least be spared going first as always. He had been a strong and righteous man, able to inspire and strengthen other men, as he had inspired Robert; to his death but not, she believed, to his loss. An idea came to her and she paused in her work, wondering how best she could carry it out. She would go to his burial tomorrow. To do so would be to pay him the only honour it was in her power to pay. She would go in Robert's place, for Robert's sake. It was a long way to Hampden, where they were to bury him, but she would ride there on Baw. Parson

Hawthyn, she knew, would come and spend the day with Margaret and the children. Yes, she would go.

She had just made up her mind when Biddy burst into the room, crimson with indignation. "Would you believe it, Mistress Froniga, here's one of those gypsies, one of those thieving, murderous Herons, at the back door! I couldn't believe my own eyes; no, I couldn't believe them! Who'd have thought that a Heron would dare to show himself in this village again? And asking for you, if you please. At least he knew better than to try and do business with me, after I'd been all but murdered by that wicked woman. I told him to be off, and I did not mince my words, but he stood there as brazen as you please. Then I slammed the door in his face, and peeped through the kitchen window, but he'd gone no further than the well. He's sitting there now, obstinate as the kitchen cat. You must come down, Mistress Froniga, and send him about his business, or we'll all lie in our blood in our beds this night."

"Certainly I'll come down," said Froniga equably. "And do you, Biddy, strain this infusion for me and then go to your mistress and change her bed-linen. I promised her that should be done tonight."

Biddy did as she was told and Froniga went downstairs. She opened the back door and stepped outside. Yoben had settled himself on the edge of the well in the sunshine, his battered old hat tipped over his eyes, combining obstinacy with comfort in a way that brought her a glow of amusement. For the first time in a week she was aware of the warmth of the sun and the scent of the flowers in the garden. "Yoben," she said.

He got up, took off his hat and bowed over her hand, then looked into her eyes with a matter-of-fact, direct sort of compassion that was as strengthening as a cordial.

"Froniga, I am sorry for your grief, and for that of Mistress Haslewood and the children, but I pity no man in his dying, excepting only those who die desperately, without faith in the mercy of God. Is there some quiet place where we can talk for a short while?"

She took him through the garden to the arbour of vine leaves where Jenny had sat with Francis, and they sat together on the seat. Though it was nearing sunset the bees were still humming among the lilies that grew just outside the arbour, and the flowers whose scents had been dulled by the heat of the day were now fragrant in the coolness of the evening.

"They say the scent of a flower is its spirit," said Froniga. "In the burden and heat of the day they sometimes forget they have them, as we do. At morning and evening they remember. What have you to say to me, Yoben?"

"The man you know as Mr. Loggin was with Captain Haslewood when he died," said Yoben. "He took such personal possessions as he had about him and has given them to me to restore to you."

She opened the small leather pouch he had laid on her lap and took out Robert's ring, the letters and the bunch of dried herbs. He noticed that she did not blench when she saw the bloodstains on the letters. She held the bunch of herbs in her hand. It was the one she had given Robert and she realised what it was that he had been about to show her when he stopped himself.

"It did not save him," she said.

"Do you wish it had?" he asked.

"I have grieved bitterly over his death, and for that of Colonel Hampden," she said, "but such grief is like a storm on the surface of the sea. When I can manage to sink below it then, like you, I shall lament only the death of those who die desperately."

She put the ring, the letter and the bunch of herbs back into the pouch and sat holding it in her hands, looking down at it. It was of supple leather with a crest, a little lion, worked upon it in gold, a rich man's toy. She saw the face of the man who owned it, steady-eyed, very honest, with the rather obstinate square chin that she had seen and remembered when she saw in the spring the face of the young man with the powdered hair.

"Please tell me all that John Loggin told you of Robert's death," she said.

"He wishes you to know, but it will make hard hearing."

"What could be harder hearing than the news of his death?"

He told her, omitting nothing except the fact that Robert had forgotten, or had not bothered, to put on his armour, for he knew how the small fortuitous accidents that appear to cause death can torment the bereaved. When he had finished he saw that she was most painfully distressed. She took her hands from the pouch she had been holding and he saw that they were trembling. "He struck in defence of the Prince," he said. "He could not help himself."

"I know that," she said. "You need not excuse him. This is civil war. It is that, one day, I shall have to tell Jenny."

"Why?" he asked.

"I shall have to tell Jenny," she repeated. "How can I tell her so that she will forgive? Who is he, Yoben? His life is bound up with ours and I do not even know his name. It will be safe with me."

"Francis, Lord Leyland," said Yoben.

"That is a great name," said Froniga, "and there will be times when she will find it a heavy burden. Yet to that she is called, as Robert to his death, and if she does not answer the call she will never find peace." Yoben was staring at her in blank astonishment but without looking at him she went on, "Where am I to find Robert's grave, Yoben?"

"Froniga, there are seldom individual graves after a battle," said Yoben pitifully, knowing how much a grave meant to her. "There is a deep hollow near Chalgrove called 'Clay-pit', and there the dead were all put together and covered over. I came that way to visit you. It is a place rich in turf and moss, abounding in curious shells, with gorse and juniper bushes."

"And marjoram?"

"I saw no marjoram."

"I will go there as soon as I can and plant marjoram," said Froniga. "But not tomorrow, for tomorrow I ride to Hampden to attend Colonel Hampden's funeral. That I must do in Robert's place, for Robert's sake."

"You will do no such thing, Froniga!" said Yoben with sudden violence. "To ride there and back will take you all day and the countryside is full of mutinous and lawless soldiery. Froniga, I forbid you to ride to Hampden."

She looked at him. "I am not your wife," she said. "You did not choose to give yourself the right to command me."

He looked at her in dismay, and with a slowly dawning realisation that the terms of love which may satisfy the man do not necessarily content the woman. He had found nothing but joy in their long friendship, but was it possible that she had found bitterness as well? He knew so little of women. Perhaps he had been causing her great pain all these years and he had not known it. He was horrified at the possibility and his dismay was so comical that her face softened. "Come with me," she said. "I shall be safe with you."

"*I* come with you to Colonel Hampden's funeral?" he asked incredulously. Then he looked down at the ground that she might not see his sudden amusement. Did she not realise that the news of Colonel Hampden's death had seemed to all ardent Royalists almost too good to be true? In him the rebels had lost their best leader up to the present time. Pym was a clever politician but no soldier. Essex had been a fine soldier once but was so no longer, and his loyalties were divided. Colonel Hampden's death had transformed the small engagement at Chalgrove Field into an important victory. Even the chivalrous King, though he had sent Dr. Giles, rector of Chinnor and a friend of Colonel Hampden's, to enquire after him, and had offered the services of the royal surgeons, had nevertheless, so Yoben had heard, been much more cheerful the last few days.

Froniga was quite aware of Yoben's amusement. "I do not mean to go into the church, Yoben," she said. "I would not so presume. It will be enough for me to stand by the churchyard wall. Surely you can stand beside me and remember what you said to me last summer—that you have no politics."

"I'll come with you, Froniga," said Yoben, ashamed of himself. "No. I am not a Royalist for political reasons. And I remember something else I said: that in the last resort what matters to a man is the war within the war, the battle that he fights within himself. To that war death brings peace, and to honour the peace of another can be a foretaste of one's own."

The darkening arbour suddenly seemed oppressive to Froniga. She got up restlessly and moved out into the brightness of the evening. She loved light above all things, and June with its long days and short nights was the month she loved best. She and Yoben walked up and down the grass path, making their plans for the morning. Then they said goodbye quietly and Yoben went away down to the warm dry hollow in the beech-woods where he had left his pony and his saddlebags, and where he had planned to sleep that night. But he did not sleep. He lay thinking of Froniga and of that wound of secret bitterness that had opened suddenly within the depth of her love for him. He had never even suspected it was there. It seemed that he must give himself the ease and self-indulgence of confession after all, for there was no other way to heal that wound of Froniga's.

CHAPTER IV

THE SUN AND MOON

I

Froniga and Yoben were away soon after dayspring, such a dayspring as Froniga had never seen in her life before. There had been no darkness that night, for the moon was at the full, and at half past three, as she was dressing, she saw a sight she loved, day and night both in the sky together. She had a corner room at the manor. Through the south window, flung wide open, she saw the full golden moon and stars in a pale sky. Out of the east window she could see far over the fields to the sunrise. The sun had not risen yet, but the brown brink of the world was turning to apricot, with a deepening blue sky above. The woods were dark against the sky and the hollow lands mist-filled. She hardly recognised the garden, it was so unbelievably enchanted in its changed colours. The grass was golden, the white flowers pearl-coloured, the trees and bushes a warm pinkish grey, the shadows on the grass the same colour. The stillness and silence were absolute and the soft rustle of her garments as she put them on seemed almost a desecration of it. Then beyond the south window she heard an owl hoot, while eastward a cock crowed; the voices of day and night. She thought of the old gypsy story of the two lovers, the sun and the moon, who might greet each other only across the width of the world, and suddenly her heart sang within her. For she was not separated from her lover. She was going to do what she had never done before, spend a whole day in his company.

She felt like a girl again as she went light-footed through the sleeping house and out through the bewitched garden to the stables. The horses lifted their heads when she went in and Diamond whinnied. She had survived the battle of Chalgrove Field. Her return home, riderless, had been seen by no one except Froniga. It was she who had taken her to the stable and tended her, expending her best herbal remedies upon her both externally and internally, for the mare had been brokenhearted and in sorry shape. It had linked them together in undying affection and she talked to Diamond as she saddled Baw. Will would soon be big enough to ride her, she said, and for her there would be no more war.

When she reached the valley in the beech-wood, Yoben rode quietly out to join her and they went on at once, for there was no time to lose. Though at first they took the same road that she and Will had taken, this seemed a very different journey. Then they had gone at a slow gentle pace, now they rode fast. And the countryside had changed utterly in two months. The cherry blossom had gone, but in the woods the bluebells were not yet over and the croziers of the young bracken were growing stout and high. Wafts of bluebell scent came to them as they rode, the hedges were a froth of cow parsley and stitchwort and the oaks were a golden green. The newly-risen sun shone through the woods in golden shafts, but out in the open spaces the blue of the morning was cool and the moon was still to be seen. The singing of the birds was so lovely that they did not want to talk. They rode through this world of glory in silent thankfulness and humility. This day, this gift, and they alone possessing it all, riding through the green and the gold, seeing the blue pools under the trees and hearing the birds. And up there the sun and the moon, alone. A man and a woman in the sky and a man and a woman on the earth. So it had been in the beginning, in Eden's garden.

As the hours passed and the sun rode high they no longer had the world to themselves. They passed fields where the haymaking was going on, groups of cottages where children were playing in the gardens and mothers were sitting at the cottage doors spinning, and sometimes they met troops of cavalry and infantry upon the march. No one molested them, though many looked curiously at the comely woman in Puritan dress and the ascetic-looking gypsy who rode beside her. Though in dress they were so sharply distinguished they were alike in their dignity and poise, and rode as a king and queen might do upon a royal progress. They had never been in such perfect accord. Yoben was not thinking of what he must tell Froniga before the day was out, nor she of what tomorrow might hold. Though they rode on a sad errand they did not think about that either, but yielded themselves to the joy of each moment as it came.

Their ponies were stout and strong, used to travelling long distances, but they stopped and rested occasionally, in the woods and fields, and let the ponies graze while they ate a little of the food that Froniga had brought and enjoyed the company of the birds. Yoben had the same sort of power over birds as Froniga had over animals. He could imitate their songs to deceive even themselves, and the brave among them would come and perch on his boots and on his shoulders while he whistled to them. Even the shy cherry-hopper would fly from a branch towards him and then back again, as though he would have liked to make friends had he dared. Of all birds Froniga loved best the little cherry-hopper with his rayed breast. For the rest of her life he seemed to her a part of the joy of this day.

It was midday when they came to Hampden and found the little village thronged with the army. All Colonel Hampden's Greencoats were there, and men of other regiments who had come to do him honour. They rode wide of the village, tethered their ponies to a tree, and then walked through a field to the churchyard wall. Here the humble folk of the village were gathered and they mingled with them, then drew apart a little and stood together under the cool shade of a yew tree. There were berries on the evergreen yew, shining like small red lamps in the deep green. Froniga never forgot them, or the depth of the blue sky seen through the dark branches overhead.

The murmur of quiet voices rose about them, talking of Colonel Hampden, recalling his righteousness and kindness, and that today was the anniversary of his wedding to his wife Elizabeth. Then the voices, the country sounds of haymaking, dogs barking and birds singing, were silenced by a rolling of muffled drums and the slow tramp of men. Colonel Hampden's Greencoats could be seen coming down the road that led from the manor to the church, six of them bearing his coffin on their shoulders, covered with the regimental banner. They marched bareheaded, with arms reversed, and when the first roll of the drums ceased they began to sing a psalm, the ninetieth. "Lord, Thou has been our refuge, from one generation to another. Before the mountains were brought forth, or ever the earth and the world were made, Thou art God from everlasting, and world without end."

The sound of the chanting grew louder as they came nearer and the drums began to roll again as an accompaniment to the singing. "Thou turnest man to destruction; again Thou sayest, come again, ye children of men." If Yoben had feared that his emotions upon this occasion might be unsuitable he had worried for nothing. For a few moments he forgot this was the funeral cortège of an enemy, he almost forgot it was a funeral at all, for there was no weeping here, no lament. Man's little life and death fell into nothingness in comparison with the omnipotence of God. "For a thousand years in Thy sight are but as yesterday when it is past, and as a watch in the night. As soon as Thou scatterest them they are even as a sleep; and fade away suddenly like the grass."

The men filed in through the gate and came tramping slowly through the churchyard. Their faces were stern, their voices rough and strong. Yoben remembered again that these men were his enemies, but remembered it without enmity. As they filed past, nearly deafening him with their singing and the rolling of their drums, he felt a brief flash of admiration for something tough and uncompromising about them and their faith. These men were at present worsted in the war, but they were not going to be defeated as easily as the Royalists were hoping. Their leader was dead in the coffin they carried, but this tough faith of theirs would raise up another in his place, a man of perhaps greater power and ruthlessness. For they would become more ruthless as they went on; that was inevitable in war. "Who regardeth the power of Thy wrath? or feareth aright Thy indignation?" They were right. Men sunned themselves too much in the thought of God's mercy and forgot His wrath. "Thou hast set our misdeeds before Thee; and our secret sins in the light of Thy countenance." They forgot the judgement. He began to tremble with some strange foreboding of it.

Froniga slipped her hand into his and as the coffin was carried into the church and the drum-rolls ceased he could hear her singing beside him. "Turn Thee again, O Lord, at the last, and be gracious unto Thy servants. O satisfy us with Thy mercy, and that soon : so shall we rejoice and be glad all the days of our life." His trembling ceased. It was also possible to think too much of the judgement and forget the mercy.

2

"It must be Colonel Hampden's funeral at this very moment," said Margaret to Parson Hawthyn. "*He* is having a fine funeral, with drums, and mourners following behind his coffin, and my poor Robert was just pushed into a pit with a lot of others like a dead dog! I cannot even weep upon his grave!"

"My dear," said Parson Hawthyn, "that is at least one thing to be thankful for."

She began to cry again, feeling under her pillow for her handkerchief. "Please to draw the curtain right across," she said weakly. "I can't bear the light."

"No, Margaret," said Parson Hawthyn firmly. "I am enjoying the sunlight and you should be doing the same."

Margaret raised herself on her elbow and looked at him with weak indignation. Now he too was turning against her. Until today his visits had been her one solace. Though she had consistently turned from all the comfort he had tried to give her, she had liked to have him there holding her hand and witnessing her grief. Nothing had comforted her like refusing his comfort. Now it seemed he had come to the end of it.

"Is that all you have to say to me?" she asked fretfully.

"No, my dear," said Parson Hawthyn. "I should very much like to ask you why you are not drinking that strengthening medicine which Froniga mixed for you."

"Froniga and her potions and spells!" said Margaret impatiently. "They are nothing but moonshine!"

"If you do not care for moonshine you must take a little honest-to-God down-to-earth mutton broth," said Parson Hawthyn. "Biddy tells me she has made you some excellent broth, but you will not touch it."

"It makes me sick," said Margaret.

"Fiddlesticks," said Parson Hawthyn.

He was delighted to see that this time he had made her really angry. She sat up in bed with two pink spots flaring on her cheek-bones. "How dare you talk to me so!" she said. "You—a bachelor—what do you know of love? And dried-up spinsters like Froniga and Biddy, what do they know? You don't understand what's between husband and wife. You don't understand what it's like to lose the other half of yourself."

"I understand very well, Margaret," said Parson Hawthyn. "My wife died of the plague six months before I came to this parish."

Margaret gazed at him in an entirely self-forgetting astonishment and curiosity. "But why did you never tell us?" she asked.

"I have always feared sympathy," said Parson Hawthyn. "I have craved it, of course, being human, but I have feared it too. Taking your grief to one person after another is like taking it to so many mouths that suck at you and drain away your strength. And God knows we need all our strength to catch up."

"To catch up?" asked Margaret.

"They seem to grow so immeasurably towards the end," he said. "They grow away from us, outstrip us and leave us behind."

Margaret began to cry again, but this time there was no self-pity in her tears. She cried merely because he had touched sharply upon a chord of memory. And presently she stopped crying and said, "That's what I thought on the morning of Will's breeching."

"What did you think, my dear?" asked the old man.

"That Robert had grown and left me behind. I thought I'd try and grow into a new woman to match his new man. But I did not, and now it is too late."

"Certainly not. That is what I am trying to tell you. This is your growing time, now, when you have no Robert to lean on. The propped never grow. You will grow now. You will have to. You have an immense incentive; nothing less than the growing up towards eternal life like a tree towards the sun. Now, my dear, I am going downstairs to see the children."

"I think I could take a little broth," said Margaret. "Will you be so good as to tell Biddy?"

3

Froniga and Yoben rode home in a more leisurely manner than they had come, for it would be a night of moon and stars and they would see their way clearly even when night had fallen. And on this homeward journey they talked more, Froniga telling Yoben stories of her wild and happy childhood with her father and mother, of the years with Robert's parents, unhappy ones because Robert's mother had disliked her, and of her escape into freedom again. "It was my father who taught me the spells of a white witch that my mother had known," she said. "Always they must be handed on from man to woman and from woman to man. To whom shall I teach my spells, Yoben? To you?"

She looked at him, laughing, and saw a comical look of dismay pass over his face. Then he smiled and said a little stiltedly, "I am much older than you, Froniga. You must teach them to a younger man, or let them die with you."

"You think it would be better to let them die with me."

"I do not presume to judge you, Froniga. I have never concerned myself with what you believe, or what you do or have done. I have been concerned only in loving what you are."

"And that has contented you?" she asked.

"Yes, it has contented me. But I am a man, and a man rather ignorant of women. I have known few women well, and have loved only yourself and Madona. I think I have perhaps been mistaken in judging you by myself. What has contented me has not necessarily contented you. The times are dangerous, Froniga, and if I should die in this war I shall leave you with very little knowledge of me. You will perhaps grieve that you have so little. Would you like to know more?"

"Only if you would like to tell me more," said Froniga.

"Up till now you have respected as well as loved me," said Yoben. "If I tell you more of myself, then you will be left only with your love."

"No," said Froniga, "for I respect the man I know today, in this present time in which we are together, not the man who lived in a past that I did not share. If it will ease you for me to share it, I shall be glad, but only if it would ease you."

It would ease him, Yoben thought. He had been thinking of this sharing only for her sake, but now he wanted it increasingly for his own. This long day together, bringing them nearer to each other than they had ever been, had seemed to lift their love on to a new place, almost into a clearer atmosphere. He had never been less conscious of her as a woman, and for that very reason had never been more conscious of her as a companion, in the sense of unity upon the same timeless journey. He realised that human love, if it is to last beyond death and approximate a fraction nearer to divine, must feed on truth. "Froniga," he said, "by silence I have deceived you. I have only just realised that."

"Don't reproach yourself. Deception that you conceived to be your duty has become second nature to you, has it not?"

"You're right. A recusant priest. A Royalist spy. I have never been able to be anything openly. You could pull off my disguises like the skins of an onion and always find another underneath. And the core rotten—fit only to be thrown away."

"And not yours either to judge or to throw away," said

Froniga. "Only our disguises are our own. Tell me about yours, Yoben. I never thought you were a gypsy. I have learnt lately that you are a spy. After that night last autumn when I angered you so with my careless speech I wondered if you had, perhaps. Papist sympathies. As to the other—of that I had no knowledge at all. Tell me what you will."

Her voice was quiet, but her face was turned away from him. He tried not to think of what her feelings might be, this Puritan woman who would have been brought up to fear the very name of Papist, but to think only of what he must say. "I am English," he said, "and was born in England. My parents died when I was still young and I was sent to the Spanish Netherlands, where my father's brother was a Jesuit priest at the English College at Douai. There I was rigorously trained as one of those missionary priests sent across the Channel year by year to keep the Catholic faith alive in England. I was an ardent and rather passionate boy, but not as physically strong or as morally courageous as I imagined myself to be. Somehow that hard discipline of the seminary, that tempered so many proud spirits, did not teach me humility. When the time came for me to leave with other priest for England I had no doubt at all about my own powers of endurance, even to the point of martyrdom. I was more than ready, I was eager, for the martyr's crown of roses and lilies. I had not laid to heart the wise words of Sir Thomas More, who would not press upon martyrdom 'lest God for my presumption might suffer me to fall'. It was a strange existence that we had in England, Froniga. We were not there to convert Protestants to the faith, and we did not try to proselytise; we were there, in the words of our mandate, for 'the preservation and augmentation of the faith of the Catholics in England'. And we had to do it hiddenly, for there was no protection for Catholics in the old Queen's days, or in the days of King James; to be caught hearing or saying Mass meant fines and imprisonment for the laity and torture and death for the priest. We lived sometimes under grim conditions of hunger and cold and poverty. It was a hard life, always with its undercurrent of ceaseless danger. After a few years it told upon me and I fell ill. I think that in my fever I must have spoken of the hidden things, for the first time I went abroad again after my illness, to say Mass in a certain Catholic house where the faithful had gathered on Easter morning, they came and found us. My congregation escaped, but I was caught."

"Do not go on, Yoben," said Froniga sharply. "I cannot bear it."

"Am I not riding beside you safe and sound?" he asked bitterly. "And do you suppose I should be so crass as to harrow your feelings with details of physical torture?"

"I should not mind if you did. What I cannot bear is to look upon a man's shame."

"You will not look on mine. It is too deeply buried. The few plain facts that lie above it I can recite as drily as a chandler pattering the price of corn, for I know them so well and have lived with them so long. I and another priest, a frail old man who later died in prison, were taken to London. For the last bit of the way we were pinioned on our horses, our arms behind our backs and our legs fastened together under the horses' bellies, and the people in the street pelted us with rubbish. We were imprisoned in the Tower, but not together. I was alone in a filthy dark little cell, so small that I could scarcely stretch out in it. I was there for many weeks, each day expecting to be put to the torture. I became ill again, and as I waited for it day by day and week by week I came to have a fearful dread of the torture. I was afraid I should fail. Yet when it came at last, and I was on the rack, I did not fail. I answered none of the questions the rack-master put to me. I was carried back to my cell and left for ten days and then, with my limbs still crippled from the first torture, I was racked again, and this time I was promised my life, and the means to leave England, if I would give the information that was asked of me. But again I kept silence and this time, though the pain was so bitter, I felt some of my old presumptuous self-confidence returning. I realised that my courage was equal to it. I could do it. I was the victor, not they. I came back to consciousness, that second time, still with that sense of confidence, and found that I was not back in my cell but still there in the torture chamber. The rack-master bent over me, asking me the everlasting questions all over again, but gently and with tenderness, praising my courage and promising me peace. It would be a pity, they said, to put me back upon the rack. And it was then, not on the rack at all but lying on my back on the floor, that I broke down completely and told them all I knew. I even told them of matters that had been confided to me under the seal of confession. They kept their word and set me free and I left England, but because of what I had told them, several good men were ruined and imprisoned and my three closest friends died the traitor's death at Tyburn. And you know, Froniga, what that death is."

There was no sound but that of their ponies' feet on the road, and the birds singing. Froniga did not speak, for she could not. For a few moments she felt the pain that the man beside her had endured for so many years. . . . Withered and dry, a branch broken from the tree, burnt up with fiery misery. . . . She had often been allowed to share the suffering of others for a few moments, but she had never shared anything like this. It passed abruptly, as such things did.

"How old were you, Yoben?" she asked at last.

"Twenty-five."

"What did you do?"

"Not the one thing I should have done—return to Douai and submit to whatever discipline was judged best for me. I was too much of a coward for that and perhaps still too proud. My instinct was to disappear, sink away from the companionship of decent men, and I followed my instinct. I became a vagabond in Europe, picking a living as best I could."

"Yoben, do you not think that the fearful results of your failure made you believe it worse than it was? It was only your nerve that failed, not your will. It was weakness, not sin."

For the first time they looked at each other. The astonishment in his eyes turned to something almost like antagonism and she realised that the relentlessness that had gone into his training had become a part of his judgement of himself for ever. Nothing she could say could soften it now. "Never mind, Yoben," she said quickly. "I do not see this quite as you do. Never mind. It is long ago now. So you became a vagabond in Europe. Where did you become a gypsy?"

"In Spain," he said. "I had always been attracted by the gypsies and now they seemed akin to me, wandering forever in expiation of their sin. I was with them for many years and then I found myself longing for the gentleness of England, the green springs and the golden fall of the leaf. I joined a ship's crew at Lisbon and sailed from there to Ireland, and from Ireland I got to Scotland, and then journeyed down through the great hills to Cumberland. There I fell in with Righteous Lee, Madona's brother, and came south with him."

"And would have given your life for him," said Froniga. "The Herons have told that story. The village know it and I know it. Did it grieve you that you were not allowed to die on the gallows for old Righteous?"

"Yes," said Yoben. "I had hoped to be allowed to suffer for another man something of what my friends had suffered for me. If we could choose our purgations, I suppose we would all of us choose to suffer as we have made others suffer, to feel every cruel word we have spoken enter our own hearts, to have withheld from ourselves what we have withheld from others. Yet that's partly pride, Froniga, the desire for that tit-for-tat that restores equality. The gift of free forgiveness would humble us more. In prison, nursing my disappointment and my sore ears, I saw that at last and managed to stop clutching hold of that hope. I gave it into the hands of God, to be or not to be as Heaven wills."

"How did you come to work for the King as you are doing?" asked Froniga.

"Both in Spain, and in England later, I always heard Mass when I could," said Yoben, "for I had never become so desperate as to try and cut myself off entirely from the mercy of God. In Catholic Spain I had been able to slip into a church among a crowd of peasants and not be noticed, but in England I could not do that. I had difficulty in finding the hidden congregations, and when I did find one the appearance of a Catholic gypsy among them was an alarming phenomenon. For the sake of their own safety they would question me and I would have to answer their questions. I became well known among them at last and it was known that I had been a priest. Before the war all the best officers in the King's army were Catholics and I came to know some of them well. When war became inevitable they thought I could be useful. Is there anything else that you would ask me, Froniga?"

"Only one thing. Have you never served as a priest again?"

"Only once. A priest was taken suddenly ill and I was asked to take his place. It seemed my duty, but it was a fearful thing to me."

Froniga would have asked him why it was a fearful thing and then something in the quality of the silence that had come between them stopped her. They rode on and gradually she understood why it was a fearful thing and felt a sudden sharp anger. If he thought their long self-denying love a sin, then she thought he was a fool, though she loved the fool no less for his folly. Hot words rose in her, but she did not speak them. They rode on for a long time in continuing silence and then by mutual consent drew their ponies to the side of the road, and forgot them. The ponies cropped the grass, and the man and the woman looked at each other.

From that long wordless look Froniga gained great knowledge of Yoben. She realised, as she had not done before, how utterly his love for her had flooded his haunted, lonely life. She had been like sunshine in cold and desolate places. She had transformed his life and he had not been able to give her up. Like the young ruler in the story, who could not part with his great possessions though his soul's life depended on it, she had been the one thing that he could not relinquish. He had yielded everything else, but not this warmth and sunshine, without which he had come to feel that he could not live. Yet looking with her far-seeing eyes deep into his spirit she saw how the weakness that had betrayed him before was betraying him again. He was not able to free himself from his enslavement to her. If she did not set him free he would die with his soul in chains. Yoben, meeting her steady, piercing glance, felt a sense of panic. His spirit wanted to recoil and creep away, to hide from her. It took all his courage to open himself to her gaze, yet not to do so was to cheat her. No good to stop short now, to reveal so much and no more. If she wanted full knowledge of him, she must have it even if it was his doom. He could not read her as she read him. He saw her face grow white and cold and it seemed that something of her beauty withered. He did not know how long they stayed there, or what sort of struggle was going on in her. The sunset had been golden when he had begun to talk to her, now it was dusk, with great moths flitting, and a silence of birds. He felt that life was draining away from them both, leaving desolation.

"It's cold," he said, and did not know he had spoken.

"We'll ride on," said Froniga.

They rode quickly now. Night came and the stars clustered thickly in the sky, and still they had not spoken to each other. Near home, in the hollow in the beech-wood where Yoben would have to turn aside to reach his camping place, they stopped. He dismounted and came and stood beside her bridle, his hand on hers, waiting for her to do what he had not the strength to accomplish for himself.

"Goodbye, Yoben," she said steadily. "I do not want to see you again. Since you knew me you have never been free to serve God with a single heart. Till the end of our lives we will long for each other, and the longing will seem more than we can bear at times, but I expect it is the one thing needful for us both, for if we do not one day find each other in God, we shall never find each other again at all."

He seemed rooted to the spot. His hand moved on hers, caressing it. "Don't, Yoben!" she said sharply. He kissed her hand, took his pony's bridle and went straight away into the darkness of the woods without looking back. She rode to the manor, stabled Baw and let herself into the dark house without knowing what she was doing. She went softly through the sleeping house to her room, undressed and got into the big four-poster bed. Unconsciously she pulled herself into the far corner of it, cowering away from the moonlight like a whipped dog. She lay with her knees drawn up, as though she were in pain, motionless for an hour or more. When she began to weep at last the sobs seemed tearing her in pieces like hands tearing a rotten sheet. The emptiness within her and all round her was appalling. She had said once to Yoben, in her ignorance and foolishness, that there are more ways than one of consummating love, and the hardest way can be the best. But she had not known it was like this. There was nothing grand or inspiring about renunciation. It was just all the years of your life stretching ahead in a long grey dreary emptiness. There was no comfort anywhere. The thought of death was too far off to bring any comfort, for she was physically so immensely strong. She would live long. If the hours were so leaden, what would the years be? They would never pass.

Yet a tract of time did pass and she could no longer refuse the compelling light. For hours it had been drenching her while she lay with her face buried in her hands. She turned over in the bed and stretched out her cramped limbs. Their aching, the discomfort of her nightshift drenched with sweat, of her face stiff and sore with weeping, seemed somehow to ease the other pain. She was aware of the moon, remembered vaguely the old story, and the loneliness of sun and moon. Her sore eyes could not bear the brightness and she shut them, but her body seemed soaking up the light and presently she slept.

CHAPTER V

A FAIR CITY

I

A month later Charles and his cavaliers were once more advancing upon Edgehill but not this time for war. Things were going so well with them that it had been judged safe for the Queen to come to Oxford and they were riding to meet her. Through the first year of the war she had been in Holland, collecting weapons and money for her husband. Then she had returned through fearful storms to England, landed at Bridlington and narrowly escaped death at the hands of the enemy. From there she had marched north to York at the head of a small Royalist army and now at last she was coming south. Rupert with an escort had gone to Stratford to meet her, and they had been entertained there by Mr. William Shakespeare's daughter Judith, and now he was bringing her to Edgehill.

The King and his boys were in splendid spirits, and so were the young men with them. They rode through the dusty lanes, and through the woods that were now dark and heavy with their dense July foliage, laughing, talking and singing. Though their swords and pistols were handy they did not wear armour, for the disheartened Parliament troops were not likely to attack so large a company. The plumes in their great hats nodded as they passed by on their splendid horses, in and out of the shadows of the trees, with accoutrements jingling and sparkling, and the sun gleamed on the shining lovelocks lying on their shoulders. When they passed through villages the children and their mothers ran out to drop curtseys to the King, and men came hastening from field or farm to cry "God save Your Majesty!" For whether they were for King or Parliament, the person of the King was sacred to them. They wished him well and they hoped this peaceful laughing calvacade was a harbinger of better things to come.

Francis laughed and cracked jokes with the rest, but he was feeling less cheerful than he appeared. For one thing, the death of Robert Haslewood was still a grief to him; and for another thing, he was about to be reunited with the beautiful girl whom his father and her father had decided he should marry. She was one of the Queen's maids of honour. She had not been to Holland with the Queen but she had joined her at York and was now riding with her towards Oxford. "And towards me, God help me," thought Francis. He had just had a letter from his father suggesting a wedding at Oxford this autumn. The exquisite airy little letter with which Barbara had favoured him a few weeks ago had hinted delicately at the same thing. A sense of doom was upon him. He was acutely conscious that the outsize in hats he was wearing did not disguise the fact that John Loggin had chopped off Lord Leyland's lovelocks, and their present state of semi-growth was by no means becoming. Also he was uncomfortably hot. He was not a self-conscious man, for his great possessions had always mitigated that sense of lack which drives a human being back upon himself, but in Barbara's vicinity he always remembered the one thing he did not possess : good looks.

In the brilliant sunshine, under the hot blue of the sky, they came out into the plain where the battle had been fought in the grey gloom of the north wind. There was nothing ghostly about it now. The crest of the great hill shimmered softly in the heat-mist and the fields were gold and green. The only reminder of the battle, the long lines of mounds that covered the trenches where the dead had been buried, were green too and flowers grew upon them.

Their arrival had been well timed. They waited only a short while and then they saw another cavalcade approaching them and could make out the two figures riding ahead of it : Rupert on his huge black horse and the little Queen on her white palfrey. The cavaliers waved their plumed hats, cheered and rode forward. The King's trumpet rang out and the Queen's answered it. Then both cavalcades quickened their pace and came towards each other like two great rippling flower-gardens carried forward by the summer wind.

In the midst of a green meadow they halted, and the King and his sons dismounted and came forward to the Queen. Henrietta Maria slipped off her horse into her husband's arms. "Dear heart," she said, for that was what she always called him. He was speechless as he kissed her. She had passed through incredible danger and was still the same.

Their courtiers and cavaliers looked on benignly. This marriage, which had begun with such bitterness and dislike upon both sides, had after a few years become a happy one. The Court had watched with amusement the King falling in love with the Queen, and the Queen blossoming into gaiety and confidence, and finally autocracy. She now did what she liked with her husband. She was a Queen in miniature, for she reached only to her husband's shoulder and he was only five feet in height, but her will was all the more dominant for her lack of inches. Apart from her flashing black eyes she was not beautiful, for her skin was sallow and her features irregular, but she was so dainty and so sparkling with vivacity that no one in her company remembered that she was not a beauty.

Francis had forgotten it now as he watched her greeting her excited young sons. He was one of the group of young men who formed an inner circle of devotion about the King and Queen. He knew her well, for she had a special kindliness for those of her husband's Court who were of her own faith. He knew her quick temper and her arrogance, and how dangerous at times was her influence over her husband, for she did not always understand the matters in which she meddled, but he loved her for her fearlessness, her wit and charm. There was only one of her ladies who did not look insignificant beside her, and she was the slender girl in cerulean blue sitting straight-backed yet graceful upon a grey palfrey almost as beautiful as herself. Her silver-gilt hair glinted under her wide hat. Her complexion was of cream and roses and on a day when everyone else was inclined to perspire she looked almost maddeningly cool. Francis groaned within himself and rode towards her.

Everyone was on the move now, for both companies were to have a rest beneath the shade of the trees that bordered the valley and partake of a delicate collation before they continued their journey, but Barbara, as always, sat her horse in a state of elegant detachment from the common herd. She was not looking for Francis, for she seldom took the initiative. She did not lack strength, she had the strength of a boa-constrictor, but she was indolent; and everything she wanted always came to her if she waited for it as she was waiting now, with apparent indifference, her lovely lips a little parted and her gaze directed towards the horizon. She was a woman who drove men mad and yet she made no attempt to attract them. It was that that attracted them. They felt that if they could not bring themselves to her favourable notice they would burst a blood vessel. Francis was almost the only man whose reason had never been affected by her. As an artist he was not very attracted by the static quality of her flawless beauty, and as a singularly creaturely man he had always secretly craved a more homely and comfortable love, the sort of love that his loneliness had glimpsed sometimes within firelit cottages upon his fathers great estate. But to that estate, and to his heirs, he had his duty. "Barbara," he said, and wheeled his horse alongside hers, doffing his great hat. Her cool blue gaze slid round to him, she smiled and gave him her hand. He kissed it and she said, "Francis, have you turned Puritan?"

The word brought Jenny almost intolerably to his mind but he laughed and said, "No, Barbara, I cut my hair short for a wager." Then he looked up at her, for even on horseback she was taller than he. There was a flicker of amusement now about her mouth, and he wondered why. She was thinking how ridiculous it was that she should be about to marry this stocky, hot, freckled young man, more like a farmer to look at than a viscount, and more ridiculous still that looking as he did he should be the one man of her acquaintance who was not mad about her. Yet the very absurdity of it intrigued her slightly. Later on, when they were married, the goading of him into some sort of emotion with regard to her, no matter what, might prove amusing. Without knowing her thought he felt a chill of foreboding as they rode together towards the trees.

Some while later the gallant company was on its way back again, the King and Queen riding side by side in the midst of the cavalcade with Rupert and their sons behind them. The rest and collation had taken rather longer than they had expected because the boys had wanted to tell their mother all about the battle, to show her where they had stood on the hillside with Rupert's poodle, where their father had stood, taking the place of his fallen standard, when Rupert had charged and where their own regiments had fought so doughtily. All the way back to Oxford it was a triumphant progress, for this time the villagers were expecting them and the children had picked flowers in the fields and in the cottage gardens and they threw them to the ladies and the cavaliers. The Queen had always been slightly contemptuous of her husband's barbarous and heretical people, but on this day of reunion, in the glorious July sunshine, she was touched by their welcome. She laughed and kissed her hand to them and catching a carnation that was flung to her she put it in the buttonhole of her riding-coat. Her ladies and the cavaliers did the same, and so flower-bedecked they rode upon their way.

Near the sunset of a golden day they came down a long winding hill and saw Oxford in the valley below them. Now that London was in the hands of the rebels, Oxford was the King's capital, the chief as well as the loveliest city in this fair realm of England. "See, dear heart," Charles said to Henrietta, "there, now, is your home and mine. Did you ever see anything so beautiful as that fair city?"

Within the strong sweep of the battlemented city walls the towers and spires, with the steep roofs and the great green trees, were all softened by the golden summer haze to the illusion of a dream. Without the walls they could see the blue curve of the river, bordered with willow trees, and the water-meadows freshly green, threaded with winding streams. As they came down into the valley and rode nearer they could hear the bells pealing and see the good people of Oxford pouring out of the West Gate to line the way.

And now the King and Queen were riding ahead, leading the rest. They rode through West Gate between the ranks of their cheering people, into the city, clattering and jingling over the cobbles, then up a winding street between the tall gabled houses towards the tall tower of Carfax at the meeting of the ways. All Oxford was out in the street to greet Henrietta, cheering and crying down blessings upon the King and the Queen. Tapestries hung from the windows and again flowers rained down upon them, and were flung upon the cobbles before the horses' feet. It was a happy hour. The little King and Queen seemed to their loyal people all the more endearing because they were such fragile and miniature figures. And yet what commanding dignity they had, Henrietta of the flashing eyes and her grave and courteous husband; King and Queen of England, this lovely city seemed made for them. And so they came up to Carfax and turning to their right rode down to the royal college of Christ Church. All the bells of the city were pealing because the Queen had come home.

2

It was a gay summer. With the King lodged at Christ Church, the Queen at Merton, Rupert at St. John's and the Court everywhere, the university city took on a surprising metamorphosis. Venerable doorways, accustomed to the passage of learned dons and sober students, now disgorged ladies and gallants tricked out in all the gorgeous finery of the most astonishing period of haberdashery that England had ever known. Silk and satin petticoats whispered up and down worn flights of stone steps, ribbons fluttered and trinkets glittered, perfume and music drifted out from mullioned windows, colour ebbed and flowed in the narrow twisted streets and over the grass lawns of college gardens. By day there were picnics, hawking and riding parties, and by night masques and dancing in the college halls. In conscious or unconscious revolt against the staidness and sombreness of the Puritan enemy the King's men and women made a sort of cult of colour and gaiety, ridiculous pranks and jokes. The dons and heads of colleges endured as best they could, supported by the thought that all things pass.

War added its own colour and excitement to the scene, for in the glorious month of July almost everything was going well. Young Prince Maurice, Rupert's brother, who had come riding to Oxford to fetch help for the hard-pressed south-west, had ridden off with it again to the victory of Roundway Down. Rupert marched out of Oxford with drums beating and banners flying to the siege and capture of Bristol. Yet still those three armies could not march on London. The army of the south-west, and Newcastle's army of the north, could not march, with Plymouth and Hull still in the hands of the enemy. There was another small cloud on the horizon, though so small that it was hardly noticed. A certain Colonel Cromwell, commanding now not a troop but a regiment of horse recruited from the godly East Anglia that was fast becoming a stronghold of the Lord's people, won a victory. His small but splendidly disciplined body of cavalry, trained after cavalier methods but with Rupert's technique improved upon by Cromwell's genius, had come up against the best of Newcastle's cavalry and with a disadvantage of ground had defeated them. But the cloud passed and was forgotten.

Francis had not marched with Rupert to the siege of Bristol, for if the coming of the Queen had brought good luck to the Royalist cause it had brought ill-luck to him. He had been betrayed by haberdashery. Dancing with Barbara at Merton College he had tripped over a great rosette that had come loose from his shoe, slipped on the slippery floor, fallen down and broken his arm. The farcical disaster had put him in a black mood. The arm, his sword arm, had been badly broken and unskilfully set, did not mend well and caused him much pain, sleeplessness and inconvenience. The Royalist victories were taking place without his assistance and he did not know when he would be able to fight again. Meanwhile he was condemned to attendance upon Barbara, and he liked her less and less. He did not know what was the matter with him in regard to Barbara. He had always thought of marriage as a necessary evil for a man in his position, and had been thankful that in his case the evil would be so well gilded by the beauty of the bride, but now Barbara's loveliness was less apparent to him than her cold egotism, and her undisguised devotion to his wealth was slightly revolting. When his father suggested that they should make a further gift of several thousands to the King's empty coffers he gladly agreed, and the resultant row with Barbara was one of the few pleasures of those days.

Another was the fact that the younger royal children had been brought to Oxford to be with their mother. He had always loved those children, and especially the Princess Elizabeth, whose portrait he had painted. She was eight years old, a serious little girl whom her father called "little Temperance". Now that her elder sister Princess Mary was married to the Prince of Orange she was, after her mother, the first lady in the land, and the honour seemed to weigh upon her. She liked to escape from her nurses, and boisterous Prince Henry with his bouncing ball, to a quiet corner of the Merton gardens, behind a hedge of sweetbrier, where she would build houses for the fairies with flowers and bits of twigs, with beds inside them made of rose-petals. Here Francis would sometimes join her and having bowed to her and kissed her hand he would assist her in her architectural designs, and when she tired of them he told her stories. She would sit beside him on the garden bench that stood there against the old wall, her eyes fixed on his face, one small hand laid imperiously upon his knee. If his attention was deflected from the matter in hand, or if he made some mistake in the telling of a well-loved story, she would slap his knee hard, for gentle though she was she had her father's acute awareness of the rights of royalty. Now that she was so important a princess she was always very regally dressed in full-skirted gowns of rose and blue brocade with bows down the front, rather stiff and uncomfortable to play in. They rustled and crackled when she bent to her fairy houses and it was easier for her to sit upon the bench, swinging her small feet among her swishing petticoats. She was like Jenny in her sweet seriousness and air of remote dignity, but she lacked the underlying happiness that gave warmth to Jenny's seriousness. Her gravity, though tranquil, was sad. She was more like her father than any of the other children. Francis remembered now that Froniga had seen death in her painted face. What was to happen to this little girl? What was to happen to her father? Perhaps his aching arm and his sleepless nights had something to do with it, but it was in these hot sunny days of victory and joy that he first began to feel a foreboding of disaster.

There was another man who liked to escape behind the sweetbrier hedge from the flood of ribbons and rosettes, intrigue and gossip that engulfed the city, and that was Dr. Jeremy Taylor, one of the King's army chaplains. He built the best flower-house of the season, of hollyhock leaves, with Canterbury bells hanging from the ceiling to give music. This mutual love of the Princess Temperance, of peace and quiet, drew the two men together, and presently they found a retreat of their own in New College cloisters. It seemed that no one ever came there, except occasionally a few lovers of quietness such as Lord Falkland, the King's secretary, who like the dead Edmund Verney was a man tormented by the war, or the King's new standard-bearer, John Smith, who had retrieved the Royal Standard after Edgehill and had now been knighted. It was one of those places that seem to hold a profound and inviolable peace. One could pace up and down on the flagstones under the arcade, or sit on a stone bench looking out at the green garth and the ilex tree, with the Founders' Tower above, and hear nothing but the sound of the great pendulum in the Tower, the voices of pigeons and the chime of bells. In this place noise was shut out, and always would be, for it could impose its own peace on all who came.

Francis, neither learned nor prayerful, yet found it easy to talk to Jeremy Taylor the scholar and saint, for he had a humility to match that of Parson Hawthyn, patience and great courtesy, and was never in a hurry. Francis could talk to him of his sorrow and remorse over Robert Haslewood's death and the hatred of the war it had brought with it, of his fear for the King and his confused grief for the breaking of that dream that once he had shared with him, troubles that no other man of his acquaintance would have begun to understand; except perhaps Falkland, but his mind now was too darkened by his own troubles for him to be able to give much help to another. Dr. Taylor had a mind full of light. His loyalty to his God, to the Church of England and to the King was strong and simple, but he could understand the confusion that civil war brought to the minds of other men and with great simplicity he counselled simplicity; that day by day waiting upon the will of God, as revealed in the events which each day brought, as the only road to sanity. Like so many men of his time, he believed that the world was drawing to its end. He quoted John Donne. "The world's span-length of time is drawn now to less than half-an-inch, and to the point of the evening of the day of this old grey-haired world." Each day was likely to be one's last, and to live it as one's last was the only way to live it.

July passed into August and the King himself marched with Rupert and the army upon Gloucester, hoping to strengthen his hold upon the west. Francis's arm was still stiff, painful and useless, and he stayed behind in an Oxford that waited anxiously for news. And now things began to go a little wrong. Gloucester held out stubbornly against siege, and a large Parliamentarian army under Essex, reinforced by Skipton and his London trained bands, marched to its relief. The King raised the siege and the two armies, moving back towards Oxfordshire, manoeuvred for battle. They met outside Newbury and there fought another bitterly contested battle that gave decisive victory to neither. And here, for the first time in a full-scale battle, Rupert and his cavalry did not sweep all before them. Rupert, on the left of the line, was in open heath country, and his first charge, with his men so enthusiastic that some of them threw away their armour, broke the enemy cavalry to pieces in the accustomed manner. But when they would have turned to roll up Essex's line they met with an unexpected check. They came up against a couple of trained-band regiments, London boys, young apprentices who had never seen battle before. But old Skipton himself had trained them and they knew what to do. For the first time in English history they formed the famous square that was to bring victory at Waterloo. Rupert charged them, but the boys did not break. Infuriated, he charged them again and again, but they did not break, and when at last they withdrew in perfect order the Royalist Cavalry of the left wing were incapable of rolling up Essex's line. On the right wing they had fared little better, for the country was enclosed with fields and hedges. They fought a grim battle, in the course of which Lord Falkland threw away his life. When darkness fell neither side had won a victory, though the King was in the better position, for his army blocked the road to London. But during the night he made a fatal mistake. Choosing between two opposing counsels, that of attacking again in the morning or of withdrawing, he chose the latter, and turned towards Oxford under cover of the darkness, leaving Skipton's boys to march home victorious to the roaring welcome of the London streets. On the way back to Oxford the King re-captured Reading, but that was a small gain to set against the loss of the victory that might have been. The cavalier fortunes had reached their zenith and now the tide had turned.

3

The re-capture of Reading had importance for Francis. The return of the King and Rupert to Oxford led to a further outbreak of festivities, but Francis had no heart for them. He had had a fever, caught he thought from the insanitary conditions of his lodgings in the old crowded city during that unusually hot summer. He had recovered from it but he felt wretched. There seemed some sort of a curse upon him. The doctor had advised him to go away for a while, but he lacked the energy, and in none of the Royalist houses in the neighbourhood where he would have been an honoured guest would he have been safe from Barbara. And he grieved for the death of Lord Falkland, whom he suspected had been as glad to lose his life as Sir Edmund Verney had been to lose his, and for his many other friends dead at Newbury. It seemed to him that the flower of Rupert's cavalry had fallen there, and he wished he had died with them.

In this mood he started out one evening to go to a party at New College, where he was to meet Barbara, and succumbing to temptation turned aside into the cloisters. Though it was now late September it was a warm and golden evening. There was no one there. With relief he sat down on the old stone bench and rested his eyes gratefully on the small green garth, the dark tree and the tower. He thought he would stay here for a while, and make his peace with Barbara later. He shut his eyes and let the peace of the place sink into his very bones.

Presently, with his eyes still shut, he knew he was not alone here after all; but whoever was here was not alien to him, for he felt a sense of increased peace in his presence. He thought it was Jeremy Taylor, but when he opened his eyes he saw that the cloaked figure walking slowly up and down on the other side of the cloister, a book in his hands, was too tall for Dr. Taylor. After a moment or two Francis recognised him, got up and went slowly to meet him.

"Yoben!" he said.

Yoben, who had recognised him as soon as he had come in, bowed and said cheerfully, "It is some while since I have seen you, my Lord."

"Not since you went on that errand for me to Mistress Haslewood," said Francis. "Must you call me my Lord?"

"Your Lordship's magnificence calls for it," said Yoben with amusement, eyeing Francis's crimson-and-silver doublet and the crimson rosettes on his shoes. "Though your face does not match your finery. Have you been ill?"

"A broken arm from falling over my finery and fever from the smell of cabbage," said Francis shortly. "Yoben, sit down and tell me news of the heathlands, and the wind up there. And the Haslewoods. Are they well? Have they recovered at all from Robert Haslewood's death?"

"I cannot tell you," said Yoben gently. "I took the things you gave me to Mistress Froniga and she was glad to have them, and bade me thank you when I saw you again, but since that time I have not been back to the village."

Their talk drifted to matters not personal to themselves, to the war and their hopes and fears for it. Francis was aware of a change in Yoben. He looked older, and as though he had passed through fiery loss since Francis had seen him last, but he gave the impression that he had been tempered by it. His humility had always had something faintly deprecating about it, but now though the humility remained the deprecation was gone. He seemed at peace.

"Where are you going now, Yoben?" asked Francis.

"To Reading."

"On the King's business?"

"On the King's business."

There was a grating sound as the heavy door into the cloister was pushed open and then closed, a gust of perfume, and a tall slender woman came swaying towards them, her stiff rose-coloured skirts rustling faintly as she walked. She wore a small fringed black mask, and there were flowers in her silver-gilt hair. She looked so lovely, and she came so quietly, that her presence should have been no intrusion on the beauty of the place, yet both men had the sensation that the serpent, and not Eve, had come into their Paradise. She glided down upon them so quickly that she was upon them almost before they had time to get to their feet.

"Francis, will you introduce me to your friend?" she asked. Her voice was extraordinarily sweet, but nowadays it reminded Francis of that very thick honey that can so often hide a wasp. Before he could answer Yoben bowed and said, "Lady, I am only a poor gypsy. I followed my Lord to beg alms of him. Lady, may God bless your pretty face." And he slipped away like a shadow and the cloister door closed behind him.

"A gypsy," said Barbara. "Those children, that silly priest, and now a gypsy. Your choice of companions is peculiar, Francis."

"You are so often enraged," said Francis gaily.

"And what effort do you make to see me when I am not?" flashed Barbara. "You were to meet me at this party. You have showed no eagerness to do so. They told me I should find you here. What a dingy place. Like a graveyard. All our friends, it seems, know more about your extraordinary habits than I do myself. I am not honoured by your confidence."

He had shamed her by his non-appearance at the party and she was bitterly angry. It had been one more of many evasions of his duty towards her of which he had been largely unconscious, but which had been all the more galling to her for that reason. He had made her feel negligible. Her resentment had reached boiling point and her usual caution forsook her. They quarrelled. It was only the second time they had quarrelled, so naturally good-tempered was Francis, so cunning was Barbara in keeping a firm hold upon what she wanted, and now all the resentments that each had secretly harboured against the other came pouring out. As quickly as it had flamed up it died, leaving a bitter taste behind it.

"You insult me by your negligence," said Barbara, returning to the point from which she had started.

Francis was so dog-tired that he said the first thing that came into his head. "The remedy is in your own hands, Barbara."

There was silence. Then she took off her betrothal ring and handed it to him. He was so astonished that he dropped it. "Pick it up," she said harshly. "It will be something else to toss into the coffers of the King instead of the service in battle that other men give. You are so fortunate in your falls and fevers."

The furious blood rushed into Francis's face. He let the priceless emerald ring lie where it was and offered her the tips of his fingers. "May I conduct you from this graveyard?" he asked.

He conducted her from it, led her ceremoniously to the Warden's house, from which lights were shining and music sounding softly, bowed and withdrew. As he strolled away he heard her call once, sharply, "Francis!" but he pretended not to hear. Out in the streets he took to his heels and ran, for she was on the verge of changing her mind and he had no time to lose. His lodgings next door to a tavern were not far, and the taverner was at home. The old man made no difficulty about providing him with a suit of fusty old clothes and his pony, though he extracted exorbitant payment. The townspeople were by this time well accustomed to the freaks of the young cavaliers and found them quite a pleasant source of revenue. Francis left a note in his room for one of his friends, saying he had taken his doctor's advice and gone out of Oxford for a short time. Then he rode his pony to the East Gate, now bolted and barred for the night, for Great Tom had sounded the curfew, but he was known to the sentry there, who made no bones about opening the gate once his palm had been greased with a piece of silver. As he rode over Magdalen bridge the stars were already growing bright in a strange green sky and the tower of Magdalen soared up among them, almost as lovely as they were. Out in the dusky fields the air came freshly, cool and clear, and he was free alike of Barbara and of the fair city that had held so many troubles for him.

CHAPTER VI

A FIGHT IN THE STREETS

I

Francis rode slowly, for now that the excitement had gone out of him he knew once more how tired he was. His head began to ache and his shoulder with it. The adventure seemed now not so good. He had no idea when Yoben was going to Reading, whether tonight or tomorrow. That he should fall in with him tonight was the merest hope, and if he did not come across him what did he propose to do? He jogged on with no idea. He had brought his pistol with him, his much-depleted purse, his water-bottle, a pipe and tobacco and a blanket, but this equipment would not support him for very long. "I can always steal and be hanged for it," he thought, and there was comfort in the thought.

But it seemed that for once in a way he was to be lucky, for presently he heard the sound of a trotting pony behind him. The rider drew abreast of him and bade him good night. "Good night, Yoben," said Francis.

Yoben exclaimed, laughed, and drew in his pony to amble beside Francis's slow-moving old beast. "John Loggin the portrait painter?" he asked.

"No," said Francis. "There was no time to collect John Loggin's equipment. Yoben, I am flying from a beautiful woman. If you yourself have ever done such a thing you will understand the desperation of my state. I hoped I would fall in with you. May I be your assistant for a while, in whatever project you have in hand at the present time?"

Yoben was glad that the darkness hid his consternation. He was to have enough on his hands in the next few days without being responsible for the safety of one of the King's favourites. Would these young men never learn that they could not prosecute war and their private affairs at one and the same time?

"If you help me now, my Lord, you are likely to swing for it," he said curtly.

"I was just thinking, before you came along, how pleasant

that would be," said Francis. "I was thinking of sheep-stealing."

To this there was no reply but silence, and Francis felt ashamed of his frivolity. And he was ashamed, too, to have been brought so low by such small misfortunes as had been his just lately. The fact was, he supposed, that he had hardly begun to know the meaning of the word misfortune. But it did not occur to him to relieve Yoben of his presence, though he was aware of the other man's unwillingness. He wanted to go with Yoben and he was accustomed to do what he wanted. "I am coming with you," he said.

He spoke with such authority, even with such arrogance, that Yoben said no more. He must do the best he could. Having accepted the burden of the young man's safety he put his misgivings from him and was once again the courteous and delightful company that Francis knew.

Having struck into the woods they rode towards Reading by bridle-paths known to Yoben, for he did not want to encounter troops upon the road. About midnight they found a deep dry dingle, lit a fire and rested for a few hours. Then they went on again, and when the sky was rosy with the dawn rode over the beautiful bridge at Caversham, crossing themselves as they passed the chapel there, and so came to the old walled town of Reading, and the north gate of the city. It was market day, and as they rode they had been joined by country folk coming in with their produce, and at the gate all who came were scrutinised by the Royalist sentries there. The gypsy tinker with his gear upon his back and the disreputable young man who accompanied him were passed in without comment. Francis noted with amusement that Yoben, after a night spent in the woods, could remain as dignified, tidy and comely as a badger or fox, while his appearance was farcical. He did not belong to the woods and possibly they felt a humorous resentment towards him.

They rode through the narrow cobbled streets to an old galleried inn, where it seemed that Yoben was well known. There the money in Francis's purse purchased them a good meal of ale and bread and bacon, and Francis could make an attempt to better his appearance with a bucket of water in the corner of the yard. Then Yoben disappeared, saying he would be back for the evening meal, and Francis was left to his own devices. With his pipe in his mouth and his hands in his pockets he made his way through the streets, thronged with citizens and soldiery, market carts and wagons, sheep and cows. Reading was a city of gabled, many-storied houses, fine churches and a grand old abbey. As at Oxford, the river curved about it and the green fields flowed up to its walls. Francis was soon tired and took refuge from the turmoil within the abbey gardens. His back against a wall he dozed in the sun for hours, waking up now and then to mourn, as a good Catholic should, on the departed glory of this place. Then, stiff with sitting, he made his way back to the Market Place, where beneath the grey walls of St. Giles's Church the booths were set out. For a little while he elbowed his way through the crowd, enjoying the rich colours of the red apples and golden pears, plums and pumpkins, and the great bunches of glowing autumn flowers, and enjoying the crowd itself, the rosy-cheeked countrywomen, farmers and shepherds, Reading housewives with baskets on their arms, dogs and cats and children. He was just beginning to feel tired again, and thinking of a bench outside the inn and a mug of ale, when a voice that he knew said in a melodious whine. "May the poor gypsy tell your fortune, kind gentleman? Cross the poor gypsy's hand with silver and let me tell your fortune."

He swung round and found that he had been accosted by Alamina. She nipped his right wrist tightly and he could not pull it away without wrenching the arm that had been broken. But he was not going to have her tell his fortune, and he closed his hand into a fist.

"Last time we met, Alamina, you took enough silver out of my pockets to cross my palm half a dozen times," he said good-humouredly. "I admired your sleight of hand."

She looked at him with so much hatred that he was appalled. He supposed that when he had flung her away from him that night he had done it more scornfully than he knew. "What a fool I was," he thought, and felt oddly terrified. But he met her look steadily and waited patiently for her to relinquish his hand. She too had altered since he had seen her last. Her beauty, though still very great, seemed blurred. He would not have thought now, as he had before, that she was neither good nor evil but elemental. Into her absence of good there had now come some evil and perhaps, he thought, it was his fault. She had no weapon against his patience. She let go of him and slipped away into the crowd. But he did not suppose that was the end of it. She had grown subtle.

During the evening meal together Francis said to Yoben, "I saw Alamina in the market. She also saw me."

"That is unfortunate," said Yoben, "for she saw me too. I was leaving Colonel Thistleton's lodgings, where I had been mending his wife's kettle."

"Why unfortunate?"

Yoben had no answer to this, but they both knew it was unfortunate.

"Are the rest of your gypsies near Reading?" asked Francis.

"They are encamped not far away. But Alamina now is not popular with them and tends to go about more by herself than she used to do."

"She has changed."

"She misses her grandfather Piramus. His beatings were salutary. We can stay here tonight, John Loggin, and get a good night's rest. Tomorrow I go to Henley. Do you still want to come with me?"

"Yes," said Francis.

Next day, their ponies left behind in Reading, they were making their way on foot through the woods towards Henley. The escape from Barbara and the clear autumn weather, warm and sunny but with a crisp edge to the warmth, had worked a miracle on Francis. His sword arm still ached and was not much use to him, but he was fast throwing off the effects of the fever. "What piece of work do we do now?" he asked Yoben. "Is there to be another Royalist raid on Henley?"

"The day for light-hearted raids on an undefended little town is over now," said Yoben. "Henley has fortified itself against them very thoroughly and since we took Reading a troop of rebel horse have been stationed there. This will be a full-scale attack to get the town in our hands once and for all. We have the rest of today and tonight in which to prepare. Before dawn tomorrow Royalist troops from Reading will attack." He paused, pointing to a bridle-path. "Lord Leyland, you see that path there? It will bring you out on the Oxford road. I very much wish that you would take it."

"No," said Francis curtly. "I am sick of doing nothing. What have you to do in Henley?"

"The usual work of a spy," said Yoben. "Find out where the sentries are posted and where and how would be the best way to attack. Take word of this tonight to our men who will be waiting in the woods."

"There's work for two men there," said Francis.

Yoben knew it was not so. This sort of work was best done by one experienced man alone. As they went on, he blamed himself that twice over now he had let his own judgement be overruled by Francis's stronger character and innate authority. He feared for Francis. With all the power of his being he offered himself for the young man's safety, with deep intention substituting himself for him.

"We must not enter Henley together," he said later. "Nor be seen together until the evening. Then we will meet, two vagabonds casually encountering each other. But not in a hidden corner, for hidden corners arouse suspicion. During the last hour before sunset I will be eating my bread and cheese by the market cross. I am well known in Henley as Bartholoways the Tinker and will spend the day plying my trade and getting information. Our Royalist friend, the landlord of the Bell Inn, will doubtless have much to tell me. There is nothing you can do to help me in this. You had better not come into Henley until the afternoon."

Francis opened his mouth to protest but met a surprisingly steely look in Yoben's usually gentle eyes. "Very well," he said. "I will stay here in the woods."

He enjoyed his hours alone in the woods that curved about Henley. For the most part he lay on his back in the beech leaves, looking up at the trees above him where the leaves were just taking the first tinge of autumn colour, watching the squirrels and the jays. He remembered the glorious red and gold of the trees when the army had marched up out of the valley to Edgehill. That was not yet a year ago, though it seemed so long. And now he was on the eve of another battle, a fight so unimportant that it would not get into the history books, yet for many it might be the most important day in their lives, their end-of-the-world and judgement day. It might be his.

After a while he ate some of the food he had brought with him and drank from his water-bottle, and then he dozed for a little. Waking up with a jerk, he had the sensation that someone had just passed by in the woods. He sat up and looked about him, but he saw no one. He listened, but he could hear no crackle of dry twigs breaking, no rustle of beech leaves, and he lay down once more. But he felt vaguely uneasy and he did not sleep again.

When the shafts of sunlight, piercing through the great trees, grew long and level, he got up and made his way towards Henley. Though it was the oldest town in the county it had no city wall, and he slipped in with no trouble. He wandered through the streets until he came to the bridge, over which he had ridden to Edgehill, and grieved to see that it had been very much knocked about in one of the raids on Henley. The lovely chapel of St. Anne was partially in ruins. Then he strolled slowly along Hart Street towards the Market Place. It was a warm, sleepy hour and there were not many people about. He passed a few Parliament troops strolling with pretty girls or looking in at the shop windows, but most people were at home. There was a smell of cooking in the warm air and smoke rose from the chimneys. No one took any notice of his shabby figure. He came to the Market Place and strolled round it. Henley market was an important one, famous for its malt, corn and cheese, and two days ago it would have been crowded, but now there was no one here but a white cat and Yoben sitting on the steps of the market cross, his tinkers' gear beside him, eating bread and cheese. Taking no notice of him, Francis walked along past the beautiful Guildhall opposite the cross, where were assembled the stocks, whipping post, pillory irons and the ducking-stool for scolding wives. Not far from the cross, at the edge of the square, stood a tall tree. At the cross-roads below the Market Place, facing down Duke Street, there was something else, but Francis made no comment upon it until, having strolled towards Yoben and accepted his offer of a share of his bread and cheese, he had been munching for a good five minutes, and then he said, "Did you know that cannon was there?"

"No. It has come here within the last few days."

"They mean to hold Henley."

"They do," said Yoben grimly. "That's a very good cannon. The troopers are well armed and so are the citizens. When you and I were here together last autumn they hardly knew one end of a pistol from the other. Now they do."

"What about the cannon?" asked Francis. "It could do terrible damage."

"We will warn our men," said Yoben. "There is no more we can do now. I know where the main bodies of troops are lodged and after dark we must find out where the sentries are posted. If you will discover that upon the western side of the town I will find out upon the south. Meet me in the woods, at that hollow tree where we parted company, when you have your information. And, my Lord, there is one thing of great importance which you must remember. You and I are not fighting men. If we were to be seen taking any part in the fighting tonight all our future usefulness as spies would be over. When we have done whatever duty may be required of us tonight we must keep out of sight, and eventually make our way back to Reading, to the inn where we spent the night. We will not wait for each other. We will go independently. I'll leave you now. Stay here for a while, then do what you like until dark falls."

He shouldered his tinker's gear, called out a cheery goodbye and strolled off. Francis sat where he was. When the sun had set and there was a chill in the air he strolled down towards the river, found a tavern there and went in to get a meal. When he had eaten he wandered about among the wharves for a while, and after dark he was outside Henley upon the western side of the little town. He did not find it easy to locate the sentries without being seen himself, but he did the best he could and then went back into the woods. At the old hollow beech tree he sat down and waited for Yoben.

At a little distance from him, behind a holly tree, Alamina also waited. She had been keeping him in sight all day, with such wild-bird woodland skill that neither he nor Yoben had seen her. Alamina had been born with an overdose of curiosity, and that skill in satisfying it which in some women amounts almost to a spiritual gift. Gathering her information like a hen gathering corn in a stubble-field, picking here a grain and there a grain, she would then put her facts together with an accuracy which was quite horrible. The other gypsies had not wanted to know where Yoben went when he left them for such long periods. They had been content to lay the patrines that he might find them again when he wished to, and had left it at that. But Alamina had not been content. She had found out long ago that Yoben was a spy, though she had kept her knowledge to herself, for Yoben had saved the life of old Righteous Heron and she was not without Romany loyalty. When Francis had come to the camp that night she had seen with half an eye that he was no countryman. He was a *Rai*, a gentleman, and a spy too, she had imagined, and she had desired him. But he had repulsed her contemptuously and so she had hated him and gone to Mother Skipton, and after that visit there had begun in her that change that Francis had noticed. Two days ago, when she had seen Francis and Yoben in Reading, first separately and then together at the inn, she had known that the time Mother Skipton had foreseen had come. Sitting gracefully among the beech leaves she waited quietly. She would kill Francis if she could. If she harmed Yoben in doing it she would be sorry, but it could not be helped. Her loyalty, like other good things in her, had suffered disintegration these last few months. After a while she saw Yoben join Francis, heard the low voices and saw them move more deeply into the wood. She followed them. Hours passed and then there was the sound of men's feet moving cautiously through the beech leaves and the gleam of a lantern. Creeping nearer she saw its light shining on the hilts of swords, and on men's grave and bearded faces. There were many armed men there, and she saw Francis and Yoben moving forward to speak to the man who led them. With a sure instinct for what would hurt Francis, she turned and ran back to Henley to give the alarm.

Under the shadow of the trees Yoben and Francis conferred with Colonel Thistleton. He decided to divide the men into two bodies. Francis would guide the smaller one in from the west, avoiding the sentries, to capture the cannon. Yoben would lead the other in from the woods on the southern side, to make a surprise attack upon a large body of troops who were lodged on that side of the town, then make their way up Duke Street to join the smaller troop. Yoben with Colonel Thistleton and the main body of men waited in the woods, for they had the shorter march before them. Francis, with Colonel's second in command, a Henley man who knew every alley of the little town by heart, moved off with the rest of the men through the wood, and then stealthily along hedges and through clumps of trees round to the west, where by way of some pigsties and a farmyard they could gain entrance to the little town.

Everything went well. They had hoped to attack just before dawn, when the town would be still asleep, but there would be enough light to see what they were doing, and they had hoped for the grey light of a clouded sky. They had what they wanted. As Francis and the young captain crept along the hedges with their men the darkness was just beginning to give way to a misty half-light. They got through the pigsties and the farmyard with nothing worse than a plastering of black mud, then went slowly and noiselessly through the alley-ways to the market. No one challenged them. Henley seemed completely asleep. It seemed too good to be true and Francis felt uneasy.

They crept up the street towards the cross-roads and then halted. Looking across the cobbles through the veils of grey mist they could just make out the shape of the cannon. The young captain gave the order and the men ran forward after him. Francis was beside him; he had entirely forgotten Yoben's remarks upon non-combatancy. Suddenly shots rang out. Men who had been crouching beside the cannon had leapt to their feet and were firing their pistols. The young captain cursed, and then shouting, "Have at them!" ran forward a few paces and fell. Francis took his place and yelling encouragement to the men charged for the cannon. The two opposing forces met and clinched about it.

For the King's men it was a grim and hopeless fight, for more and more Parliament men came running from the houses near and they were surrounded. It was very soon each man for himself, to cut his way out or die where he stood. The sound of firing to the south told them that Colonel Thistleton was fighting his way towards them, but if he too had encountered troops who were ready for him he would not reach them in time to save their lives. Francis, with no sword, laid about him savagely with the butt end of his pistol. He felt consumed with rage. Something, somewhere, had gone wrong, and all these poor fellows were caught in a trap. His weak right arm suddenly went numb and his pistol was struck out of his hand. He hit out with his fists and another fist swung out and struck him on the head. He was now on the edge of the fight, in which civilians were joining with fists and sticks. He staggered, his arm was clutched and he was jerked free of the mêlée. A tall burly fellow, still with his nightcap on, dragged him over the cobbles, flung him good-humouredly towards the pavement and then went back into the fight.

Francis lay for a few moments where he had been flung, half stunned. Then his mind began to work again, and he realised that in his rough clothes he had been mistaken for a good citizen of Henley and so saved. Suddenly he remembered the cannon. If Colonel Thistleton and his men were to advance up Duke Street now they were doomed, and the sound of musket-fire was coming from that direction. He struggled to his feet and fought his way towards it, fighting now not the rebels but his own dizziness and weakness. Blood was running from a flesh wound in the leg, but he was scarcely aware of that or of his bursting head. He seemed to himself to be struggling against a wall of mist such as one encounters in nightmares. The more he pushed against it the more it seemed to be pressing him back. He kept one hand on the house walls as he passed them, helping himself forward, and dimly saw terrified faces at the windows, and troops advancing up the street. Another fifty yards and he would have reached them, but before he could cover the distance the cannon blazed out.

After that he had very little idea of what happened. He heard the fearful noise, the cries of agony, and was vaguely aware of total disaster. The King's men who were not dead were retreating. He stumbled through a doorway and found that there were screaming women all about him. One seized hold of him, dragged him down a passage, opened a door and pushed him in. He heard the key turn on the outside. Through a high window above a window-seat he saw a green garden, and thought, how pleasant. It was his last thought for some while.

2

Once Yoben had brought the troops into Henley they had no further use for him and he had slipped away through side streets towards the Market Place. Behind him he could hear the firing and was surprised that they had met such prompt resistance. Just as he reached the Market Place the cannon was fired. An excited, terrified crowd was in front of him and only from their cries did he learn what had happened. He felt sick at heart. Somewhere, he was sure, there had been treachery. If all had gone well he would have made his way back to Reading, as he had told Francis to do, but now in this disaster he must stay and do what he could to help. If Francis had obeyed him, he would be safe by now. If he had not, if he had joined in the attempt to capture the cannon, then he might be dead beside it. As soon as he could he forced his way through the crowd in the square to the cross-roads. Men were already lifting the wounded and carrying them into the nearby houses, and he joined them. It was daylight now and he could see the bodies lying about the cannon. Most of the men who had stormed the cannon seemed to have died. He saw the body of the young captain, but he did not see that of Francis. After the fearful noise everything seemed suddenly very quiet. Colonel Thistleton's company had lost many men in fighting their way through the town and the firing of the cannon had completely routed those who were left.

As quickly as the fight had broken out it was over. A Parliament officer was directing the men at the cross-roads and Yoben worked with them. When he came back from helping to carry a wounded man away he was amazed to see Alamina clinging to the officer's arm, shaking it, pouring out a spate of low excited words. Her face wore the mad look that was hers when she wailed for the dead, or was in the midst of the *hokkani boro*, exalted and yet somehow devilish. The officer, angry and disgusted, tried to shake her off, then abruptly stopped and listened to what she was saying. Yoben's anxiety deepened and he moved within ear-shot. He knew Alamina would not see him, for she saw nothing when she was in this state. He heard her say hysterically, "I've told you—I've told you—he brought the troops in." And then in answer to the officer's sharp questioning, "The bakery. I'll bring you there."

"Bring her along, but hold her," said the officer. Two of his men seized her arms, one on each side, and she screamed in fear.

Yoben slipped through the men who were now crowding round Alamina and the officer, and ran. His mind, that had been dulled with fatigue and grief, suddenly cleared. He knew just what Francis had done, for it was what he would have done himself in his case. In coming down Duke Street to warn them he had probably been hit and carried into the bakery, and Alamina had seen it. For some reason that he did not know about, she wanted revenge upon John Loggin. One rare but familiar joy was his as he ran, a joy that purged him of all anxiety, for he knew this to be one of those moments in life when a man has only to obey. He had offered himself so entirely for Francis that he had been lifted up into that clear place where mistakes can scarcely be made. When occasionally this experience had come to him before in his past life he had recognised the plane of existence to which he had been momentarily lifted as the place where the saints live always.

He reached the door of the bakery. Inside was only a trembling frightened old woman and two hysterically sobbing young girls. "Where is the young man who came here wounded?" he asked.

"In the room down the passage," said the old crone. "She said we were not to touch him. She said she would put the evil eye upon us if we so much as looked upon him."

Yoben left them and walked down the passage. He found a

door to the left, locked, but with the key outside. He unlocked it and went in. Francis lay upon the floor and he bent over him and examined him. He had evidently lost much blood, but the wound was not serious. Roused by Yoben's handling he groaned and cursed, opened his eyes and looked at him.

"We'll get out of here together," said Yoben cheerfully. He turned to the high latticed window, wrestled with it and forced it open. Then he dragged Francis up to the window-seat, helped him through the window and pushed him roughly so that he fell into the flower-bed beneath. The pain of the fall, he hoped, would knock him out again. He had just got the window shut when he heard their feet in the passage.

The door opened and they came in. Alamina was not with them. Terrified of being hanged for a spy too she had twisted out of the men's grasp at the bakery door and run for it. Knowing her, Yoben had supposed she would do that, but even if she had not he would still have been without anxiety. He was still doing all he had to do with absolute certainty.

"Was it you who led the enemy into Henley?" asked the officer.

"It was, sir," said Yoben.

"And told them where the weapons were hidden, a year ago?"

"Yes," said Yoben.

"You've done your work well," said the officer. 'We've been looking for the Chiltern spy for more than a year."

"Then your search is over," said Yoben. "I am the Chiltern spy, and also a recusant priest."

"That crazy girl told me you were wounded."

"I have wrenched my ankle," said Yoben.

The officer looked at him curiously. "Even so, that window is not at a great height from the ground."

"I could not get it open."

"Why did you tell me you are a recusant?"

"Because I am tired of disguises," said Yoben.

"Bring him along," said the officer.

His men fastened a rope round Yoben's wrists and brought him along as bidden.

CHAPTER VII

THE TAROT CARDS

The night of the attack on Henley Froniga sat before her fire, weighed down with dreariness. The summer had passed somehow, empty and purposeless. Now that Yoben had gone out of her life she realised how much the thought of him had been in all she did and was. Anything beautiful or amusing that she had seen or heard she had stored up in her memory so that she might tell him about it. She had kept her home orderly and beautiful, looking forward to the next time he came, and she had striven to be the woman that his love thought her to be. Even her work, of which he had always been slightly sceptical, had been the more dedicated because of the dedication of which she had been almost unconsciously aware in him. The whole of her life seemed dust and ashes without him. When they parted she had spoken of finding each other again in God. Now she found she did not want God, but only Yoben. In moments of exaltation one expressed sentiments that outstripped one's spiritual capabilities by a vast span; and she knew well that unless God is sought for Himself alone, with a selflessness of which she was at present incapable, He is not to be found. She went to no one for comfort, not even to Parson Hawthyn, for unlike Margaret she got no sort of satisfaction out of displaying her grief; the only satisfaction her proud spirit could find was in hiding it. No one, except Parson Hawthyn, had seen the slightest difference in her, and he did not know the reason for her lustreless eyes. He had always loved the glow in her eyes, as though she exulted in all she looked upon. Now her eyes seemed to find nothing left remarkable beneath the visiting moon.

It grew late, but Froniga did not go to bed, for going to bed seemed as pointless as anything else. She spent many hours like this, gazing stupidly at the fire. Pen was on her lap, but she was hardly aware of the warmth and whiteness between her hands. Then very gradually something began to penetrate her dull dreariness, something sharp and pointed, the slow thrust of coming danger. As she felt the thrust her fingers curved about the white cat and found the fur soft and the body warm. She was alive again, alert, ready for what might come. She sat listening until she realised that her pre-vision was not for herself, or rather it was for herself, because Yoben had seemed for so long the soul within her body and the mainspring of her life. It was Yoben who was in danger. What danger? She jumped to her feet, spilling the indignant Pen from her lap. If she thought she had entirely renounced Yoben she found now that she was mistaken. Unknown to herself she had been clinging to the thought that he was still with her in this world, and he was not going out of it if she could help it. If he had caught the plague she would find him, wherever he was, and apply every remedy she knew.

She got out her pack of tarot cards, that had come to her from her mother, and that she had not touched since she had looked into the future for Robert and Will. She used them seldom, for though she dared to wear a green gown she doubted her right to use this most ancient instrument of power, she who was only half a gypsy. But now she had no scruples. She must find out what it was that threatened Yoben.

She lit her candles, sat down and took the cards into her hands, shuffling them gently. There was a gypsy saying, "The shuffling of the cards is the earth, the pattering of the cards is the rain, the beating of the cards is the wind and the pointing of the cards is the fire." Earth, water, air and fire. Having shuffled them she let them fall one after the other pattering upon the table, then gathered them up, tidied them into two piles and beat one softly against the other, then spread them fanwise in her hands so that the firelight glinted on their golden points. Then she repeated the process, over and over, reaching out in thought to the four elements as she did so, until gradually awareness grew in her : of the dark earth outside flowing up to her cottage walls, of the small shower that was even now pattering against the window-panes, of the wind that stirred over the thatch and the flames that leaped upon the hearth. The awareness grew deeper. Her own body was of the earth's substance, and the earth hungered for the time when its darkness would close over her in death. The rain was her tears that were even now falling upon the cards, the wind her breath and the fire the hot pulsing of her blood. It grew deeper still and was forgetfulness of self and awareness of the cards only as they shuffled themselves in her hands. For the inner life of their own that they possessed had borne down her life now, and the cards were using her hands, not her hands the cards. Then she dealt them, and the colours and symbols covered her table like one of the gleaming cloaks that the gypsy girl had woven when she had tried to save her lover's life. They covered her table, and she looked down on them as though from a great distance, dazzled by them, for her tears still filled her eyes.

She wiped her eyes, steadied herself, and came back a little to awareness of herself as a woman looking at a pack of playing-cards that had been painted by her great-grandfather and given by him to his granddaughter Richenda, her mother. They were exquisitely painted and had been kept so carefully that the gilt and the colours were as fresh as on the day he had laid them on the squares of papyrus. He had been a Chovihan and one of his many skills had been the painting of tarot cards after the pattern of the pack brought by the Romany people to Spain from Egypt four centuries ago. There were four suits—coins, cups, sceptres and swords, representing earth, water, air and fire—each with four picture cards: the King, the Queen, the Knight and his Esquire. There were twenty-one trump cards, cards of great power symbolising those things that go to make up the life of a man. The mystic number seven dominated the pack. Each suit numbered twice seven cards, the trump cards were three times seven, the total seventy-seven, eleven times seven. The seventy-eighth card was not numbered in the pack. It stood by itself, O, the mysterious Fool carrying a load upon his back, a heavy pack round as the earth that Atlas bore; only Atlas had been bent beneath his burden and the Fool stood upright with joy in his bright eyes. What he symbolised no man had ever known.

A woman looking at a pack of playing-cards that she might tell the fortune of the man she loved. . . . Yoben. . . . Froniga sat upright now, dry-eyed and in command of herself, noting the position of the beautiful symbols, the Sun, the Moon, the Star, the Chariot, the Wheel of Fortune, the Lovers, the Emperor and the Empress, and all the others in their clear and lovely colours. In the exact centre of the glowing pattern three cards came together, the Skeleton, the Angel and the Hanging Man, and the Hanging Man was between the other two. Froniga grew rigid and cold, as though all the blood were draining out of her body. The Skeleton symbolised death, the Angel was the Angel of Judgement, for he was sounding his golden trumpet over the graves, and the Hanging Man symbolised renunciation of self sacrifice leading to the secret at the heart of the world.

Froniga sat for a long time in perfect stillness, then she gathered the cards, shuffled them, pattered them, beat them and pointed them again. Her mother had taught her seven different ways of dealing the cards, and one after the other she tried six of them, but always Death, Judgement and the Hanging Man came to the same positions. At the seventh trial she broke down. She could not finish it, as the poor gypsy girl had not been able to finish the seventh cloak. There was nothing she could do. She lay with her head on the table, slumped over the cards. There was nothing she could do. It was death, and a death ordained, for always the Hanging Man had been held between Death and the Angel. There was no escape.

Then suddenly her will hardened and she lifted herself up. The cards had power, but other things had power also. She knew many spells. She was strong. She could beat down this power of the cards with greater powers. Cold and shaking but ironly determined she got up and put the cards away. They lied. She would win. She was strong. She had used her spells very little lately. Now she would use them all, and invoke every good spirit who had ever come to her aid. She blew out the candles, for the white magic was all in her mind and had never been committed to paper, and for hours she sat in the dark and wrestled by all the means known to her for the gift of Yoben's life. She had never fought such a fight. When it was over she thought, "I have surely won," and out of sheer exhaustion fell instantly asleep in her chair.

When she woke it was dawn. It was a misty morning, and over every bush, and between the branches of the trees, were spun the autumnal glory of the spiders' webs. They sparkled as the patterns of the cards had sparkled last night, when the firelight gleamed upon the colours and the gold.

The sun was well up and she was out in the garden when she heard a babel of excited voices from the direction of the inn. She ran up the lane and found a group of men outside the inn: Sam Tidmarsh and his brother, the wheelwright, men and women from the nearby cottages, and a Henley man. "There's bin a great bloody battle fought over to Henley, Mistress Froniga," they cried to her. "The King's men, they attacked last night, thousands of 'em, and the Henley men, they fired a cannon at 'em. There's not a man left alive on the King's side and not a dead man on our own."

Froniga asked the Henley man a few sharp questions, but he had drunk a mug of ale at every house where he had called with the news and was as full of exaggeration as the rest. She left them and ran back to her cottage. She would have thought it only another of the many small raids on Henley had it not been for the mention of the cannon. That, too, might be exaggeration, but if it was true, then any woman with sense and some knowledge of healing herbs would be badly needed. Never, so long as she lived, would she forget Colonel Hampden's unnecessary death. . . . Samile, milfoil and bugle. . . . She put them in her basket at once, together with remedies for shock and plenty of soft bandages. She forced herself not to think of Yoben now, for she believed that she had saved him and she must think of the wounded. When she had packed her basket she set off at once for Henley down Pack and Prime lane.

As she went the mist thinned and the autumn sun shone out in a cool pale sky. There was dew on the grass and a touch of colour here and there where the brambles were turning. On either side of the lane the flowers were golden in the hedgerows, tansy and ragwort and ploughman's spikenard. She was short of spikenard, but she could not stop to get any now. The crying of the plovers came over the fields, but theirs was the only cry in a windless silence. It was going to be a fair day, sunny and still with a cool tang in the air. Passing Mother Skipton's cottage, Froniga saw that it had now fallen into ruin. Briars and nettles had taken possession of the garden and soon they would have grown all over the fallen cottage too. The evil that had once lived there was now only a memory.

As Froniga came down the steep hill towards Henley she saw the scene below like a distant but clear picture, like one of those scenes in a Dutch landscape. She could see the church tower, the smoke rising from the chimneys, the market cross and the crowded market square. The colour was gay and shifting, the sky blue above it. The square seemed packed with people and the noise they made, though so distant, came up to her and caught her by the throat. It was an excited hum of talk, with occasional laughter, the barking of dogs, shouting and catcalls. It was not market day, but in any case the noise of market day was not like this hubbub. She had never heard or felt anything quite like this before. Down there the people were in a ferment of pleasurable excitement that somehow terrified her. She stopped and thought to herself, "They're going to flog the prisoners, or shoot them." Henley had endured an hour of terror and now its citizens were out for revenge. "I'll wait here till it's over," she thought. She knew what happened at times like these. The respectable people stayed indoors, dissociating themselves from the cruelty of other men but too cowardly or too politic to make any effort to restrain it, while all the rough elements of a town, the vagabonds, the evil cackling old women and the brutalised young boys, came running to see the fun. They made no secret of their enjoyment. To see other men suffer, while they themselves remained immune, was a poignant pleasure.

The crowd parted to let through some Parliament officers, their swords at their sides, and Froniga could see the tall tree that grew at the edge of the square, and the cart and horse beneath it. A rope was fastened to a branch of the tree. Her knees gave way beneath her, so that she slid down beside her basket, but she had not fainted, and after a moment or two the blankness of shock cleared away and her mind began to work again. They did not usually make such a public spectacle of the hanging of spies. This must be some prisoner of importance. But a spy could be important if he had been a clever man and had eluded them for some while, and if it were known that he was also a recusant the old terror of Spain and Popery would awake the old cruelty and there would be great rejoicing at his death.

Froniga got up, hung her basket on her arm and walked on down the hill. She had such a tough strength that no one seeing her would have known that her mind hung upon the point of agony. She walked with an easy stride and looked out over the scene below as though it were indeed no more than a painted picture. The crowd was packed densely a little way up the hill, swelled by many Parliament troops who were laughing and cracking coarse jokes, and when she came behind them she could no longer see. She went back a little way, climbed up a flight of steps that led to an arched doorway, and then she could see. She had not to wait long. A group of men came out of the Guildhall and there was a roar of execration. The pikemen who surrounded the prisoner, pushing the crowd back with their pikes held level, were none of them as tall as he. She could see him quite well, his head up, his hands tied behind his back, walking easily. She could not see his face clearly, but she believed he smiled. He went up into the cart so quickly and lightly that she knew he was happy. The noise died down abruptly and there was silence. A woman screamed once, shrilly, and then the silence flowed back. He stood patiently while a Puritan preacher harangued him, and then she saw him kneel to pray. The silence was absolute, for the mood of the crowd had swung round. This was a man who was dying gallantly, a rogue such as they loved, who would give them the spectacle of an edifying end, and their mood had changed to a liking for the fellow. They would not jeer at him again until he hung at the rope's end.

He got up and while the rope was put round his neck she heard his deep voice speaking. She could not hear what he said, but she thought they were Latin words and that he spoke them over and over. She turned back into the archway behind her, slipped to her knees and hid her face, for he would not want her to see further, but she knew when the cart was driven from under him because his deep voice broke off abruptly. She endured it through to the end with him, as she had with Robert. When it was over she felt one extraordinary deep gush of joy and then fell into blackness. It must have held her for some while, for when she opened her eyes again the square seemed quiet behind her. She knew she must not look back at the square and she did not. She got down the steps somehow, and somehow she walked home. It was the hour of the Angel, and now she knew the secret at the heart of the world.

CHAPTER VIII

THE WEB OF LOVE

Froniga passed through the next two weeks in anguish. He was gone. Though the other parting had been final, yet she had been final, yet she had been able to picture him tramping the lanes with his tinker's gear on his back, riding his pony through the woods, sitting at night by the camp-fire. She had known they watched the same sunrise and thanked God for the same stars. She had known that his body still lived, that others heard his voice speaking, and often she had felt his thought touch hers and had known that he still loved her. For the first few days after he died she was sure that he would come to her. With her more than normal powers, her great sensitiveness, she had always been aware of the unseen world and able to communicate with it; even sometimes, she had thought, to command it. He would come. While he still lived in the world she had set him free, and now he would reward her by coming to her. She lay awake at night waiting for him, an emptiness of longing that he would surely fill. By day she tried to force her agonised spirit to stillness and peace, for perhaps the peace that was now his could only make contact with an equal peace. But he did not come. There was nothing. He was gone. The body she had loved, the fine mind, were gone. The spirit, if there were a spirit, was gone. Not all her power had been able either to save his body or to bring his spirit to her. Her power too was gone, crumbled into nothing with his body and his mind. Somewhere within her, as well as her grief, there was a fearful humiliation.

It was two weeks to the day, and once more she sat before her fire at dusk, with Pen upon her lap. She was feeling physically exhausted. As she had told no one about her first parting with Yoben, so she had told no one about this other parting, and she had done her work as usual, but the shock and strain had told upon her body as well as her mind and spirit. All day she had not known how to drag her body from one task to another. When a knock came on the door she felt a sense of panic. If someone had been taken ill at a distant cottage she did not know how she was going to get there. It was all she could do to get to the door to open it.

Outside in the windy dusk stood a thin, stooped old woman wrapped in a worn brown cloak, a diklo over her head, wisps of white hair straggling about her brown wrinkled face. She looked frail as a cobweb. Then suddenly she smiled, and her face lighted up an inexpressible tenderness as she spoke the words of Yoben's own greeting, *"O boro Duvel atch' pa leste, Tshai."* She spoke the last word over again, tenderly. *"Tshai.* My daughter." Then, stepping into the room with decision, and shutting the door behind her, she took Froniga into her arms.

Froniga's weakness felt upheld by strength. She was in Yoben's arms and all was well. It was as though Yoben himself had come in from the dusk and now was laughing at her grief. Madona, laughing, had turned her face to the candlelight. "You are like her," she said. "You are like your mother Richenda. Once again I hold Richenda in my arms. What foolishness that I let her go from me in anger, what foolishness that I did not watch you grow from a brown acorn of a child to this tall woman whom now I see. Who shall give back to us the years that our sin has wasted? It was foolishness and it was sin. Your mother broke Romany law, marrying a gorgio, and you broke it, wearing the green gown; but those who break the law should be loved more and not less for their sin, for if we do not forgive, then is sin added to sin and the end is death. So he taught me, who would not listen to the wisdom of the gorgio. He was patient. He went back and forth between us, carrying thoughts of one to the other, spinning the web of love. Now it is a cloak that covers us both, and I have forgiven you that you wear a green gown."

Froniga found that she was sitting on the floor before the fire at Madona's feet, her head on her lap. The old woman sat as a queen in Froniga's chair and softly touched her forehead, her hair, with fingers that were light and gentle. Her voice flowed on softly, rising and falling like music, infinitely comforting. Froniga wept for the first time since Yoben's death. She wept for a long while and did not know how long it was. When it was over she was like a woman who has lived through the crisis of an illness and survived it. "Do you know that Yoben is dead?" she asked.

"Should I be here if I did not know," asked Madona. "While he lived I would not obey when he said, 'Go to Froniga,' but when, being dead, he commanded, I set out. The commands of the dead are tongued with fire, compelling as sunlight on closed eyes. We obey and cannot help ourselves."

"Have you come far, Madona?" asked Froniga.

"From near Oxford," said Madona. "We have had to seek fresh hiding-places since Alamina, that wicked one, shut us out from Flowercote Wood."

"You have come, alone, from near Oxford?" asked Froniga incredulously.

"I have taken my time," said Madona placidly. "Last night was warm and I slept snug in a deep dingle. By day I walked till my strength gave out, then I begged a lift from one or another, a gorgio with a hay-wain or a farmer on his horse, whom he told me would do no harm to an old gypsy."

"Who told you?" demanded Froniga.

"Yoben, as he walked beside me."

Froniga was silent, her face hidden in her hands, and that hidden humiliation within her grew deeper still. Then, remembering that fear of the dead was the chief tenet of the Romany faith, she said to Madona, "Were you not afraid?"

"That foolishness also I have left behind me," said Madona. "And I shall not again wail for the dead, for that too is foolishness. And if you marvel, *Tshai*, that he should come to you not directly but through the old grandmother, the *Pûri-dai*, I cannot tell you the reason. The dead, how they come, why they come to one and not another, at one time and not another time, it is a mystery. We do not know. What their life is we do not know. But this I do know, *Tshai*, who myself am near to death, that there is laughter there. Not laughter as we know it who can laugh in fear, in wickedness and scorn, but laughter like the laughter of children when they wake on a blue morning and run out into the light."

"Do you know the manner of Yoben's death?" asked Froniga.

"I know it," said Madona. "Alamina witnessed it. She came back and told me the manner of it with much wailing and tearing of her garments and her hair. She is a foolish girl, and wicked, but she can still wail when the results of her wickedness are not what she designed."

"What did she design?" asked Froniga, hardly above her breath.

"The death of a young *Rai* who came to the camp one night with Yoben and who she thought had insulted her. He and

Yoben were spies together in Henley, and Alamina betrayed the young man into the hands of his enemies, yet when she stood in the crowd to watch the death of her enemy it was not he who climbed into the cart, but Yoben. She says she screamed and fainted. How it came about that Yoben should have suffered in place of the other, Alamina does not know."

Madona's voice, that had been flowing on so surely, strong with the truth of what she had to say, suddenly wavered. She shrank in upon herself. She looked no longer a queen upon her throne but a very old woman who had just accomplished a task that had been too much for her.

"You must have food and drink at once, Madona," said Froniga, and jumped up in contrition. What had she been thinking of? Supernatural power can uphold a human being through a service to another too hard for physical strength, but does not remit the physical consequences afterwards. That Froniga knew, and she had rebelled sometimes at the seeming injustice. But that, too, was perhaps part of the meaning of the word substitution, that Madona had expressed in the Romany tongue as suffering in place of another. That Yoben had done so by choice and not by accident she was now quite sure, for she had been aware of the happiness with which he had faced death. As she moved about the kitchen, getting supper for Madona, she realised that the dream he had relinquished had been given back to him again and had been the last chapter in that book to which the patience of God adds another chapter, and another and another, and in the hour of victory closes the book. Once again, within her, the seal had broken and for a short while there was Easter in her soul.

Madona ate her supper of hot bread and milk, drank a cup of the herbal tea she loved and consented to be put to bed on a mattress and pillows and blankets on the kitchen floor. Go upstairs she would not, nor lie in a proper bed. It was bad enough to be inside a house, but stairs and a bed she would not face. Yet she enjoyed the few days she spent with Froniga. The weather turned to rain, and it was good to sit warm and snug by the fire, smoking her old clay pipe, and good to talk to Froniga, who was so like her sister Richenda that she felt no strangeness in her presence. They had loved each other deeply and at once, and the talk flowed easily between them. But Madona would not be cosseted, nor would she have her clothes washed, for they had been washed only a month ago and she thought that three of four times a year were enough. Also she was afraid that, if she took her clothes off, Froniga would find the cancer in her breast and insist on keeping her here to treat it. And she did not want that. Never having ailed at all, she had at first been astonished by the pain, but now she was used to it and had accepted her cancer with a fatalism that was not far removed from affection. And once the sun shone again she must go home. She was the *Pûri-dai* of the tribe and was needed. It was she who protected the children, composed the quarrels, dosed the sick and comforted the sorrowful. She waited until the weather was settled and then she rose to her feet and said she was going. Froniga was not surprised and did not argue the matter, for she had seen how restless Madona had become once the weather showed signs of clearing, but she was not going to allow her to walk back, and she had already arranged with one of the farmers to lend her his horse and cart.

In this they set out on a clear fine morning, Froniga driving the old white horse and Madona sitting behind her in the cart on a pile of hay. When the cart jolted over stones on the road it caused her pain, but no shadow of it was to be seen on her serene old face. About her were piled such gifts as she had been willing to accept from Froniga : bunches of herbs, comfits and cakes for the children, soft rags and medicaments for her sick. On her lap she held a bundle that Froniga of her own will had given her. It was the green gown, and wrapped within it were the tarot cards. Madona considered that, being only half a gypsy, Froniga had no more right to use the cards than she had to wear the green gown, and was removing them from her in much the same spirit as Froniga herself had removed the contents of her cupboard from Mother Skipton.

"You can still use your mother's spells, my dearie," said Madona, "for they were not Romany spells. She learned them from a good Chovihan who was a blacksmith up Dracot way. On his deathbed he taught them to her, for he said that gypsy or no gypsy she was the wisest woman whom he knew."

"I will not use them again," said Froniga. "They were good spells, and they were good spirits who came to my help, but the pride that I felt in my power to summon them was not good. And why should we trouble the spirits when the good God has planted in the earth the cure for every ailment under the sun? And is it not presumption to summon the spirits? They are God's, and will He not send them Himself at need, as He sent Yoben to bring you to me? And in the attempt to command them there may be danger too. One's heart must be pure indeed to summon to one only that which is good."

She had spoken in a low voice, brokenly, and did not look round for some while, and when she did look round she saw that Madona had dropped into a doze. They were driving now over a better bit of road, and the ease and the hot sunshine had made her sleepy. But Froniga did not mind, for heard or unheard it had been a step forward to speak aloud some of the conclusions to which she had come through days and nights of struggle, for speaking a resolve aloud is like setting a seal on it. It would be hard for her to lay aside her spells, for to do so would involve laying aside much of her power, but she had been proud of her power, and so it must go. She would bring to the sick her knowledge of the herbs, her healing hands and skill in nursing, such love and compassion as might be given her, but no magic. Magicians, sooner or later, became worshippers of their own power, and the smoke of their idolatrous incense hid the face of God.

Yoben was gone. She knew now that she would never feel him with her in the way Madona had done. In Madona he had come to her, but he would come no other way. He was dead. But in the void that he had left behind him there was new life stirring. Last night, in the hour before dawn, she had said out loud, in darkness and sleeplessness, "From the rising of the sun until the going down of the same the name of the Lord is worthy of praise." It had not seemed to be herself who spoke, though by the words spoken she was committed, nor was it the voice of that gush of joy that sometimes came to her, for the voice spoke in the depths of her loneliness. Thinking about it now, as she drove the old white horse through the deep lanes, it came to her that those had been the words that Yoben had spoken over and over as he waited for death. *"O solis ortu usque occasum, laudabile nomen Domini."* Yet it had not been Yoben who had spoken them last night. She believed it had been the spirit of God within her crying out that love to God that of herself she could not feel. The years stretched before her, a long and dusty way, yet if she could walk humbly along it she might find that life, unfolding slowly, keeps its best secrets till the end.

After a couple of hours' travelling they stopped and she and Madona ate their noon lunch under the shade of a beech tree.

They had gone along the byways and had met no one but a shepherd with his sheep, and children looking for early blackberries. Madona was alert and wide awake now and they spoke of their own children, Jenny and Will, Dinki, Meriful and Cinderella. Froniga found herself longing for the gypsy children and said to Madona, "You must all come back to the village soon. The great trick is already almost forgotten."

"We shall never come back."

"But I must see you again, Madona. We cannot be parted."

"In the ways of the world we must be parted," said Madona. "But this parting will not be as the other, when I locked you out of my heart because you wore the green gown. Now I have locked you within my heart and have thrown away the key. Come, *Tshai*, we must go on for you must be home again before nightfall."

In the midst of the golden afternoon they drove across a rough field and stopped on the brow of a hill. Below them in a deep wooded hollow they saw the drift of smoke and Madona clacked her tongue in annoyance. "I have told them to guard against a smoky fire," she said. "We were safe in that hidden place, and now they must betray it with their carelessness."

"Who would come across this field full of thistles?" said Froniga. "No harm can come to you down in that hollow, Madona."

She spoke with a certainty she did not feel. Now that the moment of parting had come she felt desolate. "Let me come down to the camp with you," she said.

"No, *Tshai*," said Madona firmly. "You took Baw the pony and are not forgiven."

"I would like to see the children again."

"Then you should not have taken the pony."

"There is so much for you to carry."

"You speak as a child," said Madona severely. "A pack of cards. A green gown. A few herbs. Wrap the herbs in my diklo and help me from the cart."

Froniga did as she was told and then Madona took her in her arms, kissed her, blessed her and turned away. Froniga stood by the cart, watching her go down into the wood. She did not look back and almost at once the trees hid her from sight, so much was she akin to them. She made no sound, moving through the wood. There was a bird-call, down in the depths of the green shade, and then silence except for the purling of a hidden stream. Froniga wept for a short while, leaning against the old white horse. Then she took his bridle and led him back through the field. All the way home she was obsessed by the thought of the children, and how they had been used to come to her like birds out from a bush.

CHAPTER IX

THE BIRDS FLY HOME

I

The autumn that changed the course of Froniga's life also changed the course of the war. Hampden was dead and Pym was dying, but a new star had risen in the Parliament sky. Colonel Cromwell, commanding now a fine body of men, well trained, well disciplined and all in a state of grace, won another victory in East Anglia at Winceby, his devout and godly men chanting a psalm as they rode into battle. He was now in control of Lincolnshire, on the flank of any possibility of the Royalist attack from the north. The King's hope of three marches on London was doomed. Then came another blow for the King. Parliament made an alliance with Scotland. The Scottish army would not be able to march for some months, but when they did and the Covenanters made contact with Cromwell's army, what then? Outwardly, that autumn, life was gay as ever in Oxford, but those who had leisure to do any thinking found no pleasure in their thoughts.

Francis had plenty of leisure and his thoughts were a torment. If his mind turned outward to the cause he had fought for, and would fight for again, there was gloom there, and if it turned inward to his own affairs there was stygian darkness. And there was no one to whom he could speak of his wretchedness, for Dr. Jeremy Taylor was now on the march with Rupert, and with his other friends he was not intimate. They thought his continual misfortunes merely farcical : a fall over a rosette, a fever, a tiff with Barbara, a wound in the leg. What were these to throw a man into such a state of gloom? Barbara was now betrothed to another young nobleman, but no one supposed that caused Francis much grief, and if his stiff leg and shoulder made him still unable to fight, surely attendance upon the King was honourable labour. They had no patience with him, and he did not blame them. They did not know what had happened at Henley a month ago.

And nor entirely did he; that was one of the worst of his

torments. When Yoben had pushed him through the window he had fainted again. When he came to himself he remembered vaguely that Yoben had said, "We'll get out of this together." Dragging himself up, he looked through the window, but the room was empty. It was physically impossible for him to climb back through the window. Entirely bewildered and incapable of commonsense reasoning, he thought that Yoben might be at the bottom of the small untidy garden. Somehow he got himself down through the herbs and currant bushes and found a door in a wall. He opened it and went through into an orchard that stretched along behind the backs of the houses. There was a pony cropping the grass and near to it he stumbled over a man lying beside an apple tree, and found him to be one of Colonel Thistleton's officers, to whom he had talked in the wood the night before. There were several men here who had escaped through one of the houses in Duke Street after the firing of the cannon. After that he remembered very little of what happened, except that they bound up his leg and gave him water to drink, and said something of staying here until dusk and then trying to get away. But after only a few hours of waiting there was a great noise from the direction of the Market Place, as though the whole town were gathered there. For the men with him it seemed a heaven-sent opportunity for escape while attention was elsewhere. He was hoisted upon the pony and they made their way into a deserted lane behind the orchard, and from there into the woods. A few hours later they were in Reading, where he was looked after with others of the wounded.

The next day they learned to what event they owed their safety. All the Parliament troops and most of the inhabitants of Henley had gathered in the Market Place for the execution of a Royalist spy. The rumour was that the man was a recusant priest and a few questions to those in authority left Francis in no doubt as to who he was.

In Reading, and back again in Oxford, Francis went over the events of that night again and again, his thoughts going round in maddening circles. He had little doubt that Yoben had saved his life, and perhaps died in his place, but he could not put the bits of the puzzle together. But of one thing he was convinced, and that was that though Alamina was doubtless concerned in it somewhere, yet it was he who was to blame for Yoben's death, for he had forced his company upon him in the first place, and he had disobeyed him in not keeping clear of the fighting. And now Yoben was dead and Froniga was in grief. It was the thought of Froniga that chiefly tormented him. For Yoben it was over, but for Froniga it was not. And he had enjoyed her hospitality, as he had enjoyed Margaret's, whose husband he had killed. He was ceaselessly haunted by his memory of the night when the three of them had had supper together and he had realised something of the depth of Froniga's love for Yoben. It was no good to tell himself that this sort of tragedy was the inevitable result of civil war, for he knew it was just as much the fault of his own character. As John Loggin he had forced himself upon the Haslewoods for a wager he had been too arrogant to refuse, and as a joke. He had forced his company upon Yoben the night they left Oxford out of determination to have his own way. A headstrong arrogance had been a part of him all his life, but he had not known it until now. Through the days and nights he suffered as he had never done before. He thought much of Parson Hawthyn and of Jenny. He longed to go and see Froniga, to tell her of his sorrow for her and to ask her if she could put the bits of the puzzle together for him. But shame kept him away. To thrust himself upon the Haslewoods now, after all the suffering he had caused, would be an insult to them.

Then came an autumn day when he was not in attendance upon the King and free to do what he would until nightfall. He had bought himself a gentle old grey mare upon whom he could ride easily, in spite of a stiff leg and shoulder, and he thought he would get out into the country for a while, away from the crowded streets of the city. He rode down the winding High Street and out of the East Gate into the meadows beyond. As he rode up through the woods towards Shotover he met no one, and the quietness began to give him a little ease. It was a grey day, one of those autumn days of dream-like stillness that can draw one within their peace. Yellow leaves fell silently about him in the woods and the carpet of gold upon the bridle-path muted the sound of his horse's feet. He climbed up until he reached the heights of Shotover and then he halted and looked back and down, over the golden woods and the slopes covered with tawny bracken and silvery traveller's-joy, down to the shorn harvest-fields and the green water-meadows and the winding river. Oxford looked a city of dreams down there, her towers and spires mysterious in the faint haze that hung over the valley. It did not seem possible that her grey walls contained the noise and confusion, the restless ambitions, the fears and cruelties and vulgarities from which he had fled; they looked as though they encircled the City of God.

He turned away from the sight of the lovely city, overwhelmed again by his wretchedness. Where could a man find peace? The world had a canker at its heart, and in himself, when he tried to withdraw from it within himself, he found these searing faults that could work such havoc in the lives of others.

He rode on, and the quiet grey day was suddenly ripped through by the sound of a pistol shot, and then another. He heard men shouting and women screaming. The trouble, whatever it might be was not very near, for sound travelled far on such a still day, and Francis instinctively pulled up his horse. Why get embroiled in something that was nothing to do with him? He had ridden out from Oxford to escape vulgar confusion, not to plunge headlong into more of it. Then with shame he changed his mind, for here was another detestable trait in himself. It was partly because he and men like him had lived for so long in ivory towers that this hideous war had broken out. He rode quickly down towards the sounds of trouble, which he thought came from a deep wooded valley not far from the village of Garsington.

At the foot of the hillside that sloped to the valley, among the bracken and gorse, he met a body of Royalist troopers riding towards the village from the direction of the valley and halted them with a sharp command. "What were you fellows doing?" he demanded. He was wearing his lifeguard uniform, and a young officer came forward and saluted.

"We are stationed at Garsington, sir," he said. "We've just found a nest of gypsies hidden in that valley. We thought there were some about, for we've had a couple of horses stolen. And we've reason to think they've been spying on us lately, for yesterday a troop of rebel horse attacked us. But we've beaten them up well and given them a good fright."

"How did you know they were in those woods?" asked Francis.

"One of the villagers told us he'd seen some smoke rising above the trees."

"How many have you accounted for?"

"Three or four, sir. The rest ran away. But now we've taught them a lesson we'll have no more trouble. They won't come back."

He grinned cheerfully, saluted and rode on with his men. As they disappeared towards the village Francis could hear them singing and whistling. Gypsies were nothing to them. They were nothing to anybody, and no one bothered to protect them. They were a persecuted people, fair game whenever they gave any trouble. And yet, thought Francis, they came of a great and ancient race and had wandered the ways of the world longer than any man knew. Suddenly he remembered the camp-fire near Flowercote Wood, and the wild beauty that he had seen, the old songs he had listened to, and Madona's face. He saw her face before him now, with its noble selfless beauty. He remembered her leaning forward and smiling at him, and he remembered the promise that he had given. So much had happened since then that he had forgotten it. Now he cursed himself that he had forgotten, turned his horse round and rode as fast as he could towards the wood. It was unlikely that they were the same gypsies. It was probable that when he got there he would find only a few dead bodies and a deserted camp, but he must find out.

He came under the golden eaves of the wood and into the deep shadows beneath the trees. All was silence and stillness, but he followed the track of the trampled undergrowth that the troopers had left in their wake. Though in this cankerous and suffering world it was a little thing, yet it grieved him to see the small plants trampled into the soil, the fern-fronds broken. Yet he did not blame the troopers. Just such a searing track had he made himself through the lives of those he loved.

He followed the track downhill into the heart of the wood and found a wide valley with a stream running through it, a hidden and lovely place. The grass was trampled and the bushes wrenched and torn, as though there had been a considerable struggle here, but there was no sign of the gypsies. Some cooking-pots lay in confusion on the ground and the fire was burning, but the camp was completely deserted. With the suddenness of a flock of birds who rise up all together and fly off to another feeding-place they had vanished, taking their dead and wounded with them, their carts and wagons, ponies and children. The speed of their exodus was a measure of their terror. He got off his horse and stood listening, half expecting to hear frightened cries and sounds of escape, but there was not a sound anywhere. The grey stillness seemed to press upon him, and he stood motionless. There was nothing he could do, but he did not go away. He was sorry for what had happened. Who were these people, so quickly overtaken by fear and disaster? He tethered his horse to a tree and walked a little way beside the stream, looking about him, and his eye was caught by a gleam of colour in the woods on the other side. There was a wagon there, almost hidden within the shadows of the wood.

He crossed the stream by the fallen log that spanned it, went across the clearing and into the woods. The gaily painted wagon stood beneath the branches of a great oak tree, its shafts trailing on the ground, its wheels deeply sunk in leaves and mosses. He climbed up and went inside. At first it seemed so dark that he could see nothing, and then, as he became able to distinguish form again, his mind played a queer trick on him. He was once more in the village church, looking down upon the carved figure of a woman lying upon her tomb. But that woman had been young and lovely and this woman was old, and she lay not upon a slab of stone, but upon a rude litter of twined branches laid upon upturned logs of wood, and the long folds of her cloak were brown, not white. But she lay as the other had lain, on her back with her hands crossed upon her breast, and though her face in death looked almost unbelievably ancient, sharpened like whittled wood, shrunken like the face of some old Egyptian queen who had been centuries dead and entombed, he could fancy he saw some echo of laughter there. He sank to his knees and crossed himself, and looked long at Madona's dead face. He imagined she had died the previous night and he was glad she had known nothing of the fight in the clearing. He was glad that his life had touched hers, if only so briefly and lightly. He would never forget her face, either as he had seen it in life or as he saw it now in death. She was one of those people, like Froniga, Yoben and Jenny, whose quality can seem to justify the human race.

As before, his eyes were drawn from the sculptured figure to the darker shadows beyond it and he saw a faint gleam of colour, orange-tawny, red and blue, and the sparkle of terrified bright eyes. The three children were huddled together behind Madona, pressed up against the wall of the wagon, and the little girl had her wooden baby hugged desperately against her breast. Dinki, Meriful and Cinderella. Their terror was pitiful to see. They panted like wild birds caught in the net, and their eyes swivelled from side to side, yet somehow never seemed quite to leave his, as they waited for what he would do to them. In the church they had attempted flight, but now they were so paralysed by fear that only their eyes moved. He felt helpless in face of their fear. What could he do? He spoke to them, telling them he would not hurt them, but they did not understand him and it made no difference. Nevertheless he went on talking to them, gently and softly, while his own thoughts whirled round bewilderingly in his head. These three, Yoben had told him, were Alamina's children. If Alamina was with the tribe now, what sort of mother was she that she had fled and left them here? Yoben had told him that the children's only refuge was Madona. They must have fled to Madona as soon as the fight started. Though she was dead she was their only refuge still. If Alamina was away perhaps the terrified gypsies would not even notice the absence of the three children, and it might be a matter of days before they could pluck up enough courage to come back here and give Madona burial. What would happen to the children meanwhile? And even if they were soon found, what would become of them in the future without Madona and without Yoben? Cinderella would become as wicked as her mother. The boys would grow up thieves and poachers and perhaps die on the gallows. All three would lead hunted, persecuted lives. His mind suddenly cleared. He had to save these children. That was the promise he had made to Madona. He must take them, tonight, to Froniga.

He stood up, bent over and picked Cinderella up in his arms. Carrying her to the front of the wagon, he sat down with her on his knees, held in the crook of his arm. Terrified, she curled herself up into an almost circular ball like a hedgehog, with her precious wooden baby in the midst of her. But presently, as he rocked her and talked to her, she uncurled and began to sob. He wiped the tears away, while within him there was a sudden explosion of laughter as he wondered what Barbara would say if she could see him now. Looking round, he saw that the boys were beside him. They were still trembling, but their eyes were steadier and they did not attempt to run away. They realised now that he would not kill them as the other gorgios had killed the men of their tribe. He remembered that he had a couple of apples in his pocket and he gave them to them and they fell upon them greedily. He did not know if they understood the gorgio speech at all, but he told them carefully and slowly that he was taking them to Mistress Froniga Haslewood, and her name at least they understood, for they smiled shakily and said it again after him . . . Mistress Froniga Haslewood. . . . Then, still carrying Cinderella, he moved back into the wagon and laid his fine leather purse, heavy with silver, near Madona's feet; for he was about to steal three children and, like Froniga when she stole Baw, he felt that some reparation should be made. Also he hoped that if there were any of the gypsies who cared at all for the fate of these children, the purse might tell them that they had fallen into kind hands. Then he made his way back to the valley and across the stream, the boys following dumbly. He sat all three upon his horse and led it up through the woods beside the stream, finding himself eventually in a lane near the field of thistles where Froniga had said goodbye to Madona.

He never forgot the journey with the three children on that still autumn day; through the drifting golden leaves under the grey sky, through the glow of a sudden fiery sunset that burst through as the sky cleared towards evening, through the deep azure mists of twilight, with the moths bumping against their cheeks, through the night under the stars with the owls calling, the first sound they had heard all through the long hours. Francis could not walk for long and he and Meriful took turns to ride the grey mare with the two little ones, and when it was Francis's turn to ride they travelled quickly, with Meriful leaping along beside the horse, quick and tireless as some fox or hare. The children soon lost their fear and gave Francis their trust. It gave him a poignant thrill to ride with Cinderella asleep in the crook of his arm and Dinki behind him clinging to his coat. Oxford and his duty there seemed utterly remote. It was this journey, although it had a dreamlike quality, that seemed real to him, and as they came near the village he realised how strong was the hold it had upon him. It was the setting of those dreams he had entertained and then tried to dismiss as moonshine. But they had their own reality, for they had refused dismissal and lived with him still.

2

Froniga was preparing to go to bed. She had set aside her spinning-wheel and was on her knees before the hearth, signing the cross in the ashes. She felt as though she signed it upon her own life, grey and dead as the ashes, or upon her heart that would not know joy again; or so she told herself in the self-pity into which her good sense and courage had momentarily crumbled. For it had been a hard day, one of the worst. Apart from Pen, who was *enceinte* and as full of self-pity as herself, she had seen no one, heard no sound in the grey stillness but the sound of her own weeping. For she had wept today, wept for the emptiness of her life without Yoben, and for Madona, of whose death she had been aware in the dark hour before dawn, and wept too for fear of the years ahead. They yawned before her as empty and silent as this day had been.

What was that? The clop-clop of a weary horse along the road that crossed the common. Sound travelled clearly on such a still night. Well, what of it? What was there in the sound of a tired farmer riding home to make her heart leap up and such a warmth to steal through her cold body? She was tugging at the front door, impatient because it stuck. Then she was outside in the little garden, standing in the beam of candlelight that shone out through the door. The moon had risen, and it was almost as clear as day. The sweetbrier hedges that hedged her garden gave out a faint perfume and one or two late roses clung to the cottage wall. The tired horse had turned down from the road into her lane. She heard the chime of children's voices and a man's footsteps, as halting and weary as those of the horse. Man and horse stopped outside her gate and she saw the three children sitting one behind the other on the horse's back, looking down at her as she stood in the moonlit garden, in the beam of candlelight. They smiled at her and she smiled back at them, holding out her arms.

Now it had happened she was not in the least surprised. The man, of whom she was scarcely aware, lifted them quickly one by one off the horse and over the gate and set them down upon the garden path. Like birds flying out from a bush they ran to her and she gathered them into her arms within the safety of this green domain, within her life and home and heart, just as she had dreamed she would. Time stopped. When she came to herself she found she had pulled them all inside the cottage and shut the door. Kneeling on the flagged floor she was hugging them all over again.

"But the gorgio, *Rashai*," said Meriful. "The gorgio who brought us here. The cruel men would have come back and killed us too if the gorgio hadn't brought us away."

Froniga ran out of the cottage and found Francis waiting humbly and wretchedly outside the gate. "Come in, John Loggin," she commanded.

"I can't come in," he said. "How can I come in? But I must tell you what happened. Mistress Froniga, Madona is dead."

"I know," said Froniga. "I knew when she died this morning, but I do not know what has happened. How was it?"

He told her briefly how he had found the children. "Did I do right to bring them?" he asked.

"You did right," she said. "With Madona and Yoben dead what would have become of them? If Alamina comes here and makes a fuss I'll buy them from her. She would do anything for gold. She is a wicked woman."

"I helped to make her so," said Francis.

"Nonsense," said Froniga. "Come in, John Loggin."

"I was the cause of Yoben's death," he said.

He spoke in dry hard tones, almost as though he did not care. His face looked blank and expressionless in the moonlight. But Froniga knew that tone and that look. He had brooded too long and become so obsessed by his grieving that now there was nothing left in his mind to share with another except what he could not share; for to speak of what was in his mind was so hard as to be almost impossible.

"I know you were," she said, "but you also gave him joy in his death, and if you will come in I can tell you why. There will also be much that you can tell me. You owe it to me to come in. Take your horse to the inn stable and then come back. I must go to the children."

She ran into the cottage, and Francis did as she told him. He lingered a little while, seeing to the comfort of his horse, that she might have longer alone with the children. When he got back to the cottage the little kitchen was empty, but he heard Froniga moving about upstairs, putting the children to bed, and he heard the murmur of their sleepy voices. They sounded happy. He hoped the novelty of being put to sleep in a real bed had driven the remembrance of what they had seen out of their minds. Or perhaps they were so used to scenes of violence that they were not frightened by them as a delicately nurtured child like Jenny would have been. . . . Jenny. . . . She was only a mile away from him, but he would never see her again. Moving restlessly about the room he noticed that the remains of the children's supper was still on the table: half-empty bread-and-milk bowls, and some apples and little cakes that they had attacked and then abandoned after the manner of hungry and weary children. He began clumsily to put the things together, with some vague idea that he was helping Froniga. He had just succeeded in breaking a bowl when she came back and took it from him. "Sit in my chair while I get our supper," she said. "You are more weary than the children. And you are limping. Why is that?"

"I was wounded in the leg at Henley."

"Badly?" she asked sharply.

"No, very slightly."

"Then why are you still limping? Had a slight wound been correctly treated you would have forgotten all about it by now. What herbs were used in the dressing of it?"

"None," he said. "The surgeon had little faith in old-fashioned remedies." He suddenly grinned and felt happier than he had done for weeks. "The death-rate was high among the wounded," he assured her.

"So I should suppose," she said coldly. "And what is the matter with your shoulder?" He looked at her in astonishment, as she put her hand to her own right shoulder. "I feel the pain just here."

"I broke a bone last summer," he said, "and it was unskilfully set. Mistress Froniga, are you a white witch?"

He spoke laughingly, but she answered very seriously, "Not now, but I expect I shall always know when others suffer, and when they die, for that is part of my healing gift, that God gave me; not like the other power that I wrested by my own will from the strange powers that are all about us. I know that you have suffered much, John Loggin, and the bodily pain has been the least of it, but we will not talk of that until we have eaten. Draw up your chair."

As they ate their supper of broth, bread, cheese and apples, she told him of Parson Hawthyn, Margaret and the children. They were all well, she said, and she and Margaret were now happier together than they had ever been. "She is changed," said Froniga, "and so am I. One is seldom unchanged by the death of those one loves. It gives one a deeper knowledge of them, and so of oneself in regard to them. Margaret and I wonder now just how much we hurt Robert by our antagonism to each other. He stood between us and must have received our shafts into himself. Now he has gone and we are drawn together by the knowledge, even as Madona and I were drawn together by the death of Yoben. Madona stayed with me here, John Loggin. I made a bed for her before the fire, even as I will make one for you tonight."

He did not protest. They had much to talk of and he knew he was far too tired and stiff to ride back to Oxford without a night's rest. After they had finished their supper they drew their chairs to the fire and Froniga said gently, "Now I will tell you all I know of Yoben, and why it was that the manner of his death was the one he would have chosen. Sit down, fill your pipe and be at ease, for you must understand that self-reproach is a thing you must put away."

Francis marvelled at her. Not only did she not hate him but she was concerned for him. He saw in her face the same sort of change that he had seen in Yoben's. What she had endured was stamped upon it, but without bitterness. Her strength was as great as ever but had lost its dominance. Even before she reached the end of her story he felt a sense of relief from the tautness of his misery, and when she had reached the end he said, "Is there a sort of divine economy that turns even our sins to some use?"

"I believe so. If not, we should despair." She smiled at him. "Though that's no excuse for sinning. But did you sin?"

"I am an arrogant man. If I had not been so Robert and Yoben would not have died."

"Tell me about your arrogance," she said, and he told her. When he had finished she too felt a sense of deep relief. She had never supposed that he could be guilty of treachery but she was infinitely glad for Jenny's sake as well as her own that she was right. He was a boyish creature, she thought, and always would be, the boy whom she had seen standing before his father at the great desk. She smiled a little thinking that Jenny in years to come would not find the gap in their ages any hindrance to the management of him.

"Why did you smile?" he asked gently.

"I was wondering whether you would ever grow into a henpecked husband."

"Whatever made you think of that at this particular moment?" he asked, slightly outraged.

"The mind goes off at strange tangents," she said. "But I do not think that your wife will ever manage you otherwise than lovingly, and for your good. Now let us put the bits of the puzzle together more clearly that we may see the pattern of it."

A little later he said, "How can you talk so calmly of Yoben's death? Almost as though it were something that happened years ago."

"Because grief like a great storm has already carried me away from it on the first stage of the journey back. When I am united again with his death it will be by my own death; and then it will be my life united with his life. The coming of the children has helped me, John Loggin. All day the journey back has seemed unbearably lonely. It is not so now."

There was a silence while Francis lay back in his chair and felt a sense of pleasure in the rosy glow of the flames, in warmth and shadows and the shapes of things. It was so long since he had felt pleasure in anything that the beauty of the firelight shining on Froniga's spinning-wheel was a profound astonishment to him.

"Tell me of your father," said Froniga, "and of your home."

"My father is safe, but my home has been destroyed by the rebels," he said. "No, don't look distressed. It was gutted by fire, but when the war is over my father and I will build it up again. He is with Lord Winchester at Basing House. It has been turned into a great fortress and he is as safe there as he can be anywhere in England. We had a fine library, and I am sorry that is gone, but I expect the whole of it did not mean as much to us as Parson Hawthyn's few books meant to him."

"You will go and see Parson Hawthyn while you are here?" she asked.

"No, Froniga. I must be gone by daylight tomorrow. I shall have to make my peace with the King, upon whom I should be attending at this moment. But I shall never forget him. Nor you. Nor Jenny."

There was sadness in his tone and Froniga said, "You will come back, John Loggin."

"I can never come back."

"When Jenny is older I will tell her about Robert," said Froniga. "When she has got over the shock of it I do not think that she will hate you. By that time she will understand better than she does now what things constitute the peculiar bitterness of civil war, man's helplessness in face of it, man's grief because of it. And she will understand, I hope, what women have to do if peace is to come untarnished by bitterness and revenge."

He looked at her wondering. "How much does she know?" and she looked back at him, thinking, "Has he understood?" Then she got up and went into the next room, and when she came back again carrying two pots of ointment and a small bottle she was briskly professional. "Take off your coat and let me rub your shoulder," she commanded. "I wish I had had the care of it when you broke the bone, but it is not too late to coax out the rheumatic humours which have settled in the joint. Did you suffer pain at the drawing of the tooth?"

"Well—a twinge or two," Francis admitted, "but no pain during the interval between your toothwort and the extraction. What is this you are using now?"

"Hog's grease and broom flowers," she said. "Keep still."

For a moment or two the probing of her fingers was painful, then it ceased to be so. She seemed to be reaching down to the roots of the pain and drawing it out. Her hands began to glow warmly and became infinitely gentle and soothing. He felt sleepy and oddly at peace. He was sorry when she withdrew her hands and handed him back his coat.

"Take the ointment with you. This other, with a little geranium and germander added, is to draw the pain from your leg. And this cordial of roses and violets is excellent for a tender conscience. Take that internally. The others are for external use only. Don't mix them up. You will soon be well again and next time the King takes the field you will go with him. You have worked through it now."

"Through what, Froniga?"

"Through this present spell of evil fortune. These black times go as they come and we do not know how they come or why they go. But we know that God controls them, as He controls the whole vast cobweb of the mystery of things."

She made his bed for him before the fire, bade him good night and went upstairs. But after a moment or two he heard her voice calling softly, "Come up a moment."

He groped his way up the stairs to the raftered room above and found her standing beside her wide curtained bed, shielding the flame of her candle with her hand. The three children lay together, Cinderella in the middle between her brothers. They were deeply asleep and looked angelic children. Meriful lay on his back straight as an arrow, Dinki was curled up sucking his thumb, Cinderella had her wooden baby clasped in her arms and her cheek rested against its head. The green curtains made them look like birds in a leafy nest, downy and soft.

"They were not afraid to get in the bed," whispered Froniga. "I thought they would be, but they did not mind. I expect they were too sleepy to mind." She turned to him and he saw that tears were sparkling on her cheeks. "John Loggin, this is what I have always longed for; these children here, safe with me. You have brought me what I have longed for."

"By day, you may not find this nestful as angelic as it looks now," said Francis grimly. "Fledglings of this sort are best asleep."

She laughed softly and happily. "I have a strong will, and when there is need I know how to use the flat of my hand."

She went with him to the head of the stairs and stood holding her candle to light him down. At the foot of them he turned round and looked up at her. Changed and aged though she was, he thought he had never seen her look more beautiful. She smiled, the smile transforming the strength of her face to a bewitching tenderness. He felt himself included in her new maternal love and smiled boyishly back at her. Then with a sudden pang he thought of Jenny. What had he done to Jenny? If Froniga was to love these children more than Jenny he would never forgive either himself or her. Not knowing what he did he frowned at Froniga. "Don't love them more than Jenny," he said.

She bent down to him reassuringly. "I can never love any child as I love Jenny. Not even these. But Jenny will not be a child much longer, and when she leaves me for the new great house among the lime trees, I shall have these. Good night, John Loggin."

She had gone, leaving him staring stupidly at the place where she had been. He went back into the kitchen and lay down before the glowing ashes of the fire, but he did not sleep. The present spell of private misfortune might be over, but not the misfortunes of his King and country that he must share until the end. He lay thinking of them, but not without hope. "The new great house among the lime trees." He did not understand tonight what Froniga was talking about, but through the years ahead he never forgot what she had said. In the blackest times it would flash through his mind like light.

When Froniga came down in the morning he had gone. She was not surprised. Their goodbye last night had been a good one to carry in memory through the years until they should meet again.

CHAPTER X

BEAUTY AND THE BEAST

Mistress Jennifer Haslewood was in her stillroom preparing cowslips for cowslip wine. It was a day of warmth and loveliness and there seemed no sound in the world but the singing of birds and the humming of bees in the wallflowers below the open window. Jenny sat near the window, and as she stripped the cowslip heads from the stalks and dropped them into the cauldron of water beside her she looked up sometimes and saw the distant woods alight with the green flames of the beech leaves, with below them the silver and gold of cherry, blackthorn and gorse. In the garden, as well as the wallflowers, the hose-in-hose and jacks-in-the-green were in flower, and soon now the honeysuckle would be out, and then the roses. Another spring, and then another summer. The winter was over and ahead lay the months of colour and delight.

And men were saying that another sort of winter was also ended. Cromwell, the Lord Protector, was dead, the years of the Commonwealth were over and King Charles the Second enjoyed his own again. But Jenny still wore her dark hair smoothed combed beneath her white Puritan cap, and a white apron over a grey gown. And so did her cousin Froniga. It was only Margaret and Will who were relaxing in colours and rosettes, Margaret because she had always secretly loved them and Will because he was in love. Politics had never at any time meant much to any of them and in their hearts all four had disliked the ranting Puritan preacher who had been sent to the parish after Parson Hawthyn had been driven away, but Jenny and Froniga had that tough obstinacy that holds to a dying cause just because it is dying, and would have done so whatever the danger. Actually there was no danger. The King had shown wisdom as well as mercy in refusing to be revenged on his former enemies and by his Act of Indemnity and Oblivion both their lives and property were protected. But being a Puritan was not fashionable now and Will kept giving her sister ribbons and laces in an effort to convert her to conformity with the times. Jenny thanked him gravely and sweetly and laid them away under her lavender-scented handkerchiefs, side by side with her box of rosemary wood, Froniga's gift to her. Parson Hawthyn had made it of the wood of Froniga's old rosemary tree. "Make thee a box of rosemary and smell to it," said the old herbal, "and it shall preserve thy youth." In the box was a faded letter that had been there for years, and a pair of exquisite doeskin riding gloves embroidered with unicorns in tiny seed pearls that had been sent to her from London soon after the King's triumphant homecoming.

Jenny had shown these gloves to no one, not even Froniga. Though there had been no letter with them she had known who had sent them and she was afraid. "Dear God, don't let him come," she had prayed. "Please don't let him come." She did not hate John Loggin. Long ago Froniga had told her, though never Margaret, how Robert had died, and the knowledge had been a more fearful shock to her than even Froniga could understand. But gradually her horror had turned to pity. These things happened in civil war and Froniga had told her how bitterly John Loggin had grieved for what he had done. And Froniga had made her see that if the wounds of civil war are ever to be healed it can only be by women's readiness to forgive and love their enemies. And she owed it to John Loggin that some chance words of his, spoken in the garden on an autumn day, had given her life a direction that had brought her peace. But she was afraid of the vividness of her memories of him, and of the memories she shared with him. They had a potential power that frightened her.

There was a clatter of hoofs and she saw Will riding down the lane from the stables. He took off his plumed hat and waved it to her. He was wearing his smart new riding clothes, and his new chestnut mare had been groomed until her coat shone like glass. He was riding to see Lettice. He seemed to go by like a burst of sunshine, so strong and happy was he, so glowing in his yellow doublet with the golden feather in his hat. A pang went through Jenny, bitter and sharp. She and Will had grown very close to each other after he left Oxford and before he met Lettice, almost as close as in their childhood before he was breeched. It had been a halcyon time for Jenny. But it was over now. What was it like, Jenny wondered, to be in love? It had transformed Will. Jenny had never loved a man and had consistently refused to consent to any of the arranged marriages that were the custom of the time. To do so would have seemed to her a disloyalty; to what she did not quite know. And now she was twenty-six, past her first youth and increasingly patronised by young matrons in their teens. She did not mind for underneath her poise and seriousness she had a gay and happy temperament and her love for her mother, Will and her home was so deep and strong that she asked nothing better than to be with them and look after them. Love of her home broke over her suddenly. It was perhaps a shameful thing to love a mere house so much but this one was the white unicorn, the warm and living body of the spirit she had seen once in the woods, the spirit that was to her a symbol of that other-ness that called out the deepest loyalty of which she was capable. But would Lettice want her to go on living here? Lettice would soon be the mistress of this house. Lettice and Margaret liked each other, and Margaret was fast settling down into one of those plump and placid elderly women, sweet, lazy and understanding, who are a welcome ornament to any hearth. But her daughter, Jenny knew, was not that sort of woman. She was serene when her hand was on the helm, but not otherwise.

And for that reason, though she loved Froniga as dearly as ever, she did not think they would be happy living together. Froniga's hand had been accustomed to the helm from a very early date, and not accustomed to sharing it with another. And Froniga, Jenny knew, had lately found great happiness in solitude. Her three adopted children were married now in homes of their own and though they lived near her, came to see her often and loved her as dearly as ever, she had nevertheless come back full-circle to a loneliness that could scarcely be called loneliness any longer, so deeply had she found union with the source and end of her being and so companionable did she find the Way that led from one to the other. Sometimes she tried to speak of this livingness of the Way to Jenny, and in spite of her halting words Jenny understood something of her experience for she too in her different manner had had knowledge of love not as an emotion but as a person; and she understood too that though Froniga was more loving than she had ever been, that though she toiled for the sick more selflessly than she had ever done, yet at the same time this companionship contained within itself all that she longed for.

So what of herself? She was not ready yet for Froniga's sort of solitude for she had not travelled far enough. What she wanted was the particular experience that had been ordained for her to bring her there. She did not know what it was, and the darkness of her ignorance frightened her, but yet she wanted it.

Her thoughts went suddenly to Parson Hawthyn and she wished she could go to his little house in the beech-woods and talk to him as she had done so often through the years until he died. He would have understood her fears for there had seemed nothing he did not understand. When, like other Royalist priests, he had been deprived of his parish he had not gone overseas or taken to a secular way of life in another county, but had made himself a little shelter in the woods. He still considered himself the parish priest and he would not leave his people. Here, secretly, he lived and secretly they came to him. The men of the parish rebuilt his shelter for him, making quite a stout little house of it, and here he worked at his woodcarving, making dolls and toys, wooden platters, stools and the like, which his people sold for him at the local fairs. In this way he kept himself alive, and if he was sometimes hungry, cold and suffering in the long winters he let no one know it. He was sturdily independent and only when he was really ill would he let Froniga take him to her cottage and look after him there. He was poorer than the poorest of his people, his clothes were shabbier than theirs and his lot harder, and they opened their hearts to him as never before. He had never been so happy. Lying in Froniga's green-curtained bed during his last illness he had said to her, "In true poverty I found my greatest happiness. When I am dead, Froniga, I would like you to write to Francis, Lord Leyland and tell him that this is the truth. I should like you, also, to send him my blessing."

Froniga had been astonished, for never in all the years had he mentioned Francis, but she did as he told her. She wrote the letter, then wondered where to send it, for Cromwell was still Lord Protector and all notable Royalists were either dead or in exile. She did not know what had happened to Francis, though she was sure he was not dead. Finally, thinking that an Oxfordshire man would be willing to help her, she sent it to Lord Saye and Sele. He was still a Puritan but the execution of the King had so horrified him that he had gone into voluntary exile at his castle on Lundy Island rather than have anything to do with the regicides. For months she heard nothing, and wondered if the Earl had merely destroyed her letter, and then at last, by way of Lundy Island, she had Francis's answer.

It filled many pages, an outpouring of bitterness and grief that she was glad to have because it must have eased him in the writing. He told her of many things. Of the sack of Basing House, that black stain on the name of Oliver Cromwell who had ordered it, and of his father's murder there, of the King's escape from Oxford, and of that midsummer day of 1646 when the garrison of Oxford had marched out of the town through the lines of Parliament men that extended all the way to Shotover, with colours flying, drums beating, matches burning and bullets in bouche, to lay down their arms at Thame. In all the bitter story there had been for him only one happiness, the fact that the strength Froniga had restored to him had enabled him to be with the King as long as it was possible, to fight through all the tragic battles until the end, to come through privations and dangers physically unscathed and at last to escape to Europe to join the young King in exile. "Until your letter came the darkness seemed stygian," he wrote, "but the remembrance of that old man has lightened it. As a young man I always dreaded poverty but I think I could have borne this sort of poverty, honest-to-God poverty of the clean winter woods, with a merry heart. It is this sort of poverty, this shoddy boredom of the court in exile, this empty mind under a dirty fantastic wig, this queasy stomach under a shabby doublet stained with wine that seems to me a good imitation of hell. But now that I have the old man's blessing I will try to find some good in it. I serve the King. If I cannot love him as I loved his father he is still the King and I shall serve him till I die and find in the distasteful service, God helping me, the doing of His will. And I have two great possessions (what poor man has not got something?) the memory of my father and the memory of Jenny. I look sometimes at a memory I have of my father, sitting at the desk in his library when I was a boy, as though it were a scene before me, and in the same way I look at Jenny saying goodbye to me through a hole in the hedge. I love what I look at with my entire being and in that love there is companionship."

A few days later, after some thought, for Jenny was still only twenty and it was a bitter letter, Froniga gave it into her keeping and Jenny had kept it ever since in the rosemary box. She knew it now by heart, but even before she knew it by heart she had begun to share Francis's memories, not in a visual manner but in the way of suffering and emotion, as though she and this man who was a complete stranger to her shared one life. It had terrified her.

Froniga had come into the garden and was talking to her mother. She heard Margaret's pretty childish voice chattering of her small affairs and Froniga's deep voice gently answering. It was a music to which she was accustomed and she went quietly on with her work. And then she heard something else, something not heard by the two women in the garden. She still had her childhood's gift of acute hearing, if it concerned anyone who was a part of herself. What she heard was the rumble of coach wheels and the trot of horses, the crack of a whip and the high cry of a postilion. For a few moments the sounds were intensely clear, as though heard in crystal-cold air, and yet they were far away, as though some princely cavalcade was travelling the roads of another world. She listened intently, and there was only the singing of the birds and the voices of the two women in the garden. She would have thought she had imagined it had it not been for the beating of her heart. She steadied herself and went on working and thirty minutes passed before she heard again the sound of wheels and trotting horses coming down from the further common into the beech-wood, muffled in the depth of the beech-wood, then mounting the hill. She did not know if her mother and Froniga had heard it too for she had forgotten them. She was standing up, straining to see from her high window the place where the road came out of the beech-wood under the arching trees, that arch where she and Will had stood once to welcome her father.

They came out from under the arch, looking from this distance like a fairy cavalcade, one of those cavalcades that as a child she had read about in the book of fairy tales John Loggin had given her. Four white horses pulled the coach, the sun glinting on their curved necks and shining flanks and on the blue and silver liveries of coachman and postilion. The body of the coach, swinging on its leather braces, was blue and silver too, with a pretty domed roof and blue curtains. In days when great men travelled in almost royal splendour, with outriders and a large retinue of servants, this was a very humble cavalcade but to Jenny it would have been awe-inspiring had it not been for the softness of the colouring, the blue and white and silver that seemed spun out of the beauty of the day.

Somehow the beauty touched her heart, appealed to her love of otherness. It had come out of a far country. She leaned at her window, watching it come along the road, listening intently to the music of the jingling harness and the rolling wheels. It stopped at the gate. She heard her mother give a few sharp, excited little cries, like the cries of a bird, and saw Froniga moving with unhurried dignity towards the gate; and knew instantly that Froniga was expecting this arrival.

Yet she was not angry for Froniga seemed suddenly strangely unreal, an almost misty figure. Nothing seemed real except the man getting out of the coach. She was unaware even of herself as she watched him. He only existed. The stocky figure was the same and so was the way he moved, gracefully assured and a little arrogant, as he took off his great hat and bowed over Froniga's hand, then moved to the fluttering Margaret and bowed to her also. She had not analysed these things as a child but she recognised them now, for just in that way had this man moved through her memories and her dreams. But these things only were familiar. Apart from these things the man was a stranger. John Loggin had been young and this man looked old. She leaned far out of the window that she might see him better as he stood talking to her mother and her cousin. The small pointed beard he used to wear was gone and the fashionable periwig shaded a clean-shaven face, sallow and lined, with pouches of ill-health under the eyes and no beauty to commend it. His shoulders sagged a little. He used his hands as he talked, in the French manner, and the artificiality of it offended her simplicity as much as the flash of his diamond ring and the lace at his wrists. This foppish creature was not her idea of a man and she thought he looked dissipated. He was utterly alien to her. Yet still he alone was in the garden. He looked up and saw her at the window. For a moment he gazed at her unsmiling, then he smiled and bowed, sweeping the grass with the plumes of his great hat.

Jenny fled in terror. Gathering up her skirts she pelted down the back stairs as though she was a child again, nearly upsetting old Biddy at the bottom of them, out through the kitchen to the back door, down through the vegetable plot that was behind the house to her beloved herb garden beyond. She had fled to it instinctively because it was the place where she always went when she was frightened or unhappy, but on this occasion it had not been a good choice because thick yew hedges enclosed it and there was no way out except by the way she had come. "Cousin Froniga will find me," she thought childishly. "Biddy will have told her where I went. She'll be furious." Her knees giving way beneath her she sat down on the narrow grass path between the herb beds and hardly knowing what she was doing stretched out her hands to her beloved herbs, that she loved only a little less than Froniga loved hers. She picked rosemary, southernwood, marjoram and costmary, and then more rosemary, crushing the fragrant little bunch together in her hands, and presently, as the rosemary did its accustomed work of strengthening the spirits, she began to be ashamed of herself. For what, after all, was required of her at this moment? Nothing but common politeness to a morning caller. No, a little more than that; generosity to a man who had caused her family such grief through no fault of his own and suffered sorrow and self-reproach because of it. And as for the rest of it; perhaps that was nothing but a lonely woman's over-active imagination. For she had sometimes been lonely in spirit through the years, as those upon whom others lean must often be. Her quick hearing caught the gentle sound of garments brushing against the lavender bushes that bordered the vegetable garden. It was Froniga coming to fetch her. She got up and went courageously to meet her.

But it was not Froniga, it was Francis walking slowly up the grass path that divided the vegetable garden, his hands behind his back, his head a little bent. And his back was towards her. He was walking away from her. Again she knew what Froniga had done, and by this time she was angry, thoroughly angry. Froniga had sent him by himself to look for her and it was the last thing he had wanted to do. He was as terrified of her as she was of him. It was not easy for him to confront, grown to maturity, the little girl whose father he had killed. Froniga should have known that. The way Froniga managed them all for their good was absolutely infuriating.

She came quickly up the grass path and called softly, "Mr. Loggin!"

He swung round and saw her. The rather severe young woman he had seen at the window had been a profound shock to him, for he had scarcely realised in how short a space of time a child can not only grow up but cease even to be young. He had realised in a moment of humiliation how ridiculous had been the dream with which he had been secretly comforting himself all these years. But now, with her cap awry and her cheeks flushed, he could see the old Jenny in her. She was clasping a little bunch of herbs tightly in her hands, as though she was as frightened as he was. He stood before her as embarrassed as a schoolboy, conscious of his age and ugliness that were in no way mitigated by the ridiculous great wig and the fantastic clothes that were *de rigueur* at the court of Charles the Second. Then he looked in her steady brown eyes and forgot himself. The bitter-sweet scent of the herbs floated up between them.

As for Jenny, she no longer noticed that in him which had antagonised her for it fell away like the pelt of the beast in the old fairy tale and she saw the man himself standing clear of it all, standing clear even of time and change. For a few moments she lived intensely and saw deeply. This man might have retained the habit of arrogant manners but in himself there was a humility far deeper than her own, and the trappings of his rank hid poverty. In the years since she had seen him last he had been stripped of all material things and now that they had been given back to him he found among them nothing that his profound loneliness was able to value. Jenny had discovered when Will first left her long ago the essential loneliness of human beings but she had discovered also the comfort in loneliness that companionship can give. All human beings have their other-ness and it is that which cries out to the heart. Jennifer Haslewood felt within herself the first faint stirrings of a great love.

"Have you forgotten me, Jenny?" asked Francis.

"No," she said. "I never forget anybody."